"You are not a virgin."

Julia shook her head, mesmerized by the dark burning eyes above her.

"It lowers your value, still you have hair which, when cleansed and rubbed with unguents, will shine like the morning sun. You have the eyes of a sorceress fit to destroy men's souls or lead them to search for the treasure therein. Your body has the grace of a gazelle—it is a poem of tender symmetry. In such rare beauty great men will accept a small flaw. Failing that, others will pay handsomely for the honor of possession of so novel a woman."

Julia said nothing. She was a slave, with no hope of escape. And she wanted to live.

She would do whatever she had to. . . .

The
Storm
and the
Splendor

Jennifer Blake

FAWCETT GOLD MEDAL • NEW YORK

THE STORM AND THE SPLENDOR

© 1979 Patricia Maxwell

Published by Fawcett Gold Medal Books, a unit of CBS Publications, the Consumer Publishing Division of CBS Inc.

ISBN: 0-449-14282-5

Printed in the United States of America

First Fawcett Gold Medal printing: December 1979

10   9   8   7   6   5   4   3   2   1

For my mother,
who taught me to love reading,
and for my father,
who never had a chance to be a journalist.

Part One

Chapter One

Julia Marie Dupré paused in the doorway and looked back. The light of a girandole attached to the wall beside the door frame caught her in its flickering rays, giving her the look of a gilded Madonna. Her high-piled hair, shining through a mantilla of blond lace, had the burnished gleam of old gold coins. Beneath winged brows, her eyes were a shadowed and mysterious amber, like the sun penetrating into the depths of a woodland spring. She was taller than most French Creole women, with a regal bearing that went well with the classic mold of her features. Still, there was nothing cool or severe about her. Her eyes could flash with sudden life, with anger or mirth, and the curves of her mouth were both sensitive and sensuous. There were those in New Orleans who claimed that a misalliance such as the marriage between her French Creole father and American mother could produce only mongrel progeny lacking the attraction of either nationality. That they never made such claims in the presence of Julia Dupré was not because of her admittedly hot temper, but because she could shatter their argument with a single bewitching smile.

She gave a slight nod to herself. All was well. On the dais at the end of the long room, made by throwing the grand salon and the petit salon together, the musicians played with a will. Her guests swung to the strains of a lively *contredanse,* the ladies in light gowns of pastel muslin, the gentlemen in dark cutaway coats and knee breeches. Music, the scuffle of dancing feet, the murmur of conversation filled the air. At a sideboard at the end of the room, a footman in black-and-gold livery served liquid refreshment from silver bowls. For those who found the damp air of the rainy spring night a trifle cool, there was a small fire in the Carrara marble fireplace. The chairs lining the walls were occupied only by the older women who were acting as chaperons. Julia had seen to it that no young girl was left to sit making tapestry while her more fortunate sisters cavorted on the floor. Julia herself would not be missed if she slipped away for a time.

Like most houses in what was becoming known as the Vieux Carré of New Orleans, the Dupré mansion was built around a courtyard. Because of dampness and the danger of flooding, the lower floor was not used for living space but was rented out as shops and offices on the side fronting the street and used as stabling, kitchens, and laundry in the interior of the court. The family living quarters were on the second floor, where wide galleries protected the high-ceilinged rooms from the sun and the courtyard could act like a funnel to draw every passing breath of air through the French windows. On the third floor under the eaves were the servants' quarters.

Most of the family rooms opened into each other, but some, for the sake of privacy, did not. To reach the chamber known as the library it was necessary to venture out onto the dark, rainswept gallery and follow its turnings until the last room on the end of the right wing was reached.

Picking up her skirts of white tissue silk shot with gold thread, Julia hurried along. The rain drummed on the tiled roof, running from the eaves to splash into the paved courtyard below. The night air was cooler than she had expected, and she shivered a little as she ducked her head to avoid the blown spray. She should have had one or two flambeaux lit in the court, she thought, though it would not have done to draw too much attention to the need to see in these back regions of the house.

She was rounding the corner where a flight of stairs rose

from below when two dark shadows loomed in her path. With a small cry, she tried to sidestep and found the stairwell nearer than she had realized. Her stomach gave a sickening lurch as empty space fell away beneath her feet, and then she was caught in a bruising grip. An arm like a band of steel compressed the air from her lungs while hard fingers sank into the flesh of her upper arm. As the yielding softness of her body came up hard against a masculine chest, the man who held her gave a startled exclamation.

Beside him the other man chuckled. "Your pardon, captain, but I believe you have there my daughter Julia. She is no threat, at least not in the way you must have imagined. Permit me to present you. Julia, *ma chère,* this is our guest, Captain Rudyard Thorpe. You will have observed his ship, the *Sea Jade,* anchored in the river."

The instant her feet touched the floor Julia pushed free. Her skin burned where he had held her. Curiously shaken, she retreated behind what was left of her ruffled dignity. "Captain," she said, acknowledging the introduction in a tone as cool as she could manage. "I believe I must thank you for your quickness and presence of mind."

"Not at all," he replied. "It was no more than a reflex action."

"Nonetheless, I am grateful."

"The pleasure was mine."

A more perfunctory gallantry Julia had never heard. The man spoke in the cultivated tones of a gentleman. His French was fairly fluent, though his accent was less than perfect, marking him unmistakably as being of English upbringing. One thing more Julia detected in his deep voice: a rough note of impatience. She realized that he was waiting for her to excuse herself and allow him and her father to go about their business. It gave her great pleasure when her father took her hand and tucked it into the crook of his arm, drawing her along with them.

"Captain Thorpe has just arrived, and we are going to meet with the others," M'sieu Charles Dupré said. "Won't you join us?"

"I would be delighted," Julia said dryly, for she had

never for a moment intended otherwise, and well her father knew it.

A pair of bookcases standing on either side of the fireplace gave the back room the right to be called a library. They did in fact hold a number of books, ancient leather-bound volumes moldering in the damp climate, a Bible, and a collection of the children's books Julia had used in the nursery. They also held a miscellany of yellowing news sheets and farming periodicals prevented from cascading to the floor only by the glass doors, plus dust-coated brass figures of soldiers and statesmen, an astrolabe, a molting stuffed owl, and a Meissen china bowl filled with string, fishing flies, broken hairpins, rusty needles, and corroding coins. The books that Julia wanted for her consultation and enjoyment she kept in her bedchamber, since her father was jealous of the privacy of his library and seldom allowed anyone to intrude, even to clean.

With a rueful twist of her lips, Julia noted the layer of dust that coated the center table, which served her father for a desk. The brandy decanter holding pride of place on the gritty surface had left a definite imprint, and by counting the rings it was possible to see how many times it had been lifted to refill the glasses of the four men who sat around it.

At her entrance the gentlemen got to their feet. One, her father's old friend, General Montignac, came forward and took her hand, raising it to his lips. "Mademoiselle Julia, such a pleasure, though not an unexpected one."

General Montignac, late of Napoleon's *grande armée,* was a gray-haired, craggy-featured veteran. He had sacrificed a foot and an eye for his emperor and hobbled about on a specially fitted boot with the aid of a cane, while peering around the protection, or so it seemed, of a rakish black eyepatch. He was the accredited leader of the Bonapartist following in New Orleans, a post he enjoyed immensely. His pleasure in it did not prevent him from being deadly serious about the goals they espoused, however.

"You are too kind," Julia murmured as she met his one flashing black eye without evasion.

"Not as kind as I would be were I twenty years

younger," he replied with a gusty sigh and a shake of his head. "I see you have made the acquaintance of Captain Thorpe."

Julia had not until this moment glanced at the man who stood beside her. He was tall, as she knew he must be. For some reason she had expected him to be in uniform; instead he wore excellently tailored evening clothes, which clung to his wide shoulders and molded the muscular length of his thighs. A cloak damp with rain hung from his arm, and in his hand he carried a curly-brimmed beaver. Despite the trappings of a gentleman, his skin was burned as mahogany brown as that of any sailor, contrasting strangely with the vivid, deep sea-blue of his eyes. His hair was cut short and brushed back without the artifice of careful disarrangement practiced by the dandies. Though it appeared fine in texture, it had the crisp vitality and midnight color of a swamp panther's pelt.

In that quick, comprehensive appraisal, she discovered one thing more. She was also being inspected, though Captain Thorpe's attention seemed to be centered upon the décolletage of her gown, where the creamy curves of her breasts were covered by a tissue-thin layer of silk.

"Yes," she said more sharply than she had intended. "We have met."

"Then if your father permits, I will make known to you the two gentlemen gathered with us who may be strangers —M'sieu Marcel de Gruys, a fervent admirer of the emperor recently arrived in our city, and M'sieu Eugène François Robeaud, lately in the service of the emperor. M'sieu Fontane I believe you know."

"Please be seated, messieurs," Julia said, taking the chair her father held before she acknowledged the two men. With a smile and a nod she greeted the fourth, an old acquaintance of her father's with ties in the commerce of the city. M'sieu Fontane, the general, and her father constituted the leadership of the Bonapartist following in New Orleans.

Marcel de Gruys she had seen about the city often in the last few weeks. He appeared to have an entree into the normally closed French Creole society and was popular with the hostesses of the *ton*. It was said that he had inherited his money, a family fortune, though no one seemed to know anything about his family—a black mark in New Orleans, where identifying relations was a favorite pastime. Exquisitely turned out, he had the heavy-lidded eyes and slightly protuberant lips of the confirmed roué. He raked her with an exploring glance as he inclined his head, a glance prevented from being offensive only by its habitual nature. M'sieu Robeaud was entirely different. A self-effacing man, he was short and tended to corpulence. His gray eyes held a worried look, and he did not quite meet Julia's amber gaze. Still, her attention was caught and held. There was an attraction in the man's symmetrical features, a suggestion of steadfast character. And there was something more which teased at her mind, something she could not quite capture.

"Brandy, Captain Thorpe?" M'sieu Dupré, the elegant host with silver gleaming in his white hair, waved the captain to a chair. He splashed the fiery liquid into a balloon glass and pushed it toward the other man, then replenished his own glass before he joined them around the table.

General Montignac tapped on the floor with his cane for attention. "Messieurs, mademoiselle. I believe we are all aware of why we are here. There is none among us who has not waited, dreamed, and hoped for this day. Three long years, since the moment of inattention at Waterloo, we have stood in readiness to aid the emperor. Now, at last, the summons has come. Napoleon has laid his plans. He has need of us to bring them to fruition. Soon the eagle will fly his cage. In days to come we will be privileged to say to our grandchildren that we, here in New Orleans, helped forge the key which set him free! Let us drink to the flight of the eagle!"

Ladies did not drink anything stronger than a glass or two of wine with their meals, but Julia repeated the toast with the others. There was a tightness in her throat, the result partly of the emotional tone of the general, partly of her own deep sympathy for the man who was being held on the barren island of St. Helena. Head held high,

13

she smiled, proud as any to be a part of the moment. Let him who thought he could keep her from this quest dare to try!

When the echoes of the salute had died away, General Montignac went on. "As some of you know, I have been in direct contact with the emperor. A letter, smuggled out in the baggage of a young officer aboard a ship which touched at Jamestown harbor on St. Helena, came to my hand not a week ago."

"How does he go on?" asked the elderly banker, M'sieu Fontane.

"His morale is good, honed by his constant battle of wits with this English dog set to watch him, Sir Hudson Lowe—your pardon, Captain Thorpe, but one may condemn as a dog a single man without maligning a whole race, *n'est-ce pas?* But to proceed, the commissioners, these *canaille* of England, Bourbon France, Austria, and Russia, indulge in petty tyrannies. They refuse to give the emperor his correct title, calling him merely General Napoleon, a name he left behind after the African campaign twenty years ago! They censor his mail—that which is sent directly as a camouflage for that which is not! They search for messages in the packages of food and wine sent to him by friends and relatives, and they send away anyone on the island who they think may be too sympathetic. But our emperor is not beaten. He retaliates by making certain the viands shipped to him are more sumptuous than any the petty English officials ever dreamed of consuming. By refusing to admit into his presence anyone who fails to address a request for an audience in the proper terms, he denies himself to the commissioners, but holds court for every other visitor to the island."

"They do not force themselves into his chambers?" M'sieu Fontane asked, frowning.

"They dare not. Napoleon has armed both himself and his retinue. They are sworn to defend the environs of the court at Longwood with their lives. If Sir Hudson Lowe caused death or bodily harm to come to the emperor, he would face the outrage of Europe, as well as the strictures of his own government. Public opinion is beginning to swing in the emperor's favor. The thought of a man's being tied to a rocky island for life, like Prometheus with the carrion birds pecking at his flesh, does not sit well on the consciences of the world. But enough. We have important matters to decide."

Captain Thorpe let his gaze wander from the speaker and sent Julia an oblique frown as he cupped his brandy glass in his fist. When his attention fastened on the gold bee, Napoleon's symbol of royalty, that was pinned to a black velvet ribbon at her throat, the blue of his eyes darkened. And then, catching Julia's inquiring gaze, he looked deliberately away.

Julia's fingers tightened on the arm of her chair. It was a novel sensation to find herself unwanted. Most gentlemen of her acquaintance were overjoyed to be in her presence. She recognized that she was privileged above most women in being accepted in the councils of her overindulgent father and his friends. Still, she knew that she was also accepted for her own sake and the contribution she was capable of making. It was irritating in the extreme to be judged on appearances alone and found lacking. That Captain Thorpe did not trouble to conceal his opinion she considered nothing short of an insult.

Turning from the captain, she encountered the gaze of Marcel de Gruys. Smiling, his eyes closed to slits, he raised his glass in homage to her beauty. The gesture was not unusual, but she was surprised to find herself unmoved by the flattery. What ailed her that she could not be pleased by either appreciation or the lack of it?

The one-eyed general drew his chair nearer to the table and lowered his voice. "The emperor, messieurs, mademoiselle, plans to leave St. Helena by August, at the latest, of this year. By October he will have reached Malta, the first way station in his return as master of Europe."

"By August!" Fontane exclaimed, blinking rapidly. "That is less than five months away. How are we to mount a rescue, procure a ship, recruit men, and arrange for weapons and all such necessities in so short a time when the prison is half a world away? Have reason, *mon ami!*"

15

"Everything has been planned. All these details and many others you have not dreamed of have been taken care of by our emperor, the master of logistics such as you enumerate. First the ship—indeed a necessity, as you say. This is why Captain Thorpe, so fortuitously arrived in the city, has been invited to join us. Men? Weapons? If you envision an army, such will not be needed. The emperor does not intend to risk the lives of his faithful followers in a contest of arms at this date. How then, you will ask, does he expect to make his escape? Does he intend to hide himself in an empty wine barrel or dress himself like a common stevedore or sailor? No, a thousand times! Such conduct is beneath the dignity of a man who has felt the mantle of empire about his shoulders, a man who has bought and sold kingdoms, given crowns and coronets away as gifts!"

The banker, a man with little appreciation for eloquence, looked sour. "Must he take wing, then?"

"You are a pessimist, my dear Fontane," the general accused. "He walks away, *naturellement,* like an emperor and a gentleman, strolling beneath the noses of those who think they have him fast."

"And books his own passage on a ship of the East India Company, I presume?"

"Non, mais non! It is more complicated than that, though still of a great simplicity. It is a brilliant plan, truly brilliant, and a major portion of its success depends, as I have said, on the men with us now, Captain Thorpe and also M'sieu Robeaud."

"I am sure this plan is a marvel, general. We require only to be told what it is for a proper appreciation."

General Montignac, enjoying the moment, smiled and shook his head. "Such impatience. I am coming to that."

With sudden decision Captain Thorpe sat forward, placing his empty glass on the table. "Before we begin, General Montignac, may I ask if everyone present has given you a personal guarantee of loyalty? This is a dangerous conspiracy we are about to embark upon. We would be foolhardy to jeopardize it at the beginning by allowing the details to be either deliberately revealed or bandied about in careless chatter."

As he spoke Julia felt his glance sweep over her once more. His words might seem to be directed to the group at large, but she was well aware of their focus. Men did not ordinarily consider their conversation chatter. That was a word reserved for the conversation of women.

"If you are referring to me, Captain Thorpe," she said, keeping her voice firm with an effort, "I assure you that I have been privy to the secrets of this group for some time and they have not yet become common knowledge." To his credit, the captain made no attempt to deny the obvious. "I meant no offense, mademoiselle," he replied, his head tilted on one side. "In England it has never been the practice for men to burden females with matters of political significance, or those which may become hazardous."

"Your concern is commendable, captain, but I must point out that this is New Orleans and that I am not, I believe, your typical English female—"

"Here, here!" General Montignac said to a rumble of laughter from her father and his friends.

Smiling a little in response, she went on. "I do not intend to take a direct part in this affair, but you may be certain that what is said in this council will be safe with me."

M'sieu Fontane also championed her. "There can be no objection to Mademoiselle Julia Dupré. Napoleon has no more staunch supporter and friend. In any case, she would soon have the entire tale from Dupré or one of us, so she may as well stay and hear the correct version."

The captain surveyed the amused faces around the table almost as though he was doubtful of the wisdom of becoming involved in a plot undertaken with so light an attitude. "And the others?" he asked curtly.

"With the exceptions of Messieurs Robeaud and De Gruys, I have known these men all my adult life," Julia's father said with a gesture of one white hand that was as graceful as it was impatient. "M'sieu Robeaud will be the one most endangered should anything go wrong. You cannot expect a greater assurance of his cooperation. De Gruys I have known for some months both personally and in the realm of commerce. He is willing to contribute handsomely to the mounting of this expedition. It is elemental that one does not finance an expedition one expects to betray. It would be to cast a fortune away for nothing."

The astringency of her father's tone, subtle though it was, was not lost on Captain Thorpe. This was a country where men had been killed for less obvious slights to honor. The captain was a plain-spoken man, and under the circumstances the men gathered in the library were willing to indulge him, but the cemeteries of New Orleans held many men who had dared to express their doubts too plainly.

Julia watched Rudyard Thorpe's tight-lipped struggle. It went against his grain to bow to the will of others, that much was clear. No doubt he had the habit of command, and of accepting responsibility for his subordinates. It would do the man no harm to discover that he was not in charge here, nor in any way superior to the others.

"I take it we may proceed, then?" General Montignac inquired. After a moment Captain Thorpe gave a reluctant nod. Once more the general launched into speech.

"The instructions of the emperor are set out so simply that there can be no misunderstanding. Some small portion of them has been carried out. However, if you will allow me, I will refresh your memories. We of Nouvelle Orleans have been given the great responsibility of contacting M'sieu Robeaud and arranging transport for him to England aboard a ship of American registry. I think there is no problem there, Captain Thorpe?"

"None at all, general. The *Sea Jade* was owned originally by my father, who was an American. It was his wish that she never fly the Union Jack. By birth I am British, and my mother's people still reside in England, but I have honored my father's wish."

"Very good. In fact, if I may say so, it could not be better. Once in England, M'sieu Robeaud will take passage on a ship of the English East India Company, which will have as its destination Rio de Janeiro via St. Helena. The emperor has arranged for General Baron Gaspard Gourgaud to travel to London for the purpose of facilitating this voyage—"

"Gourgaud?" M'sieu Fontane asked. "I understood he had quarreled with Napoleon and demanded, in a positive fit of histrionics, to be allowed to leave St. Helena. An unstable fellow, descendant of a family of actors, I believe."

"Indeed yes, just the man to carry out a ruse. That is all it was, this quarrel, you perceive? A ruse to convince the commissioners that he was done with Napoleon. All these denunciations and intimate details and supposedly secret information you will hear from Gourgaud will be so much bombast to cover his true purpose. I think we here in Louisiana will be in a position to give greater aid to Gourgaud than was at first envisioned, however. Perhaps, Captain Thorpe, you will be so good as to tell the others what you confided to me when we met a few days ago?"

"Certainly," the Englishman said, straightening in his chair. "The main problem which confronts Gourgaud is to assure that an East Indiaman will be sent out to St. Helena at the proper time. The difficulty arises because, as you are undoubtedly aware, the island is owned by the East India Company, which has leased it to the crown as a place of detention for Napoleon. Only company ships, and British ships of the line, are allowed to anchor in the harbor at Jamestown, St. Helena. I believe I may be in a position to be of service here. My mother's eldest brother is a director of the East India Company. Since he has no sons of his own, it has long been his wish that I settle down and take an interest in the India trade. If I could manage to convince him that I intended to do so, I might be able to discover the sailing schedule for Indiamen going to that part of the world, or even influence a voyage at the proper time, should it prove necessary."

"Now that should be of value," Fontane said, nodding his white head.

"Yes," General Montignac said dryly. "And, of course, the captain will sail from England for Rio de Janeiro with the *Sea Jade* and await the coming of Napoleon in that city. The instant the emperor arrives and boards, he will put out to sea, with Malta as the destination."

Marcel de Gruys, an observer until now, shifted in his seat. "One is forced to wonder what Captain Thorpe hopes to receive for all this," he drawled, his cynical black gaze measuring the large form of the Englishman.

"What I hope to receive," Rudyard Thorpe replied as he swung to face de Gruys, "is money."

A small silence fell. The men at the table glanced at each other.

"Well?" General Montignac said, a trace of bluster shading his voice. "What did you expect? Not everyone can be depended upon to serve the emperor out of love."

"I suppose not," M'sieu Fontane said unhappily. One or two of the other men murmured a dubious agreement. Julia sat forward. "That may be so," she said, her voice earnest, "but is it wise to trust so much to one who is of the same nationality as those who have been Napoleon's most implacable enemies and who are now his jailers?"

"She has a point," M'sieu Fontane said.

"Indeed, yes," Marcel de Gruys agreed, his eyes approving as he flicked a glance in her direction. "I believe it would be in order for the rest of us to require from this English captain some proof of his loyalty to the cause he hopes will bring him a profit."

A muscle corded under the sun-bronzed cheek of the Englishman, and his blue eyes seemed to darken. "In matters of business my word has always been my bond," he said with slow deliberation. "I did not ask to be a part of this; I was approached by General Montignac and M'sieu Dupré in Maspero's Coffee House after they had overheard me say I intended to return to London at short notice. I care not a tinker's damn whether Napoleon Bonaparte lives out his given years as the despot of Longwood or the master of Europe. I owe allegiance to no man and idolize none. The sea and the *Sea Jade* are the things I hold highest, and the welfare of my ship is my first concern. Whatever benefits her has my strictest fidelity. More than that I cannot say. However, if any of you harbor doubts, they can best be resolved by sending some one or two from among you on this voyage."

"An excellent suggestion," M'sieu Dupré said in a thoughtful tone.

Marcel de Gruys gave a nod.

Julia looked from her father and de Gruys to find herself the target of the captain's hard stare. There was a tightly held anger in his expression, combined with a deep aversion to being forced to defend himself. Julia waited for the satisfaction of a score settled. Without precisely planning it that way, she had had her revenge for Rudyard Thorpe's attempt to exclude her from the conference. The sensation did not come. Instead she felt a shrinking feeling in the region of her stomach. Despite her father's presence beside her, a shiver of something like fear ran over her. An instant later it was ousted by a redeeming rage which allowed her to lift her chin and return the Englishman's gaze without flinching. And yet, within herself she was never as aware as never before in her life of her vulnerability as a woman.

"There now," General Montignac said, sweeping a comprehensive glance around the table, "if all are satisfied we will proceed. There are still a few points to be explored—some of the more important ones, I might add."

"I should think so." M'sieu Fontane snorted. "It is all very well to speak of needing no armament and risking no lives, but what happens when the emperor's absence is discovered? Pursuit will be immediate, pursuit by English warships carrying heavy guns. The ship carrying the emperor will be blown out of the water the instant they come within range. An escape attempt—what else could give them such an excellent excuse for ridding themselves of Napoleon?"

Captain Thorpe answered. "What you say is true, sir. I have been given to understand, however, that this will not be a problem."

"Not a problem?" the other man exclaimed, staring at

Rudyard Thorpe as though he suspected him of being mad.

"Precisely," the general said with grave humor. "There is no reason to believe Napoleon's absence will be discovered until he appears to make a public announcement of the fact. By that time the English will be too busy defending themselves to worry about trying to recover their prisoner?"

"Bah," M'sieu Fontane said with a wave of his hand. "You talk in riddles."

The general smiled. "Not at all. The absence of the emperor will not be detected for the simple reason that M'sieu Robeaud will take his place, as he has many times before."

Fontane slewed around in his chair to stare at the plump little man sitting so quietly among them. "It is true?" the banker demanded.

Robeaud inclined his head.

"Why do you do this?" Marcel de Gruys asked, his drawling tones sharp with suspicion. "For money, like our good captain?"

Robeaud frowned over his answer. "That is a question of some difficulty, m'sieu. For money, yes, but also for many other reasons. It is permitted that I explain?"

"Not only permitted but required, I think," de Gruys answered with an encompassing glance at the others.

"Merci," Robeaud replied, bending his neck a curiously humble bow once more. "I was born a peasant, m'sieu, in the little town of Balaincourt in France. As a young man I was conscripted into the army as a *voltigeur*, a light infantryman of the Third Regiment. Soon I came to the notice of an intelligence officer, Colonel de Rochalve, because of my resemblance to the emperor. One night I was called into his quarters and told that I was being sent to Paris for a special assignment, M'sieu Fouché—"

"Minister of police," General Montignac murmured.

"Yes, m'sieu. The minister of police had been requested to find a man who could relieve the emperor of some of the more tedious duties which are the lot of a ruler, someone who could attend assemblies and balls,

inspect troops, put in an appearance at the endless cere-
monies of the city fathers. There were so many demands
of this sort on the emperor's time that he had little left
to govern the country or to plan his campaigns. It would
not be good to disappoint the public or the civic leaders,
but the emperor's patience could no longer abide such a
waste of his waking hours. I, messieurs, was considered
to be the man most nearly the same in features and coloring to Napoleon, though I am somewhat shorter, and a
trifle younger. The first could be remedied by my wearing
special boots with built-up insoles and also by arranging
that I remain seated as often as possible, upon a dais, a
carriage, a horse. As for the second, the emperor was not
averse to appearing somewhat less advanced in age than
he really was."

"Amazing," M'sieu Fontane said, a sentiment echoed
by the others. General Montignac and M'sieu Dupré, the
only two of those present to have heard the tale, exchanged a smile.

"Perhaps," Robeaud agreed with a small shrug. "In any
case, I received the blessing of the emperor. At once I
was taken into the palace of Versailles and hidden away
while I was taught to speak, gesture, walk, and dress like
Napoleon. Here General Gourgaud, with his theatrical
background, was particularly helpful. I was instructed in
reading and writing, of which I was ignorant, and set to
copying the emperor's writing style, particularly his signa-
ture. I believe I can say that my performances gave satisfaction. For four and a half years I helped to relieve the
burden of office for my emperor. Then came defeat and
abdication. I was given a sum of money and sent away.
But after tasting the richness of life at court, how could
I return to being a simple peasant? In the years while I
was away from Balcicourt my parents had died, leaving
my only sister alone in the world. The two of us decided
to emigrate to the new world, and a new life, in Louisiana.
We prospered, after a fashion, although the money given
to me was soon spent. And then a few months ago, I began
to have a pain in my belly. The doctor I consulted told
me I have but a few years to live, two, possibly three. My

sister, she has never—that is, she was not blessed with talents or intelligence. Without me she will have to go into a poorhouse or beg for a living. In my desperation to provide some meager existence for her, I wrote to the emperor. For a time I received no answer, and then a letter came, brought by a sailor of a foreign ship. If I would come to St. Helena and spend my last days there in comfort and plenty, Napoleon would provide a pension to be paid to my sister for the remainder of her life. Such a joy, messieurs! My emperor needed me, I would be useful again, and my sister would be taken care of. How could I refuse?"

"How indeed?" General Montignac said, reaching over to clasp Robeaud's shoulder. "It is a great honor, one I envy you, mon ami."

"You are too kind, general," Robeaud said. "To end my tale, I was instructed to contact General Montignac here in Nouvelle Orleans. I have done so and now await further orders."

"You see the beautiful simplicity of it, my friends?" the general said, spreading his hands. "M'sieu Robeaud will take a trip to England in the role of a merchant, or perhaps a planter, seeing something of the world. His return journey will be via St. Helena and Rio de Janeiro. On reaching Jamestown, St. Helena, he with perhaps one or two others will request an audience with the emperor. At Longwood he and the emperor will exchange places, and Napoleon will continue on to South America. From there, Malta and Europe. If the English do not realize their prisoner has escaped, there will be no alarm, no pursuit. The masquerade can be kept up indefinitely, or for as long as it takes for the emperor to organize his return to power."

Julia's father cleared his throat. "The point has been raised more than once the need of additional persons on this roundabout voyage to St. Helena, first of all to serve to make M'sieu Robeaud less conspicuous, and also to—forgive me, captain—to ensure the integrity of the mission. I find within myself a great desire to be a part of this undertaking, as I am sure we all do, and since I have the leisure to indulge my whims, I would like to volunteer both my daughter and myself to accompany M'sieu Robeaud."

For an instant Julia, her eyes sparkling, met her father's bland gaze. It was no sudden impulse which had dictated his suggestion. Only that morning her father had told her that they would go, that there was a special reason for their presence. It was clever of him to seize the opportunity offered by the captain's proposal to introduce the idea, but then her father was a clever man, one who could attain much if given a position of responsibility under a strong and dynamic ruler. Unconsciously her fingers strayed to touch the gold bee at her throat.

"I also find this adventure exciting," Marcel de Gruys was saying, his smooth lips twisted in an ironic smile. "Perhaps three passengers other than Robeaud would not overcrowd the *Sea Jade?*"

Thus applied to, Captain Thorpe threw a glance tinged with contempt at de Gruys. "There is space enough, yes, but may I remind you that this is not a pleasure outing? The list of things which can go wrong is endless. The existence of Robeaud cannot be a complete secret. If he is recognized in England and picked up by the authorities, everyone with him will also be subject to arrest. Suppose a guard or some official becomes suspicious at Longwood? You will be lucky if arrest is your only danger in that event. And what if the unthinkable happens and the exchange is discovered? If it occurs while he is aboard the East Indiaman, that will be the end of it. If he is traced to the *Sea Jade,* then we may be able to elude the British warships, but we will probably be prevented from putting into our port of call, forced to run before constant danger."

"You would prefer to make this voyage alone after all, captain?" Julia said, her chin high as she made the challenge.

"I would certainly prefer to make it without a woman aboard," Captain Thorpe countered, his voice as hard as his eyes.

Julia opened her mouth to reply, but her father forestalled her. "We are happy to know where you stand, captain," he said smoothly. "I am sure that if we decide to go we will absolve you of all responsibility for our safety."

"I am afraid that will not be possible," the captain returned. "Once you are on my ship I become accountable for your well-being, whether you wish it or not."

"It is good to know you take your duties so seriously," M'sieu Dupré said, though Julia did not think he looked at all pleased.

"I, for one, have no wish whatever to risk my comfort on this journey," M'sieu Fontane said. "However, I fail to see that the presence of M'sieu Dupré and his daughter, or for that matter of M'sieu de Gruys, will affect the outcome of the voyage one way or the other. *Le bon Dieu* knows the price of the passages will be high enough."

It might have been thought that the banker was referring to the cost in anxiety and nervous apprehension for the success of the mission. Those around the table were under no such illusion. They all knew that M'sieu Charles Dupré, using the great wealth gained from his sugar plantation, Beau Bocage, was the heaviest investor in the expedition, with Marcel de Gruys a close second.

The captain leaned back, a scowl drawing his heavy brows together. The banker's meaning was not lost on him. If he had not realized before who held the purse strings, he did now. That it went against the grain to allow monetary matters to order his policies was plain, but after a moment he gave a short nod.

"Very well, then. Don't forget you were warned. We sail for England within the week. Anyone not on board the *Sea Jade* when we weigh anchor will be left behind."

Julia wanted to protest. As much as she wanted to go, she had not dreamed they would be leaving so soon. The time was too short. She would not only have to assemble clothing and other belongings for months at sea, but also prepare for a climate vastly different from that of southern Louisiana. Moreover, she would have to oversee her father's wardrobe, cancel their engagements for the remainder of the season, close the house in the city, and see that the plantation house at Beau Bocage did not suffer from their absence. It could not be done, she thought, until she saw the sardonic expectation in Rudyard Thorpe's eyes. She forced a smile to her lips. It would be done, she vowed. She would do it all and arrive on board the ship well within the allotted time if it killed her!

General Montignac was on his feet. "To the emperor!" he cried. "And to those who will sail to set him free!"

When the chorus of voices had died away, Julia pushed her chair back, rising to join the men, who were already standing. "Forgive me, gentlemen," she said, "but I must return to my guests or they will think I have deserted them. I trust you will not be long in following?"

"Certainly not, *ma chère*," her father answered. The general and M'sieu Fontane indicated their compliance with a smile. De Gruys lifted his glass as she turned away.

"Messieurs, I propose a toast to the most beautiful Bonapartist in New Orleans!" he exclaimed.

Julia laughed, swinging back to drop a curtsy as glasses were raised, enjoying the warmth of the admiration and approval directed toward her. But as she left them and started back along the rainswept gallery, it was the brilliant blue gaze of Captain Rudyard Thorpe that remained with her. Admiration there might have been in it, but if so it was neither warm nor approving. It was instead cool, and touched with a deliberate appraisal.

Chapter Two

The sedan chair swayed along the muddy street. Rain lashed in windblown sheets at its glass windows, obscuring the forms of street vendors and pedestrians huddled beneath the protection of the overhanging galleries. Though it was still early in the evening, the coffee houses and cafés spilled lamplight into the street, bright, warm beacons to the chilled and damp unfortunates who had to be out in the dismal weather.

Inside the chair, Julia clung to the velvet hand loop, her lips compressed into a thin line as she peered through the fogged glass. Her father had said that he would meet her at their home on Royal Street before proceeding to board the *Sea Jade*. He had gone out to the Café des Ameliorations, to bid *au revoir* to his friends there over an *apéritif*. Julia had waited nearly three hours for his return, but when he still had not put in an appearance she decided to go down to the levee without him. It would not do to present Captain Thorpe with an excuse to leave without them. True, the Baltimore clipper was not due to sail until the morning, but the Englishman, to the highest degree reluctant to have them on his ship, might seize on any pretext to deny them passage.

Charles Dupré was not the most punctual of men. Time, whether his own or that of others, meant little to him. Still, it was not like him to delay his coming so long. He treated his daughter as he would any other gently bred female, with a certain reverence and an exaggerated concern for her peace of mind. Something of an unusual nature must have occurred to keep him from at least sending a messenger to explain the delay.

As Julia craned her neck, peering up and down the street, the front bearer of the sedan chair slipped in the muddy street. The chair lurched forward, throwing Julia from the cushioned seat into the glass. With an unladylike sound of wrath she picked herself up and flung herself back on the seat. She ached in every muscle from the unaccustomed labor of the past few days. Her eyes burned from lack of sleep and the candle smoke of her midnight toil. These last days had been a nightmare. Though her fingers were permanently stained, she feared, from the ink of the hundreds of missives she had sent flying here and there all over town, she was by no means certain she had accounted for all their obligations. The packed trunks and boxes were following along behind the chair in a wagon, but she could not claim to know what all of them held. Her maid of fifteen years, Minna, a faithful and dependable henchwoman, had been distracted by the tidings, after seven years of marriage to the Dupré butler, that she was to be a mother for the first time. The woman had gone around in a daze, her mind occupied with visions of tiny white garments rather than the clothing of her master and mistress. It was obviously impractical for an expectant mother to set out on an ocean voyage of several months' duration, another problem. Rather than face the task of training a new maid, a young girl who would no doubt be seasick and unhappy once they reached the chill climate of England, Julia had decided to fend for herself. She would miss her maid, of course, but she had often done her own hair and dressed herself. The main problem would be seeing to her own laundering. No doubt something could be arranged; it would have to be.

Table linens, cutlery, bed linen, toilet articles, an outfitted writing box, playing cards, visiting cards—these and a dozen other items had been bought and packed, and yet the inescapable feeling that she had forgotten something nagged at the back of Julia's mind. She was damp and chilled from standing about in the courtyard waiting for the sedan chair to be summoned. If her father had come the carriage would have been put to for the short drive to the levee, but as it was, that vehicle had to be left behind in case her father returned after she had set out.

The chair came to a halt. Gathering up her reticule and scent box and pulling her cloak of blue velvet about her, Julia looked out. The bulk of a ship rose above her. Its sleek hull was painted black, with a white band above the waterline edged in scarlet. Upon the band was set in script the name of the vessel. Beneath the bowsprit, which thrust out over the levee, was the figurehead. It was a surprisingly delicate piece of wood sculpture, the torso of a woman, the flowing mane of her hair masking the generous curves of her nakedness. The face was finely cut, the lips smiled, the eyes invited, and yet there was a coldness in the expression, as though the promise behind the invitation was false.

Julia averted her face, turning her attention to the rail of the ship. There was no sign of her father, nor indication of any activity, beyond a trio of coatless seamen who appeared to be securing a cargo hatch. A gangplank stretched steeply down from the ship to the levee.

Drawing back her skirts, she pushed her slippered feet into pattens, then stepped gingerly down into the mud. The rain had slackened somewhat, but she had no faith that it would not begin to pour again at any moment. Head down, she hastened toward the end of the gangplank. As her pattens clattered on the wet and slippery wooden boards they began to sway. Reaching for the rope railing, she looked up. Captain Thorpe, clad in breeches and an open-necked shirt, his uncovered head wet with rain, came toward her. With the ease of long practice he adjusted to the movement of the gangplank, striding as though he trod solid, level ground. As he came abreast, he took her arm without a word, assisting her up the incline.

The courtesy was unexpected, but welcome. The mud-coated pattens had not made the best of footing for such a climb. The instant she reached the deck she kicked them off, as much to keep from soiling the white holystoned deck as to rid herself of their weight.

"Thank you, captain," she said as they paused in the shelter of the entrance to the companionway. Her smile was genuine, and her amber-gold eyes, behind lashes tangled with raindrops, were warm.

"Not at all. Your cabin is the second door to the left. Watch your step down the companionway." With a curt bow, he swung away.

"Captain?" she said, her voice sharper than she had intended.

"Yes, mademoiselle?" he inquired. There was a frown between his brows as he turned back.

"Is my father on board?"

"No, not as yet."

"Could I be informed when he arrives? Also, our baggage is coming behind me."

Rudyard Thorpe looked past her to where a man in the uniform of a ship's officer approached. "Here is the man to handle your problems, mademoiselle. May I present First Mate Jeremy Free from the port of Baltimore. Jeremy, this is Mademoiselle Dupré, who will be sailing with us. I leave it to you to see that she has everything she needs."

A brief look of surprise registered on the first mate's face as Captain Thorpe walked away. Then he smiled down at Julia. "Welcome aboard the *Sea Jade*," he said in a pleasant baritone. "In what way may I be of service?"

Interested and concerned, Jeremy Free did much to soothe Julia's ruffled sensibilities. Of average height, he seemed with his sandy coloring and hazel eyes to suit the buff-and-blue uniform he wore. His tanned skin carried a sprinkling of freckles. His chin was firm and his mouth strong, though it curved easily into a cheerful grin.

Promising to send word as soon as her father arrived and to see to the stowing of their baggage, he escorted her along to her cabin. He pushed open the door, stepping back to allow her to enter.

The cabin was incredibly tiny, little more than a box.

31

The low ceiling seemed to press down, constricting the small space. There was a single bunk against one wall, a washstand holding a basin and stoppered water carafe, with a closed space below for the necessary pot, and a small desk which was fastened to the floor with a chair in front of it. A corner offered the only space to hang a few essential items of clothing, and there might be room for a single small trunk beneath the porthole, but if she had brought her maid, poor Minna would have had to resort to a sailor's hammock or sleep on a pallet on the floor.

It occurred to Julia as she glanced about her that the cubicle had a masculine air. That was not unusual, perhaps, on a seagoing vessel, where accommodations were utilitarian, but the lack of any concession to a female passenger troubled her. "I hope, Mr. Free," she said slowly, "that I am not inconveniencing anyone by coming on this voyage?"

"Why, no, ma'am—that is, not to any great extent."

She put the hood of her cloak back before she said wryly, "I take that answer to mean that I am. On the few trips I made to Europe as a young girl, I noticed that the second cabin next to that of the captain is usually occupied by the first officer. Tell me, Mr. Free. This isn't by chance your cabin?"

The first mate colored a little. "A clipper isn't set up for many passengers, ma'am. I don't mind bunking with the second mate for a spell. I'll be happy to think of you in here. That is to say—"

"Never mind. I appreciate your meaning," Julia said, giving him the smile touted as bewitching by the most accomplished *beaux sabres* of New Orleans. "I also thank you for the gesture."

"It was Captain Thorpe's idea, ma'am. Your father will be across the hall with Mr. Robeaud, and the other passenger will be in with the ship's surgeon."

"I had no idea it would be so crowded."

"The *Sea Jade* is fitted out to be a cargo ship. That's about all she has carried since the day she came off the slips, ma'am."

"I see."

A commotion overhead claimed the attention of the first mate. "That will be your baggage, I expect. Is there anything you would like brought directly here?"

After carefully memorizing the description of a small hidebound trunk and a pair of matching bandboxes, he took his leave.

Mercifully, her father put in his appearance directly behind the baggage wagon. "Don't scold, *ma chère*," he said as he greeted his daughter in the companionway outside her cabin. "It was unavoidable. An emergency meeting had to be held to discuss a new development. I will tell you all about it as soon as we are settled."

There was no time for more. The small passageway was filled with seamen carrying trunks on their backs or laden with boxes and crates. From all sides came demands to be told where each piece was to be put, and only Julia could sort out the tangle.

It was perhaps an hour later when Julia, dressed for dinner in a simple gown of white muslin with a red-and-gold paisley shawl draped about her shoulders against the chill left by the rain, went along to the dining saloon. She expected to find her father ensconced there with a before-dinner drink in his hand. Instead, the room appeared empty and silent, dimly lighted by a lantern swinging gently from a hook above the green-baize-covered table. An instant later, Captain Thorpe stepped from the shadows at the end of the room. Behind him, through the porthole, could be seen the lights of the town blooming like fire flowers in the deepening dusk.

"Good evening, Mademoiselle Dupré," he said formally. "Won't you sit down?"

Julia took the chair he held for her. As she settled her skirts and the fringes of her shawl, she touched the golden bee which held the triangle of paisley in place, a habit, making certain it was safe. In the uncomfortable pause which followed, she gave a fleeting thought to propriety. Seldom in her twenty years had she been alone with a man not related to her by birth. Surrounded as she was going to be by men for the next months, she must put

33

such considerations out of her head. She was no longer an unfledged miss. At her age most girls were not only married but mothers. There were many in her circle who, if she had not been quite so obvious an attraction to prospective suitors, would have been ready to call her an old maid, one who no longer needed the protection of a chaperon. Not that she could possibly need protection in any form from Captain Rudyard Thorpe. For all his awareness of his opportunities, they might as well have been in a crowd—an irritating observation, since she was herself so conscious of his tall presence in the room. He had changed from his wet garments into a dress uniform similar to that worn by the first mate except for additional decoration of gold braiding. Julia wondered if she could congratulate herself that the effort had been made for her sake, but she dismissed the thought for lack of encouragement.

"Has it stopped raining?" she asked as he moved to take a seat at the far end of the table from where she was sitting.

"Yes, it's beginning to clear."

"Then there should be no difficulty in sailing in the morning?"

"None whatever. I believe your father boarded the ship safely after all?"

Ignoring the hint that she might have been unduly concerned, Julia agreed. "He was detained at a special meeting. Some emergency, I believe, though I have no idea of its import."

Interest narrowed his eyes so that his thick lashes provided a screen for his thoughts, but he did not comment.

Casting about in her mind for a topic which might interest a seafaring man, she said, "I suppose you will be happy to be putting out to sea again?"

He leaned back in his chair, his arm lying along the edge of the table. "It has a few advantages."

"Oh?" she said encouragingly.

"At sea I am master of my ship and everyone on it."

"Surely in theory only, captain?" she said, suppressing

a smile. It still rankled with Captain Thorpe, then, that she and her father had insisted on a place on his vessel.

"Not at all," he corrected. "Beyond the sight of land my word is law."

Julia stared at him, sensing a purpose behind his words, though she could not discern it. She raised her chin a fraction but before she could demand an explanation the door opened to admit Marcel de Gruys.

He advanced a few paces, then stopped. "Do I intrude?" he inquired, a smile which just missed being offensive on his face as he looked from the captain to Julia and back again.

"Happily, yes," Captain Thorpe replied with a look of sardonic amusement as his blue gaze rested on the color which stained Julia's cheekbones.

Speculation gleamed in de Gruys' black eyes before his heavy lids came down to hide it. Moving forward, he took the chair beside Julia. "You look charming tonight, mademoiselle," the Frenchman observed.

Julia murmured something appropriate. De Gruys was himself dressed for the occasion. In his dark coat with satin lapels the silvery color of polished steel, stiffly starched linen, and white breeches, he was a shade too resplendent for the shipboard meal. Beside Captain Thorpe he looked rather like a dandy in mourning. In retaliation for the moment of embarrassment he had caused her, she swept her gaze over his somber raiment and asked, "May I offer my condolences, m'sieu?"

"What? Oh no, no, mademoiselle. They are not at all necessary. My friends are all well. As for my family, I have none for whom to grieve."

"Forgive my mistake," she said, veiling her eyes with her lashes, though not before she had seen the twitch of Captain Thorpe's mouth.

"You, I would forgive anything," de Gruys replied punctiliously, if with a certain stiffness in his manner.

With both men on the defensive, Julia found it a labor to make conversation. It was a relief when they were joined by Jeremy Free, M'sieu Robeaud, and her father.

The other ship's officers would not be putting in an appearance, since they were in town, making the most of their last night on shore.

The new arrivals were followed by a steward bearing a tray containing glasses and a bottle of sherry. When all had been served and the steward had departed, Captain Thorpe spoke. "I understand, M'sieu Dupré, that you have news?"

"Indeed?" the older man said, his gaze moving significantly to the first mate.

"You need not fear speaking in front of Jeremy. As first officer of this ship he must naturally have some knowledge of where she is sailing and for what reason. He is also a friend who has my implicit trust."

Julia's father hesitated a moment, then inclined his head. "Knowing your concern for the secrecy of this mission, I bow to your judgment. This afternoon a new message was received from St. Helena. Cipriani Franceschi, *maître d'hôtel* to the emperor and a man of considerable use to him as a spy and confederate, has been poisoned. It is not known whether he was killed because of his usefulness to his master as an organizer of informants and counteragents against the English, or whether he partook of a dish intended for Napoleon himself. On the night he was stricken, Franceschi was serving dinner and became incapacitated during the course of it. He died a week later after days of excruciating pain."

"Does the emperor consider that an attempt was made on his life?" Robeaud inquired.

"The emperor has not made known his thoughts. Regardless, it becomes of the utmost importance to remove him from such an—unhealthy atmosphere."

"Of a certainty," Robeaud agreed, his gray eyes gentle. "I never considered otherwise."

They were immediately reminded that to remove Napoleon from this new danger meant exposing Eugène Robeaud to it. That the quiet, self-effacing man did not shrink from the possibility seemed to make it worse instead of better.

"Forgive me, my friend," M'sieu Dupré said, frowning.

"Such a death—no one could be blamed for withdrawing from it."

Robeaud shifted his gaze to the swaying shadow pattern made by the overhead lantern on the table. "It makes no difference. Compared to some, such an end would be swift."

Captain Thorpe put a merciful period to that line of thought. "Will this development affect the emperor's plan?"

"There was nothing in the message to indicate that it will. However, common sense tells us that time has become an enemy, which, like the jailers of the emperor, must be combated with whatever means are at our disposal."

The *Sea Jade* loosed its moorings in the gray light of dawn and, borne on the breast of the river's current, turned its siren-eyed figurehead toward the turquoise gulf. Julia, lying sleepless in her bunk, heard the shouted orders. The feel of the ship floating free gave her a peculiar sensation, as if she were being torn away from the shore, set adrift without purpose or direction. Experimentally she reached out to touch the bulkhead. It vibrated with tension, as though the ship were a living thing. The sound of wavelets against the hull came with the regular cadence of a heartbeat, disturbingly close and insensibly threatening.

In the hope of escaping such fantasies, Julia threw back the covers and slid out of her bunk. She did not trouble to light a lamp, but dressed in the dark, pulling the first gown she came to, a rose cambric, on over her convent-embroidered chemise and underskirt. Napoleon's bee at her throat, her cashmere shawl about her shoulders, she was ready.

A thin blanket of fog lay over the river, and the trees of the shoreline seemed to grow from a cloud. Already New Orleans had dropped away out of sight. The only sign of habitation was cleared fields of waving sugar cane, appearing like gaps among the trees.

The mahogany ship's rail was wet to the touch. Julia

tucked her damp, chilled fingers beneath her crossed arms, lifting her face to the moisture-laden breeze. The dank smell of the river was in her nostrils with the scent of new hemp, fresh paint, and tar. The activity on deck had slowed as the sails were set. One or two of the men who made up the crew glanced with interest in her direction as she stood alone, but they quickly averted their eyes when she looked their way. A sudden show of industry on their part was enough to alert her to the approach of their captain.

"You are up early, mademoiselle," Rudyard Thorpe greeted her.

"The sailing woke me," she replied. She had not realized how cool the wind was until she found herself in the lee of his body. The warmth emanating from him was oddly disquieting, as if it had a magnetic quality which she had to resist to keep from drawing nearer. It required an effort of will to keep from flinching as he took her arm and led her toward the bow, out of hearing of the ship's crew.

"Not regretting leaving?" he queried, turning to her as he came to a halt.

She shook her head, managing a smile despite her earlier misgivings.

"Certain? Think carefully, while there is still time to put back into New Orleans."

She swung her head to stare at him. "Would you really do that?"

"I would," he answered, meeting her amber gaze squarely.

"I had not realized you wanted to be rid of me quite so badly, captain, in spite of everything. But I'm sorry. I'm afraid you will have to learn to live with me."

A slow smile curved his mouth. "That is an idea," he told her, and watched in amusement as the color of embarrassment tinged her skin.

"I see nothing comical," she snapped.

"No? Perhaps you lack a sense of humor?" he suggested. "Or maybe you're just not used to people laughing at you." As she opened her mouth to refute both charges, he held up his hand. "Oh, I know all about you; I've made it my business to know. Your mother died when you were thirteen, your father took you out of your dull convent school and made you his housekeeper and boon companion. Your accomplishments are legion, from the feminine and social graces to more masculine arts like cupping wafers with a pistol, driving a curricle and pair, riding horses astride, playing euchre, faro, poker, and chess to win. Beautiful, graceful, intelligent, bilingual, if not trilingual, grounded in the classics and the sciences—there is little there to provoke ridicule, and yet we all have our faults."

"It is gratifying to see that you include yourself among the imperfect."

"High temper disguised as acid wit, that's the first fault. For myself, I've always considered a woman without temper a pathetic creature, but some consider it a blemish."

She longed to slap the condescending smile off his face, but that would be to show the temper he accused her of. "Perhaps I should be flattered by your interest," she mused.

"Spoiled by men. No doubt that's the fault of your father and his elderly friends. Did you notice that when I extolled your virtues just now you neglected to voice a word of appreciation?"

"I was not aware that I was being complimented. As for being spoiled, you have not known me long enough to judge."

The corner of his mouth twisted in a smile. "I'm certain that you are thoughtful and considerate and self-sacrificing, but I'm also sure that you extract your quota of homage. If not, why are you still unmarried? Isn't it because no one man can satisfy your vanity?"

She turned to face him, gold flecks of rage glittering in her amber eyes. "Are you certain we are talking of me, captain, or is it of some other woman who has disappointed you? I have not married because I have never met a man I could not live without. If it is being spoiled to have a father who will permit me to make that decision for myself instead of choosing a husband for me, then I suppose I must plead guilty. As for my vanity, it is not so colossal as to lead me to think I can understand a fellow human being from a few hours' acquaintance!"

If he felt the prick of her riposte, he did not show it. "Bravo," he said softly, a reluctant gleam of approval in his eyes. "I begin to hope you may not be such an encumbrance on this voyage as I feared."

"You—do you mean the things you said were merely to provoke me, to see what I would reply? That is the most despicable trick I have ever seen!"

"Is it? Then I can't say much for your experience. In an expedition such as this, we are as weak as the frailest member. It is well to test the steel of your allies, as well as your enemies."

"Weak? This is a strong expedition, heavily financed, organized by Napoleon himself, and supported by his sympathizers on two continents, to say nothing of St. Helena!"

"From where I stand, mademoiselle, it appears that I have set out to free a man guarded by the naval power of the greatest seagoing nation in the world with the aid of an elderly gentleman, a popinjay, a young woman, and a dying man. Can you truly blame me for being cautious?"

"Come, captain," she said in dulcet tones. "You must not underestimate your own strength."

"Nor yours," he said, and pushing away from the railing, he left her.

In the days which followed, they slipped imperceptibly into a routine. M'sieu Robeaud and Marcel de Gruys seldom appeared for breakfast. Julia's father, normally an indolent man who kept late hours and late risings, seemed invigorated by the sea air and the excitement of their purpose. He made it his habit to eat with the ship's officers, and he insisted that Julia join him. She was happy to do so. The camaraderie of the dining saloon in the early-morning hours was a pleasure, and she was able, without too much difficulty, to coax many details of the running of the ship from Jeremy Free and the second mate, an Irishman by the name of O'Toole. What the

Irishman lacked in manly beauty—he had flaming red hair which the damp salt air made to stand on end like a wire brush, a wide split between his teeth, and a seamed face displaying every one of his forty years—he made up for in audacity. Before they had left the muddy silt of the Mississippi River behind them Julia had ceased to be Mademoiselle Dupré and become "Julie me darling." Frown, correct, forbid as she would, nothing short of downright, hostile withdrawal seemed likely to prevent him from taking that liberty with her name, and his company was much too entertaining to be deprived of it by standing on her dignity.

Strolling about the deck, sitting with a book in a chair contrived of canvas, rinsing out a few articles of clothing and placing them before the porthole to dry—these things whiled away the morning. Unless she could avoid him by staying in her cabin doing needlework or napping, Marcel usually took up her afternoons. It was not that she was averse to his company. He was a most gratifying escort, lavish in his praise of her superior qualities. At first it seemed natural that he should consider her, her father, and himself as above the others in some way, but she soon grew tired of his constant complaints, his harping on the defects of the ship, and his attempts to vilify its officers. He gravitated so surely to her side that she began to suspect that it was her status as the only female on the ship rather than her charms which attracted him.

Gradually, a familiarity began to creep into Marcel's manner also. Once, when he had run her to earth where she sat alone in the dining saloon, she gave him her hand in greeting. Instead of bowing over it in the accepted manner, he carried it to his lips palm uppermost. The grip of his hand was tight and faintly damp. His smooth lips touched her palm, and then she felt the flick of his warm, wet tongue across that sensitive surface.

The shock of it traveled up her arm. She snatched her hand away and an instant later swung it with a cracking slap against the side of his face.

Rage flared in his eyes for a brief moment, then was

deliberately snuffed out. He allowed a hurt look to move over his countenance. "Why, Mademoiselle Dupré. What have I done to offend you?"

"You know very well," Julia said. Disbelief jostled with fury in her mind, and unconsciously she rubbed the open palm of her hand on her skirt.

"I protest, I have not the least idea."

Gold flecks glittered in her eyes at his effrontery. She opened her mouth to denounce him, and then the difficulty of putting his exact crime into words held her mute.

"Can you not explain? Do not attempt it. As a man of some experience I understand the odd humors of young ladies very well. I do not hold your moment of temper against you, I assure you. In fact, I do most earnestly beg your pardon for whatever small error I may have made to raise your ire."

A young woman less certain of herself could have been forgiven for doubting the evidence of her senses under the effect of his suave denial and forgiving air. Julia was not fooled, but short of accusing him like a fishwife she could do nothing. Her head high, she retreated into a cold disdain which, while an unsatisfactory release for her feelings, had the desired result. Though he still denied any knowledge of how he might have offended her, Marcel begged her pardon with every appearance of sincerity. Returned to her graces, he behaved himself with the utmost propriety, though occasionally Julia caught him looking at her as though mentally stripping away the fragile muslin which covered her.

She debated whether to speak to her father about Marcel. He had so much on his mind, was so involved in conferences with Captain Thorpe and M'sieu Robeaud, that she hesitated to burden him further. It could be argued that her problems were her own fault, since she had insisted on coming on this voyage without a maid or suitable female companion. There was also the possibility that her father might feel called upon to reprimand Marcel. If he clung to his plea of innocence, there would doubtless be a quarrel, which could cause much unpleasantness in such close quarters. In addition, de Gruys was known for his skill with rapiers; it was even rumored that he had killed his man and been forced to flee France for Louisiana. If the tales were true, she certainly did not wish to risk a meeting between him and her father. While M'sieu Dupré had boasted a certain skill with blades in his youth, he no longer had the stamina required for a match which featured foils without buttons.

The clash of arms on deck one warm, lethargic afternoon brought her topside in a rush which left her out of breath. Eyes wide, she stared at the men circling each other, coatless and in their stocking feet on the foredeck. An instant later, she sagged against the door of the companionway in relief. One of the men was Marcel de Gruys, the other Captain Thorpe. Her father, eyes bright with interest, stood to one side with M'sieu Robeaud and the majority of the crew. There was a great noise among the assembled men as bets were placed and the merits of each man candidly discussed. From what Julia could gather, the captain was favored for his longer reach and greater strength, though a vocal group opted for the Frenchman. Marcel might be smaller, but was fast on his feet and wielded his weapon with a dexterity seldom seen outside a *salles des armes,* the fencing schools for young men.

The men circled, feinting, parrying, their blades scraping together with the singing rasp of fine steel. A look of narrow-eyed concentration masked the captain's face, while de Gruys allowed himself a confident smile. Once or twice it seemed the Frenchman's sword had slipped under the guard of the other man, but Thorpe always recovered. In each case de Gruys redoubled his efforts, certain of momentary victory. Slowly they moved over the deck, the captain retreating before the flashing brilliance of the other man's swordplay. But as de Gruys failed to touch his man, a flush of anger mounted into his face. His smile faded, to be replaced by a grimace of determination. Beads of perspiration gathered on his forehead and trickled down his temples, though Captain Thorpe seemed unaffected by his exertions.

As the seamen moved to keep the combatants in sight,

Julia drew nearer to her father. "What is it, Papa? Why do they fight?" she asked in an undertone.

"Who can say? For sport, perhaps, or boredom, or to test their comparative skill."

"Then—it is not a duel?"

Her father frowned without taking his eyes from the two men. "It did not begin so, but I think it cannot end now without a loss of pride for one of them."

Had Captain Thorpe set out to test the mettle of de Gruys as he had tested her? If so, it appeared that he had gotten more than he bargained for. De Gruys was a formidable opponent. She would have liked to feel glad, but instead she was prey to the beginning of an angry helplessness. Their mission was too important to risk it in such rivalries. As annoying and overbearing as Captain Thorpe was, he was indispensable to the success of that mission. De Gruys was not.

As her eyes followed the glinting steel of the two swords, she considered and discarded methods by which she could put an end to the fight. There seemed no way short of stepping between them. Before she could shift her position, there was a sudden change in the offensive. Captain Thorpe ceased to retreat, pressing forward against the weakened defense of the Frenchman. There was a flurry of steel, and the light sword spun from de Gruys' grasp to clatter on the deck.

Quiet descended, a quiet marred by the creaking of the rigging above them. Captain Thorpe lowered his sword. And then a resounding cheer rose from the seamen.

De Gruys, a white ring about his mouth, inclined his upper body in a stiff bow. "My congratulations on your skill, captain, and your strategy."

Julia drew in her breath, fully expecting Thorpe to take exception to this veiled suggestion that he had won by guile. He did no such thing. Tucking his own blade under his arm, he bent to pick up de Gruys' sword, presenting it to the man over his arm. "One is seldom of any use without the other," he said easily. "Come, let me give you a drink."

"Permit me to join you in a few moments, after I have repaired my appearance in my cabin," de Gruys replied.

"As you will," Thorpe said, and ordering a round of grog for the seamen, swept the others down the companionway to join him in a glass of wine. If he had looked back, as Julia did, he might have seen de Gruys staring after him, his lips drawn back in a grimace and his black eyes glittering with hatred.

They reached the port of Havana on the island of Cuba four days later. It was midafternoon when they dropped anchor. Captain Thorpe went ashore immediately to deal with the port authorities and arrange to have fresh water and victuals brought to the ship. Julia's father went with him. There were Bonapartists in the city, he said, but Julia thought he was feeling the confinement of the ship and was more interested in the thought of congenial company in the warm, wine-sour atmosphere of a café or cantina.

When dusk fell and he still had not returned, she was not too concerned. De Gruys and the ship's surgeon, a thin-featured little man named Hastings with a receding hairline and jaundiced complexion, had also gone ashore during the late evening and had not returned either. Captain Thorpe put in his appearance in time for dinner. He had left her father, he said, some hours before in front of a cantina not far from the waterfront. No doubt he had lost track of the time and would be along as soon as it occurred to him that his daughter would be growing anxious. Julia accepted this with a stiff nod, but she was grateful for the suggestion put forth by Jeremy Free a bit later that she take a turn about the deck. It was pleasant to stroll with the uncomplicated presence of the first mate beside her, and there was always the chance that she might catch sight of her father hastening back to the *Sea Jade*.

She did not like the view of Havana afforded from the ship, an area of ancient unpainted buildings squatting in the mud, leaning drunkenly against each other for support. Patches of lamplight gleamed here and there, the centers of much loud music and laughter. The light appeared to attract the women of the streets like moths, for they paraded up and down at the perimeter of the glow. Their breasts, revealed by low-cut bodices, gleamed pale, and their hips swayed beneath long skirts slit to the thigh. Once, as Julia watched, a sailor dragged one of the women into an alley, where he pressed her to the wall and there in the semidarkness began to demonstrate the purpose of the slit skirt. Quickly, Jeremy led Julia toward another section of the ship and remained there, talking and pointing out places of interest in the town spread out before them until it was safe to perambulate once more.

They had been on deck perhaps an hour when Julia caught sight of the figure of a man coming toward them along an ill-lit street. The slim shape, the jaunty, almost arrogant way he carried himself, made him instantly recognizable as her father. Though he was still too far away for her to make out his features, he was swinging his cane in the way he had when he was feeling pleased with himself. Captain Thorpe had been right; she had been needlessly worried, she told herself as she followed her father's progress through the refuse of the dirty street.

She was about to call Jeremy's attention to her father when two men erupted from an alley behind the elderly man. They were upon him before he could turn or cry out. A knife flashed high and fell once, twice. Her father's knees buckled and he pitched forward. The two men went down beside him, fumbling at his clothes. An instant later they were up, his purse in one hand, his watch and fobs in the other. Before Julia could draw in her breath to scream they had taken to their heels, and their fleeing shadows were lost among the maze of night-blackened alleys.

Jeremy would not let Julia go to him. He was brought aboard on a litter, and it was discovered that he still lived. The ship's surgeon was still in town. It was Captain Thorpe who stanched the flow of blood, dressed the wounds, and saw that the elderly gentleman was made comfortable in his bunk. Julia assisted him. Nothing he
46

said could stop her; when she informed him roundly that she was no stranger to blood, having, as mistress of her father's house, overseen the binding of the wounds of his slaves and the birthing of their babies, he ceased to try.

Mercifully, her father had remained unconscious through the ordeal. There was a gray cast to his skin, and his breathing was uneven, as though the rise and fall of his chest hurt him. Propping him on pillows seemed to help, but there were long nightmarish moments when his chest ceased to move at all. Julia, trading bunks with M'sieu Robeaud so that she could be with her father, lay for long hours listening to his struggles to breathe, her own chest aching with the desire to help him.

Toward morning he regained consciousness. He was weak and pale but lucid. Calling for the captain, he made it plain that he expected no concessions because of his injuries. He did not wish to be left behind in Havana, nor did he want to attempt to book passage back to New Orleans. He refused to allow a piece of ill luck to cause him to be left out of such an epic event as that in which they were involved. He did not expect the expedition to be delayed on his account. Such a thing would, in fact, cause him great distress. He had his daughter to care for him, and if the worst happened, it would at least happen while he was engaged in doing something worthwhile.

Captain Thorpe looked at Julia where she stood with her hand on her father's shoulder. "You agree?" he asked, his voice curt.

How could she not? The struggle to impose his will on them was draining her father of his precious strength; she could feel his trembling under her fingers. "It will be as my father wishes," she answered, her eyes dark with pain.

"Even if it is not in your own best interests?"

"That doesn't matter."

"You think not now," he said, his mouth set in a grim line. "Later, when it is too late to turn back, you may change your mind."

What was he suggesting? That her father was more

47

likely to die if they continued? That past a certain point it would be impossible to turn back, even if they wanted to, and still keep to the schedule set out by the emperor?

Lifting her head, she said, "Neither my father nor I would dream of jeopardizing this expedition."

"Doubtless, but that was not my meaning."

His gaze rested on her with a peculiar intensity, as if trying to convey some message without putting it into words which might disturb the injured man.

Abruptly she realized the implication of his words. In the event of her father's death, she would be alone on this ship without a guardian or protector. The thought was far from pleasant, but she thrust it aside. Her father was going to live. Moistening her lips, she said, "We appreciate your concern, captain. However, we urge you to proceed as if we were not aboard the *Sea Jade*. Nothing must be allowed to interfere with the rescue of Napoleon."

"Very well," he agreed, and with a short bow he left them.

When the sound of the captain's boots had faded along the companionway, her father turned his head on the pillow. "My daughter—" he began, then stopped.

Julia moved to where he could look into her face. "Yes, Papa?"

He stared at her for long moments, his forehead drawn together in a frown that was not totally the result of pain. At last he shook his head. "Nothing," he said. "It was nothing at all."

They sailed at dawn. Five days later they ran into rough weather. The tossing of the ship reopened her father's knife wounds. Feverish, in delirium, he began to cough blood. Nine days out from Havana he died and was buried at sea.

Chapter Three

There was something so final about death aboard a ship.
One moment her father was there, the next he was gone,
dropped overboard to sink beneath the waves without a
trace. When she returned to New Orleans she would have
a requiem mass sung for the repose of his soul and a
monument erected, but for the moment she was aware
of a great emptiness.

The last thing she had thought to pack in her trunk for
this adventure was mourning clothes. That would have to
wait until she reached London. For the time being she
made do with a band of black velvet about her neck,
worn with the most drab of the gowns she possessed. Not
that any were precisely subdued, but she did have a
lavender-blue muslin and a brown cambric which would
serve, especially when paired with the gray velvet of her
pelerine cape.

Clothes. Thinking of them distracted her mind from the
last painful hours of her father's life—hours in which he
had tried time and again to give her some important
message. What had he been trying to say through the
blood which foamed in his throat? What intelligence had
he been trying to convey with his staring eyes?

Tonight she would wear the brown cambric. This would
be the first time she had taken a meal in the dining saloon
since her father had been attacked. She could not bear to
sit in her cabin alone, at the mercy of the endless round

of her thoughts. In addition, it would not do to give the gentlemen with whom she was traveling the idea that she was fearful of coming out among them.

They had passed through the storm, but there was still a swell on the sea. Julia made her way toward the saloon with some care, holding to the rope which served as a railing along the bulkheads. She was too early for dinner, but she had brought with her the small woven sewing basket containing her embroidery. It would occupy her hands and give her a means of retreat from masculine conversation. There had been a time when she had enjoyed setting stitches, watching patterns come to colorful life under her needle. In the past few years there had been little time for such a solitary pursuit, but she had thrown the basket into one of the boxes as she was packing in case it was needed to while away the long voyage. It had proved its worth during the hours spent at her father's bedside.

Her mind clouded with memories of those helpless hours, Julia had almost reached the saloon before she realized there were voices issuing from the open door. At a note of anger in the tones she stopped, reluctant to intrude on what might be a matter of ship's discipline or a quarrel among the officers. The sound of her name held her motionless.

"You can't do that to the girl," Second Mate O'Toole protested. "It's not human."

"What else do you suggest? Her safety must be assured, and at the same time we must guarantee the secrecy of this mission." Exasperation laced the voice of Captain Thorpe and the measured tread of his footsteps as he paced sounded on the hard wooden floor. Julia had not realized that O'Toole was privy to the details of their mission. Captain Thorpe, it seemed, placed an inordinate trust in his officers. That could, of course, be all to the good, since they must eventually be on terms of intimacy with the emperor.

"But to clamp her in irons!" O'Toole protested.

"I don't call restricting her to the *Sea Jade* while we

are in England putting her in irons. She will be perfectly free to move about."

"Come, sir, when you can't leave a place it's a prison, no matter how you describe it."

"O'Toole is right, captain," came the voice of Marcel de Gruys. "I know you gave your word to her father that you would care for Mademoiselle Dupré, but he can hardly have envisioned such drastic measures."

"Doubtless, but as her father he was able to keep a much closer watch on her movements and the people she talked with than I can manage."

"I'm thinking the old gentleman didn't bother to keep too keen an eye on her," O'Toole said.

"Then more fool he," the captain said shortly.

"Softly," the second officer cautioned, "the man is dead." Captain Thorpe made no reply.

After a moment, Jeremy Free spoke, making his presence known for the first time. "It might be best to consult Mademoiselle Dupré. She may wish to return to New Orleans as soon as we reach port."

"That would simplify matters," de Gruys said, "but I would not set my hopes on it. From my knowledge of the lady, I would say she is most unlikely to relinquish this quest, especially now that her father has been forced to do so."

"I don't like the idea of her traveling alone," O'Toole said dubiously. "Such an attractive woman—"

"A companion could be hired, a nice widow," Jeremy suggested.

"If the lady had a companion, someone who could be with her day and night, the captain might even consider letting her go on with the thing as planned." O'Toole put forth this tentative proposal.

If he expected Captain Thorpe to answer he was disappointed. The sound of the captain's pacing halted, however.

"How to find a companion who can be trusted, this becomes the next problem," de Gruys said. "We cannot afford to encompass many more people in our circle, or soon all of Europe will know what we intend!"

Still Captain Thorpe said nothing.

Jeremy, his tone reflective, spoke up. "If she stays on the ship, then what? From England the *Sea Jade* sails direct to Rio. Does she go with the ship?"

"What?" the captain said, coming out of his absorption. "Yes, I expect so. The wait may be a long one before Napoleon makes port aboard the East Indiaman, but she will be able to see her hero and discourse with him on the voyage to Malta. After that, the *Sea Jade* will be at her disposal if she wishes to return home."

There was the sound of a hearty backslap. "Jeremy, me boyo, are you thinking of applying for the post of companion then?" O'Toole inquired, the suggestion of a leer in his voice.

"No, certainly not," Jeremy protested, but there was a general laugh at the first mate's expense.

"There is something to be said for the suggestion," Marcel de Gruys mused, adding, apparently at random, "I expect mademoiselle is her father's sole heir?"

"To the best of my knowledge," Thorpe answered, his voice cold.

De Gruys made some further remark, but Julia did not quite catch it. Behind her someone was descending the stairs of the companionway. She could not be caught eavesdropping. In the present mood of the men aboard the ship she might be hung from the yardarm as a spy if they learned she had overheard any part of their conversation, she told herself with tight-lipped cynicism. Such a convenient excuse for removing her would be too good to let pass. Swiftly, silently, she retraced her steps to her own cabin door, pulling the panel open just as the ship's surgeon came into view.

"Good evening, Dr. Hastings," she said as he drew nearer.

He looked at her in surprise, as well he might. She had found him next to useless during her father's illness and had at last pushed him forcibly out of the cabin. His mournful yellow face, like a monkey's, had driven her to distraction, and she had nothing but contempt for his

52

suggestion, made again and again, to bleed a man already drowning from internal bleeding.

"Good evening, Mademoiselle Dupré."

"Is it my imagination, sir, or does it grow colder?"

He blinked rapidly. "Yes, mademoiselle, the weather is indeed colder. The captain used the storm to good advantage and we are already leaving the temperate regions behind us."

"Then I had better keep my pelerine with me," she said, indicating the garment which hung over her arm. "Do you join the others?"

He nodded.

"Then perhaps you will give me your arm against the pitching of the ship?" she said, smiling with a shade of wanness.

Wordlessly he proffered it. Sewing basket held before her like a shield, she walked beside the surgeon back to the saloon.

By exercising every ounce of self-control she possessed and stretching her skill as a hostess to the utmost, she managed to get through the evening. There was a sense of constraint among the men which made it impossible for her to relax. Captain Thorpe retreated into a brooding silence. Jeremy Free, despite her bereaved state, was too obviously sympathetic in his attitude, and O'Toole too hearty. M'sieu Robeaud appeared to have trouble meeting her eyes, concentrating on his dinner. As for Marcel de Gruys, he was cloyingly attentive. Strange; not so long ago she would have found his pose perfectly natural. Now she felt suffocated by his nearness as he hovered over her chair trying to anticipate her every need. His manner of speaking of her father, intimate, insinuating, set her teeth on edge.

She made idle conversation, trying to ease the atmosphere, and smiled until her facial muscles began to quiver with the effort. When she could bear it no longer she made her excuses and escaped, refusing escort.

Once in her cabin she took off her pelerine, hung it on a hook on the wall, and sat down on her bunk. Only then did she allow herself to think. The arrogance, the sheer arrogance! To discuss her, to settle her future, make plans to curtail her freedom—it was not to be borne! This was not the first time it had been hinted that as a female she must be lacking in discretion. The insult of it when O'Toole, the most talkative of men, had been taken into their confidence! The next thing would be to make the weasel-faced surgeon one of them, though to her he looked the type to give way at once to either threat or bribe.

What was she to do? She found it hard to believe that Captain Thorpe would actually keep her a prisoner on the *Sea Jade,* and yet, she recalled only too well his insistence that beyond sight of land he was master of his ship and everyone on it. Beyond sight of land—

A soft tapping at the door brought her head up. She hesitated an instant, then moved to stand behind the panel. "Who is it?"

"It is I, Marcel," came the low voice, almost a whisper, of the Frenchman. "May I speak with you for a moment?"

"I—was just going to bed," she told him.

"I will not keep you long from your slumbers."

Reluctantly she lifted the latch and drew the door open. Marcel de Gruys pushed inside. Before he shut the panel behind him she could hear the sound of O'Toole's concertina coming from the saloon. Above it his rich tenor was raised in a bawdy sea ballad.

Taking a few paces into the tiny cabin, Julia turned to face Marcel. "Well?" she inquired with the lift of winged brows above the amber pools of her eyes.

"I fear, Julia *ma chère,* that you have tried to deceive me," he said, allowing himself a smile as he stood with his back to the door. "You do not appear to be prepared for bed."

"No. I would not have let you in, else," she said, her voice cool. "May I know what has brought you that would not wait until morning?"

"Such impatience," he murmured, moving toward her. "I wonder how you will survive being imprisoned."

54

"Imprisoned?" she asked quickly, the importance of what he was saying overcoming her momentary alarm at his change of attitude.

"But yes, has Captain Thorpe not told you? You are to be mewed up on the *Sea Jade* while she is in London harbor, kept here in your cabin to await his pleasure."

"I don't believe you," she said, allowing a trace of scorn to color her tone.

"Do you not? I have it from the captain himself. You will never set foot on English soil. I will wager that by the time the good captain's business in England is settled you will not speak so calmly of making ready for bed."

Julia turned away from him. "You are very free with your language this evening."

"I am only trying to make plain to you the danger in which you stand."

"For what purpose? You do have a purpose?"

The disbelief in her tone brought a flush to his face. "Naturally. I have come to offer you my protection, my name. Since the objection to your being at liberty is the lack of a companion to guard you from accidentally betraying the cause, or from falling prey to those who might seek to cultivate you for the sake of discovering what you may know, then I propose to offer myself in that role."

"You wish to be my companion?" She allowed a small smile to curve her mouth.

"If you would have it so. I rather expected that you would prefer to become my wife."

"I see," she murmured. "And you do this, I am to assume, purely out of compassion for me, to prevent me from being imprisoned aboard this ship?"

"Not entirely," he replied, easing closer. "You are a beautiful woman, beautiful enough to fire the blood of any man. I had not thought to rush my suit in this way, but I believe it would have come to this in any case."

"You believe? Aren't you certain?"

"I am certain of my own heart. Given time I might have waited for some sign of your feelings, some encouragement, before proceeding."

She swung around to fling him a look of scorn. "And

you would have waited also, I don't doubt, for a more exact accounting of my inheritance!"

"I protest, what have I ever done to give you such a poor opinion of me?"

So certain was he of himself that her words scarcely ruffled the surface of his assurance. His prominent eyes darkened as his gaze rested on the quick rise and fall of her breasts. He was much too close in the confined space of the cabin, but to retreat would be to allow him to come between her and the door.

"Suffice it to say I have it," she said, nervousness adding a sharp edge to her voice. "It is impossible that there could be anything between us."

"Impossible? Never say so. I cannot accept so final an answer without good reason." He reached out to take her arm in a light clasp, brushing his thumb over the silken surface of her skin.

"Don't!" she exclaimed, jerking her arm away, stepping back until she touched the edge of her bunk.

A trace of anger made his smile tight as he followed her. "Gently, dearest Julia. Don't shy away like a frightened doe from what you don't understand. You might discover you like being near a man."

His smooth fingers touched her jawline and moved lower to press against the pulse that throbbed in her throat. She swallowed, aware with every taut-stretched nerve that to repudiate him too harshly might bring a violent reaction, and yet she could not do nothing. His practiced caress was just as great a danger.

He laughed softly. "You are trembling, my sweet Julia, and your eyes, they grow enormous."

Her voice low, she said, "If you do not go now, this moment, I will scream."

"I think not. Consider the embarrassment for both of us, the questions and sly remarks. You would not like that. Sailors are an earthy lot. Perhaps they will not blame me, perhaps they will wonder aloud what encouraged me to think I might take liberties?" His fingers dropped lower, to the soft curves at the round neckline of her gown.

56

Abruptly she slapped his hand away, lunging under his arm for the door. She twisted the knob, opening it a crack before he was upon her, slamming it shut once more.

"Let me go," she panted, struggling against the arm which pressed her elbows to her sides. She was wrenched around to face him, her wrists caught in a swordsman's iron grip.

"Not yet," he told her, a ferocious smile drawing his lips away from his teeth.

An instant later a knock sounded on the door. "Mademoiselle Dupré?"

It was the voice of Jeremy Free. Marcel released her and stepped back, straightening his clothing with precision. Automatically, Julia did the same, even touching a hand to her hair.

"Yes?"

There was a pause on the other side of the door as though the first mate suspected something was amiss. At last he spoke. "Captain Thorpe's compliments, mademoiselle. He regrets disturbing you but requests a few words with you in his cabin at your earliest convenience."

"Thank you, I will be only a moment," she replied.

"Very good."

Marcel waited until the footsteps of the first mate had receded, then came forward, an expression very near triumph lighting his dark eyes. "You did not give me away," he murmured. "Think carefully on why you kept silent, and also on my proposal. We will talk again—soon."

"I did not betray you because I did not want to cause an uproar," she said, her face flushed with anger, "but if you come into my cabin again I will kill you."

"Such passion," he told her, "can have only one cause."

"You are mad!" she cried, but he had slipped out of the door and was gone.

By the time she had repositioned the gold bee at her throat and smoothed wisps of hair back into the chignon low on the nape of her neck, the color had faded from her face, leaving it pale. Pushing the incident with Marcel from her mind with determination, she left her cabin and walked the few steps to that of Captain Thorpe.

"Come," he called in reply to her knock. At her entrance he got to his feet, moving from behind a medium-size oaken desk, which was fastened to the floor, to show her to a chair.

When he had seated himself again, she moistened her lips. "You sent for me, captain?"

"Yes," he said, picking up a pen made of a seagull's wing feather and drawing it through his fingers. "The bulkheads on this ship allow a certain amount of sound to carry. I could not help being aware you had a visitor. I trust my intervention was not untimely?"

Julia flicked a quick glance at his impassive face, her fingers tightening upon each other in her lap. After a moment she answered simply, "No."

"Good," he said, tossing the pen aside. "I have known since your father's death that I was going to have to speak privately with you. Tonight seemed as good a time as any."

She murmured an agreement. Now that she was still, she was aware of a shaken sensation under her ribs. Never in her life had a man laid a hand on her in violence. She must not think of it, however—not now.

"I realize what the loss of your father must mean to you in a personal sense, and—we all respect your bereavement. But I wonder if you have considered the effect his death has had on the expedition."

If she chose she could save him a great deal of trouble in leading up to his plans for her. She did not choose. "I don't see that anything has changed," she said.

"You realize that we are too far advanced in our time-table to turn about and carry you back to New Orleans?" At her nod he went on. "Willy-nilly, you must go on to England. Once there, you will be alone, on your own for some weeks until the East Indiaman carrying M'sieu Robeaud to St. Helena is ready to sail. That, let me be frank, is a dangerous state for a young, attractive woman."

She drew a deep breath. "Your concern does you credit, captain. However, I believe I can manage for myself."

"The stews of London, the cribs and brothels, are filled with women who thought they could manage for themselves."

"Really, captain! There must be some respectable hotel that will take me, some agency which will provide a maid or some elderly woman to go about with me and lend me the proper degree of consequence."

"Such a thing might be arranged if you had the money," he agreed.

"Well?"

Captain Thorpe got to his feet and moved around the desk to sit on one corner. In the light of the swinging lantern the mahogany planes of his face were angular, as if they had been carved from some exotic wood. He towered above her, making her acutely uncomfortable as he stared at her through narrowed eyes.

"Mademoiselle Dupré, did it ever occur to you to wonder where your father found the money to finance this expedition?"

"He—he never discussed such matters with me, but he was not a poor man. And of course several others contributed."

"No one contributed as much as Charles Dupré. The donation of the others, taken all together, amounted to less than half. To obtain the necessary amount your father mortgaged his holdings, everything he owned."

"I—see," she said slowly. She might have guessed, remembering the busyness her father had displayed in the days before they left. Plantation owners, for all the value of their estates, were seldom able to command large amounts of ready cash. The vast majority of their transactions from year to year were made by the transfer of credit.

Captain Thorpe was speaking again. "I am sure your father expected to be reimbursed when Napoleon returns to power, but in the meantime, you are in an awkward position. Under the circumstances it is doubtful that his bankers will be willing to advance anything more against the estate. Considering the risk involved in repayment of the loan your father made, you may find that his bankers will foreclose in order to protect themselves when news of M'sieu Dupré's death reaches New Orleans."

"What you are trying to say is that I am not only alone, but penniless."

"Naturally I am not informed as to the exact state of your father's finances—"

"The purse taken by his murderers contained every penny, every picayune, he had brought with him. Except for some small change I had with me at the time, I am indeed penniless." The moment the words were said Julia regretted them. He might have guessed at her lack of resources, but he could not have been certain if she had remained silent. It was just that the shock of the knowledge was so great. She had no money. She was poor. No matter how she phrased it to herself, the words seemed to make no impression on her numb mind.

"Can I get you something?" Captain Thorpe was saying. "A glass of wine? A drink of water?"

Julia shook her head. Poor Papa. This must have been what he was trying to tell her before he died. How distressed he must have been to know that he was leaving her in such straits. Tears pressed achingly against the back of her throat, but she forced them down.

The captain slid off the desk and went to stand at the porthole, staring out into the blackness of the heaving sea. Julia watched him covertly from the corner of her eye, noting the crisp way his hair curled on the nape of his neck and the hard muscled width of his shoulders beneath his uniform jacket. The things that Marcel had hinted at came back to her. It was impossible, she told herself. The self-possessed captain of the *Sea Jade* had no designs upon her, no nefarious reasons for wishing to keep her a prisoner aboard his ship.

He turned to face her, propping his shoulders against the wall a little as though he needed to put as much distance as possible between them. "The question is, what are you to do? What would you prefer to do?"

"I take it that the arrangement my father made included our passage out to St. Helena with M'sieu Robeaud when he goes?"

He inclined his head in assent.

"Then I see no alternative but to proceed. If my father expected to recoup his losses by applying to the emperor, then he must have had good reason. I can only do the same."

"And if the attempt to release the emperor fails?"

"Then my losses will be nearly as great as Napoleon's, won't they?" she said with a smile for such an unlikely eventuality.

"You have relatives in New Orleans, someone you could go to if the worst happens?" he asked, a frown between his heavy brows.

"No," she answered, lifting her chin in a proud gesture. "My mother was an orphan, the child of German immigrants who died of fever a few months after coming to Louisiana. My father's people did not approve of his marriage to one they called an *americaine*, and he was cast off. They would not acknowledge me when I was affluent; they certainly would not recognize me if I appeared on their doorstep with nothing. One or two of my father's friends might help me, such as General Montignac, but most either keep bachelor establishments or live with their married children. I could not burden them with my problems."

"Out of pride, or from concern for the extra expense they must bear?" he asked.

Though she failed to see the reason for the question, she answered readily enough. "Both, I suppose."

He nodded as if she had confirmed something for him. When he spoke again, it was to take a new tack. "You realize that the place held by your father aboard the Indiaman will now fall vacant? The more I consider it, the more necessary it appears that Robeaud have companions on his journey. It is not that I doubt his stomach for the task, but he is a sick man. What would happen if his illness should need treatment? What might he not let fall if he should become feverish, even delirious? Even if it could be arranged for you to travel alone, you would not be able to attend him, and de Gruys, I'm sure, could not be depended on to turn a hand."

"What are you suggesting?"

As he glanced at her she thought she saw a flicker of indecision in his deep-blue eyes. An instant later, it was gone. "I am suggesting that I take your father's place. Jeremy can take charge of the *Sea Jade* on the run to Rio, where we will rendezvous and transfer once more to this ship."

"Yes, I can see the advantage of that," she said after a moment's consideration.

"Good. Can you also see the necessity for a certain—intimacy between the members of our party, an intimacy which in my case, since I am neither American nor of French ancestry, can only be explained by a close association with one of you?"

"A—close association, captain?"

"Such as marriage, Mademoiselle Dupré."

For the space of half a minute she could not speak. "Are you suggesting—? You must be mad!"

"Not at all. I have thought this through with great care, and I assure you the proposal was not lightly made."

"But—but surely something less drastic would serve as well?"

"You have in mind the role of infatuated suitor or a fiancé?" he asked, a grim smile tugging at one corner of his firm mouth. "I don't think so. That kind of thing draws attention, causes speculation among the other passengers, besides limiting the time when we could have speech together to the daylight hours. In addition, you would almost certainly have to share a cabin with another female on the Indiaman, making it well-nigh impossible for you to make a move without some busybody knowing about it. And then there is the question of Robeaud. A married woman could, with her husband's permission and presence, help ease a sick man's pain, but not a young single lady."

"You certainly seem to have thought of everything," she told him. "But are you certain there is not another reason you have failed to mention? Are you certain you are not afraid I will feel the need to unburden my maidenly breast to this female who is to share my cabin? Are you positive you are not doing this because you are still afraid I will betray you?"

He straightened, a small frown between his eyes as he surveyed her flushed face. "These things must be taken into account also," he said finally.

"So you do not deny it?" she demanded.

"No."

She would never have believed a gallant denial, so why she was nonplussed at his answer she could not understand. Perhaps she had hoped for some explanation that would make his attitude seem more reasonable. Obviously, none would be forthcoming. It was disconcerting to find her anger overlaid by disappointment.

Speaking with measured slowness, she asked, "Is there no way I can convince you that I am to be trusted?"

"It's not a question of trust," he said, flinging out one hand in an impatient gesture. "It is simply that you may unwittingly give someone more information than you realize."

"A question of intelligence, then, I take it!"

"Take it how you will," he grated. Moving to the desk, he flung himself into the chair and faced her with the width of the polished surface between them. "You have two choices in this situation. The one we have just discussed, and one other. This second is to remain on board the *Sea Jade* while she is at the London docks. I give you my word that you will be perfectly safe and comfortable. Then when she sails for Rio de Janeiro you will be with her, remaining aboard until Napoleon arrives."

"While you take my father's place, seeing after M'sieu Robeaud?"

"Exactly."

"You realize you are speaking of months of confinement in my cabin on this ship, without friends and with precious little to occupy my time?"

"You will be fed and you will have a warm and comfortable place to sleep, which is more than many in your position can say."

Gold flecks of rage glittered in her eyes. "I find I cannot work up a proper gratitude for food and comfort provided by the money my father paid out to commission your ship for this venture!"

"That's as may be," he ground out, his face hardening at the suggestion that he was battening on the money borrowed by her father. "Nevertheless, these two are the choices you have."

"To marry you or to be left on the ship at the mercy of your men?"

"I will undertake to guarantee your safety."

"Will you indeed? And how do you propose to do that when you will be thousands of miles away?"

"If it troubles you so, then I suppose you had best choose marriage!" he said, his voice climbing as hers rose.

"I think not!" Even as she threw the defiance at him she knew that it was futile. What else could she do? She could not go back to New Orleans, abandoning all chance of placing her plight before the emperor to throw herself on the doubtful mercy of her estranged relatives. Nor could she hope to exist alone in London without money for the weeks that must elapse before the East Indiaman sailed.

Her head came up. "There is one other possibility," she said slowly.

"I am waiting to hear it," he said when she did not go on.

"I could marry Marcel de Gruys." The moment the words were out she regretted them. It was as though she had made a dangerous commitment.

The chair creaked as Captain Thorpe leaned back. "I assume he has made you an offer."

"We were—discussing it when you sent Jeremy for me."

"And yet I think you said you did not mind being interrupted."

Julia felt the flush of rage mount once more to her hairline. She clenched her hands together to stop their trembling. "I was not aware of the necessity for haste in making him an answer."

"You mean because of your financial straits? I wonder

if de Gruys is aware that you will come to him, for all purposes, a dowerless bride?"

She wished there were some way she could remove the sardonic smile from his face. "I don't think that need concern you," she managed without allowing the quiver in her throat to be heard in her voice.

"You are mistaken. Your father, before he died, realized the problems you would have to face. He asked me to look after you, and I accepted that responsibility. I don't believe he would have approved of Marcel de Gruys as a husband for you, and therefore I cannot allow you to marry him."

"You—you can't do that!" she exclaimed incredulously.

"I think you will find I can. I told you once before—aboard this ship my word is law. If you are wise you will forget de Gruys and confine yourself to making one or the other of the choices I have outlined."

"You are insufferable! You know no one could tolerate being incarcerated on this ship for months on end."

"Then it appears you will have to marry me, doesn't it?" he said softly, but without joy.

Back in her cabin Julia snatched her nightgown from her trunk, slammed down the lid, and tossed the length of dimity onto her bunk. She jerked the pins from her hair, showering them over the top of the washstand. Taking up her silver-backed hairbrush, she brushed her hair with vicious swipes, a frown of fury drawing her brows together as she thought of the things Rudyard Thorpe had said to her. She would not marry him. She would not! She would not meekly give in and accept his solution, no matter what he said. There had to be another way. How, oh how she wished she were a man. She would snap her fingers in Captain Thorpe's face and walk away. She would need no one's aid or protection, she would be self-sufficient, able to make her own way in the world. A dream, only a dream.

Marcel. He was her best chance of escape. She could not visualize herself married to him, could not think what kind of husband he would make, but anything was better than taking the hard, supercilious captain of the *Sea Jade* to wed.

Why was he so determined to be her husband? She could not believe there was not more to it than he had deigned to tell her. Still, what it could be she could not imagine. She could not flatter herself that he could not live without her. Surely if that were so he could have found a more convincing way of couching his proposal. Persuasion, courtship, would have been much likelier ways of going about the matter. She tried to feature the captain in such a gentle guise and failed dismally. She knew very well that the more violent emotion of lust could be cloaked under courtship also, but she had seen little indication of an overwhelming passion. He had looked at her as if he would rather wring her neck than take her into the marriage bed. She suspected that he did not care much for women.

Julia, mistress for more than six years to several hundred slaves in New Orleans and at Beau Bocage, was not ignorant of the nature of human procreation. Called upon to treat cuts and bruises, dispense medicines, settle family disputes which might include infidelity, adultery, even bigamy, help the midwives deliver babies, and close the eyes of the dying, she was no stranger to the foibles of men and women. She was aware of the pleasure which could come to women through marriage, and of the pain. She could not bear to think of submitting to either from a man who was not only uncaring, but antagonistic.

But suppose she had misread the intention of Captain Thorpe? What if he had been offering her a marriage of convenience, one which could be dissolved by annulment when it no longer served a useful purpose? If that were the case his conduct became much more reasonable. It was possible she had been too hasty. She should have questioned him in more detail. Or should she? If that was what he had in mind, why couldn't he have said so? As soon as Napoleon was in power and the money her father had expended had been returned to her, the responsibility Captain Thorpe took so seriously would be at an end. With her fortune restored she could return to New Orleans—or perhaps buy a house in Paris, where in the fullness of time, with a respectable dowry to offer, she could choose a man to suit herself. It would be a marriage of affection and trust and comfort. She would be loved and cherished instead of treated with suspicion and threatened into obedience.

She would not obey. It made no difference what kind of marriage Captain Rudyard Thorpe envisioned, she would have no part of it. No matter what she had to do, she would not be his wife.

Carefully she laid down her hairbrush. Stretching, she undid the small buttons which fastened her gown, then pulled it off over her head. She removed her underskirt and chemise, then slipped her nightgown down over her breasts and hips, smoothing it into place. A quick puff of air extinguished the candle burning on the washstand, and its afterglow lasted long enough for her to step to her bunk and lie down, pulling the sheet over her. For a long time she lay with burning eyes, staring into the darkness. The ship rose and fell, rose and fell. She could hear the waves as they washed along the hull, a sighing sound. She thought of her father somewhere behind them, turning in his cold waterlogged canvas, never still, never warm. Slowly her eyelids fell, and from beneath their gritty weight slid the hot and salty tears.

"*Tell me, Mr. Free, why it is that your captain has such a dislike for women?*"

Julia strolled with her fingers in the crook of the first mate's arm. A fresh wind flapped her pelerine about her and filled the white sails overhead to bursting. The sun glittered on the deep-blue water and streaked with silver the small flying fish which leaped about the ship.

"Dislike, ma'am? Where did you get that idea?" He grinned down at her, willing to be amused.

"Is isn't an idea. I feel a distinct chill in the air when he speaks to me. If I am not to credit him with a dislike of women in general, I will be forced to concede that it is only me he cannot abide."

"I'm sure you are mistaken."

"And I'm sure I am not!"

"Rud—that is, Captain Thorpe—has a certain reserve about him. He isn't an easy man for anybody to get to know."

"And yet you stand on terms of friendship with him," she pointed out.

"Yes, but I've known him for years. As boys we used to play together, though he was somewhat older—six years my senior, in fact."

She glanced up at him in perplexity. "How does this come about? I understood that Captain Thorpe was an Englishman."

68

"It's my belief he holds dual citizenship. His father was an American, but he was born in England of an English mother. His father's people were early settlers in Baltimore. During the Revolution they remained staunch Tories and lost a great deal of their fortune because of it. When the conflict was over they sent their son, Rud's father, to England to round off his education. What they failed to realize was that their son did not follow their political leanings. He was first of all an American, and the treatment he received as a boorish colonial did nothing to change that. While visiting with friends he met and married a young Englishwoman. She refused to leave her parents or her country, and for a time her husband was content to work with her brother in the offices of the East India Company. A child was born, Rud. When the boy was ten, his father left England for America, went into a shipbuilding enterprise, and set himself up in competition with the East India Company for the tea trade. In 1811 he laid the hull of the *Sea Jade,* though she was christened the *Felicity* when she came off the slips. She was ready just in time for the hostilities that broke out between England and the United States the next year, and was commissioned a privateer with Rud's father as captain."

"And all this time his wife and son were in England?"

"His wife still refused to join him, but she did allow his son to spend several months out of each year with his father. That was when I got to know him, during the summers when he stayed with his father and grandparents in Baltimore. Then, as he grew older, he didn't come as often. He was at Oxford, then we heard he had joined the army, a dragoon regiment. Odd to think about, but a few years back he must have been fighting the emperor."

"Odd indeed," she echoed, frowning. She could not imagine why it had not been mentioned before.

"It was the winter of 1814, Rud was on leave in London, while the *Felicity* was patrolling the Irish Channel on blockade and doing a fine job of it. The privateers had nearly brought English shipping to a standstill. Some were bolder than others. Rud's father actually landed on the coast of England and made his way to London to see his wife and son. As he made his way back to his ship after one of these visits, he was ambushed and killed."

The toneless quality of Jeremy's voice made Julia turn her head quickly to stare at him. "He was discovered by naval patrols?"

"There was, of course, no official report of the incident. Rud has always believed that there was information lodged against him. You see, Rud's mother had been involved with a certain gentleman, some say an intimate of the prince regent, and it was a little inconvenient to have a husband dropping by unexpectedly."

"You mean she betrayed him?" Julia exclaimed.

"So Rud believes. After Waterloo he left the army and came back to the United States, where he gradually stepped into his father's shoes. The *Felicity* was standing offshore when Rud's father was taken, and the ship escaped without hindrance. Rud took her, renamed her, made a couple of runs down to the West Indies. He was planning to deliver a cargo of cotton to Liverpool, then set sail in the direction of China, when he was approached by your father."

"I think I begin to understand," she said. "I take it the name of his ship has nothing to do with the color green?"

"You have that right. A jade is a faithless woman, and I suppose all sailors view the sea as female, hence the *Sea Jade.*"

"And you still contend your captain has no grudge against women?"

He shook his head. "He never has much to do with the harbor women when we're in port, but I've always thought that was because he preferred quality, if you take my meaning, ma'am, and not intending any offense. There are a lot of us like that."

Julia sent him an oblique glance. It was nice to know that Jeremy Free wished her to think well of his friend, and also of himself, but it did little to ease her mind. She supposed she would have to be satisfied with the information she had managed to draw from the first mate.

"You—you won't tell Rud I spoke of his mother, will

you? He's a bit touchy on the subject. I should never have mentioned it, and I wouldn't have, except I, well, I was thinking out loud."

"Oh no," she answered with great certainty. "I would never mention it, I wouldn't dare!"

"Wouldn't dare what?"

At the sound of the captain's voice behind her, Julia swung around. Jeremy looked over his shoulder with an awkward smile, a trace of red showing beneath the freckles which dotted the bridge of his nose.

"Nothing of importance," Julia replied, her voice holding a sulky note even to her own ears. She had not seen Rudyard Thorpe since the interview in his cabin. What had passed between them at that meeting effectively prevented her from the kind of light, smiling retort which might have passed over the pause gracefully.

"As my fiancée, everything you do or say is of importance to me," Captain Thorpe said, lifting her hand to carry it to his lips. She felt the warmth of his firm mouth through her kidskin glove. The tightness of his grip warned her it would be useless to resist. She let her hand lie where he placed it, covered with his own, on his arm.

"Your fiancée?" Jeremy Free repeated.

"We reached an agreement last night," Captain Thorpe said, smiling down at her with a look which made her want to scratch his eyes out.

"I see," Jeremy said, though the expression in his face as he glanced at Julia was puzzled and a little hurt. "My congratulations to both of you."

"Thank you. And now, though I hate to mention such a word as duty—"

"Yes, of course," Jeremy said, his flush becoming more pronounced. Inclining his head, he walked away.

"I am not going to marry you!" Julia said in a furious undertone. She tried to remove her hand from his arm, but he would not release it. Face bland, he moved off in the opposite direction from that Jeremy had taken. She was forced to walk beside him.

"Why didn't you say as much to Jeremy just now?"

"I was taken by surprise, but in any case it will be much more diverting to see what you will have to say in explanation when I fail to become your wife."

"A shame that you will never see it, since it would have amused you."

Julia mistrusted such affability on his part. She glanced at him without answering.

"There is a point I would like to make, however. As much as it may give you pleasure to try to circumvent me, you will be well advised to leave Jeremy Free out of your calculations."

"I don't understand you," she said, staring out over the rail to where the flying fish played.

"I think you do, but I will speak plainer. Don't enlist his aid in your cause. He is the kind of young man who takes things seriously. He is too earnest, too kind, for his own good, and much too valuable to me to risk coming to blows with him over a woman."

"Shouldn't you look at your own conduct, then?" she suggested.

"I would, if I thought it would serve. Unfortunately, he would take it amiss, I'm sure, if I now spurned you. He is also a romantic."

"Something no one could accuse you of, captain."

"I trust not," he answered, a lifted brow lending the sting of irony to his words. He allowed a few minutes of silence to slide past as they walked. At the door to the companionway he stopped. "Since you are my bride-to-be, it will look better if you call me by my given name, don't you think?"

Annoyance at his ability to have the last word made her unwary. She turned on him, her eyes flashing, voice rising. "I am not your—"

She got no further. He reached for her, sweeping her hard against his chest. The breath left her lungs in a gasp. His lips stopped the words in her throat. Firm, burning, they possessed hers, driving all thought from her mind as in shock and confusion of the senses she clung to him.

A ragged cheer followed by a catcall signaled the interest of the crew in the spectacle. Julia stiffened, resisting

72

the arms which held her. Slowly, almost reluctantly, Rud raised his head. Without acknowledging the audience in any way, he pushed open the door of the companionway and urged her inside.

From the bottom of the stairs she looked back, a growing wrath darkening the amber of her eyes. He had not descended but stayed where he was, one hand still on the door, the other braced on the jam. A peculiar tension seemed to grip him and a mirthless smile twisted his mouth. He inclined his head. "I will see you later," he said, and swung the door shut above her.

Julia took a deep breath and let it out slowly. She could not cause a scene. The last thing she wanted was to face the seamen on the upper decks again. She was not even certain she wanted any further contact with Rudyard Thorpe at this particular moment, but he would not, she vowed, get away with his highhanded treatment of her.

Straightening her pelerine, which had been twisted over her shoulder, she turned in the direction of her cabin. She checked, one hand going to her hair, at the sight of a man lounging in the doorway of the saloon, then, schooling her features to composure she continued toward Marcel.

"I thought from the noise topside that we were being boarded by pirates at the very least," he drawled.

"Nothing so desperate," she answered, her voice tight. "The men were merely celebrating the betrothal of their captain."

"The betrothal? You cannot mean—?" He came to attention.

"Can I not? I assure you every man jack aboard the *Sea Jade* is now certain that their captain expects to wed and bed me, we may hope in that order!"

"Perhaps you had better tell me what took place," he said, stepping aside for her to enter the saloon.

The room was empty. Julia took a chair, unbuttoning her pelerine and throwing it back. Marcel sat down beside her. With one hand on the back of her chair he leaned toward her. "How did this come about?"

His sympathy, his interest, was soothing to her ruffled dignity. The only jarring note was the uneasy remembrance that Marcel had only the night before been prepared to treat her in much the same manner as Rudyard Thorpe. A shiver passed over her as she realized how alone and unprotected she was among this company of men. It seemed that New Orleans and everything familiar was dropping away into the distance behind them, and the more it receded, the less the conventions which operated there held. Soon they would have no validity at all and she would have nothing except her own strength and wits to aid her.

Pushing such despairing fancies to the back of her mind, she gave Marcel his answer. When she had done, he sat frowning until with an abrupt movement he doubled his fist and slammed it down on the table.

"Species of a dog!" he breathed. "Do you still say you have no physical appeal for him? It is as I said, he means to make you the prisoner of his desire here on this ship."

"He has given me an alternative," she reminded Marcel.

"One he knows you must refuse! A child would not be taken in by his protests of duty and philanthropy. Why should he care that Robeaud reaches St. Helena in good health? He has been paid to see that Robeaud reaches England and embarks on an East Indiaman, and for having the *Sea Jade* at Rio at the appointed time. More than that enriches him by not so much as another centime. Money, so our Captain Thorpe asserted in New Orleans, is his sole concern. Why should he volunteer his services for anything less?"

"Perhaps he has become caught up in this enterprise and does not wish to see it fail?"

"Does our success or failure depend on him? Bah! It is a hoax designed to convince you that you have no choice other than to stay on his vessel, dependent on his good-will."

She shook her head. "I cannot believe it. There was not the least sign of any such overwhelming attraction last night when the offer was made."

"No, possibly not. The English are famous for their

reserve. But this morning? How do you explain this morning?"

"I don't want to explain it, I don't want even to think about it! And I certainly don't want to be married—to anyone! All I require is a way of removing myself from this ship when we reach London, and keeping myself until such time as the arrangements for proceeding to St. Helena are complete."

"I will not press you for an answer to my suit then, my dearest Julia, at this time. I can wait. Until then, I am at your service, as you must have known that I would be. I see no difficulty in securing your release, one way and another. Once free, the question of maintaining yourself for as long as necessary should not be pressing for one of your means."

With a guilty start Julia realized that Marcel was unaware of her straitened circumstances. But why should he have to know? If she did not marry him—and she had no intention of it—the subject of a dowry did not enter into it. From all accounts he was not without funds. Surely he would not expect to be paid for whatever services he might perform for her?

"No," she answered, and managed to smile as he turned to stare at her.

Later, in the privacy of her cabin, she was assailed by doubt. A cynical part of her brain questioned if Marcel, finding her dependent on his charity, would exact any less from her than Rudyard Thorpe. Probably not. Still, what was the point in worrying about it? If she could not stay without submitting to the dictates of the captain of the *Sea Jade,* then she must go, using whatever means were available to her.

The remainder of the day she spent in her cabin going through her jewel box and trunks, and listing those items she thought she might sell. It was a painful process, not one calculated to leave her hopeful. She had the usual seed pearls and garnets bestowed on girls when they left convent school; she had a parure of topazes and a pendant and earrings of baroque pearls, but she had never been attracted to gems purely because of their value. It was doubtful if selling every bauble she possessed would keep her above a month. The golden bee could not be sold, of course. Its value could not be calculated in difficult English currency.

The day was waning, and she was thinking of resorting to the tinderbox to light her lantern, when a knock came on the door. She closed her lap desk and swung her feet off the bunk. She was a bit rumpled, but it scarcely mattered. Crossing to the door, she drew it open.

The tall frame of the captain filled the doorway. As he stood surveying her without speaking, she lifted her chin.

"Sulking?" he asked at last.

"Certainly not."

"We missed you at noon, and I thought I had better see if you were ill or just—ill-tempered."

"I did not feel like company," she said through clenched teeth.

"Catching up with your correspondence, I see?" He picked up her hand, studying the inkstains on her fingers. From there his gaze traveled to the crumpled pages of foolscap which lay on the coverlet of the bunk.

"Not at all," she denied.

"Having trouble deciding what to put in your journal concerning this morning, then," he suggested. Without waiting for permission he stepped over the threshold and moved to the bunk, where he took up a ball of paper. He spread it out with strong, capable fingers. Looking up, he said, "Not very impressive."

Julia stepped forward and twitched the paper out of his hand, her face tight with close-held anger. "It was not meant to be."

Hands on his hips, he watched as she swept the other papers together and pushed them away out of sight in the lap desk. Reaching for a scattered piece, she brushed against his uniform jacket, then drew back as if she had been burned.

"I wonder," he said, a hard note entering his voice, "if you could be persuaded to heed a word of advice?"

"For my own good, I suppose?"

76

"Yes, whether you believe it or not. Don't do anything foolish, like trying to leave the ship unescorted."

"Don't leave the ship? That sounds very much as if I am your prisoner, captain. Will you prevent me from going?" She stood straight, her hands clasped tightly before her.

"I will, if it is the only way I can guarantee your safety."

It was intolerable. What right had this man to interfere in her life? "You will forgive me if I doubt your concern is for my safety as much as for your convenience!"

His eyes narrowed, and she thought for a moment that she would be called upon to explain her meaning. Such a thing would have been impossible. Nothing could have prevailed upon her to put Marcel's suspicions into clearer terms. There was no need. With an impatient movement of his shoulders, he shrugged aside her allegations and her anger, turning to the door. "Either way," he said quietly, "the means of securing it is the same. We will expect you in the dining saloon in ten minutes."

Long after the cabin door had closed behind him Julia stood staring at the hardwood panel. She wished with sudden passion that she knew if he had understood her meaning. He might have; he was not slow. On the other hand, he could have thought she was referring to the convenience of securing a berth for himself on the India-man as her husband. Again, there was the even more innocuous interpretation—that he was determined to make her wait until he was ready to escort her ashore. A lady would naturally not have referred to anything approaching her meaning, and Captain Thorpe may have taken that into consideration. Julia was finding it increasingly hard, under her present circumstances, to cling to such refined conduct and thought processes. They served little useful purpose when it came to a need for self-preservation.

Moving to the washstand, she lifted the carafe and poured water into the basin. She took up a cloth and, wetting it, began to bathe her face, making ready to join the gentlemen for dinner.

The final days of the voyage were uneventful. Thirty-seven days out from New Orleans they came to rest at the dock in the port of London. Chill rain was falling from a leaden sky, making the day seem more advanced than it was. Though it was only midafternoon, lamps shone here and there in the gloom, marking the entrances of shipping offices and the windows of alehouses. Drays plied up and down the wharf, men shouted, and there was a great coming and going from the other ships tied up alongside them. Despite the activity, the city of London was still some distance away up the Thames.

Toward the latter part of the evening, two men in sober business dress came aboard the *Sea Jade*. Shortly thereafter, Captain Thorpe departed with them, getting into a carriage, which pulled away in the direction of the London Road. Before he was out of sight, Marcel de Gruys descended the gangway and, with portmanteau in hand, set out into the rain-lashed dusk.

A half hour passed, an hour. More lamps glowed into life in the fast-encroaching darkness. From the shelter of the companionway Julia watched for Marcel's return. The chill, damp air felt more like winter than spring to her, and she huddled, shivering with mingled cold and excitement, into her heaviest cloak. The deck of the ship was deserted as the seamen took their ease in the forecastle, awaiting the captain's return. A watch had been posted, but they were sheltering on the lee side of the vessel, out of the blowing rain. Now, her instinct shouted, now was the time. Still there was no sign of Marcel returning with a carriage.

At last the dark shape of a hackney materialized out of the mist, coming to a splashing stop at the gangway. The instant it appeared Julia took up her bandbox, which had been hidden by her cloak, felt to be sure her bonnet was secure, and made a dash for the gangway. The rough planks swayed beneath her hasty tread. Behind her, she thought she heard a shout, but she did not look back. Marcel had stepped down and was waiting to hand her into the hackney.

The interior of the ancient vehicle smelled of dust and stale sweat and the moldy straw which covered the floor. Julia hardly noticed. Tumbling onto the cracked leather seat, she laughed as she righted herself, then moved her box from the seat so Marcel could take its place. He called something she did not understand to the driver, then swung in beside her as the carriage jerked forward. Craning to see out the window, Julia looked for signs of pursuit. There were none.

"We made it, we have escaped!" she cried, placing her gloved fingers on the arm of the man beside her.

Quickly he took her hand, placing it in the crook of his elbow, clamping it close to his side. She was drawn against him, his thigh pressing hers on the seat, her shoulder rubbing his. "Yes," he said, his voice rich with satisfaction. "We have escaped."

The carriage lantern gave a faint illumination to the inside of the hackney. Julia could not see the expression on Marcel's face, but she knew he was staring down at her, waiting perhaps for her response. Pushing a decided unease to the back of her mind, she schooled her features to reflect nothing more than careless joy. "I wonder what Captain Thorpe will say when he finds his prisoner gone."

"Let's not think of the good captain. Nothing need concern us now except ourselves."

"Yes, of course. It will be so exciting seeing London. I've never been here before. Do you know it?" Leaning to peer out the window served as a good excuse for putting some small distance between them. When she settled back he had moved nearer still, retaining his hold on her hand.

"It has been some time since I was here," he answered. He seemed to speak at random, as though his thoughts were elsewhere.

"You—you have the direction of the Bonapartists here in London. We must not lose touch."

It was an unfortunate phrasing, for he immediately gave a low laugh and passed his hand beneath her cloak, over the curve of her waist and upward to her breast. "I have it," he murmured deep in his throat.

She could have assumed a stern demeanor and demanded that he cease taking such liberties, but she sensed something different in his manner. There was a recklessness about him, an aggressive force that she had not seen before, though she had caught a fleeting glimpse of it the night of his proposal in her cabin before Captain Thorpe had intervened. If he chose to ignore her demand, what could she do? Scream? Fight? Futile exercises, both of them. Her tongue might be a more potent weapon of defense. "It—it would be disappointing if we should miss the sailing of the Indiaman for St. Helena," Julia said, hastily placing her hand on his, stilling his movements.

"You need have no fears," he answered smoothly.

"But I would never forgive myself if that happened," she said a little wildly as with a twist he freed his hand, sliding the fingers beneath the lace of her décolletage.

"Compose yourself, my love," he said, his lips against the blue-veined skin of her temple.

Recognizing that succumbing to hysteria would give him a valid excuse for restraining her still further, Julia forced herself to relax. She took a deep breath. "Yes, no doubt you are right. I'm sure everything will be resolved for the best. Tell me. Where do we stay? Have you chosen some respectable hostelry for me?"

"There's an inn I used to know—the Dog and Partridge —just outside the city," he said, trailing kisses along the angle of her jaw. "We will make our way there, if you have no objections?"

She managed a light laughter. "None whatever. One place is as good as another to me."

"And to me," he said, his voice dropping lower, "so long as you are there."

He was waiting for some reaction, some answer to his declaration. She hesitated, uncertain what she should say. Was it possible that frankness would extract her from this coil? It was worth trying. "Please, Marcel," she said at last. "I told you I have no interest in being married."

"I remember very well, Julia my love, but I think you will realize how foolish such ideas of independence are for one of your loveliness. You are a constant temptation, and someone must protect you from all those who find it impossible to resist."

"Very pretty," she mocked. "I have no desire to exchange one jailer for another."

"Jailer? Not I. You will find me a most conformable husband. We shall deal well together with your fortune as well as my own behind us. We can move among the *beau monde,* maintain a townhouse in Paris and perhaps a small chateau in the country. I am not at all of a jealous nature, and if you will not mind my small peccadilloes then I will look the other way while you amuse yourself."

As he squeezed and fondled her breast Julia could feel her anger rising. The need to slap his hand away was almost overpowering. She could not bear it much longer. Something had to be done. "Fortune?" she exclaimed. "What ever gave you the absurd idea that I can command a fortune? Why, nearly all I own in the world is here with me in this carriage."

This announcement had the desired effect. Marcel drew back, his hand falling away as he stared at her in the darkness.

"What are you saying? Your father was one of the most wealthy men in New Orleans."

" 'Was' is correct. His estate and his property in town were all mortgaged to finance this expedition. You were there when the affair was discussed, you contributed to the monetary backing. You must have known."

"Hardly. Your father did not confide in me," he grated. "I was allowed to contribute my money and make one of this expedition, nothing more. I was too much the stranger to be privy to the details, though Thorpe, who is not even of the same nationality, was taken into their intimate council without a murmur."

Her father had been a good judge of men. He would not have slighted Marcel without reason. Now was not the time for examining her father's motives, however. "I— I'm sorry if this upsets your plans."

"My plans? I have none."

"I take it there will be no chateau, no Parisian townhouse?"

He gave a bitter laugh. "Did you think to batten on my wealth? I dislike to disappoint a lady, but my funds are also—invested. We are a pretty pair of fools, are we not?"

"I never pretended to want anything from you except aid in escaping Captain Thorpe," Julia said, sending him a cold glance. "If you will set me down at an inn I will be happy to see to my own comfort."

"No, no, I wouldn't think of it," he told her, his voice growing hard. "We may have to readjust our thinking, but it is possible something may yet be salvaged from this escapade."

"I don't believe I take your meaning."

There was a fixed expression in his overlarge, staring eyes. He did not reply.

The Dog and Partridge was not a large hostelry. It might once have catered to a sporting crowd in its long history, as the name suggested, but from appearances outside and in, its patrons were mostly seamen and draymen, and it had become more alehouse than inn. The smoke-filled common room resounded to a half dozen foreign tongues. Men with tarred pigtails and weathered faces jostled at the scarred and stained tables with the barrel-chested, beef-shouldered drivers of London's dray wagons. The sour reek of ale filled the house, overriding the cheap scent of the barmaids who made their perilous way between the tables and outstretched, grasping hands.

The place possessed a small and grimy private parlor that, from the close, musty smell, had not been used for many a long day. The blackened grate of the fireplace was filled with caked ash containing not a single lump of coal. A layer of dust covered the table and mantel like a coating of fur, and a spider had firmly attached the room's single candle to the wall behind its girandole of rusted tin.

The innkeeper's hunchbacked slattern of a wife showed Julia into this depressing chamber. She lit the candle from the greasy taper she carried, then went out, closing the door behind her without inquiring if Julia would like so much as a glass of water.

Marcel, engrossed in a low-voiced discussion with the innkeeper, did not join her at once. For this Julia was grateful. She needed to collect her thoughts. Marcel's great passion for her had suffered a more violent reversal than she had expected. She was glad of it, and yet it argued that every word he had said to her was a lie. Could it be that the money had been her only attraction for him? Why should that be so when he had, or so rumor said, more than adequate means? He had asserted that his funds were also invested, but the words had lacked conviction. The answer to the question she had posed might give her the key to persuading him to abandon her completely.

The chill in the room was so great that Julia kept on both her bonnet and her gloves as well as her cloak of gold-brown velvet. She was standing with her arms wrapped around her beneath her cloak when Marcel entered. Following behind him came a gangling lad of sixteen or seventeen carrying a coal scuttle. From the stains on his apron he served not only as parlormaid but as kitchen help and potboy in the common room as well. He had the vacuous expression and drooling mouth of a halfwit, but he proceeded to make a fire with clumsy dispatch.

Through the open door came also the inkeeper's wife bearing a decanter of liquor on a tray with two glasses. This she placed on a side table, then, bobbing the merest suggestion of a curtsy, went away again. When the boy had also taken himself off, Marcel shut the door and came toward her, rubbing his hands.

"Now, this is better, is it not?" he asked. "I have ordered dinner to be served in here. By the time we have had something to drink, the fire will have taken the chill from the room and we shall be most comfortable."

Taking the stopper from the decanter, he filled a glass to the brim, then moved to the other glass. From the look of the liquid and the smell which permeated the room, Julia knew it was brandy. She would have liked to refuse to partake of it, but she needed something to warm her and sustain her spirits.

With fingers which trembled a little, she took the glass Marcel offered. The muscles of her throat contracted as the drink burned its way to her stomach. She watched with trepidation as Marcel downed the contents of his glass, then refilled it before flinging himself into a chair before the fireplace. After a moment she followed his example by perching on the edge of a time-blackened settle opposite him.

She cleared her throat, turning her glass in her fingers. Watching the swirling liquid, she said, "Having something to eat here will be well enough, but I don't believe I would choose to stay for any length of time."

"No? And I was so sure it would just suit your purse."

"There must be another inn somewhere that is reasonably priced. Perhaps an inn which takes its custom from country people, farmers and their wives?"

"An excellent notion, no doubt, but I feel not the least urge to venture out into the night again. It is as cold as the devil's heart out, and there is a fog rolling off the Thames as thick as cotton wool."

"I take it you have arranged for rooms here, then?"

He took a deliberate swallow of his brandy before answering. "Room. A single room."

"What do you mean?" she asked, her head coming up sharply.

"Exactly what you think," he returned. "Why should money be paid out for two rooms when one will do? I have been considering our problem and I believe the solution is to pool our resources—I assume you do have something to add, some small amount which you expected to use to keep yourself for a time."

Julia shook her head. "My contribution will not be large. I have only a small cash holding, and my jewelry, which I was going to sell."

"Jewelry?" he said, his eyes running over her as if he expected to find her wearing it. "Let me see it."

"The pieces are not particularly valuable," she said hastily. The bandbox holding her jewel case was sitting on the table. Deliberately she kept her gaze from that direction, staring into the orange glow of the fire. Such tactics were useless.

Marcel set his glass aside. Getting to his feet, he went to the bandbox. "It is in here?" he asked, giving the silk-covered box a shake. Setting it down, he jerked apart the ribbons which held it closed. "Ah, yes, let's see what we have."

"You have no right," Julia cried, springing up and moving quickly to his side.

With one hand he held her back as he emptied out her chased-silver jewel case. Abruptly he released her. "Trinkets!" he sneered. "Nothing but trinkets. We could not live a fortnight on what they would bring. If this is what you hoped to use to pay your reckoning between now and August, you would be out on the street before summer comes."

"I told you they were of no great value," she said, pushing him aside to replace her treasures.

"So you did," he agreed, his tone vicious as he took up his glass and emptied it once more. "For the sake of my curiosity, tell me: what did you intend to do when you had no more money?"

"I don't know. I had thought perhaps the Bonapartists here in London would advance something to me in respect of my father's enormous contribution. I would repay them, of course, when Napoleon comes to power."

Marcel laughed. "My sweet little innocent, do you really expect to be reimbursed by the emperor? The man will need every penny he possesses to put an army into the field if he is to regain his crown. Why should he worry his head over the plight of one young woman, be she ever so beautiful?"

Julia, touching one hand to the golden bee which fastened her cloak at the throat, saw no need to enlighten him. "He will," she said. "He—he must."

"Never argue with a fool or a woman," he quoted, and reached for the brandy bottle once more.

Any reply she might have made was forestalled by the arrival of the loutish potboy with their dinner. From the tray he took two dull pewter plates and a pair of double-tined forks, clattering them into place on either end of the table. Between these he set a steak-and-kidney pie in a blackened dish, the pastry of which was a dirty gray. The aroma of boiled cabbage arose in clouds from a bowl which glistened with grease. Thick slices of ham crowned with fat sat on one side. On the other was a loaf of bread showing a rind of blackened crust.

What little appetite Julia had had vanished in the face of this repast. Though she removed her gloves and took up a fork, she could make no more than a pretense of eating. She could not force a morsel past the constriction in her throat. Covertly, she glanced at Marcel. He had spoken of sharing a room as if it were the most natural thing in the world. There could be little doubt that he expected them also to share the same bed. At the thought she shuddered, the grip on her fork tightening until her knuckles turned white.

The urge to jump on her feet and run to the door was almost overpowering. She had tried that with Marcel once and failed, however. He was deceptively swift, and strong. Beneath his bottle-green coat and embroidered waistcoat he had a full quota of muscles. Added to that was his present uncertain temper. Between the effects of disappointment and brandy, he had lost his urbanity, and there was an ugly look about his mouth as he stared at her across the greasy remains of his meal.

What if she succeeded in escaping? Where could she go? In the dark, cold, fog-filled streets there was as much danger as inside the inn. To return to the *Sea Jade* would be to face the wrath of Captain Thorpe.

For some reason the latter course filled her with a greater dread than dealing with Marcel.

Suddenly the man across the table pushed back his chair and got to his feet. "Shall we go up and see what kind of bedchamber has been given to us?"

Julia looked at him, seeing the grease he had not bothered to wipe from his over-red lips and the weave of his stance. "No, Marcel," she said with abrupt resolution.

"I believe I will stay here. The settle by the fire should make me a comfortable enough bed."

"What are you saying?" he demanded, leaning with his hands on the table.

"I am saying I will not share the chamber upstairs with you." Her voice trembled, but the words came out plainly enough.

"Is that so, my fine little—" He stopped, senses alert despite the brandy he had drunk, as a shuffling sound came from outside the room. While they watched, a slip of paper was pushed under the door. Scowling, he shoved his chair aside and went to pick it up.

The contents seemed to give him no satisfaction, for his frown grew blacker and he crumpled the paper into a wadded ball before stepping to toss it into the fire. He stood watching it flame up before turning away with an oath to find his hat and coat. He swung the greatcoat about his shoulder and clamped his high-crowned beaver upon his pomaded locks. At the door he stopped, looking back. "I have to go out," he said in phrases so clipped it was obvious he was laboring under a sense of ill-usage. "I will return shortly, and when I do I expect to find you tucked up in the bed in the chamber upstairs!"

When he had gone Julia breathed a long sigh of relief. A moment later she uttered a grim laugh. Why should she be relieved? Soon he would return. Nothing would have changed. She would have no one to defend her but herself.

Her gaze moved about the room, returning once more to the table in front of her. On the platter holding the sliced ham lay a knife, a sharp knife with a long, dull steel blade and a thick wooden handle. Reaching out, she took it up and wiped the grease from the blade with a chunk of stale bread. Face impassive, she tucked the knife into the inside pocket of her cloak, then went to sit upon the settle.

For a long time she sat staring into the dying embers, feeling the chill creeping back into the room. At last she sighed, and reaching up, untied her bonnet. Taking it off, she laid it to one side, then leaned her head back into the corner of the high wooden bench.

She was shaken awake some time later. The jerking knocked her head against the wooden backrest. She came awake to a red haze of pain laced with a saving anger. Without stopping to think, she hit out with her doubled fist, catching Marcel a blow to the chin.

Enraged, he snatched her to her feet, smashing a ringing slap across her face. As she gasped with pain, he twisted her arm behind her, saying through his teeth, "What you need, *ma chère,* is taming, starting with a lesson in obedience. If you will not have the nice comfortable bed, then let it be the settle!"

He forced her back down on the hard wooden bench, tearing at the closing of her cloak with one hand. Struggling in his grasp, she kicked out at him. As her slipper came into contact with his shin, he grunted, giving the pin at her throat a savage jerk. The catch of the gold bee gave way. Julia cried out, trying to save it, but he threw cloth and pin aside. His fingers dug into the soft valley between her breasts, ripping at the fragile silk faille. She felt the cold touch her bared skin as her bodice and chemise parted to her waist. And then he was pressing her back full-length along the settle. Her skirts rode above her knees and he swept them higher, his fingers raking along her thighs. Surging beneath him, she freed a hand to claw at his face, making red furrows down his cheek to his neck. He raised a hand and struck her once, twice. With the force of the last blow she felt her teeth cut into her cheek, and she went mad.

"Get off!" she screamed, heaving, twisting, her movements carrying them over the edge of the settle to the floor. Her cloak slid with them, and through the fog of her hurt and fear and fury, she heard the knife as it struck the floor. Rolling, she felt it under her, and for a moment she thought it was too entangled in the cloak for her to free. But then the wooden handle was in the palm of her hand.

His weight drove the air from her lungs. His hot, brandy-fouled breath was in her face as his mouth covered hers. She felt the wet probing of his tongue against her clenched teeth, and her breasts ached from his merciless grip. His knee pushed between her legs as he ground the hardness of his loins against her belly. The knife was turned like a sword, blade uppermost in her hand. She gritted her teeth, drawing a sobbing breath, then drove it into Marcel's side. With every nerve and sinew in her body she recognized when the blade struck bone and tore through the thinness of skin into the muscles of his back.

He screamed, writhing. Arching his back, he flopped away from her to his side, reaching back for the knife. In mad haste she scrambled from him, getting to her feet. Her legs would not support her. She fell to one knee, grasping at the edge of the table. In the light of the one guttering candle in the wall holder, she watched as Marcel floundered like a gaffed fish, blood from his wound soaking his coat, staining the floor.

Far away, beyond the confines of the parlor she was aware of a clamor, of shouting and a banging noise which barely reached her. She paid no heed. Her eyes never left Marcel. He had ceased to struggle, but lay half on his side, his panting breath loud in the small room. He had not quite been able to catch the knife, buried at a slant in his back, though one arm was twisted behind him. The fingers of his other hand twitched, and his mouth hung open though his eyes were closed.

Carefully Julia drew herself to her feet. She took a hesitant step toward him, circling slowly to his injured side. With a swift dart forward, she grasped the handle of the knife and pulled it out. She backed away before he could move, the knife held tightly in her fist. He groaned and settled to his back. With dragging steps she moved closer, peering into his face.

When the door crashed open behind her she whirled, her free hand going to her torn bodice. The tall form of Rudyard Thorpe filled the doorway, with the innkeeper and a seaman from the *Sea Jade* close behind. The captain took in the scene at a single glance, his eyes lingering on the bloodstained blade in her hand and the sprawled body of the man at her feet.

"Forgive the intrusion," he drawled. "I am sorry if my interruption is untimely."

Chapter
Five

The wedding *ceremony passed in a gray haze of un-*
reality. The priest stood before them, his lips moving in
what might as well have been a foreign language. The
altar cloth behind him, illuminated by candles, an oddity
at midday, was edged in beautiful handmade lace. Julia
stood in the place of honor with little realization of how
she had come to be there. There was some mention of a
special license, and she seemed to remember a long drive
in a carriage, but the name of the church and the identity
of the people around her were unknown.

Of the night before she recalled even less. She had no
memory of leaving the Dog and Partridge, nor of arriving
back at the *Sea Jade.* The first thing she could recall was
lying naked in her bunk in the pale light of dawn, watching
without interest as Captain Thorpe had dragged from her
trunk the white tissue silk shot with gold she had worn
on the night of the soirée, the night they had met so long
ago.

"Put it on," he had instructed, and like someone lacking will of her own, she had obeyed. Once started, she
had completed her toilette as a matter of course. She had
dressed her hair high in a coronet of curls, applied a pink-
tinged salve to her lips, and dusted her pale face with
rice-powder papers in an effort to disguise the bruise
which discolored her cheek.

She had exhibited a flash of animation when she had

90

discovered her golden bee dangling from a thread on her cloak as she donned it. And though the life had soon faded from her face, she had refused to put the pin away, holding it clasped in her hand until Rudyard had taken it from her to pin on a length of black ribbon at her neck.

Words, solemn and questioning. The faces of Jeremy Free and Second Mate O'Toole. Rudyard Thorpe's warm brown hands holding hers. The cold slide of a gold ring. When Rud drew her close for the bridal kiss, she stiffened, her eyes growing wide, clearing with the sudden onrush of fear. But his touch was gentle, the kiss he placed beside her mouth without ardor.

He released her to Jeremy Free, who kissed her cheek with an air too bashful to be frightening, and cleared his throat before he spoke his congratulations. O'Toole gave her a hearty hug and a "Bless ye, me brave darling!" Then M'sieu Robeaud was there to take her hand and carry it to his dry lips, the salute due a married woman.

A document to sign, and then she was leaving the church on Rud's arm. The sleeve of his uniform jacket was rough to her fingers, but beneath it she could feel the strength of his support. Wind, fresh and cold, fluttered her cloak around her, bringing color to her cheeks and causing her eyes to tear. Overhead a fitful sun poured its cool light down upon the street and the carriage drawn up before the gray stone church.

For the first time Julia really saw the equipage which awaited them, though she realized she must have traveled to the church in it. It was a barouche, its black sides glistening and its silver fittings reflecting like mirrors. A coachman in claret livery sat upon the box, while a footman, also in livery and a powdered wig, stood beside the folding steps, ready to swing the door open for their entrance. Four matched black horses stood stamping their hooves in impatience at being kept standing. Their leather harness was supple with polish and highlighted with silver, while nodding above each of their heads was an upstanding plume dyed claret.

"The property of my uncle, Thaddeus Baxter," Rud

said, keeping his voice low. Julia nodded and permitted herself to be handed in.

Inside, she discovered the luxury of claret velvet seats and squabs, swing-down footrests, and tiny flower vases of silver. On this occasion the vases held a single white rose, a touch which pleased her far beyond what was normal.

The coachman gave the horses their office to start. Through the window Julia caught a glimpse of Jeremy and the others and leaned forward quickly to wave. Then they were drawing past, pulling out into the street.

She settled back. Her hands fell into her lap, and unconsciously she began to turn the ring on the third finger of her left hand. She was married. The man beside her was Captain Rudyard Thorpe, and he was her husband.

"Are you warm enough?" Rud asked.

She sent him a sharp glance. "Yes, I—I'm fine."

The hustle and noise of the city was closing around them again. They threaded through narrow streets, then left them behind for an open thoroughfare.

"If you are interested in our destination, we are bound for the house of my uncle in Berkeley Square. My Aunt Lucinda has arranged to give us luncheon. I hope you will feel up to a civil conversation, for I'm sure she will wish to know all about you. She is not a gossiping sort, but she had a large hand in raising me, and takes a proprietary interest in me and my affairs."

"I understand," Julia managed. She was being warned, if that was not too strong a word, that she must be congenial to his relatives.

"My uncle and aunt have offered us the hospitality of their home while we are in London. Because of my uncle's interest in the East India Company I felt it politic to accept."

"Yes, I see." It would doubtless be convenient if the captain was to persuade his uncle to send an Indiaman to St. Helena at the proper time.

"Naturally they will be curious about the swiftness of our wedding. I recommend that you give the excuse of your father's death. You could not stay in London without protection. If you can manage to indicate that ours is a love match of overwhelming intensity, it would be all to the good. We were married very quietly because of your mourning, of course."

"Of course," she echoed, a hollow feeling in the pit of her stomach.

"You need not be too apprehensive. I will not leave you alone for any length of time."

Was she supposed to be grateful for that consideration? Try as she might, she could find no hint of gratitude within herself. She flicked a glance at the man beside her from the corner of her eye. His face was set in a masklike expression, his blue eyes staring unseeingly ahead. One arm rested on the window ledge, while he thoughtfully rubbed his chin with his thumb. His other hand lay on his muscular, buff-covered thigh. Between them on the seat was his tricorn hat with its dull gleam of gold braid.

The carriage ride was such a contrast with the one she had taken the day before with Marcel that she shivered a little, comparing them in her mind. The action, small as it was, attracted Rud's attention.

"You are all right?" he inquired.

Unconsciously she drew back into her corner of the carriage. "Yes. Yes, I'm all right. It is just that I can't seem to remember, Captain Thorpe, how I came to be here with you. Oh, the wedding is plain enough in my mind, but I don't seem to recall agreeing to marry you."

"Don't you?" he inquired, his voice calm, quiet.

For an instant Julia thought she saw a shadow of sympathy flit over his face. Before she could be certain, it was gone, replaced by a faintly ironic interest.

"No," she answered baldly. "I don't understand how it comes about, but I can bring to mind very little that happened after—"

When she did not go on he prompted, "After—what?"

She closed her eyes without answering, her face paling as the memory of Marcel, writhing on the floor with the knife in his back, returned.

"Julia?" he said, reaching out to touch her clasped hands.

Immediately her eyes flew open. "Marcel," she gasped, removing her hands to touch the bee at her throat. "Is he—is he dead?"

"Not when I last saw him," Rud answered, leaning back once more. "He will live to take in other foolish young women."

"You were there. You thought I was going to stab him again. I remember."

"Yes, so I did. You will forgive my arriving at that unfortunate moment. A few seconds later would have done just as well."

"How did you know I would be there of all the inns in London?"

"I am afraid I must admit that I set a watch on you. One of my men followed you when you left the ship. He had been given no instructions except to discover where you put up. When he saw you ensconced for the night at the Dog and Partridge he returned to the ship to report to me. Since I was away in town it was some time before he could make his report. I left at once for the inn, but arrived too late."

"Not too late to take me back to the ship, if that was your purpose."

"I would have preferred to spare you the kind of unpleasantness you had to endure because of my tardiness."

The abrupt tone of his voice inspired belief. An answering honesty compelled her to say, "The fault was mine. It would not have happened if I had not left the *Sea Jade*. You must realize the reason I left. It was because I objected to being married against my will, and yet I find myself now in exactly that position. Again I ask you, Captain Thorpe. How did that come about?"

"Are you accusing me of taking advantage of you in your moment of weakness?" he asked. "If so, I can only plead that last night you were not unwilling."

"Next you will be saying I was eager!" she exclaimed, anger kindling in the depths of her golden eyes. "Well, I refuse to believe it."

"And next I expect to hear you denying that you asked

me to spend the night in your cabin," he drawled, his eyes oddly intent as they rested on her face.

She would have liked to oblige him. Instead, she found the memory returning of herself lying unclothed beneath the coverlet of her bunk while Rud made himself free in her cabin, rummaging in her trunk for a gown. That was in the clear light of morning. What might have taken place during the night?

"What are you saying?" she asked, keeping her voice even by an effort of will.

She was not to receive an answer. Before he could reply, the carriage drew in at the curb of a Palladian mansion. By the time the wheels had ceased rolling, the footman had appeared to swing the carriage door open and let down the steps.

If Rud had acquired the use of his uncle's carriage, it stood to reason that he had already called upon the Baxter household. It was not surprising, then, that the elderly butler who opened the door to them accepted their arrival with perfect composure.

"Good morning, captain, madam," he said, taking Rud's hat. "On behalf of the staff and myself, may I offer congratulations on your nuptials."

"Thank you, Masters. Don't bother to announce us. I can find my way." Rud clapped the butler on the back, and as the man beckoned to a footman to convey their baggage from the carriage, he touched Julia's arm, indicating a pair of doors which opened off the wide entrance hall to the left.

Throwing open the door, he ushered her into a sitting room done in shades of pale yellow and green. Julia received an impression of cool elegance, of polished furniture, shining crystal, and bouquets of spring flowers. An instant later her attention was caught by the man and woman who came forward to greet them.

Thaddeus Baxter was a large, solidly built man with a high forehead exposed by receding, sandy-gray hair, and a merry twinkle in his blue eyes. Some resemblance between him and his nephew could be traced in his features, but there was an openness about his expression which went well with his ruddy complexion and hearty manner. His wife was a slight, rather wispy woman who, when she stood to come toward them, tumbled the book she was reading, one of Miss Austen's romances, from her lap. A lavender morning gown with flowing sleeves contributed to the fly-away impression. Despite this beginning, before Julia had been in the lady's company for a quarter of an hour she was convinced that Rud's Aunt Lucinda was sharper than she appeared.

A bottle of champagne was broached in honor of the occasion. Rud, standing with his back to the fireplace, his wineglass in his hand, made what Julia felt to be a credible explanation of their romance upon the seas. Hearing him, one would have thought he had spent months making himself known to her family in New Orleans so that nothing could have been more natural than a dying father's benediction upon their union. The smiles he sent her as she sat beside his aunt, his handsome gesture of a silent, loving toast, would have been enough to convince a less levelheaded woman that he was as smitten by her attractions as he pretended. Indeed, to have him smile at her in that warm, sincere fashion was a revelation for Julia. It softened the harsh planes of his face and brought a more gentle, almost sensitive look to his eyes. At one point he addressed her as his darling Julia in such an intimate tone that she found herself blushing like a convent-school miss. Under the indulgent gaze of his uncle and aunt there was no hope of open reprisal. The best she could do was send him a look of such languishing adoration that he stared, momentarily losing track of what he was saying to his uncle.

Not long afterward, her hostess offered to show her to the rooms prepared for Rud and herself. Leaving the gentlemen behind, they mounted the stairs to the upper level.

The rooms allotted to them consisted of one bed-chamber, a dressing room, and a sitting room. The suite was exquisitely decorated with cream damask walls and velvet drapes of deep azure blue at the windows. Rugs of an oriental design in cream and blue and black were scattered on the polished floor. Nothing had been neglected for their comfort. The sitting room was supplied not only with the normal settee and chairs, but also a desk outfitted with paper and quills and sealing wax. A dish of fresh fruit sat upon a small table suitable for private dining, and a bookcase held a selection of choice volumes. The dressing room was commodious, with plenty of space for a hip bath, Watteau screen, toweling rack, and shaving stand, in addition to the dressing tables.

Still, it was the bedchamber with its enormous Elizabethan tester bed, hung with a tapestry of shepherds and shepherdesses a-Maying, that claimed Julia's attention. She stared at it in consternation. Through some peculiar disorder of the senses, she had not had time to recognize the implication of her early-morning marriage. Now it struck her like a blow.

"My dear, are you feeling unwell?" the elderly woman asked, moving to draw the drapes, letting in the bright light of a southern exposure.

Julia turned away from the other woman's searching eyes. "I have a slight headache. Nothing worth mentioning."

"But you should have said something. You must lie down here on the chaise, and I will send for a glass of hartshorn and water."

"No, please," Julia protested. Though her headache was real enough, she did not like to make too much of it. The thing she required most was the thing she was least likely to be allowed, a few moments alone.

The other woman hesitated. "I don't like to pry, my dear, but I am not constituted to ignore the physical hurts of my guests, particularly when that guest is the new bride of my dearest nephew. I have been studying the bruises which mar your lovely complexion for this past hour, and despite the fact that I know men are unpredictable creatures at best, I cannot believe that Rud inflicted them upon you."

"Oh, no! You must not think that," Julia said, truly dismayed that Rud should be falsely suspected. "I—we

97

encountered bad weather at sea and I stumbled over my own feet."

"That does not explain the bruises on your wrists. However, I will not press you. Our acquaintance has been short, but I like you, Julia, and I would like to say that should you decide to give me your confidence, I would be honored. With that out of the way, let me say that if I may be of help in any other way you must not hesitate to ask. My carriage is at your service for any little errands you may have. If you require a maid, there are several girls in the house who would be happy to serve you while you are here. If there is anything else you need for your comfort, do not be shy. You have only to make your wishes known."

Unaccountably, Julia felt tears well into her eyes. She blinked them back with an effort, but there was still a constriction in her throat when she expressed her appreciation. "There is one thing," she continued. "I must go into black for my father, but I did not come prepared."

"Naturally not," the other woman answered with understanding. "Such a sad loss, and so unexpected. We must see what can be done. Perhaps my modiste will have something made up. These things always catch one unawares, do they not? Not at all in the mood for deciding on materials and trimmings."

From the style of the gown Lucinda Baxter was wearing, Julia knew the modiste used by Rud's aunt would not be inexpensive. "I must warn you, madam, that I do not have a great deal to spend."

"You must not be so formal, my dear. Call me Aunt Lucinda as Rud does, if you like. As for the expense, I am positive my nephew will not begrudge a few gowns, even if they are mourning wear. Black is notorious for flattering ladies of your blond coloring. A pity the conventions prevent you from going much into society, but I think a small dinner or two to make you known to my closest friends will be unexceptionable."

Julia smiled without further protest. Rud must disillusion his aunt; she could not. As for the rest, she allowed herself to appear delighted at the expected dinner parties. In truth, she dreaded the thought. In her present state, meeting a collection of strangers could be nothing but a chore. She felt like seeing no one, doing nothing, only shutting herself away somewhere where no one could disturb her. That would never do. She must control such longings. For her own sake she must put everything that had happened, her father's death, Marcel's brutal treachery, behind her. And yet, how could she? She was trapped in a loveless marriage that was the direct result of those things.

When the luncheon gong sounded, Julia splashed water on her face, applied another dusting of rice powder, and with Rud's aunt beside her, descended the stairs.

The meal passed without incident. The conversation was carried for the most part by Rud and his uncle and aunt as they tried to catch up on the events of the past three years. Now and then one of the three would stop to include her pointedly in the discussion or apologize for speaking of people she did not know. It did not matter at all to Julia. The headache she had claimed earlier was growing worse. The food before her, though beautifully prepared, could not tempt her appetite. She pushed it around on her plate in a halfhearted attempt at eating, though every bite she took seemed to stick in her throat. It was an immeasurable relief when Aunt Lucinda, after sending Julia a shrewd glance, placed her napkin beside her plate and announced that she had lately taken to having a short nap after luncheon every day to recruit her strength for the evening. When her husband stared at her in amazement, she merely returned him a limpid look and shepherded Julia from the room.

In her bedchamber Julia took the pins from her hair and brushed the lustrous golden-blond strands into smooth order. She removed her gown, and wearing only her chemise, slid between the sheets scented with lavender. A cloth soaked in cologne had been recommended for her brow by her hostess, and since Rud's aunt had been kind enough to send a maid to her with the compress, she settled it in place. Aunt Lucinda had offered to have a fire made in the bedchamber, but Julia had refused. Now she wished she had not been so hasty. Her feet were like ice. Despite the pale spring sunshine outside, there was a chill within the thick walls of the mansion.

Lying flat on her back and gazing at the carved headboard and turned posts of the Elizabethan bed did nothing to help her troubled senses. There was a voluptuousness in the representations of shepherd and shepherdesses in courting poses, in the soft mattress and coverlet, that disturbed her. As time passed, the turnings of her imagination presented images of Rud and herself between the linen sheets which left her appalled. With determination, she pushed them from her. She must not succumb to what was without doubt a *crise de nerfs*. Searching through her mind, she discovered what must surely be the cause of such a mental trick as her mind had played——the suggestion that she had invited Rud to remain with her in her cabin. There were some important questions which required answers concerning the night before. She must face them. Avoiding them solved nothing.

Was it possible that she had taken the man into her bed? She did not feel within herself that it could be so; still, she was aware of a certain tenderness between her thighs. It could be explained away by her struggle with Marcel, the prodding of his knee as he sought to spread-eagle her beneath him. She could not believe that after fighting so desperately to protect her maidenhead from one man she would give it up without a struggle, or at the very least without some memory of the process!

True, Rud had not mentioned lovemaking between them. What he had said was that she had invited him to stay with her in her cabin. But what if his failure to put the deed into words had been mere politeness, the reluctance to embarrass her? Such a possibility must cast a new light on their relationship. What had happened to the marriage of convenience he had hinted at so short a time ago? Had he found her more attractive than she had guessed?

No. No, she would not admit the prospect even for a moment. Every instinct resisted it. She could not, would not be the wife of Rudyard Thorpe in anything except name. Her wits must have been wandering indeed for her to permit this ridiculous arrangement of a single bedchamber between them. What did she care what his aunt thought of their marriage? Many husbands and wives had separate quarters. She would demand that she be given another room. Let her husband make what explanations he would!

It was amazing how much better she felt following this decision. The agitation deep inside her grew calmer. Even her headache began to loosen its grip. She was just drifting into sleep when the door of the bedchamber swung open. Through slitted eyes she saw Rud enter, closing the door softly behind him. At the sight of him, her resolution nearly misgave her and she lay still, allowing her lashes to rest on her cheeks.

He came closer, moving silently, only his clothing rustling in the quiet room. The side of the bed gave as he sat down. "Julia?" he said in a low voice.

For a long moment she did not move, and then, goaded by the cowardice of her action, she opened her eyes, reaching up to sweep the cologne-soaked cloth from her forehead. "Yes? I'm not asleep."

"How is your head?"

"Well enough," she answered, the difficulty of concentrating on what she intended to say making her sound ungracious. To make amends she gave him a small, polite smile. Lying full-length while he sat over her left her feeling at a disadvantage. She drew herself erect, keeping a firm grasp on the sheet and coverlet, and leaned back against the headboard. There was something of a disadvantage also in being caught in a state of undress, one she felt greatly as Rud's gaze moved over her bare shoulders.

"If there is anything you would like—a glass of water or a cup of tea—you have only to pull the bell rope."

She nodded. "I—I'm glad you came in. There is something we must discuss."

"By all means," he replied.

She glanced at him through her lashes, wishing he were not quite so close. "Are you familiar with these rooms your aunt has given us? If so, you must be aware that the suite contains only a single bedchamber. If we put our heads together surely we can find some pretext for requesting separate sleeping accommodations."

"We might," he agreed, "if there was a reason for putting ourselves to the trouble."

"You must know there is. No matter what we pretend to your aunt and uncle, ours is not a love match. Why must we continue the farce even into our private moments?"

"Because the private moments, as you style them, are some of the most enjoyable in marriage, with or without the sentimental affection most women call love. No, my girl. You'll not be rid of me so easily."

"I don't understand you," she said, frowning as she stared at him. "You yourself suggested that ours would not be a true marriage."

"Did I?" he murmured. "Foolish of me—if I ever said it. Are you quite certain you took my meaning, or did you take only what you wanted to believe?"

"Are you saying that you always intended to—to—"

"To consummate our marriage. Yes, I will plead guilty to that."

"But you don't even like me," she protested.

"Not so. In any case, what does it matter? Liking is a feeble reaction to a woman compared to others a man may feel."

"I must say I have seen little sign of these strong emotions you hint at," she said, looking away across the room to where a Queen Anne wardrobe took up a major part of the far wall.

"Have you not?" he queried so softly that she was reminded against her will of that afternoon on the deck of his ship when he had claimed her as his fiancée, sweeping her into his arms before all his men.

"I had the distinct impression," he went on, "that my advances would not be welcome. If this discussion is in the nature of a complaint on that score I will do my best to make amends." He moved closer, leaning to rest his weight on his hands on either side of her body.

Staring up into his eyes bright with laughter, she thought she saw a hint of mischief in their depths. It was galling that he found her attempt to alter the situation amusing, but she could not prevent her startled reaction as he came nearer. "No!" she said sharply. "I meant nothing of the kind."

"You are quite certain?" he asked, shifting his weight in order to take up a strand of her honey-gold hair, placing it so that it curled across her breast where the sheet had slipped lower.

As his finger brushed the soft exposed curve, every nerve in her body contracted. Without conscious thought, she brought her hands up and pushed with all her might against his chest. He rocked backward, but even as he fell, his strong hands caught her forearms, pulling her with him. The generous width of the mattress cushioned their fall. For an instant she lay flushed and furious against his chest, and then before she could catch her breath she was heaved up and over onto her back.

Tangled in the bedclothes with his weight pressing down upon her, she could not move. She opened her lips, and his mouth, warm and vibrant, came down on hers, smothering the cry she had been about to make in her throat. It was an invasion of her senses more probing than she had ever known. Her heart pounded with a primitive mixture of rage and fear and helplessness. She could feel the rasp of his beard on her chin, the press of the buttons and braid of his coat into her side. Urgency mounted to her brain with the shattering force of panic. A tremor passed over her body, and then she began to tremble as with an ague. Tears rose behind her eyelids and squeezed from the corners of her eyes into her hair. She had not meant to cry; it was a weakness she deplored. But in her mind's eye she could feel the marauding hands of Marcel upon her in drunken lust once more.

Abruptly Rud raised his head. When she opened her eyes he was staring down at her. The laughter had fled from his expression, leaving it dark and still as he studied her bruised and tear-stained face. With a soft imprecation, he levered himself up and pushed off the bed. Turning his back to her, he adjusted his coat and ran his hand back over his hair. He stood for a moment with his fingers gripping his neck, then moved to the door.

With his hand on the knob, he turned back. "I would advise you not to trouble my aunt with our sleeping arrangements," he said. "From now on, your place is with me."

When the door had closed behind him, Julia sat up. She wiped her eyes on the corner of the sheet, taking a deep, trembling breath, then sat with the material clutched between her fists. Arrogant, insufferable man. She hated him, she told herself. He was so sure of himself, so certain of what was best for her. If he expected compliant gratitude for what he was doing for her, he was going to be sorely disappointed. She suspected that he had taken advantage of her mental malaise following Marcel's attack. She was not by nature a vindictive person, but if she was ever able to prove her suspicions, one Captain Rudyard Thorpe would live to regret what he had done. It did not matter that she had no means of living otherwise. If she had wanted to trade her favors for financial advantage, she could have been wed any number of times these past five years. She had not taken that degrading course and she did not propose to do so now.

With the effects of her agitation still coursing thorough her veins, it was impossible to compose herself for sleep once more. In a defiant mood, she slid out of bed and gave the bell pull a hard tug. By the time she had searched her dressing gown out of the wardrobe, a neat, trim maid was tapping on her door.

Julia greeted the girl with a pleasant smile. "I would like a fire, if you please, and then a bath."

"Yes, mum," the girl replied as if carrying water up the servants' stairs for a bath was a regular afternoon occurrence. "Will that be all, mum?"

"A little extra hot water would not come amiss. I would like to wash the seawater from my hair."

"Certainly, mum," the maid answered, and went away to do her bidding.

Until she stepped into the hot, steaming tub, Julia had

not realized quite how caked with salt she had felt. The only fresh water on the ship had been reserved for drinking. The passengers had been forced to perform their ablutions in seawater or go unwashed. She sighed, reaching for the cake of soap scented with attar of roses as she sank lower into the copper tub.

Taking advantage of her wakefulness, the maid whisked in and out of the room, returning freshly laundered clothing and taking the lavender muslin that Julia indicated she would wear downstairs to dinner away to be pressed. From behind the bath screen set to protect her from the drafts and reflect the heat of the fire, Julia could hear her moving about the room. When she called out that she would be back in a few minutes to pour the rinse water for Julia's hair, Julia gave a languorous assent.

It was the cooling temperature of the silken water which spurred her into action. Closing her eyes tightly, she ducked her head to dampen her hair, then worked rose-scented lather through her long, honey-colored tresses. Rinsing it by submerging, she soaped her hair a second time. At the sound of the door opening and closing she called out to the maid, "I'm ready for the final rinse."

The girl did not reply, but footsteps drew nearer. There was a metallic clank as the can of water left ready nearby was taken up. The water cascaded over Julia's head in a perfect, steady stream which enabled her to free her hair of the last vestige of lather before the can was empty. Blindly, she reached for a towel to dry her face, and it was placed into her hand. She opened her eyes, smiling a little as she turned with a ready compliment for the maid, reaching to blot the water from her hair.

Abruptly her smile died. It was Rud who stood with the can balanced on the edge of the tub and one hand resting on his hip. She brought her arms down, crisscrossing them over her breasts. "What are you doing in here?" she demanded.

"I noticed all the coming and going, and decided to see the cause of the commotion. Seeing it, I stayed for the view—"

"You—" She stopped, unable to find the words to express her outrage. A flush burned its way upward to lie crimson across her cheeks. "Get out," she whispered, then cried louder, "Get out!"

The maid, choosing that moment to enter once more, turned smartly and went out the door again, closing it behind her.

"Temper," Rud said with a shake of his head. "Mustn't yell at the servants."

"I wasn't yelling at the servants," she said, through her teeth.

"I'm glad you realize it at last," he answered. "You won't be surprised if I don't follow orders too well."

Setting down the water can, he turned his attention to the folding screen. "I'll just move this out of your way," he murmured politely. Closing it, he set it back into the dressing room whence it had come. That done, he strolled back into the bedchamber and took a seat on the velvet-covered slipper chair, stretching his long legs before him.

Without the protection of the screen the chill air of the room wafted about Julia's wet shoulders. She shivered a little as cold water from her hair trickled down her bare back. "I would like to get out of the tub—if you would step outside the room. Please," she added as a closed look came down upon his face.

He stared at her, his eyes on the pearl sheen of her skin as the firelight played over her shoulders and struck highlights across the curves of her breasts. His throat moved as he swallowed. "It pleases me to stay exactly where I am."

Tension seemed to vibrate in the air between them. Julia clenched her teeth, holding onto her anger like a shield. "I cannot get out with you in the room."

"Have you forgotten? I am your husband."

"How can I forget?" she asked, bitterly aware of the water fast growing cold around her.

"I will admit that it seems difficult to me under the circumstances. Could it be that is the problem?" he mused. "Perhaps you have some blemish you would like to hide from me, bowlegs or six toes on each foot!"

She flashed him a fulminating glance. "I have no blemishes," she informed him without the least inclination to prove it.

"No, I thought not, from what I could see last night." He gave a slight shrug. "Of course, the light was not the best."

"Last night?" she said warily, her eyes wide as she stared at him.

"When I put you to bed," he explained in a matter-of-fact tone that was belied by the intent look in his eyes as he studied her face. "Could it be," he went on before she could open her lips to speak, "that I am being dense? Could it be that you are waiting for me to offer my assistance in removing you from your bath? Such gallantries are beyond the knowledge of a mere sea captain. I am afraid you will have to prompt me if I fail to move quickly enough in these matters."

As he gathered his feet under him and started toward the tub, Julia's eyes widened with alarm. "No," she said, holding out a hand as if to ward him off. "I was waiting for no such thing. I—I can get out myself."

Her words had no effect. He continued to advance. Julia scrambled to her feet, sending water splashing over the rim of the tub. The linen hand towel she held was woefully inadequate for the task she expected of it; still, she did her best to pull it about her. Her gaze on Rud, she stepped back, making ready to leave the tub on the side opposite her husband, hoping to place its width between them. She had forgotten the cake of soap. As the sole of her foot came in contact with it, she slipped. Flinging her arm out for balance, she dropped the towel. Her cry of despair was cut off as Rud sprang forward, one hard, sinewy arm catching her about the ribcage. An instant later she felt his other arm beneath her knees as she was lifted, wet and dripping, against his chest.

For long moments she kept her lashes lowered while the heat of a furious blush suffused her. Her embarrassment was so acute she could not move. She felt clumsy and bedraggled with her wet hair coiling snakelike about her shoulders. If she could have caused herself to vanish she would have done so instantly.

At last she raised her eyes to a point where she could see the damp stain on his chest. "You are getting wet," she said in a low voice, touching her fingers to his jacket as if to be certain of the actuality of her statement.

"So I am." There was a peculiar tightness in his tone that was not caused by the effort of supporting her weight.

"You can put me down."

"I wonder."

The muscles of his arms were corded like steel. She could feel the hard, steady beat of his heart. His breathing was deep, not quite even.

Almost against her will, she lifted her gaze higher to where a pulse throbbed in the strong column of his neck. The muscles of his jaws were ridged. From behind the screen of his lashes his eyes burned fiercely blue. As they raked over her, an uncontrollable ripple of gooseflesh moved in their wake. Despite the warmth of his body where she lay against him, Julia felt chilled. Her eyes grew enormous, deepening to amber pools, and her nerves stretched, teetering on a scream.

Soft and warm, his breath drifted over her as he let out the pent-up air in his lungs. He set her feet on the floor, reached for a Turkish bath sheet which lay warming near the fire, and wrapped it around her. His hands moved over her, brisk and hard, bringing a welcome rush of warmth to her cold flesh. An instant before such a ministration became unbearable he drew back. Stepping to the bell pull, he gave it a yank.

It was plain that the maid had been waiting outside in the hall from the promptness with which she answered the summons. There was a passive look on her plain face, and over her arm she carried Julia's muslin gown, freshly pressed.

Rud swung from the window at her entrance. He surveyed the gown with grim displeasure. "Madame will not be dressing for dinner," he said. "Convey our regrets to my aunt and tell her that we require a meal—a high tea will do—to be served in our room. And request a footman to come and take away this cold water and prepare a hot bath for me."

The maid bobbed a series of curtsies in token of her understanding of this spate of orders. She was at the door when Rud called her back.

"Before you go, my wife needs her dressing gown."

"Yes, sir."

With deft hands, the maid searched out the required garment, divested Julia of her towel, and, standing as a screen, wrapped her in the garnet velvet dressing gown with its deep cuffed sleeves. As an afterthought she handed Julia her silver-backed brush and comb.

When the girl had gone, Rud unbuttoned his jacket and stripped it off, flinging it at a chair. He began to slip the studs from his shirt, his gaze on Julia as she stood watching him.

"I would advise you to take advantage of the drying effects of the fire for your hair," he said, dragging the tail of his shirt from his breeches. "Unless, of course, you would like to perch on the side of the tub while I take my bath? No? I was afraid you would not find that suggestion appealing!"

Chapter Six

The window of the bedchamber allotted to the newly wedded couple looked out over a small park. The soft green of new leaves shone like jewels on the gray branches of the trees within the iron fence, while nearer the house was a single apple tree, white with blossom. Yellow daffodils nodded along the brick walks, their heads heavy with rain. A fine mist had begun to fall once more from the gray sky. It glistened on the tree trunks and speckled the puddles on the walks. The clouds seemed to press down upon the house, bringing an early twilight. There was an intimacy about the gathering dimness, the rain, and the warm room behind her that Julia found disquieting.

The footman who had brought the water for Rud's bath had also brought a brace of lighted candles. As Julia stood at the window staring out, she discovered that the glass panes with the deepening dusk behind them formed a mirror. In their reflective surface, she could see Rud, his long length folded into the tub, sluicing his arms and shoulders with the steaming hot water. There was a certain fascination in the way the muscles of his back rippled as he leaned forward, reaching for the facecloth. The broad expanse of his shoulders was sun-bronzed, as though he was used to going without a shirt in sunny climes or when he had no female aboard his ship. The red glow of the coals in the fireplace lent a copper sheen, giving him, with his dark hair growing low on the back of his neck, the look of a red Indian.

That impression was dispelled the instant he stood up. Below his waist the skin was pale, leaving a sharp line of demarcation across his flat belly. Broad chest tapering into slim hips and muscled thighs, sculptured planes and hollows; for an instant Julia was aware of the strength and symmetry of masculine beauty. Then as Rud glanced in her direction, his eyes on her rigid back, she dragged her eyes away to concentrate on the lily pattern of the spiked iron fence below.

Nevertheless, she was conscious of Rud moving about behind her, of the casual, almost deliberate way he reached for a length of toweling to wrap about his waist, the way he ran his fingers back through his sleek, wet hair. It was an inexpressible relief when he tossed the towel aside and strode to the bed to don the dressing gown of snuff-colored velvet which had been laid out for him. By the time the heat had left her face and she had regained her composure, the high tea Rud had ordered had arrived.

They sat down to a small table between two chairs in front of the fire. The room had been tidied and all sign of their baths cleared away. The only reminder was in the damp carpet beneath their feet. The hot tea was delicious, and, after her light lunch, Julia found herself well able to do justice to the smoked ham, hot buttered scones, and dark fruitcake which accompanied it. The iron restraint Rud appeared to have imposed upon himself might also have had something to do with the revival of her appetite. Twice he had broken through her defenses, and twice he had drawn back. Should she credit him with the instincts of a gentleman, or was he intent on some deeper game? Glancing at him as he lounged across from her with his hair falling in a close-cropped curl onto his forehead and his dressing gown open to the waist, she could not guess.

She picked up the silver teapot and looked inquiringly at his cup. He held it out to her, and she filled it before pouring her own half full. Setting down the pot, she leaned back with her cup in her hand. The room had grown comfortably warm. The hiss of the fire was loud, though it had burned away to no more than a bed of glowing embers. Warily, Julia recognized a sense of intimacy growing between herself and the man across the table as the rain continued its gentle music and the night drew in. An unrelieved black shrouded the window now, and shadows hung in the corners of the room. The canopied bed loomed large as the candles on the table shrank into their sockets.

Slanting a glance at Rud once more, she discovered him staring at her in brooding seriousness as he swirled the tea in his cup.

"Have—have you spoken to your uncle about the ship?" she asked. It was difficult to force the words past her stiff throat, but she had to do something to return their relationship to its proper footing.

"An East Indiaman, the *David,* is due in port in a couple of weeks. There is a chance that she can be routed to St. Helena. She has made the run before."

"Your uncle did not find your interest in the ships of the East India Company unusual?"

"Possibly, but I suspect he credited it to my increased responsibilities as a family man."

An ironic smile tugged at one corner of his mouth. Julia saw nothing amusing. "How will you explain your sudden desire to leave the *Sea Jade* and sail in the *David* when the time comes?"

"I'm not certain," he answered. "What if I say it is a whim of my lady wife's?"

"I hardly think your uncle can be expected to believe that."

"Why not?"

"It must be obvious," she said tartly, unable to put her meaning into words.

"Not to me. You are a beautiful woman. I must have been besotted with you, must I not? Or I would not have married you out of hand the instant my ship touched shore. You may think my uncle and aunt have seen little sign of affection between us. That, my dear Julia, can be easily mended."

There was a devilish gleam in his eyes she could not like. She had the distinct feeling that she was being baited. Her best course, it seemed, would be to refuse the challenge. "Surely there is some other excuse you could use —business in Rio de Janeiro, for instance?"

"A possibility, though the question arises as to why I did not travel there in the *Sea Jade*. Since we are to meet my ship there, we can still say you preferred to travel out in the larger, more comfortable ship, and like a doting husband, I decided to indulge you."

"Besotted and doting," she said, falling in with his mood of cynical amusement. "I wish I may live to see it!"

Tilting his head to one side, he inquired, "Do you indeed?"

She would not be drawn. "Oh, very well, make me the villainess of the piece. I suppose if you can bring yourself to appear in such a ridiculous light, I can bear to play the spoiled and pampered bride."

"I trust it may not be too much of a hardship," he said, though the smile he gave her sent alarm scurrying along her veins.

Their meal finished, Rud rang for a footman to clear away the remains. When the door had closed behind the silent-footed servant, he stepped to the fireplace, turning his back to the coals.

"Shall we order the fire replenished, or would you prefer an early night?" he asked.

"As you wish," she replied, "though I suggest you make some kind of arrangement for a bed for yourself first." She had been waiting some time for the right moment to make this suggestion. It was a relief to have it finally arrive.

He lifted an eyebrow. "Are you trying to tell me you are a restless sleeper? Or that you snore? Never mind, I'm sure there will be compensation enough in sharing a bed with you to make up for any little peculiarity."

"You know very well that was not what I meant," she said in frustration. He was so certain of himself that it was maddening.

"You found this ancient bed too uncomfortable to be borne, then? It's good of you to want to spare me the discomfort, but I assure you I am used to it, and besides, I would not for anything distress my aunt by refusing to occupy it. She actually thinks she is honoring us by allowing us the use of it. Good Queen Bess slept in it, you know."

Goaded by embarrassment as well as exasperation, Julia said roundly, "I don't care who slept in it, I don't intend to sleep in it with you!"

"No?" he inquired, shedding his air of banter like the dropping of a cloak.

"No!"

"Can it be," he asked in that same soft, slow tone, "that you are afraid of me?"

She realized suddenly that as annoying as his teasing had been, it was infinitely preferable to this direct attack. His deep-blue eyes held steady on hers, demanding an answer. Pride and the strength of her spirit would allow only one. "No," she said.

The briefest hint of satisfaction flitted across his face and was gone. "I thought not."

"I'm not afraid of you, but I don't trust you either."

He stared down at her, his gaze moving over the determined tilt of her chin, the firm corners of her tender mouth. His voice was abrupt as he said, "You stand in no danger of rape from me."

This was plain speaking. If that was what he wanted, he could certainly have it. "My relief would be greater if it were not for what took place this afternoon."

"You have a point," he conceded after a moment, "though I think something must be allowed for provocation."

"Provocation! I deny any such thing!"

"Perhaps it was not deliberate."

"How kind of you to say so," she flared. "I refuse to be held in any way accountable for your reactions!"

"No," he agreed unexpectedly. "What troubles me is whether you can be held accountable for your own."

His meaning escaped her. Did he refer to her instinctive repugnance for being close to a man, her horror at being overpowered? Or was he harking back to the night before, after he had returned her to the ship, when, he had hinted, her response to him had been quite different?

"I don't understand you," she said at last.

"Probably just as well," he said. smiling with a wry twist of the lips that suggested the humor was directed at himself. "The problem that concerns us at the moment is where we are going to sleep. If you are not afraid of me, and if you accept my given word that I will not force myself upon you, why can we not both be comfortable in yonder bed?"

"I could never sleep."

"You are more likely to find sleep there than on any other bed or pallet you may improvise. Oh, yes, you heard me right. Since I have no objection to sharing the bed with you, I think you must be the one to seek another arrangement. Unless you want to cast suspicion on our marriage and the reasons for it. I would not call a maid or a footman for help, however. My aunt would certainly learn of it, and she is a curious woman. The less attention paid to the circumstances of the voyage from New Orleans the better, don't you think? There may be an extra blanket you can use, if you are determined to be a martyr."

Julia bit her lip. Was it possible that questions concerning their marriage might lead to the uncovering of the purpose of the expedition? She had not considered it in that light.

Rud, with a fine show of unconcern for whatever decision she might reach, stretched, smothering a yawn with his fist. Shoving one hand into the pocket of his dressing gown, he strolled to the bed and whipped back the covers. Beneath the goose-down comforter was a soft, lightweight blanket. He tugged this free and held it out to her, a quizzical look in his eyes.

Julia stood up, taking the step which would allow her to accept the blanket. In the small sitting room was a settee she could use, though with the falling rain that room was chilly and damp. An armchair by the fireplace might be best. She had been looking forward with such longing to a night's sleep in the soft width of a bed instead of narrow ship's bunk—well it could not be helped.

It might be something less than gentlemanly of Rud to appropriate the bed; still, as he pointed out, it had not been his decision that she leave it. While she could admit the justice of this, that did not make it any easier to accept. Turning her back on him, she shook the blanket out with a vicious flap and swung it about her shoulders. She pushed the armchair nearer to the remaining warmth and sat down, drawing her feet up under her.

Though she kept her back firmly turned, she knew when Rud extinguished the candles, threw aside his dressing gown, and slid into the bed. It took a moment for her to realize that he had dispensed with the nightshirt worn by most men. It was nothing to her, of course. It served mainly to remind her that she had never had the opportunity to don her own nightgown. The extra thickness would have been appreciated.

Trying not to make noise, she drew the blanket closer about her throat and tucked the extra length in around her knees. It would have been a help if the chair had been larger. If she felt wedged in after only a few minutes, what would it be like after an entire night?

The rain died away, leaving a deep stillness to settle over the house. Occasionally, footsteps passed outside the door, muffled by the hall carpet, but these too ceased at last. The coals died away to black ash. Each shift of position brought a draft of cool air sifting through her blanket. Once she dozed, only to be awakened by a cramp in the calf of her leg. To ease it, she had to stretch her legs out straight. Her tiredness was so overwhelming, her need for rest so great, that she closed her eyes while sitting bolt upright and was instantly asleep. When she slipped sideways and grazed her head on the carved wood which outlined the back of the chair, she made a small sound of pain but did not open her eyes.

The feel of swinging movement invaded her dreams. For a moment she was back aboard the *Sea Jade* in her bunk, though there seemed to be a band of iron constricting her shoulders and her knees. Then she felt the yielding softness of a bed beneath her, and the cold rush of night air as her dressing gown was deftly drawn open.

She came up from the bed with a rush, lunging away from the dark form she sensed rather than saw beside her. Her arms were still entangled in her robe, but she slipped free after an instant's struggle and rolled, scrambling for the far side of the bed.

The bed jounced heavily on its springs as Rud dove across it, pinning her to the mattress. "Be still, dammit!" he said through his teeth.

She lashed out at him, catching him a sharp blow across the bridge of his nose. He swore again, and shifted his weight so that he lay along the length of her body. Warding off another blow, he grabbed her wrists, dragging them down until they were crossed over each other between her breasts. Panting, she strained away from him, suffocatingly aware of the hard rasp of his bare thigh against hers and the pressure of his chest against her breasts.

His chest expanded as he took a deep, steadying breath. "Lie still," he said, his warm breath fanning her cheek. "I only wanted to make your rest easier. Your hands and feet are like ice, and it would be ridiculous for you to freeze to death when I am here to warm you. Besides, all that twisting and turning was keeping me awake."

It was the touch of exasperation in his voice which reached her. Slowly the tension left her muscles and she subsided. His grip grew less painful on her wrists, and bit by bit he eased his weight from her. When he was certain she was not going to make any violent moves, he released her and reached for the sheet and coverlet, drawing them up over her. She flinched a little as his arm encircled her waist once more beneath the bed coverings, but he only drew her closer against him.

The heat of his body touched her like a caress, its intensity a gauge of how chilled she had become. She lay still, staring wide-eyed in the dark as an unwilling gratitude washed over her. Not the least of what she was grateful for was the way that his breathing slowed, then fell into a regular cadence. For all the difference her naked form beside him made, she might have been a child in need of comforting. It was this which allowed her to let fall her eyelids and accept the surcease of sleep.

Julia descended the stairs with Aunt Lucinda beside her. The older woman held a beaded reticule under one arm and a sunshade under the other while she smoothed gloves of celestial blue kid over her hands.

"Mark my words, there will be a change in the shape of women in the next few months, and I for one will greet it with joy. Do you realize it has been nearly thirty years since women have shown a normal waistline? At least in public, my dear!" Rud's aunt gave a light laugh, then continued. "The classical style is marvelously flattering to a pretty bosom, and a great convenience for women who are increasing, but since I have never been able to congratulate myself on either I am no devotee!"

The more Julia saw of Lucinda Baxter the more she liked her. Rud's aunt was completely unpretentious, and she possessed a droll wit that made it impossible not to laugh with her. Julia was quite looking forward to their shopping expedition this morning.

The opening of the outside door as they neared the foot of the stairs drew her attention. Though the bell had not rung, the butler had hastened to admit the master of the house and Rud. Dressed in riding clothes, they brought with them the fresh smell of the spring morning.

"There you are," Aunt Lucinda greeted them. "When they told me you two had already breakfasted and gone out I could not believe it. I take it the weather has cleared?"

"A beautiful morning, warming to admiration," her husband declared, saluting the cheek she offered.

As if reminded of his role of doting bridegroom, Rud took Julia's hand and drew her to him. His eyes holding a look that was both a reminder and a warning, he lowered his lips to hers. The pressure was firm but brief. Why Julia should be so affected by it she could not tell, except that it seemed to set a seal on their marriage, making it more real. It also brought to mind their closeness the night before, something she had tried to forget. That had not been too difficult. She had awakened in the bright light of morning to find herself alone in the Elizabethan bed. Rud had already dressed and gone.

Aunt Lucinda surveyed Julia's heightened color with fond amusement. "Charming," she said. "Now perhaps you could say a few words, my dear nephew, to convince Julia that she need not be too cheese-paring with her purchases this morning. I have had a terrible time convincing her, despite your inheritance from your Grandfather Baxter and the extent of the fortune you had from your American father, that you are not a pauper."

Rud's displeasure was evident in the frown which drew his brows together. "Have you?" he inquired.

"You need not take that tone with me, my dear Rud," his aunt informed him. "I have no patience with men who keep their wives in the dark on financial matters. They have only themselves to blame if they discover they are wedded to dowds or else paragons of extravagance."

"And I take it you are afraid Julia will fall into the first category?"

"Hardly," his aunt told him, her voice tart. "However, you must admit it is bad enough for her to have to go into black the day after becoming a bride, without having to settle for mourning wear less becoming than it could be!"

"I would rather she did not wear black at all. I suppose that is too much to ask?"

"Of course it is," his aunt answered for Julia. "It would look odd indeed if she did not wear mourning for her father."

"Then you leave me nothing to say except buy what you will, my darling wife, and have the accounting sent to me."

"Very handsome." Aunt Lucinda applauded.

"Thank you," Julia said, since from the other woman's glance in her direction it appeared some comment was required.

"You needn't expect me to echo the sentiment," Uncle

Thaddeus said in a jovial manner. "You know to the last penny how much I am worth, and I will expect you to keep it in mind."

"So I shall, to the last penny." Aunt Lucinda laughed, and pulling the strings of her reticule over her wrist, she swished out the door. Julia would have followed close behind had Rud not detained her with a hand on her arm. He tilted her chin with one finger and brushed a kiss across her lips. That vibrant touch, and the strange, slow smile which went with it, lay disturbingly in her memory long after the black-and-silver carriage that awaited them had pulled away from the mansion.

Why had she been misled about his fortune? Why had they all been misled, if it came to that? Rud had given the impression of a man with a need for money at that first meeting at her father's house in New Orleans. The money, he had said, was his sole reason for his part in the mission. Had he meant only to ensure that he would be compensated for his expenses? Or had he deliberately set out to portray himself as an adventurer, an opportunist interested only in what he stood to gain? Why would he do that? It certainly could not make him more acceptable to the Bonapartists of New Orleans. Or could it? Might a hard-bitten adventurer whose main loyalty was to gold be a better choice as a conspirator than an Englishman who, despite his American father, had lately been a soldier of his majesty the king, fighting Bonaparte on the soil of Belgium?

A feeling of sickness moved over her, and she clenched her hands together in her lap until it passed. No, it was impossible. Her father could not have made such a mistake. Besides, General Montignac and her father had acted on instructions from the emperor himself, received only days before the meeting. An English spy's arrival in New Orleans at the proper time would mean that Napoleon's correspondence was being intercepted at some point before it was smuggled off St. Helena. That the emperor would allow such a state of affairs she could not credit.

The sights of London rolled past the carriage windows

—magnificent homes, parks, and carriages of every size and description. Some of the equipages were tooled by their owners, gentlemen in caped coats with their tigers, young boys whose duty it was to hold the horses when their masters stepped down, while others were driven by top-lofty servants all in identical white wigs. As they left the better district behind them, pedestrians filled the streets, soberly clad merchants and clerks brushing elbows with vendors of hot pies and flowers, candy confections and hand puppets, ribbons and glass beads. There were a scissors grinder and a tinker, an old-clothes man and a trio of jugglers, all luxuriating in the balmy day as the sun ascended toward its zenith.

Julia stared about her and even exchanged a remark or two with her hostess, but she scarcely registered what she was seeing. If Rud was wealthy he could have loaned her an amount sufficient to have set herself up in a comfortable boardinghouse with a companion. That he had not made the offer could mean one of two things: either he did not expect Napoleon to reimburse her, making it impossible for her to pay back the loan, or else he had planned to make her dependent on him for the purpose of collecting a different kind of repayment. Supporting the last theory was the fact that he had even married her to make it legal.

No, that did not quite dovetail. Given the circumstances, he need not have married her at all. He could just as easily have set her up as his mistress and taken taken what he desired by force. He had not. Instead he had made her his wife, presented her to his relatives, and treated her with every respect and consideration. If he desired her, it was not an overpowering emotion. He insisted on a certain show of intimacy between them; still, she would call his attitude toward her a strange combination of compassion and exasperation.

Compassion was another word for pity, something she did not need. Marcel was not dead. She had suffered no permanent hurt at his hands. Already the bruises were fading; soon they would be gone. There were other things that required her attention. The man who had made himself her husband, for instance. Whatever his reasons for it, he might find, before all was said and done, that he had gotten more than he had bargained for.

The morning sped past in an exhausting round of fittings. Julia chose three day gowns, a pair of gowns for evening, and a traveling costume, plus the undergarments to complement them. The addition of a dozen pairs of black silk stockings, several pairs of gloves, two bonnets, one with upstanding plumes and one with knots of lute-string ribbon, a nightgown, and a fine woolen shawl in shades of white, gray, and black would, she was certain, not only fill out her wardrobe, but also give Rud a disagreeable surprise when it came time to pay the bill. Leaving the shop of the modiste, they frittered away another two hours ordering kid slippers from a cobbler's shop and strolling through a warehouse, putting themselves in the way of irresistible bargains in ribbons, mantillas, lace berthas, handkerchiefs, and sundry other small items which could be expected to enhance the fashionable appearance of the purchaser.

It was midafternoon before they turned homeward. Julia, though pleased to have completed an unpleasant task, was tired and hungry. She leaned her head back on the squabs of the carriage with a sigh.

"Yes, I know," Aunt Lucinda said with sympathy. "It is most fatiguing. Still, I believe the gowns you ordered, especially the twilled French silk, will prove vastly becoming. If one must go into black it is a great comfort to know that one is at least wearing the latest mode. I hold no brief for those who recommend retreating into dowdy melancholy. What good does that do? The purpose of fashion is to make a woman feel better, and when could she need it more than when in mourning?"

Julia smiled in polite acquiescence, though she was not so sure she agreed. She would have liked nothing better than to retreat into private grief, dowdy or otherwise. Unfortunately, events prevented such a course.

"I am somewhat concerned about the nightgown you chose, my dear," the older woman went on. "Surely it was not necessary to go so far? You are a bride, after all.

One could not blame Rud for objecting to the observance being carried into the bedchamber."

Julia had not considered that possibility. After a moment she shook her head. "I doubt he will mind."

"Perhaps he won't," Aunt Lucinda said, though without much conviction. "I am a meddling old fool, I know, only I can imagine what my Thaddeus would say if I should dare!"

Julia tried to visualize Rud's easygoing uncle making a scene over a nightgown and failed. She could not help smiling at Aunt Lucinda's expression of comic dismay, however. "I suppose I will have to wait and see," she said.

As she spoke she glanced out the window at a carriage that had swung out to overtake them. It was a nondescript vehicle with nothing about it to distinguish it from a thousand others. Mud spattered the body, clinging to its cracking paint, and though the horses were strong and swift, they were not noticeably fine. It was the passenger, leaning to peer into their carriage, who attracted her attention. He was a burly man, with a large chest and a huge flat face edged with a scraggly beard. A dark hat was drawn low on his narrow forehead, shading small black eyes narrowed to the slits of a hunting animal.

Involuntarily, Julia drew back. Aunt Lucinda turned her head, attracted by her sudden movement.

"Dear me," the older woman said. "What a fright it is, to be sure. Servant class, from the cut of his clothes. I wonder what he can be doing dashing along the roads, forcing people to give way to him? Nothing good, I'll be bound."

With a small sniff, the other woman dismissed the man, but Julia found she was unable to do so. That searching, malevolent stare remained with her long after they had reached the mansion in Berkeley Square and she was safe inside.

Rud was not in when they returned. He had received a message during the morning and, immediately afterward, had gone out. "Business with his ship, I suppose," Aunt Lucinda had said, and Julia had not contradicted her, but she was certain the message had been from the Bona-partist following in England. The next step of the great adventure had begun.

Julia was sitting before the dressing table with the maid, Rose, engaged in putting up her hair when Rud returned. One of the gowns she had ordered, an evening gown of Armesin taffeta, had been delivered about tea-time. It, along with a morning gown of tussah silk, had been put together for just such an emergency as that faced by Julia. They had required no more than the taking in of a few seams to be ready to wear. She had whiled away the afternoon trying on the two gowns, then as the dinner hour drew near, bathing and making herself ready to go downstairs. When Aunt Lucinda had offered the services of the maid to do her hair, she had accepted gratefully, since a style less severe than a knot on the nape of her neck had appeared in order. She might have contrived something presentable without help, since she was quite capable of dressing her own hair, but it was easier to allow the nimble-fingered little maid to give her a coiffure of London elegance.

A frown drew Rud's brows together as he saw the black underdress she was wearing, then he strolled toward her. The maid moved aside at his approach, busying her-self with pins and the combing box.

Stepping behind Julia, Rud took her bare shoulders in his hands. As her startled gaze met his in the mirror, he smiled, then leaned to press his lips to the smooth curve of her neck. Though the spot his lips had touched seemed to burn, Julia schooled herself not to move. She could not control the color that stained her cheekbones, how-ever.

"Where have you been?" she asked, as he raised his head.

His glance flicked to the maid and then held steady on hers. "I'll tell you about it later."

She nodded, realizing that his reticence confirmed her suppositions.

Moving away, Rud rang for a bath, then threw himself

into a chair. With his feet stretched out before him, he watched the finishing touches being applied to her hair.

"I see you had a productive morning," he commented, indicating her underdress with a curt gesture.

"Yes, I found everything I needed."

"I didn't realize you would plunge into it at once."

Her voice carefully neutral, Julia explained how that came about, adding, "Naturally I must begin wearing black as soon as possible. I have felt guilty enough in colors these past weeks since my father's death."

When he did not comment, the maid seized the moment to say, "There, madam, that is done. Shall I help you into your gown now?"

"That will not be necessary," Rud answered for Julia. "I will give my wife any further assistance she may need."

Julia sent him a swift glance, but his face was impassive. She could hardly argue with him in front of the servant. With a nod and a smile, she dismissed the girl. The instant the door closed behind her, Julia got to her feet. Back stiff, she moved from the dressing room into the bedchamber.

Rud followed, standing in the doorway, leaning with one shoulder against the jamb. "I thought you were interested in my whereabouts today," he said, his tone mocking her retreat.

Julia swung to face him. "You made contact with the Bonapartists here, didn't you?"

"I did. I was given the address of a rooming house, and a time. If you had been here we could have gone together. As it was—"

"I understand," she said, though she could not disguise her disappointment. "Who was there? What is happening?"

"There were a number of people there, not all of whom were known to me. Our host was General Baron Gaspard Gourgaud. Robeaud was there, also Marcel de Gruys, though he seemed to be a bit stiff in the back. It appears he is still with us despite the lack of encouragement from you. I expect the size of his investment weighed heavily in his decision to adopt a sporting attitude." Ignoring her flash of indignation, he went on. "He was not at all happy to see

125

me. The announcement of our marriage which appeared today in the *Times* had made him somewhat resentful of my presence."

"Announcement? I haven't seen it," she said, frowning.

"I assure you it is there."

"Are you certain that was wise?"

His face bland, he said, "I don't know what you mean."

"What I mean is," she said with care, "won't making a public announcement now cause difficulties later?"

"Difficulties? Of what nature?" he inquired, folding one arm over the other.

"With an annulment," she cried, feeling as if she had been pushed into a corner.

"There will be no annulment."

His voice had a hard ring, a final ring. Julia stared at him, trying without success to find some meaning other than the obvious one in his words.

"I don't understand you," she said at last. "You cannot wish to remain tied to a woman you hardly know for the rest of your life."

"I have known you for several weeks now. By the time this is over I will know you better still."

Was that a veiled threat? "You may not like what you discover," she said tartly.

"I'll take my chances."

She would not be daunted. "Don't say you weren't warned."

"I appreciate that," he said, a slow smile rising into his eyes. "It should help me to remember to keep a sharp eye on the carving knives."

He lounged in the doorway, his tall form filling the opening, the image of assurance and leashed strength. The teasing light in his sea-blue eyes gave him a perilous attraction. For a fleeting instant Julia was aware of an unsuspected danger.

She turned sharply away, saying over her shoulder, "How is M'sieu Robeaud?"

"Well enough, the same as when you saw him last. He has settled into a rooming house not far from where

Gourgaud is staying, and he assured me he was quite comfortable there."

"This meeting today—what was the purpose of it?"

"In the main, to make de Gruys, Robeaud, and myself acquainted with the others. Baron Gourgaud also outlined his progress in persuading the British that he had truly broken with Napoleon. He read the drafts of several articles which will appear in the news sheets, articles denouncing his former master. He told us also of the questioning he has undergone by Lord Bathurst of the Colonial Foreign Office, and of the carefully constructed bits of information he had been instructed to place before the gentleman, items of little value, or else known to him already."

"Poor Gourgaud—it must be terrible to be looked upon as a traitor to all except a chosen few," Julia said.

Rud agreed with a nod. "He feels the stigma of it greatly, I know, for he said even the British who seek to use him do not bother to hide their contempt."

"It will only be for a few months. By the end of August he will be able to tell the truth and take his rightful place beside the emperor."

"And claim his reward?"

"To serve the emperor is reward enough for some," she said with a lift of her chin.

"It may have to be," he replied almost to himself, and moved to open the door as a knock heralded the arrival of his bath water.

The acute embarrassment she had felt the day before, when Rud had undressed before her, had faded, but still she retreated to the dressing room. There she busied herself with rice-powder papers, rouge pot, and hare's foot while he indulged in his daily ritual of cleanliness.

It was unusual, to say the least, to find a man so fastidious in his habits. Her own father, in the sweltering months of summer in New Orleans, seldom troubled to bathe more than twice a week. He had been amused by the time and trouble the captain expended for such a purpose on board the *Sea Jade*. To Julia, every bit as particular as the captain, the ease with which he could order salt water heated for his tub had been a source of envy. She had disliked asking the man who acted as Rud's servant to perform the same service for her, but, being without a maid, she was forced to make the request. At last Rud, discovering the difficulty, had given instructions for a tub to be prepared for her each day at the same time as his own.

That was all very well when they could repair to separate cabins, but such a habit had done nothing but cause difficulties since they had begun to share the same room. With a wry shake of her head, Julia turned from the mirror.

Her task had not lasted long enough. She emerged from the dressing room while he was still chest-deep in the copper tub. With barely a glance in his direction, she moved past him. She had borrowed a novel from Aunt Lucinda that afternoon, which should serve to pass the time and give her someplace to look. Locating it, she turned in the direction of the sitting room.

"Where are you off to?" Rud asked. "Stay and keep me company. Tell me about your outing this morning."

Without turning, Julia said, "You would not be interested. We only visited the milliners and modistes."

"And the cobblers, if I know my Aunt Lucinda. Her small foot is one of her few vanities, I believe. There, you see how much interest I can summon if I make the effort?"

The sardonic tone of his voice told Julia plainly that he did not expect her to stay. It had also the effect of putting her on her mettle. With sudden decision she stalked to the slipper chair and sat down upon it.

"Very well," she said. "What do you want to know?"

She had the satisfaction of seeing him hesitate, though the moment was so brief she could not have noticed if she had not been watching for it. She caught also the hint of satisfaction that moved across his face before he took up her challenge.

"Whatever there is to know," he said. "I am ready to take an interest in anything you do."

"Well said," she told him, her tone shaded with sarcasm. "You must remember how you did it for when you have an audience."

He shook his head. "I think it needs a bit more practice first."

Her wintry smile failed to ruffle his composure; he only sat waiting for her to begin. Sighing, she complied.

With some idea of preparing him for the amount of money she had spent, she began by telling him of the gowns and hats and shoes she had ordered. She omitted nothing, describing every item in minute detail, even to the underclothing and nightgown Aunt Lucinda had viewed with such doubt. If Rud was going to find fault with the last item, it was as well to get his objections out of the way before bedtime.

He frowned, casting what she could only describe as a disparaging look at the black underdress she was wearing, but when he spoke it was on another subject entirely. "After your exertions, I'm surprised you didn't take to your bed and have dinner served on a tray."

She smiled a little. "The thought crossed my mind. Your aunt has invited guests for this evening, however, and we are expected to put in an appearance."

"I should have known," he said with a groan. "If I don't make a move we will be late downstairs, and then we will be in her black books." He surged to his full height with effortless ease. "Toss me a towel, will you? I believe it's your turn to play handmaiden."

Julia did exactly as he had requested. Taking up a towel from where it lay across a chair, she threw it at him. Though she instantly averted her eyes, she was aware of the brief, wolfish grin he sent her as he caught the length of linen in one hand.

She had been on the verge of telling him about the strange encounter that morning with the hideous man who had overtaken their carriage. Now the incident went completely out of her mind. She swung away, her eyes searching for something, anything, with which to occupy herself until he had donned his clothing.

Her gaze fell on her gold bee, which lay on the table beside the bed, gleaming in the light of a candle. That

129

morning she had worn it fastened to her shawl; tonight it would look better on its usual ribbon about her throat. Grateful for this small task, she moved to pick it up.

"You are attached to that piece of jewelry, aren't you?" Rud said in a conversational tone.

"Yes, I must admit I am. It—belonged to my mother."

"Your mother? Odd. If I had been going to guess I would have said it had something to do with this campaign to free Napoleon. The bee was his symbol, was it not?"

She had worn the bee for so long without anyone commenting on it, beyond its obvious ornamental value, that it came as a shock to have someone recognize its significance. She had schooled herself to discretion regarding it to such an extent that it was difficult for her to speak naturally concerning it.

"You are right, of course," she admitted.

"It doesn't have the look of an heirloom," he said critically.

How much could she safely tell him? Surely he had a right to at least a part of the truth. "No. It was a gift from the emperor to my mother."

"A valuable one. It looks like purest, unadulterated gold."

Something in his tone touched a nerve. "You needn't look so disapproving. There was no romantic involvement, though as you say, the gift has great value. My mother was given the bee in recognition of a service she performed for Mamère, Napoleon's own beloved mother."

"It sounds like an interesting tale. This took place in Paris, I assume."

Julia nodded. "We were on a visit, my mother, my father, and I. I was five years old, perhaps, and Napoleon had been emperor for little more than a year. We had traveled through the countryside, spent some time visiting relatives still living in the provincial town where my father's family originated many years ago, and my father and mother had been presented at court. All that was left to do was to enjoy the amusements of Paris. Trouble, riots, conspiracy against the lives of the emperor's family, prison—these were the last things on my parents' minds.

And yet, they became involved with them one spring afternoon."

Rud had stepped into his breeches and drawn on stockings and highly polished Hessian boots. When she stopped, he looked up from fastening his shirt studs and nodded for her to continue.

"My father left us alone, my mother, my nursemaid, and me, while he went to visit with an acquaintance he had made in the city. We became bored. We left our lodgings and walked along the street a short distance to a confectioner's shop. We had just emerged when we were engulfed in a mob of shouting, screaming people, one of those sudden disturbances that were all too common in the years following the Revolution. We never knew their grievance. Some said a butcher's high prices, others the low price paid for cabbages in the market. It did not matter. Also caught by the rioters was a carriage with the Bonaparte emblem on its side, though there were no outriders, no guards, and the only occupant was an elderly woman. Regardless, the rage of the crowd centered on the carriage. They attacked it, dragging the coachman from his box and pulling the old lady out into the street. When my mother saw her, she recognized her as Mamère, Napoleon's mother. She was a Corsican woman of great courage and pride, but her belligerence only inflamed the crowd. They would not listen to her, pulling her this way and that, spitting on her, striking her. My mother could not bear it. Leaving me with my nursemaid, she fought her way to the woman's side, took her arm to support her, and pushing and screaming with the best, tried to make her way back to where we stood against the shop wall. At that moment a troop of cavalry rode down upon the crowd, scattering them in all directions. Those who did not take to their heels were arrested, my mother among them. Mamère was helped with all solicitude back into her carriage, and in minutes the street was quiet again."

"I hope your nursemaid had the good sense to get you out of harm's way," Rud said.

"Yes, she scurried with me back to our lodgings as soon as she saw my mother taken away. A message was sent to my father posthaste. He went immediately to the prison where my mother was being held, but his efforts to explain were ignored. They would not release her. In desperation, he went to the emperor. Mamère, who was shaken but not seriously injured by her ordeal, confirmed my mother's innocence and heroism. My father had always been an admirer of Napoleon, but the swiftness with which the emperor acted on the information he received to obtain my mother's release gained him my father's allegiance for life. The golden bee was presented to my mother in a private ceremony in recognition of her service to the Bonaparte family. With it went a promise of instant aid if it should ever be needed."

"I begin to see why you value your bee," Rud told her, a thoughtful look in his eyes as he stared at her over the cravat he was tying under his chin.

Did he? Fear fluttered along her nerves, the fear that she had revealed too much. Keeping her eyes on the soft golden sheen of the bee's upheld wings, she made herself smile. "It has been many long years since Napoleon presented the bee to my mother. I expect it is foolish of me to hope that he will recall it."

"He has a reputation for having a long memory." Rud's smile held a mild encouragement. Moving toward her, he took the bee on its black ribbon from her hand and tied it about her neck, making a perfect bow in the back. The action was casual, as if he had been doing such things for her for years.

Julia let her breath out in a silent sigh as he turned away. He was not going to question her further. Later, when they neared St. Helena, she would have to tell him, but not now, not yet.

Automatically, her hand went to the bee in the hollow of her throat, Napoleon's golden bee, which was to have identified her father and herself to him and now must serve for her alone, the double precaution which, with Robeaud, would signal the beginning of the emperor's flight to freedom and his return to power.

Chapter Seven

"*Pirates, bloody pirates, that's what they are! Let them* call themselves the Algerian navy or the scourge of the Mediterranean as they please! I tell you they are nothing but pirates who should be hunted down and exterminated like vermin."

It was a small dinner party with an even dozen at the table. They had eaten their way through soup, fish, game, and poultry, with at least three more removes to go. The candles in the chandeliers overhead and in the candelabra that lined the table had burned down half their length. Crumbs, wine stains, and crumpled napery marred the perfection of the table, though the scent of the roses in the centerpiece could still be detected above the odor of the food. There was only one title represented at the board, that of the man who had spoken; still, it was obvious that the other guests lacked nothing in the way of wealth or social position. Julia, watching them, was glad she had allowed herself to be guided by Rud's aunt in the choice of a modiste. She did not feel at all out of place, even though it had begun to be borne in upon her that Thaddeus Baxter was something more than the merchant Rud had called him. She would not have been at all surprised to learn that the Baxters were used to moving in the first circles of London society.

The man who had denounced the Algerian pirates had been introduced as Lord Holland. A vitriolic man in his middle forties, he was the nephew of the great Whig politician Charles James Fox. He was well known in his own right as a politician, an impressive figure who showed every indication of having been a handsome youth.

"Algeria is not the richest country in the world," his host answered from his place at the head of the table. "Piracy has been a way of life with them for centuries. When you kill off a few they only come back thicker than ever, and more daring. The India Company has waged war on them for decades. This ship listed as lost to them today makes only three this year, but I know any number of smaller shippers who have been wiped out by their repeated attacks."

"The Americans had the right idea," Lord Holland declared. "Send in the marines, shell their towns, and take back the Christian men and women sold into slavery by force of arms."

"And go to war for the sake of a few?" Thaddeus Baxter inquired. "Algeria is a vassal of the Turkish Ottoman Empire. We might find ourselves fighting a larger enemy than we imagine."

"The United States did not bring a war down on themselves when they attacked the Barbary pirates of Tripoli a few years back. Besides, my good man, we are talking about more than a few slaves. The number of men of European blood who have died under the lash, the number of white women incarcerated in the harems of Islam, is incalculable. But I forget that there are ladies present. Allow me, Mrs. Baxter, to beg your forgiveness."

"I'm not sure I want to give it, not sure at all," Aunt Lucinda said with mock severity. "Have you ever noticed, ladies, how the gentlemen always change the subject just when it is beginning to be interesting?"

"Often," Lady Holland agreed. "And they never ask our opinion on any of these interesting matters, either. On the subject of slavery, for instance. Regardless of the news today, why should we single out Algeria? There are men and women in slavery on every continent. True, they may not have European blood in their veins, but they are slaves no less for that."

Farther down the table one or two of the other guests exchanged glances. Lady Holland, according to Aunt Lucinda, was well known for her radical views. She had been seen taking chimney sweeps to task for forcing their climbing boys into hot chimneys, chastising carters who abused their horses, and haranguing mill owners who worked children under the age of twelve at their machines. It was even rumored that she had visited Bedlam, the Hospital of St. Mary of Bethlehem, where London's insane were kept hidden away.

"We cannot argue with your sentiments, Lady Holland," Rud said, playing with his wineglass, "but it is my understanding that armed intervention usually results in the death of Christian slaves in Islam. Their masters would rather kill them than see them go free. Their only hope of escape is to embrace the Muslim religion, since one true believer cannot enslave another. The rub is that a slave must first be offered the opportunity to become a Mussulman by his owner."

"You are very knowledgeable, Captain Thorpe," Lady Holland observed.

"Not at all. I am afraid you have just heard the sum total of my knowledge, which is only what can be picked up in any Mediterranean port."

Aunt Lucinda pursed her lips. "In spite of all that, I agree with Lord Holland that it seems cruel to leave them languishing in their prisons while we do nothing."

"Just as Islam holds no monopoly on slaves, it also has far from the worst prisons in the world," Lady Holland said.

"True," Rud agreed, flicking a quick glance to where Julia sat listening before turning back to the wife of the peer. "I understand you and your husband disapprove of the way England is treating the defeated emperor of the French?"

"We do indeed," her husband answered for her. "It is a disgrace that we could not be more generous in our victory."

Down the table another of the gentlemen, also a director of the East India Company, interrupted. "We were generous once. We gave Bonaparte his private kingdom at Elba, with a small army to defend it, and what did we get? The Hundred Days, that's what! And the loss of the lives of fifty thousand young men. I say the man is where he belongs, where any power-mad dictator belongs, as far away from the rest of humanity as he can be sent. He should count himself lucky he still has his head on his shoulders!"

"You sound as if he were a criminal," said Lady Holland. "When Napoleon abdicated and took ship voluntarily for Elba, it was with the understanding that the country he had made great would remain as he had left it, intact. And yet, only a few months later there were England, Austria, Prussia, and Russia, all his old enemies, picking over it and dividing it up like so many carrion birds. Was he supposed to watch the desecration of all he had accomplished without lifting a hand?"

"Well," the gentleman said, "as a woman you cannot be expected to understand these things. For my part, I say the man is more comfortable than he deserves to be. He lives in state, kicking his heels in idleness at the expense of the English people while consuming the most delectable food and wine that can be procured for him by a peer of the realm."

Lord Holland leaped to the aid of his wife. "If you are referring to the consignments sent to Napoleon in the name of my wife and myself, I can only say that I have never seen the least reluctance on the part of the East India Company to accept the cargo, or the profit it gains from carrying it to St. Helena. In fact, I expect the company turns a tidy profit supplying the garrison and the commissioners set to guard the emperor!"

"Come, come, gentlemen, let's not descend to personalities," Thaddeus Baxter admonished them, and with more determination than tact, managed this time to turn the subject.

Despite the controversial overtones, the conversation had given Julia a warm feeling. It was good to know that there were highly placed English people who felt as strongly as she did about Napoleon's imprisonment. At

136

the back of her mind there was a niggling worry as to what the British government would do to those who were left behind on St. Helena when the emperor escaped, those who would still be in its power when it was revealed that Napoleon was at large. Surely if enough people could be brought to see the injustice of his incarceration, there would be no reprisals against those who had conspired in his escape.

Later, when the ladies had retired to the drawing room, leaving the men to their port and claret, Julia sought out Lady Holland. They sat talking with the liveliest of interest until Julia was summoned to Aunt Lucinda's side.

The elderly woman drew her down beside her. "There is something you must tell Rud," she said in a low voice. "I meant to warn him earlier, but the two of you were tardy in putting in your appearance before dinner. I don't know if he has spoken to you of his mother? You realize she has remarried since his father's death, and is now Lady Cathcart? I received a note from her this afternoon. She is in town and means to call on me. I do not know if she is aware that Rud is staying here, for she did not say, but I see no way that he can avoid seeing her if she is determined upon a meeting."

"Perhaps she saw the wedding announcement," Julia suggested.

"Doubtless that is it," Aunt Lucinda agreed.

"Then she will want to come and inspect me. Any mother would."

"Any mother except Georgina. I doubt very much that her curiosity is maternal." Aunt Lucinda smiled grimly. "I can think of three reasons why she may be coming, none of them to her credit."

"I am afraid I don't follow you."

"First of all, she may be coming as a whim, secondly, she may want something of him, and thirdly, she may wish to cause either embarrassment or trouble."

Julia stared at her, shocked by the venom in the voice of this usually mildest of women. At last she said, "Rud has never confided in me concerning his mother. What little I know of her I learned from the first mate aboard the *Sea Jade,* and I was not certain how much faith I could put in his version of the story."

"I have made the acquaintance of Mr. Free, and in my judgment he is not a young man prone to exaggeration."

"No," Julia said. "That being so, can you tell me if it is true that Rud's mother arranged the death of his father?"

"I wish I could answer that positively for you, my dear, but the truth of the matter is, no one knows. We can guess, but no more than that. What is more important, however, is what Rud thinks, and that I can tell you. He believes it with all his heart."

It was not long afterward that the gentlemen rejoined them. As a partial repayment for the welcome Aunt Lucinda had extended to her, Julia allowed herself to be persuaded to display her skill on the pianoforte for the assembled company. Rud was not backward in offering to turn the sheets of the music portfolio for her.

The instrument was located in an alcove at the end of the drawing room, well isolated from the others. Under the cover of a Mozart melody Julia said over her shoulder, "You need not have sacrificed yourself. I could have turned my own pages."

"I don't doubt it," Rud replied, reaching to adjust the candle in its bracket beside the music stand as an excuse for leaning over her. "But how could I resist the opportunity to play the adoring husband again?"

"Easily, I imagine, if we had no audience."

"I thought the audience was the point of the thing. Still, if you would like me to continue when we are alone, I'm sure it can be arranged."

"I never said—" The gleam in his eyes was enough to halt the words on her tongue. Taking a deep breath, she said, "As much as I appreciate the offer, I am afraid I must decline."

"Why must you? The classical reason does not apply. We have both secular and religious sanction."

She struck a wrong note and recovered, though the interested glances turned in their direction did not help her composure. Her color high, she flashed him a furious look. "How can you make jokes? You know that a true marriage between us is impossible."

"Careful," he warned. "You will have them thinking we are having our first quarrel."

"They could well be right!"

"I don't think so," he said, stretching to turn the page at her signal. "An exchange of views is not a quarrel."

"How can it be an exchange of views when you haven't asked for mine?"

"Your pardon, Madam Thorpe! I've been so used to receiving your views whether I wanted them or not that I never thought to ask." When she did not reply immediately he said, "Well?"

Julia frowned, searching for words. "Marriage should be based on love and trust and respect," she said. "Three things I think neither of us has for the other."

"So many complications," he murmured. "I thought all you wanted was a man you could not live without."

His last words had a familiar ring. She had spoken them to him aboard the ship in the early dawn of the morning they had left New Orleans. Ages ago. How odd that he had remembered.

"That too," she replied, her voice as hard as stone.

"It's a pity you ever came on board my ship, then," he said abruptly, and did not speak again until the piece was ended and he could lead her back to the others.

Rud was still in a black temper when the last guests had stepped into their carriage and he and Julia were free to retire. He held the door of their bedchamber open, and when she had passed through, slammed it behind them. Without a word he stripped off his coat and began to untie his cravat.

Julia sent him a nervous glance from the corner of her eye before moving to the wardrobe. Opening its doors, she took her black nightgown from the shelf and shook it out, tossing it on the bed.

Rud threw a quick look at the voluminous garment. Julia thought his brows drew closer together over the bridge of his nose, but he said nothing.

More disturbed than she would have liked to admit,

Julia untied her gold bee and set it aside, then took the pins from her hair. She tossed the loose waves behind her, reaching back toward the row of tiny buttons that closed her gown. Rud had fastened them for her earlier, before she went downstairs, but she was in no mood to ask for help now, especially with him in his present humor. At the thought of the maid who could have been waiting to assist her if Rud had not refused the offer, she gritted her teeth in exasperation. In silence, she struggled, her arms bent nearly double behind her back.

Abruptly Rud rounded the end of the bed. Before she could move, his hands were on her hair, gathering the silken mass and placing it out of the way over her shoulder. His fingers were warm and vibrant on her bare skin. Involuntarily, she flinched, taking a swift step away from him.

His hands came down on her shoulders, wrenching her back into place. "Be still," he growled, holding her until she ceased to resist.

She stood with head bowed while his hands traveled slowly, almost caressingly, down the smooth length of her back to the low top of her underdress. Even through that thin fabric she could feel his touch as he dropped lower, to the level of her waist and below it. In the French fashion, she wore nothing beneath the underdress. For the first time in her life she was grateful that the underdress tied at the waist in front with tapes.

"Thank you," she said in a strangled voice when he was finished at last. Swinging away from him, she moved a short distance away before she slipped the sleeves of her gown down her arms. The bulk of the wardrobe was near. She held to its side as she lowered the gown still farther and stepped out of it. Her legs were trembling so that for an instant she overbalanced, nearly falling before she caught herself. Her hair sliding forward made a perfect screen for her features, and she refused to look in Rud's direction.

The black nightgown was in truth an ugly thing. Composed of yard upon yard of opaque lawn gathered to a high yoke, it had enormous billowing sleeves caught at

140

the wrist by a narrow band, and a wide white collar turned down over the yoke like a limp medieval ruff. Embellished with ribbon and rosepoint lace, it still looked to have all the charm of a court jester's costume.

In the shop of Aunt Lucinda's modiste, the nightgown had seemed to Julia a form of protective covering; now it merely appeared ludicrous. She slipped it over her head, fighting to find the neck opening. Her head protruding like a turtle from its shell, she stepped out of her underdress and tossed it aside. Back straight, she moved toward the dressing room with the black folds billowing around her.

At the dressing table, she stared at herself in the mirror, shifting her shoulders uncomfortably as the material bunched about her neck scratched her skin. For a long moment, she considered taking the fright of a gown off, bundling it up, and sending it back to the dressmaker.

Then Rud spoke from the doorway. "What in the name of God is that thing?"

"It's the latest thing in night apparel," she said, catching up a fold on either side between her fingers and pirouetting before him. The spirit of defiance lent a hard edge to her tone. "How do you like it?"

"I don't."

"Why? I believe it is unexceptionable for someone in mourning."

"Possibly, for a fat burgher's widow. It hardly suits a bridal bed, however."

"I fail to see how that matters, or what concern what I choose to wear is of yours."

"Do you?" he said, a distinctly unpleasant edge to his voice.

Her head came up. "Yes, I do. In any case, it is what I have bought to sleep in and what I shall wear!"

"Must I remind you that I will be called upon to pay for that monstrosity? I warn you, Julia, I do not intend to waste my money in that fashion."

"I don't understand you," she cried. "If you mean to choose what I can and cannot wear you should have come shopping with me this morning."

"Perhaps I should," he countered, his voice rising. "My choice for you would have been the merest nothing, nothing at all. In the meantime you will take off that nightgown."

"I won't!" she said, spinning around, crossing her arms over her breasts as she pressed her lips tightly together. She gave her hair a toss, anger glittering in her eyes.

"Oh, won't you?" he queried softly, advancing with slow controlled strides. "Would you prefer that I took it off for you?"

"You wouldn't dare!"

"You think not?" Rud drawled.

There was such menace in his voice that she hastily abandoned her defiant pose. Wariness entered her gold flecked eyes. "You—you can't!" she said a little wildly. "Besides, what difference does it make?"

"I can," he said, "and the difference is, I refuse to share my bed with someone who looks like a pregnant nun."

The calculated insult stung her into action. With sudden speed she darted to one side, ducking underneath the arm he flung out to stop her. Her bare feet were nimble. She dodged as he lunged for her, then swung through the door into the bedchamber.

In the middle of the room she paused. She could not go running out into the hall in her nightgown. What if she were seen? It did not matter. With Rud pounding after her she could not stay!

In an instant she was at the door, twisting it open. She sped down the hallway toward the marble stairs that rose to the third floor. Up there were other bedrooms, closed, unused, where she might hide or even pass the night. As she neared the flight of wide steps she yanked up her nightgown with her left hand, her right reaching out to grasp the banister so that she could pull herself upward. Her feet slapped on the cold, hard treads. Her breath rasped in her throat as she strained her eyes in the darkness to see where she was going.

Despite the lifted hem, the excess fullness of the nightgown flapped and twisted about her feet, dragging over the stairs. Once, twice, she stepped on it and recovered.

And then she stumbled, her feet entangled in the treacherous lawn. There was a rending sound as her knee went through the fragile cloth. Tearing at the gown, searching for purchase, she looked over her shoulder.

Rud was on the stairs behind her, taking them three at a time. At the sight of his dark form bounding toward her, her heart leaped in her breast. Careless of damage, she surged to her feet, making a half dozen more steps before the trailing material tripped her again. She fell headlong, a small scream of fury and despair and pain forcing its way past her lips as her ribs struck the sharp-edged marble.

And then Rud was upon her. He grasped her wrist, dragging her upward, passing her arm behind his neck. Like bands of tempered steel, his arms encircled her waist and clamped about her knees. She was lifted as though she weighed nothing.

As her feet were disentangled, she kicked out, pushing against his chest with such strength he had to shift to keep his balance. His hold tightened with a jerk, crushing her against him, burying her face against his neck.

The uselessness of her flight, the ease with which he had caught her, added fuel to her anger. "Let me go," she hissed, raking his chest with her nails, reaching for his eyes.

Abruptly he loosened his grip, letting her sink toward the floor before tightening it again. Her clawing hand caught at his shirt, clinging to him. A hard note in his voice, he said, "Try that again and I will drop you indeed, over the banister."

"Put me down at once, or I'll—"

"You'll what?" he said, his voice low. "Scream?"

How could she? The last thing she wanted was to call attention to her humiliation. Even if she did, what then? The servants would not dare interfere with the pleasure of the nephew of their master and mistress. There were few of any class who wished to intervene in a quarrel between a husband and wife. Aunt Lucinda, for all her kindness, could not be expected to take her part against Rud. Doubtless Thaddeus Baxter would think the whole thing vastly amusing. "No," she answered at last, "but I will make you sorry if it takes the rest of my life."

He laughed, an almost exultant sound. Without answering he strode down the stairs and back to their room. The bedchamber door was standing open as he had left it. He shouldered through and kicked it to behind them. Crossing to the bed, he dropped her on the smooth counterpane.

The springs jounced with the force of her fall, and she gasped for the deep, lung-filling breath of air that had been denied to her by the pressure of his arms. Before she could recover enough to move, he placed one knee on the bed and leaned over her. He inserted his fingers at the neck of her gown and with a mighty wrench tore it open to the yoke. Her hands came up, clutching at his wrists, but it was too late. Another effort and the nightgown was split to the hem.

He pushed his hand beneath her back, lifting her as he pulled the sleeves down over her arms. Stripping her of the black lawn, he let her fall while he rolled the offending garment into a ball and threw it across the room.

Rage pulsated in a red haze behind Julia's eyes. She pushed away from him. "All right!" she cried. "I hope you are satisfied!"

His hand shot out to catch her shoulder. "No," he said, his eyes growing dark as he stared down at her. He allowed his gaze to roam over her blush ivory skin, to linger on the pink-tipped mounds of her breasts, the smooth indention of her waist and the curve of her hips, before he spoke again. "No, I'm not."

She flung out a hand to ward him off, catching him a blow on the chin. Immediately her wrist was grasped and jerked above her head. His weight came down on her and she was pressed into the pillows.

Julia heaved against him, turning and twisting, digging her heels into the bed. He shifted so that the hard length of his body lay along hers, making movement impossible. The studs left hanging in his shirt bit into her skin, while one arm was trapped between them. Still she did not give up. Eyes glittering, she drew in her breath, jerking at her confined wrist until the skin felt bruised and raw, arching her back and neck, wriggling, trying with every ounce of her strength to dislodge him.

That useless, prolonged effort left her almost spent. In that instant of weakness his mouth captured hers. Light-headed from strain, she felt her senses beginning to whirl, drawing her down into a whirlpool of feeling. His mouth moved on hers, firm, demanding, ruthlessly invading her being. Her eyelids fluttered down. Her tingling lips parted with a naturalness that sent a tremor of surprise and dismay through her.

It was too late to raise her guard. He tasted the sweetness, probing deep. The pressure of his lips lessened, becoming more gentle as she ceased to resist him. His thumb moved, caressing the inner surface of her imprisoned wrist. Her fingers clenched, then slowly relaxed. She felt a sense of detachment creeping over her, paralyzing her will. A remote portion of her mind identified the taste of wine on his lips, the steady jar of his heart against her, and the muscular hardness of his thighs as they pressed into her.

By imperceptible degrees his hand moved from her wrist downward, exploring the tender turning of her arm, the hollow of her shoulder, pausing at the crested peak of her breast. She shivered as he brushed his open palm across it, gently cupping the fullness. And then as his caress moved lower, over the flat expanse of her belly, her stomach muscles tightened in mingled dread and anticipation, and a small moan of distress sounded in her throat.

Rud raised his head. He drew a deep breath, his eyes on her face in the candlelit room. She opened her eyes, staring up at him in bewilderment, the tender curves of her mouth moist and tremulous.

With violent decision he flung himself away from her, rolling to land on his feet on the floor. He watched her a moment longer, the expectancy of his expression fading to a look of doubt. With an abrupt gesture, he turned on his heel and strode to the window, where he braced one hand on the frame. He leaned his head on his forearm, clenching his other hand into a fist, resting it on his hip. The sound of his breathing was harsh in the silence as he strove for self-control.

Rud, she thought, had not passed unscathed through their encounter. That was some consolation. She needed any she could discover, for she was forced to confront the treachery of her own body. Staring at the silhouette of his tall frame against the window in horrified fascination, she allowed the truth to seep into her brain. Before he had left her side she had lost the will or even the desire to resist him. At some time, not tonight or tomorrow, but someday, there could come a time when she would not want him to leave her at all.

Her movements were clumsy, her legs heavy as she slid from the bed and turned down the coverlet. Climbing back onto the mattress, she burrowed into its softness, curling into a ball, pulling the linen sheet and the fat comforter over her head. But she could not hide from herself. It was a long time before she slept.

She awoke to pitch darkness. The mattress sagged away from her, and as she lay still she heard the muffled thump of Rud's boots striking the floor and the rustle of his clothing as he undressed. Scarcely disturbing the covers, he slid into bed beside her. A tingling sensation ran down the length of her body as his bare skin touched hers. She turned her head on the pillow, staring blindly in his direction.

At the sound, he shifted to his side, reaching for her. He ignored her murmur of protest, nesting their bodies together with her back against his chest. Julia lay stiff and unyielding long after his chest had begun the steady rise and fall of sleep.

His skin, though it had quickly grown warm, had been cool to the touch when he had first come to bed. Had he been all this time staring out into the night, conquering his lust? It seemed laid to rest, but she did not dare believe it. She was acutely uncomfortable, she told herself; her shoulder was stiff from lying upon it, the weight of his arm constricted her breathing, and the hair that covered

146

his body rasped against her skin. And yet she could not risk waking him by moving.

A sense of ill-usage gradually took possession of her mind. She was not Rudyard Thorpe's plaything or his bedwarmer. Why should she lie where he placed her? Slowly, carefully, she inched away from him until she could lie flat on her back. For all her efforts, when daylight filled the room she awoke to find herself enclosed once more in his embrace.

Her eyes flew open and she turned her head. Rud was staring down at her with his head propped on one hand while the other measured the fit of her breast.

"Perfect," he said softly, almost to himself.

In a flurry of bedcovers, Julia slapped his hand away and rolled beyond his reach. He made a swift movement, then checked as she stopped, hovering on the edge of the bed.

"Careful," he said, letting his hand fall. "You'll land on the floor."

"That would be better than some places I can think of," she snapped.

His eyes narrowed briefly, and then a smile wry in its self-mockery curved his firm mouth. "That's right, Madam Thorpe," he said. "Put me in my place. Give me not the slightest shred of encouragement. I want you as I have wanted few things in my life. You are everything soft and warm and beautiful that I have ever lacked. Making love to you would be like standing at the wheel of my ship, racing before a strong wind on a fine, clear day; a glorious excitement in the blood, endlessly pleasurable. I crave that the way I crave the feel of my ship's wheel beneath my hands when I am away from her. Still, I have given my promise; I will not take you against your will. But I warn you! I will take advantage, instant and complete advantage, of the least sign of weakness. So, sweet Julia, make up your mind to resist me with all your strength— or surrender, now."

His words vibrated through her, leaving her curiously shaken. She recognized the painful honesty of his warning, but was unable to appreciate it.

"Leave me alone," she said, her golden eyes unconsciously pleading. "Just leave me alone."

His gaze held hers like a trap. "Never," he answered. "Never as long as I live."

The days slipped past. The English spring advanced, turning the countryside into a wildflower garden. Though the days continued cool and rainy with fitful outbursts of sun, no one seemed dissatisfied with the slow progress toward summer.

Julia could not help thinking that at home in Louisiana it would be hot already during the day, and warm enough at night to sleep with the windows and doors thrown open to the heady scents of roses and magnolias, of honeysuckle and lush new growth. It was the time of year when everyone moved from New Orleans into the healthy country air at Beau Bocage. How her father had loved it, riding in the fields to oversee the planting of the new crop, counting over the half-grown calves, colts, and lambs, the baby chicks that ran peeping everywhere, even the new additions in the quarters. What pleasure he took in the fecundity of his land and the season! In the evening he would preside over his table groaning with the fruits of the plantation. Friends, neighbors, even stray travelers were made welcome. No one was turned away, not even the Methodist circuit riders who dared to attempt to turn him from his Catholicism, preaching parsimony while they enjoyed the bounty of his board.

What did London have to offer compared to the rich earth, the friendly smiling faces, and the marvelous sense of freedom that were Beau Bocage? Julia yearned for home, still the mere thinking of it gave her courage to continue with the mission she had embarked upon. If she did not, there was every chance she would never see Beau Bocage again.

Rud, when he was not off on matters of business with his uncle, did his best to entertain her. Together they rode in the park, trotting sedately along Rotten Row. They visited the declining wonders of Vauxhall Gardens, and hired a discreetly placed box for a viewing of *The Duchess of Malfi* at Covent Garden. When Rud was not available, Aunt Lucinda acted as her guide for a few of the historic places about the city, though she had a tendency to duck out of sight when she thought she might be seen in them by any of her friends. The elderly woman was so ill at ease doing such a countrified thing as viewing the sights of London that Julia usually allowed herself to be dissuaded, accepting the offer instead of the latest issues of the *Journal des Modes* or a small, intimate tea party. On the whole, she discovered, she preferred Rud's company. For all their skirmishing, or perhaps because of it, he was a stimulating companion who cared not at all who might see them, or what they might think.

Gradually, as time passed, Julia grew used to his constant presence in her bedchamber also. It was odd how quickly a way of living she would have found unthinkable only a short while before had become commonplace. The intimacies of everyday life, dressing and undressing together, bathing and sleeping, had, little by little, ceased to be embarrassing. Occasionally Julia would find herself watching Rud as he shaved or stepped into his breeches. Or else she would turn suddenly from brushing the long blond strands of her hair and discover his eyes upon her. At night he insisted on drawing her close to sleep, and sometimes she would awake between midnight and dawn to find his hands exploring the curves and hollows of her body. The instant they were both fully conscious he always released her at once. At times he would turn to his side and lie for the rest of the night unmoving, at others he would remove himself from the bed and, taking an extra comforter, sleep in the sitting room on the hard, silk-covered settee. On those particular nights, Julia, wanting to relax and enjoy the unexpected boon of being alone, would be troubled by the unaccustomed emptiness around her and a vague guilt for Rud's discomfort.

Lady Cathcart, Rud's mother, did not put in an appearance. It was just as well. When Julia had informed Rud, belatedly, on the morning after the dinner party of the possibility, he had stared at her. "For what?" he asked. "What does she want?"

"I have no idea, nor did Aunt Lucinda."

"She knows what I think of her. If she comes here dripping tears and mouthing her innocence, I will not be responsible for the consequences."

"She is your mother," Julia protested.

"She is a faithless witch who cares for no pleasure, no convenience, except her own. She led my father a merry dance, but I have watched her use her wiles on people for too many years to be taken in by them. I am amazed she would even think of trying."

Greatly daring, Julia asked, "Are you certain you are being fair to her? Have you ever listened to what she has to say?"

"I suppose Aunt Lucinda could not resist telling you the sad tale, though what she expected to accomplish with it I cannot imagine. I would be grateful if both you and she would allow me to handle this affair of my mother in my own fashion. I assure you I have no need of help, however well intentioned."

There was nothing more Julia could say. Her curiosity concerning the woman who had borne Rud would have to go unappeased. Though it was not her nature to do nothing when she thought someone was wrong in his attitude, she could not force Rud to see his mother. He had not forbidden her to see Lady Cathcart, however. If the opportunity arose to make the lady's acquaintance, Julia did not think she would be backward. But no such opportunity presented itself to her, and then an event occurred which pushed all else from her mind.

It was a gray afternoon. Aunt Lucinda had gone out to make a round of calls. She had invited Julia to accompany her, but Julia had refused, pleading a headache. It was a valid excuse. She had spent so much of her free time in the last few days doing embroidery or reading that she had strained her eyes. She sat now in the small sitting room with a piece of Berlin work on her lap, though her hands lay idle upon it. Rud had gone out with his uncle before luncheon, and she was alone. Soon it would be time to ring for tea. With that out of the way, she would ascend to her bedchamber and while away the hours until dinner dressing. Since she had by now worn every one of the new mourning creations twice over, that occupation offered little promise of entertainment.

The sound of the door opening behind her brought Julia's head around. "Rud! I didn't hear the carriage."

"You must have been daydreaming," he answered with a smile, closing the door behind him as he came toward her.

As he neared, Julia raised her lips for his kiss as unselfconsciously as if she had been doing it all her life. It had become a ritual between them when they parted and when they met again, something Rud expected of her. She had learned that if she omitted it she would find herself subjected to a passionate public embrace. Now he put his finger under her chin, his warm mouth lingering on hers longer than usual.

"I have good news," he said a trifle thickly as he raised his head. "The *David* is making her way into port."

"Oh, Rud," she breathed, "at last."

"Yes, the waiting is over. A few days in port, a week, two at the most, for loading, and then we will be on our way to St. Helena." A shadow crossed his face and he straightened, moving to stand with one arm resting on the white marble mantel of the fireplace.

"Is—is anything wrong?"

"No," he said with a shake of his head. "What could be wrong?"

"I don't qnow. It must have been my imagination," she excused herself. But she was sure she had not been mistaken. For an instant she had seen regret on his face, and also worry.

"Gourgaud and the others will have to be informed. I have already sent messages for a meeting to be held tonight. Would you like to come?"

"Try to keep me away," she exclaimed. "But is it certain the *David* will be routed from London to St. Helena?"

He nodded. "To St. Helena, and then on to Rio de Janeiro. It has all been arranged, thanks primarily to the help of Lord and Lady Holland, who have a consignment of food and drink to be shipped to the emperor."

"Bless them! I do like Lady Holland, don't you?"

"Even though she is a divorcée?" he queried.

Julia had heard that bit of scandal, of course. Lady Holland, with her constant round of charities and worthy causes, was prone to stirring up things the aristocracy had ignored for years and preferred to continue to ignore. Since they did not intend to act on her appeals, they excused themselves, and her, by pointing out the faults and weaknesses of her past. It did not matter that she was warm and lovely and had been much wronged. Julia could not help taking up the cudgels in her defense. "A young woman far away from the restraints of home in the eternal city of Rome, tied to a doddering old fool of a husband, must have found it difficult to resist a handsome young man like Lord Holland."

"The stuff of fairy tales, in fact?" he asked, amusement lacing his tone.

"No, not -really," she answered in all seriousness. "Merely human frailty."

"Is that what you call it?" He lifted an eyebrow. "In that case I could wish you had more of it!" Without giving her time to reply, he stepped to the bell pull hanging beside the mantel. "I think this latest development calls for a celebration. Will you join me in a toast to the arrival of the *David* and the successful conclusion of its next voyage?"

"Gladly," she said, and wondered at the grimness of his smile.

It was late when they started for the meeting of the Bonapartists. The streets were quiet, almost deserted. The reason was not hard to find. The London season had come to an end. The *beau monde* had packed its trunks, bags, and boxes, taken the knockers off its doors, and retreated either into the country, to Bath, or to Brighton with the prince regent. More than that, the evening had turned cool and fog was rolling in from the Thames. In the light of their carriage lanterns, it swirled around them like silken ghosts.

It was a night to notice other carriages, for the simple reason that there were so few of them abroad. As they turned the corner into the main thoroughfare leaving Berkeley Square, Julia saw the driver of an ancient hooded hackney spring to life. With the fog and darkness, she could discern no more than the shape of the man, but she thought he stared fixedly at their own barouche as it bowled past. A few minutes later she heard the echoing rattle of another carriage following them.

She turned her head in the direction of the man sitting close beside her. "Rud? Do you hear—"

She got no further, for he swooped upon her, drawing her into his arms. His lips met hers in a thorough kiss that forced her back against the claret velvet squabs. He

153

lingered at the sensitive corner of her mouth, then trailed fire along the curve of her cheek to the tender hollow of her neck. He pressed his face to the high-piled curls of her hair, breathing deep of its fragrance, before returning once more to the honeyed sweetness of her lips. His fingers moved to the bodice of her dress, unfastening the row of gray pearl buttons. Her breasts swelled, straining against the material as he drew it aside to expose the soft, deep valley between them. He lowered his head, and as Julia felt the searing heat of his mouth she drew in her breath, one hand going to the crisp waves of his hair. When he tugged her bodice wider in order to direct his attention more closely to a single warm globe, she suddenly sank her fingers into his hair, giving it a tug.

"What are you doing?" she gasped.

He sighed, and then as she released him, raised his head with slow reluctance. He settled back on the seat, though he did not let her go. "You looked so aloof, as virginal and untouched as a novice in a convent, and so unaware of me that I could not stand it."

"There are other ways of attracting my attention," she said through clenched teeth.

"Can I help it if I prefer my own?"

She refused to succumb to his drollery. "Yes, I think you can."

"I might, if I set my mind to it," he agreed unexpectedly. "But I am so easily distracted." With deliberation, he allowed his gaze to fall to the white curves presented by her still-gaping bodice.

Her right hand flew to the front of her gown. Snatching her left from behind his back, she began to refasten her buttons with feverish haste. "There," she said when she was done. "Now you have no excuse."

"I think," he said, his voice tinged with melancholy, "that absence is going to make the heart grow fonder."

In the confused emotions of the moment, and the peculiar exhilaration of their sparring, she forgot the other carriage.

General Baron Gaspard Gourgaud was just as Julia had imagined him to be. Suave, polished, he had a flamboyant air derived, no doubt, from his theatrical background and a frivolous manner that made an admirable cover for his basic strength of character. Though he bore the highest rank possible in the French army, he was only thirty-four. Since saving the life of the emperor at Brienne following the Russian campaign of 1812, he had enjoyed Napoleon's highest confidence.

Though Julia had attended one other of the infrequent meetings of the Bonaparte faction in London, Gourgaud had not been present. This was their first meeting.

"I am charmed, Madame Thorpe," he said, carrying Julia's hand to his lips with Gallic grace as he was presented to her. "One has heard so much about you, your courage and beauty. It is a great honor to have you with us in this magnificent endeavor."

"The honor is mine," she replied, smiling despite her awareness of Rud standing stiff with disapproval at her side.

M'sieu Robeaud did not look much changed to Julia, though he had begun to grow the beard and mustache that would play a part in the exchange of identities with Napoleon. They gave him a surprisingly fierce look, belied by his manner. He greeted her with quiet pleasure, then moved humbly aside so that the others crowding around could be introduced in their turn.

One of the last to come forward was Marcel de Gruys. Julia's smile became fixed as she faced him. It was all she could do to bring herself to extend her hand to him; she could not manage to summon a smile, however false.

"We meet again," he said, an unpleasant edge in his voice. As he bowed, he appeared to favor his right side.

"Yes." She had to force the single syllable past her lips.

"We must renew our acquaintance. We have much unfinished business between us," he told her with snide insinuation. "Perhaps there will be time on the voyage outward to St. Helena."

His eyes raked over her in a look that left her feeling naked. His thumbnail dug into the palm of her hand before she could drag it from his damp grasp. Glancing to

155

where Rud had been standing only moments before, she saw him in close conversation with Gourgaud.

"Oh, yes," de Gruys said with a sly nod. "I know you are married to the fine sea captain. He makes a formidable bodyguard, I will admit. Still, he cannot be with you always."

She lifted her head, her eyes blazing. "Take care," she said, allowing a small, ironic sneer to curve her lovely mouth. "When my husband is not with me, I make it a habit to carry a knife."

He stiffened, a rush of blood staining his face an unhealthy red. His lips writhed in a vile epithet he dared not pronounce aloud with the others so close around them. "Save your warnings for yourself!" he hissed. "Even shecats like you can be disarmed." Spinning around, he stalked away.

Julia could feel the trembling along her nerves. As slowly and as casually as possible, she turned. Moving to Rud's side, she slipped her hand into the crook of his arm. He pressed it to his side, sparing her a quick glance. At the set paleness of her face he lifted a brow of inquiry, but she shook her head, summoning a smile.

It should not have mattered, then, that he returned to Gourgaud, falling back into their discussion of the difficulties of the thousand-mile trip from St. Helena to Rio. Somehow it did.

After a time Gourgaud reached into his waistcoat pocket and drew out a pocket timepiece as large as a turnip. "Messieurs, madame, time speeds. Let us be seated. I believe Captain Thorpe has an important announcement to make."

With alacrity they moved into the dining saloon. Rud stood with his fingers resting lightly on the table as he told them of the *David*. He was a commanding figure, standing broad and tall under the crystal chandelier. The candleglow shone in the blue-black waves of his hair and gave a bronze cast to his features. His rugged attractiveness seemed, by contrast, to give every other man present a soft look that was almost effeminate.

Julia, returning her attention to her husband after

glancing around the table, discovered he had finished speaking. With a sense of shock she realized she had not heard more than a few words of what he had said.

No one else had been woolgathering. A buzz of joyous congratulations filled the room. The feeling was one of suppressed euphoria. The emperor had his ship! It was as though he had reached out across oceans to make things happen in the way he desired. It did not matter that others had made the arrangements; Napoleon had set them in motion.

Gourgaud got to his feet as Rud sat down. "I thank you, Captain Thorpe. I am sure I speak for everyone here when I say you could not have brought us more welcome tidings. Words cannot express our joy, nor can they convey our gratitude to you for your efforts in behalf of him who waits on St. Helena."

There were a few more items to be decided. These were dispatched with a minimum of disagreement, primarily because Napoleon's instructions were so explicit for every eventuality.

"Before we part," Gourgaud said finally, "there is one thing more to which we must give our attention." With a flourish, he presented a curling sheet of foolscap. "Messieurs, Madame, I have a message from the emperor!"

The main body of the letter was devoted to a barrage of last-minute instructions. Toward the end Napoleon Bonaparte wrote:

I sit here on this rock and attempt to visualize all that can go wrong. This exercise is designed to see that nothing will. I am confident of the future. Its promise shines clear. I have had time while accepting the hospitality of the English to regroup my forces, to survey the strengths and weaknesses of my position. The former outweigh the latter. For three years France has known the ineptitude of the Bourbons and the contempt of the members of the Convention of Paris—Austria, Russia, Prussia, and England. The people remember their past glory and pray for its return. It shall return! I shall!"

The roar of approval was loud and long. Flushed with the excitement of the moment, clapping her stinging palms together, Julia looked down the table. She was so proud to be a part of the effort to free the emperor. It was disconcerting to see Marcel de Gruys with the hard edge of cynicism curling his mouth as he stared at the foolscap being passed from hand to hand. An instant later he was applauding, smiling as broadly as any.

They did not linger long after that. One by one, the Bonapartists departed as quietly and inconspicuously as they had come. Marcel, much to Julia's relief, was among the first to go. She and Rud tarried a few minutes behind the others as he and Gourgaud discussed the best route to send word to the emperor of the impending departure of the *David*.

The fog had grown thicker in the hour they were inside, so thick it almost hid the coachman on the box of their own carriage from view as Julia and Rud stepped inside. Its dampness touched Julia's face with wraithlike fingers, and she shivered, wishing she had worn her pelerine.

"Cold?" Rud asked, throwing himself onto the seat beside her as he slammed the door.

Before she could answer, the door on the opposite side of the carriage, away from the flambeau-lit entrance to Gourgaud's lodging, swung open. A horse pistol was shoved at them.

"Hold!" a hoarse voice growled. "Sit still there and nobody'll get 'urt. No screechin', mind."

The last was directed at Julia as she swung to face their assailant. He was a short, squat man with beady eyes in a round face which sprouted a straggly beard. Her eyes widened in disbelief as she recognized the man who, more than three weeks before, had driven past her and Aunt Lucinda as they were returning from their shopping.

"What do you want?" Rud demanded, placing his arm across Julia to shield her as much as possible. It was not a great deal, since she was between him and the man with the pistol.

"Yer valuables," the man answered with an obscene

laugh, "startin' with this pretty piece right here!" His hand shot out to grab Julia's wrist, jerking her off the seat.

"No!" Rud shouted, his fingers digging into her ribs as he pushed her back. For an instant she was torn between them, then Rud lashed out with his booted foot, sending the pistol spinning from the thief's grasp.

Cursing, the man let Julia go to scrabble on the floor for the pistol. Rud reached for it at the same time. The two of them grappled back and forth in the rocking carriage. The stout man's arms bulged with muscles and his face twisted in a bestial rage. He had, in addition, the advantage of standing on solid ground instead of having to kneel inside the carriage. Rud was a match for him in strength, but there was something ruthless in the man's grunting efforts to bring the gun to bear on Rud's chest, or to use teeth and nails to gain the upper hand.

Julia did not think Rud was in need of her help, but still the fear spiraling up into her throat compelled her to join the fray. Setting her lips, she kicked out, catching the burly man a fine blow in the ribs.

The action did not go unnoticed. The man flinched. Rud flung her a tight grin. "Julia, my pistol, side pocket!"

She had not known it was there. In frantic haste she lunged across the seat, searching in the shirred pocket on the side where Rud had sat. Her fingers closed over cold metal.

Behind her their assailant hollered out, "Gov'nor! Help me here! I can't hold this 'un!"

Pistol in her hand, Julia swung around to see a second man shoulder into the open carriage door. He was cloaked in black, with a hat pulled low over his face.

"Bungling idiot," he hissed, bringing the pistol he had been holding on the coachman up level. There was a flash, followed by a deafening explosion.

Rud was thrown backward as from a hard blow, blood pouring down his face, the horse pistol he had wrenched from the other man's hand at last clutched in his fist.

Julia did not stop to think. Using both thumbs on the stiff mechanism, she cocked the pistol she held and fired. The man in black took the ball in the side, spinning backward out of sight. As Julia threw the now useless weapon to one side and leaned to take the other from Rud's limp fingers, the first man backed away, then turned and ran. Julia watched him for a brief instant before she slid to her knees beside Rud.

The door of the lodging house flew open and Gourgaud appeared. He hurried toward the carriage. "Madame Thorpe! I thought I heard gunfire! What has happened?"

"Two men—they attacked us," Julia flung over her shoulder.

In the added light thrown from the open door, the two men could be seen, one helping the other climb into a hooded hackney standing across the fog-filled street. The door slammed and the dilapidated vehicle rattled away.

"I will catch them," Gourgaud vowed.

"No, no, there is no time. Rud has been shot. A doctor —he must have a doctor!"

Gourgaud pulled the door wide to look down at the unconscious man. "No need for that."

"You don't mean he—he is dead?" Julia breathed, her fingers tightening on the broadcloth of Rud's coat beneath her hand.

"No! Forgive me, Madame Thorpe. I did not mean to frighten you. I only intended to indicate that I have had a great deal of experience with wounds of this nature on the battlefield—far more, I daresay, than any London physician you might find who earns his living from midwifery and female complaints. If you will permit me?"

"Very well," she said with quick decision. It might be the better portion of an hour before a physician of any kind could be summoned, and every moment counted. "Go ahead, only do something quickly. He is bleeding to death."

Blood, so much blood. It soaked through layer after layer of bandaging from a long furrow that slanted across Rud's temple.

"Head wounds always bleed profusely," Gourgaud told her, but she could not believe any man could lose so much blood and live.

Even after the bleeding was stopped, Rud did not regain consciousness. He lay on the bed in the bedchamber of Gourgaud's lodgings in perfect stillness, his face drained of color and vitality. Julia sat beside him with her hands clasped tightly in her lap. He looked so lifeless, so vulnerable, lying there. She felt she should be doing something to help, but there was nothing to be done. She had tended enough deep cuts as mistress of her father's plantation to know that the French general had done everything possible, everything a physician was capable of doing.

A dozen times she was on the verge of sending a message to Rud's aunt and uncle, but to do so would bring too much attention to Gourgaud and the late-night meeting at his lodging. True, he was supposed to have broken with Napoleon, and was, in his own fashion, currently cooperating with the English, but still this was a complication he did not need.

In spite of this, she had almost made up her mind to take the risk, to ask their host for paper and pen to send a note around to Berkeley Square, when Rud groaned and shifted his head on the pillow. An instant later he opened his eyes.

"Julia," he whispered.

"I am here," she said, rising to move into his line of vision. She took the hand that lay with fingers curled on the coverlet and held it between both of hers.

Rud's gaze focused on her face. His mouth tugged in a brief smile. "The men got away?" he asked in a voice so low she had to lean close to hear him.

In answer, she told him what had happened after he was shot.

"So, you got one of them? I knew you would. I am still at Gourgaud's, then?"

The general had been resting in his sitting room. Now he stepped into the bedchamber. "Yes, *mon ami*. You are still my guest, and also my patient, due to your carelessness."

Rud smiled. "My thanks for your efforts, but I must not trespass on your hospitality any longer. If you will help me to my carriage—"

"You are certain you are able?" Gourgaud asked.

"I must be, since I can't stay," Rud said, and shifting to his side, pushed himself up on one elbow.

Gourgaud gave an unhappy nod. "I do not like it, but you are right, *mon ami*. You have, I think, the concussion, and should lie still for a time, but I have seen men with worse injuries walk with help from the battlefield."

"So have I," Rud agreed, "but not in the same army."

"This has been made known to me," Gourgaud said, a reserve coming into his face. "Strange, is it not, the fortunes of war?"

In Berkeley Square the mansion was dark, though the butler was still on duty to answer their ring. With his aid, and that of the coachman, Rud was finally established in his own bed. Masters, with a slight cough, suggested that he make Rud comfortable. With no more than a moment's hesitation, Julia agreed. The poor man fairly bristled with curiosity, but she told him only that their carriage had been set upon by robbers. When Rud was stronger he could tell the butler, and also his aunt and uncle, anything else he wished them to know. The coachman could provide the truth, of course, if anyone chose to ask him. Julia suspected, however, that Rud had chosen him originally for his discretion. She had no choice except to rely on his judgment.

It was odd to see Rud attired in a nightshirt. She could only suppose Masters had borrowed it from Thaddeus Baxter's wardrobe and slipped it over his head while he was too weak to protest. She fully expected that at the first opportunity it would land, like her black nightgown, in the corner, thereafter to be relegated to the bottom of the wardrobe.

It did not. By morning Rud was caught in the grip of a high fever. For three days he lay, his skin flushed and his eyes burning bright as they followed her about the room. Sometimes he dropped into a fitful sleep; more often he tossed back and forth, a prey to the throbbing of headache. There was often a faraway look in his eyes, as if he were listening to other voices, and Julia thought when she approached him on those occasions that he prevented himself from sliding into the raving of delirium only by strength of will.

He was not entirely successful. On the third night, as the fever began to break, she stood beside his bed, testing the heat of his forehead with her hand. He opened his eyes, staring up at her. Reaching up, he captured her fingers, holding them against his cheek.

"Such cool hands," he said, his voice a whisper of sound. "Give me rest and peace. The pure face of a nun with hate in your eyes. Don't look at me that way. I won't hurt you."

She drew in her breath, pain swelling around her heart. Once she might have been glad to see him reduced to helplessness. She was not. The sight hurt her in some peculiar way she could not explain. Perspiration dewed his forehead beneath his bandage. His lips were dry and cracked. With her free hand she stretched to take up the damp cloth left lying beside the bed after they had bathed him to lower the fever. She wiped his face with slow, gentle strokes. "No," she said soothingly. "I know you won't."

By morning he was rational and free of fever. At Aunt Lucinda's insistence, Julia left him for the first time since he had been shot. In a spare bedchamber, she enjoyed the relaxation of a hot, scented bath and then fell into bed to sleep the clock around.

When next she saw Rud, the nightshirt had vanished and the dressing on his head, freshly changed, had not only shrunk, but had acquired a rakish tilt. His docility was a thing of the past. His head, much against his will, still ached, and he was far from satisfied with the thin chicken broth which had been brought to him for luncheon. More than these, he desired to know the whereabouts of his wife. No one else could do anything to suit him, whether it was smoothing the bedcovers or stirring his tea. Everyone else was too rough, too clumsy, too noisy—and much too likely to go away in a miff if he did not thank them properly for their efforts.

After a further forty-eight hours of this treatment, Aunt

Lucinda barged into the bedchamber and swept Julia away with her for an afternoon drive.

"My dear, you must be descended from the angels," Aunt Lucinda said when they were well away from Berkeley Square, bowling along with the folding top of the barouche thrown open.

Julia denied it with a smile and a shake of her head.

"Ah, well, make light of it if you wish, but I don't mind saying I have been touched by your devotion. For many years, here in England, there has been a lamentable tendency to marry for money and position and seek love elsewhere. It is good to see a marriage in which the two are combined. Rud has been like a son to me, as I think you know. I am proud to think that he has found as much happiness in his marriage as his uncle and I have found in ours."

Julia would have liked to deny this conclusion, but to do so would only cause his aunt needless distress. The truth was, it was guilt which caused her to appear so devoted. If it had not been for her, their carriage would not have been attacked and Rud would not have been injured. All too well she remembered that horrible man putting his hands on her, trying to drag her out of the carriage. It had been a daring plan, the second carriage waiting, one that was old and without visible identification. Two men, one to hold the coachman at gunpoint while the other persuaded Rud to part with his "valuables" —his money and Julia. Without false vanity, she was positive that of the two she had been the preferred prize. She was certain that out of lust or a twisted need for revenge, the purpose of the attack had been to kidnap her. She was certain, for though she had told no one as yet, she had recognized the voice of the second man, the man she had shot. It was Marcel. That she had failed to kill him she regretted exceedingly.

If Rud had recognized their assailants, if he realized their purpose, he had given no sign. For all he had said to her or to anyone else, he was content to leave it as a robbery attempt. Julia sometimes thought he was so reticent out of a desire to save her distress. Certainly she had no wish to disturb him by mentioning it, not when he was unable to go after Marcel or to send the authorities to question him. Soon, when Rud was more nearly recovered, Julia knew she must discuss the matter with him. Together they would have to decide what was to be done.

Rud's aunt and uncle had accepted the incident without question as a robbery attempt. For this much Julia was extremely grateful.

Aunt Lucinda beguiled the remainder of the drive with the kind of quiet, undemanding chatter which needed little reply. They moved sedately through the deserted park where only a few weeks before they had bowed left and right to acquaintances. It was a clear day. The sun shone down with a warmth they could feel. Aunt Lucinda resorted to a sunshade against its strength, but Julia lifted her face to its rays, enjoying its gentle touch.

"You will freckle, my dear," Aunt Lucinda protested.

Julia only shook her head. "I never freckle," she said.

The breeze of their passing was soft and sweet on her eyelids, and she realized that Aunt Lucinda was right; she had been shut up inside too long. How then must Rud feel? An inactive life was completely foreign to him. He was used to being out in the elements, the sun, wind, and rain. She wondered in sudden contrition if he ever felt that she was his jailer.

It was obvious there was some truth to that supposition when they returned. In defiance of Gourgaud's advice and Julia's entreaties, Rud had gotten out of bed. The most dire of threats on his part had produced a hot bath for his enjoyment and a change of linens for his bed. The paraphernalia of sickness—the laudanum drops, the pans of water, the excess bandaging and various powders used as a preventive against gangrene—had been swept out of the room. The windows and doors had been thrown open to rid the place of the last lingering closeness of the sickroom. Last of all, he had cajoled the woman who presided over the kitchen belowstairs to send up a large sirloin steak with vegetable side dishes and a tankard of ale.

His efforts had served to convince him that he was not quite as strong as he had thought, however. Or perhaps he had taken care to preserve what was left of his strength. The breeches he had ordered laid out still decorated a chair, while the patient himself was back in bed, propped high on pillows.

"There you are," he greeted Julia when she stepped into the room. "I have been waiting for hours for you to come and shave me!"

She eyed him with misgivings. He certainly did not look any worse for his exertions. The bandage on his head had been reduced to nothing more than a sticking plaster. His broad shoulders were braced against the headboard of the bed, and though he lay still with his fingers knitted over his flat stomach, he had the look of a panther at rest, watching his next victim.

"Shave you?" she asked doubtfully. Masters had attempted to perform that service the day before and been roundly cursed for his pains.

"That's what I said."

"I don't think I can," she said, moving closer. "I would probably cut your throat."

"Better you than Masters," he answered, unperturbed.

"From the looks of it, you had quite a busy afternoon. Why didn't you shave yourself while you were about it?"

"It crossed my mind," he replied with a slow smile, "but I decided it would be more pleasurable to have you do it for me."

"Oh, you did?" she said with the lift of an eyebrow. There was something in his manner that sent a quiver of alarm along her nerves.

"I did. The water has been heating below for some time, if it hasn't all boiled away. Be a love and ring for it?"

There seemed nothing else to do. Julia complied with as much grace as she could muster. By the time she had draped a towel around him and brought out the razor and soap, the water had arrived.

Dipping a linen cloth in the steaming pan, she squeezed out the excess water and laid the wet towel on his face.

"That's hot, woman!" he said, slinging it off.

"Isn't it supposed to be?" she asked innocently.

He made no reply, but there was a smoldering look in his eyes as he lay back and allowed her to continue.

The straight-edge razor with its bone handle was sharp enough to split a hair. Rud had relaxed somewhat under her firm but gentle touch as she worked lather into his beard. Now he turned a wary eye in the direction of the blade in her hand. Seeing her watching him, however, he hastily assumed a waiting air, sticking his chin out.

Carefully she scraped his face, wiping away the accumulated soap and stubby hairs on the dry towel about his shoulders. So intense was her concentration that it was a moment before she noticed the stroking hand moving on her back. After an instant's consideration, she decided to ignore it. What could it hurt? Without doubt it was a good sign that Rud was getting well.

Making such a resolution was easier than keeping it. The easy slide of his fingers on the tussah silk of her fitted bodice was more distracting than she had expected. With a deep breath, she leaned across him to reach the area just under his ear. The fullness of her breasts pressed against his chest, making her aware of its muscled hardness. His other hand came up to test the supple indentation of her waist, moving to the buttons down her back. She rose up, staring at him, but his face was bland. Once more she turned her attention to the taut skin beneath his chin.

"Ouch!" he exclaimed.

"Serves you right," she told him. She had not meant to nick him, but she was positive he was stealthily easing the buttons of her gown from their holes.

"Witch," he muttered.

"Fiend," she replied, her lips suspiciously tight.

Suddenly they both broke into a wide grin. Taking the razor from her hand, Rud finished the job in a few deft strokes. Tossing the blade aside, he removed the last traces of soap with the wet towel. Julia took it from him and, dropping it into the pan of warm water, moved to set both outside the door to be picked up.

Fingering his chin, Rud said, "Nice job."

Julia stepped back to the bed to take the dry towel from him. "Maybe I should try for a post as a valet."

"You have a post already," he said as he caught her wrist. "As my wife."

As he drew her down beside him his eyes searched hers, a look both serious and questioning in their dark-blue depths. His fingers went to her hair, probing the soft waves, removing the pins. The thick chignon at the nape of her neck uncoiled, spilling in a golden cascade down her back and releasing its special perfume. He smoothed the lustrous strands, spreading them out, trailing them through his fingers before he pushed them aside to reach the few buttons still fastened on her gown. Her eyelids fluttered shut. His lips sought the tender shape of her mouth, molding it to his. He tasted the sweetness of her response, the gentle surrender as her lips parted.

The confinement of her bodice eased. Obedient to his guiding hands, she moved to allow him to bare her shoulders and release her arms from the clinging folds of her gown. A touch on her naked breast alerted her to the fact that he had loosened her underdress also, pushing it down around her hips.

Her eyes flew open and she tried to push away from him, but he held her fast. His kiss deepened, growing more demanding. His hands moved over her breasts, teasing the nipples to firmness, sliding down over her stomach. Crossing his arms behind her, he rolled off his propped pillows, pulling her with him, easing her to her back. A few swift moves and she was free of her trailing skirts, lying half beneath him.

"Rud—" she breathed in supplication, her hands braced on his chest. He smothered that weak protest against her lips.

It sank into her mind that this time he would not be stayed, this time he had no intention of drawing back. Fear tightened the muscles of her abdomen; still, at the same time a heady surge of something like anticipation mounted in her. Brushing aside her resistance, he held her against his lean frame. He drank in the fragrance of

168

her hair, the wild, sweet tang of vetiver and jasmine, while his lips felt the smooth silken texture of her skin.

The hard urgency of his need made itself known against her thigh. His hand moved to her breast and his mouth followed. Slowly, with care, he explored her body, leaving a tingling excitement behind. He was her husband, a part of her mind whispered. It was his right. She could not prevent him, was no longer certain she wanted to try. A tremulous sigh escaped her parted lips.

Rud's arms tightened around her. His caress grew more intimate, pressing deeper. She put her hands on his shoulders, opening and closing them as flame leaped within her. The surface of her skin seemed to grow hot to the touch. Her breath caught in her chest.

Then Rud loomed above her, his arms trembling with strain. His knee eased between her parted thighs. His mouth possessed hers with hot, passionate longing. Her senses reeled as she felt the first iron probing. Close upon it came an instant of sharp, rending pain that made her gasp, her nails biting into his shoulders. For a fleeting moment they were still, the frantic beating of their hearts shaking them, and then he eased deeper, filling her being, sending radiating waves of warm pleasure through her. He moved above her, gently at first with many kisses and caresses, and then more strongly as his lust, so long contained, burst the bounds of his control. She moved to accommodate the shock of his thrusts, accepting in wonder the sharp mounting of her own burning enjoyment. It scaled higher and higher, a white heat, glowing in her blood, consuming her, fed by the one thing that could quench it. They soared, their bodies fused in a mystic union. Ecstasy caught them, hurling them higher still. Julia clung to Rud, certain in the dark recesses of her mind that she could not bear it. Then came the perfect, easy descent by gentle steps to stillness.

Their breathing was loud in the quiet. Rud entwined his fingers in her hair. Julia thought he carried a strand to his lips, though with her eyes half closed she could not be sure.

The mattress was depressed beside her head as he

169

raised himself on one elbow. "I would apologize," he said, his voice husky, "but I am not sorry."

Julia felt none of the hate and resentment she had expected. It was as though what had happened between them had been inevitable from their first meeting. The tension and tiredness of the past days were gone, leaving her drowsy with content, and oddly grateful. Slowly she opened her eyes. In their amber depths shone a clear golden light. "Neither am I sorry," she whispered.

A fierce gladness blazed in his face. Setting his mouth to hers in ruthless exploration, he swung her over so that she lay on top of him, the fullness of her breasts pressed against his chest, her hair falling in a curtain about them, the full length of her body resting on his.

She lifted her head, trying to breathe. For some strange reason she felt the ache of tears in her throat. "You—you are uncommonly active for an injured man," she accused him.

"Experimenting with a new treatment," he said.

"I see. And was it effective?"

"Miraculously so. I am much better, though I am afraid the effects are going to be short-lived. I feel sure I will need to repeat the performance frequently."

Julia knew a quickening inside her at the promise in his voice, though she had no intention of letting him know it. "Not, I hope, before dark. What if someone came in now? It is the middle of the afternoon."

"No one will come in without knocking," he replied reasonably. "Besides, I am a sick man; I am supposed to be in bed no matter what the time."

"I am not supposed to be in it with you!" she reminded him.

"Aren't you?" His voice dropped to a low note. His hand on her back began to move, stroking, squeezing.

"No," she answered, though with less certainty.

Pushing his fingers under her hair, he pulled her mouth down to his. Their tongues touched, hers meeting his hesitantly at first, then with growing boldness. Her cool, shapely arms came up to cradle his head, while his hands took fullest advantage of the higher movement of her hips. She felt the stirring of his manly ardor.

A knock fell on the door.

Julia raised her head. Rud muttered something blasphemous, a scowl drawing his brows together, though he did not release her. "Who is it?" he called.

"Masters, sir," the butler said, coughing respectfully.

Julia broke Rud's grasp, scooting, sliding from the bed. She bent to retrieve her gown and underdress. Noiseless in her stocking feet, she flitted into the dressing room and started to shut the door. Abruptly she noticed her slippers tumbled beside the bed, looking just as though she had kicked them off before climbing in.

Rud was hurriedly straightening the rumpled covers. At her frantic motion he leaned over the side of the bed and batted the slippers out of sight underneath it. Lying back, he said in an irritable tone in no way feigned, "Come in, then!"

"Your pardon, Captain Thorpe," Masters said, stepping into the bedchamber. "You have visitors below, sir."

"And who might they be?"

"The name given was Lord and Lady Cathcart, sir."

"What! Tell them I am not receiving visitors."

Julia, listening through a crack in the door, paused in tying the tapes of her underdress. The expected visit from Rud's mother at last, and he was not going to see her.

She ducked into her gown, letting it billow down over her shoulders, pulling it into place about her waist. She listened a minute to be certain Masters had gone, then stepped back into the other room.

Her color a trifle high, she moved across to the bed. Rud watched her approach with a possessive smile, his gaze on the gentle swing of her hips. She turned her back, presenting her buttons.

"So you aren't going to see your mother," she said over her shoulder.

"No."

"Why? To punish her, to make her pay because she would not live with your father, wouldn't make a home for you to enjoy."

"You know nothing about it," he said in easy dismissal.

"You think not? Well, perhaps you are right. I have no idea whether your mother was innocent or guilty of the death of your father, but I do know that you cannot be an impartial judge. When I was a child I used to hate my mother for dying, for going away and leaving me with no one to chaperon me, or to give gay little entertainments for my friends, no one to talk to about becoming a woman."

His busy fingers paused at the small of her back. "The two cases are entirely different."

"Are they?" she inquired gravely. "My motives were based on self-pity. What is the basis of yours?"

Catching her elbow, he swung her around. "That woman downstairs arranged to have my father killed. What am I supposed to do? Pretend it didn't happen?"

"You are not her judge, but even if you were, don't you think it would be best to be absolutely certain of your facts before you pass sentence?"

"My mother was the only one who knew my father was on English soil."

"How can you be so sure? His message to her might have been intercepted, or a patrol may have come upon him accidentally. He was a Yankee privateer on enemy soil, indulging in a dangerous, even foolhardy escapade. The wonder is not that he was found out, but that he could think that he would not be."

The angry scowl that drew Rud's brows together was an indication of how close her thrust had come. "There is more to the matter than appears on the surface."

"If that is so, then enlighten me," Julia said, meeting his gaze squarely.

"I would prefer that you accept my word, and my judgment."

"On faith," she asked with a lift of her chin, "like the word of God?"

"Bravo! Oh, bravo!"

The cry of approval came from the doorway. A woman stood in the opening. In their involvement with their argument they had not heard her enter. Behind her stood Masters, his face as well as his upper body stiff with disapproval and offended dignity.

The woman advanced a few steps into the room. "Well done, my dear," she said to Julia, her eyes moving with a wry amusement over her unbound golden tresses falling about her shoulders and the still-open back of her gown. "He has needed just such a set-down for sometime. You must forgive the intrusion. I rather suspected Masters of prevarication when he told me Rud was not in a condition to receive visitors. I see, however, that he spoke nothing more than the truth. Still, you need not be embarrassed on my account. Such scenes are not precisely unknown to me, and as strange as it sometimes seems to me, the man who is handling you in such a familiar manner is my son."

Chapter
Nine

*L*ady *Georgina Baxter Thorpe Cathcart was surpris-*
ingly small, not quite as tall as Julia, and had the slender
frame and aquiline features of a thoroughbred. Her hair,
though elegantly dressed, was a henna brown, while her
blue eyes lacked either the depth or the intensity of
Rud's. The only feature she had bequeathed her son was
the firm turn of her lips. Dressed in the height of fashion,
in a walking costume of écru taffeta trimmed in silk floss,
and a modish bonnet with braided ribbon and dyed
plumes, she did not look her fifty-odd years in spite of
the fine lines radiating from her eyes. Regardless of her
audacity in entering where she was not wanted, and in
carrying off the situation as she found it, Julia thought
she was not so self-assured as she appeared. Her eyes, as
she turned to her son, were overbright; the lace fan and
silver calling-card case in her hand were clutched a trifle
tightly.

Something had to be done. They could not stand there
forever without speaking. Rousing herself, Julia gave a
nod to Masters, who went out, closing the door behind
him. "Won't you sit down, Lady Cathcart?" she said.

Rud's mother glanced at the deep armchair near the
fireplace. "Thank you, no. I prefer to stand. In any case,
I will not be here long. Cathcart is waiting for me below."

Rud spoke at last. "Ah, yes. Cathcart, the new husband. Permit me to congratulate you." There was such a

cold light in his eyes that Julia was surprised the other woman did not wither under it.

"Thank you," his mother answered, her composure intact. "He is my new husband but an old friend. You must not forget that."

"You may be certain I have not," Rud replied.

His mother looked down at her hands, visibly relaxing the grip on her card case.

Julia, uneasy, put a hand to her hair, pushing it behind her back. She was acutely aware of her bare feet and the crushed look of her gown. She would be much better able to cope with this if she did not feel quite so bedraggled. "Perhaps you would like to be alone?" she suggested. "I can wait in the dressing room—"

"No," Rud said, reaching out to place his hand on her forearm.

His mother shook her head. "That will not be necessary. As I said, I will not be long. News came to me of the shooting incident. I wished merely to satisfy myself that my son had come to no harm. Despite everything, I do still have some maternal feeling."

"I am well enough," Rud answered when she did not go on. His tone was clipped, shaded with suspicion.

"I have come also to ask a favor. I find it uncomfortable to have people saying behind my back that my son and I are estranged because he feels I am responsible for his father's death."

Rud's grip slipped from Julia's arm to her hand. "Go on," he said to his mother, though his attention was on the slender fingers he was toying with as he ran his thumb over the smooth knuckles.

"I thought that as soon as you are well enough to be seen out and about, you would not mind being a bit more, shall I say, attentive? There should be time enough to scotch the rumors before you are ready to sail."

"Sail?" Rud said as if such a course were the furthest thing from his mind.

"You need not pretend with me," Georgina Cathcart said. "If you will remember, I have my sources of information in the Foreign Office, usually most reliable. Becoming

175

Lady Cathcart has not changed that. A few other interesting rumors have come to my ears of late concerning your activities, my dear Rud. Must I go into details?"

"No, I think not," Rud said slowly.

His mother glanced at Julia, with an odd smile curling the corner of her mouth. "I rather thought it would be unnecessary."

Frowning, Julia stared at the other woman. Was she suggesting that she knew of Rud's association with the Bonapartists? If so, she must not realize his wife was also involved, for Julia was certain the woman was hinting that she could mention things Rud would prefer his wife not to hear.

"Who else is in possession of this information?" Rud was saying.

"No one. Naturally the person who informed me thought I would be interested beyond the ordinary, and he has long been in my debt. Beyond that, he is the soul of discretion."

Rud released Julia's hand and sat up. "You are certain?"

To Julia he had become once more the man she had met aboard the *Sea Jade,* alert behind a pleasant mask, armored with cynicism and hard self-reliance.

"I am certain," his mother answered, smiling a little, though her light blue eyes remained watchful. "Under the circumstances, I believe you can understand my feelings, and my need to have you pay me some small attention?"

"I believe I do," Rud answered, his voice grim. "What exactly do you want of me?"

"Only to be seen once or twice in public with me, and to attend a small reception I will give for you and your new bride. That is not so much to ask, is it?"

"I never thought to hear you admit to needing the countenance of anyone else."

The woman drew herself up. "That is neither here nor there. Do you intend to fall in with my wishes?"

"You leave me no choice," Rud said with a mocking half bow from where he sat in the bed.

"That was my intention," his mother answered. "We will call it settled then. I will not stay longer. Only let me tell you once more how delighted I am to see you so well, my son, and express my pleasure in making the acquaintance at last of the charming young lady you have married, and I will leave you to your rest."

There was a definite shading of irony to that last word. Julia, catching that pale-blue glance, lifted her chin.

The other woman smiled a little, with something like pity in her gaze. "You needn't ring for Masters to show me downstairs. I can find my own way."

As the door closed behind her, Julia let out her pent-up breath. She had known many women, but none with quite the confidence, the quiet power, of that one. "How much do you think she knows?" she asked after a moment.

"That," Rud said, staring with narrowed eyes at the closed door, "is a good question."

"You don't really think she would betray you to the authorities?"

Rud glanced up at Julia. "With scarcely a qualm."

"But you are her son!"

"Yes," he answered, his tone grim, "so I am."

It appeared Rud was right. Any woman who could threaten her son with the exposure of an offense punishable by imprisonment, even death, could well have caused the demise of her husband. How much easier to betray a partner in a loveless marriage than a son! What a terrible woman; without heart, without any of the tender feelings that would make such a thing impossible. And yet that woman had actually pitied her. Why? How dared she?

"Don't frown so," Rud said. "The *David* sails within the week. A few more days, and that will be the end of it. It will not hurt us to do as she wants until then."

"I suppose not," Julia agreed. "But I would like to be sure that she will remain silent if we keep our part of the bargain."

"Oddly enough, I believe she can be trusted to do that. My mother's political beliefs are not strong. Her first loyalty, now as always, is to herself."

His voice was dispassionate, as though the words he

spoke had long since lost their power to wound him. In spite of that, Julia said, "I'm sorry."

"For what?" he inquired lazily, brushing the blue-veined underside of her wrist with his thumb.

"Sorry that your mother is the way she is, sorry I doubted what you had to say of her."

"Turn around," he said, giving her arm a tug so that her back was to him again. His arm slid like a hawser around her waist, making her sit with a bounce on the bed.

Julia, thinking he intended to finish the job of doing up her gown, was obligingly still. Within seconds she discovered her mistake.

"What are you doing?" she asked, reaching back to feel the bareness of her back where the buttons had been undone once more. Twisting, she tried to rise, only to find herself firmly held.

"I thought you might like to demonstrate precisely how contrite you are," he said, nuzzling the skin above the top of her underdress, brushing it with his lips.

She stiffened as if she had been stung. "I can't imagine where you got that idea."

"Can't you?" he murmured, his strong teeth nipping gently at her flesh through the thin silk.

The grip of his arm tightened. Julia lunged forward to grasp at the table beside the bed, her fingers sliding over the surface as he exerted a steady backward pull. "Is this all you think about?" she asked between laughter and exasperation.

"Of late," he admitted.

The pressure at her midsection was becoming unbearable. "It will be dark soon," she gasped.

"I know," he said, a quiver of amusement in his voice. "I'm looking forward to that time too."

He slipped his free hand under the bodice of her gown, his fingers busy at the tapes of her underdress.

"Rud—"

"Yes, my sweet?"

She drew a deep breath, letting it out in a sigh as all resistance left her. She leaned back against him. He released her, and raising his head, turned her in the circle of his arms. He pressed her close as his mouth, warm with promise, sought hers. Reaching out, he flung back the covers in unsubtle invitation.

Julia, already beginning to slip her arms from the clinging folds of her bodice, glanced across the sheets. She went still, her gaze fastened on the reddish-brown stain that marred the wrinkled expanse of the bedding. Anger and revulsion swept over her in a wave, routing her languor like a strong wind. She pushed away from Rud, springing to her feet.

"You lied to me," she hissed.

Her loosened gown slid slowly down her hips to lie about her feet. With a furious gesture she stepped out of it and kicked it aside. The low-cut underdress allowed a generous view of her charms. Its ebony color made a breathtaking contrast to their ivory perfection, while the quickness of her breathing threatened momentarily to reveal the coral-pink aureoles.

Rud swallowed, bringing his gaze with difficulty to her face. "About what?" he asked, his voice thick.

"You told me that you—spent the night with me, slept with me, aboard the *Sea Jade* on the night before we were married."

"So I did," he answered, a frown beginning to draw his brows together.

"You didn't, you couldn't have."

"I did, and I could!"

Julia waved her hand in a derisive gesture toward the bed. "Then how do you explain that?"

"I never said I made love to you," he answered after a brief glance in the direction she indicated.

"Oh no?" she queried. "You certainly allowed me to think so!"

"What I said, if I remember correctly, was that you invited me to spend the night in your cabin, and that the morning afterward you were not unwilling to marry me."

"I woke up with no clothes—"

"True, but if you will think back you will remember that it had been a foggy night that turned into rain. It was impossible to avoid getting wet climbing in and out of the carriage between the inn and the ship. I could not let you catch pneumonia from sleeping in damp clothing, could I? You were chilled with the weather and the shock of what had happened. You did not want to be alone. Was I supposed to leave you in the dark with your trembling and your fears?"

It sounded so plausible, and yet she knew she was not mistaken. "Do you deny that you deliberately set out to let me think that I—that I had allowed—even invited you to—"

She floundered under his considering gaze, knowing full well that he would not come to her aid.

"Yes?" he said in false encouragement.

"You know what I mean!" she cried wrathfully.

"Yes, I do," he said, smiling a little. "Why do you think I would do such a thing?"

"I'm not sure, though I think possibly to make me resigned to our hasty marriage, less likely to cause a row in front of your uncle's servants, or even your uncle and aunt."

"Right enough, as far as it goes. In my conceit I also thought you might prefer to dwell on what might have happened between us during the night instead of harking back to Marcel's rough wooing at the inn."

The flush that dyed her cheeks gave mute evidence of the success of that gambit. Ignoring it, she placed her hands on her hips, tossing her hair behind her shoulders. "Am I supposed to be grateful to you then for that low, despicable trick? Am I supposed to thank you for using my weakness and distress to make a fool of me?"

With a swift movement like a panther rising, he came up off the bed. Before she could recoil, he caught her about the waist, drawing her against him. He appeared not to notice her hands pushing without effect at his shoulders. "No, no, sweet Julia. The last thing I want from you is your gratitude. On the morning of our wedding I saw your beautiful bruised face and the haunted look in your eyes. I felt you shrink from me, unable to bear my nearness, much less my touch. The night before had been different. Your mind had closed off what had taken place and you were like a child, gentle, confiding, and entrancingly lovely as you turned to me for comfort. I held you in my arms, and I could not face the thought that you might never willingly lie there again. I could and would give you time for the memories of the ugly side of a man's desire to fade. But would that be enough? I told myself that if you could be made to think, even for an instant, that you had yielded yourself to me once, it would not be so difficult for you to do it again."

She remained rigid in his arms, ignoring, as much as possible, the hard masculinity of his body against hers and the straightforward appeal in his eyes. Her lips tightened, and then she said, "All in all, it was done for the sake of your own future pleasure, then?"

"And yours," he said in a low voice, bending his head to seek her lips, tasting, teasing them with the promise of sensual delight.

Her mind warred with itself, one half standing back, viewing his appeal to her intellect and her senses with derision, encouraging her to feel used, manipulated for some nefarious purpose she could not discern. The other half registered an overpowering need to believe him, to rest content in the circle of his arms, drowning in the warmth of his kiss, malleable to his desire and obedient to her own amorous instincts. As his hands wandered over the curves and hollows of her body, she could feel her hostility melting away.

With an abrupt movement, she twisted out of his arms, backing away from him. "You must think I'm a simpleton to be taken in so easily," she told him, scrubbing her hand across her lips. "Do you think I can stand for you to touch me now, knowing what you have done? You are an unscrupulous beast. You care for nothing except the satisfaction of your carnal appetites!"

"You may be right," he drawled, stalking her in magnificent, rampant nakedness like the animal she had called him.

Her eyes widening a fraction, she retreated before him. With a few quick steps, she put the high-backed armchair between them. Rud swept it aside with one muscular arm, sending it skating across the polished floor.

Julia dashed to one side, escaping his grasping fingers by a hair's breadth. Face grim, she swung around the foot of the bed, flinging herself into the sitting room. On a marquetry table was a chess set of carved stone sent to Thaddeus Baxter from the Far East. Julia swooped down upon it, gathering up the pieces with both hands, clutching them to her. The moment Rud came through the door, she shied a queen at his head before dropping back to the cover of the settee.

He ducked the first chess piece instinctively, and side-stepped the second, but a bishop glanced off his shoulder and a pawn caught him squarely on the cheekbone. With an oath, he braved a hail of knights and pawns to charge her position. The settee rocked with his weight, teetering on its back legs as he swarmed up and over it.

With a small scream, Julia dodged the frontal attack. She would have slipped past him if his fingers had not closed on the silk of her underdress. The material held, and an instant later he grasped the ends of her hair. Quickly he wrapped the long strands about his wrist, and coiling the hair like a rope, he drew her to him. When she was close enough, he released her hair with a flip of his hand and closed his arms around her.

Swift as a striking snake her hand came up, the fingers spread like claws to tear at his face. Within inches of their target he caught her wrist, jerking it down, twisting it behind her back. Her other hand was pinned between them. Julia closed her eyes, fighting sudden tears of frustration and chagrin.

Rud's arms tightened around her. "Julia," he said, his voice low and insistent. "Look at me. Am I such a monster? Have I hurt you in any way?"

She flicked him a look of scorn, but did not answer.

"Of course, it could be that I have spoiled you by being too gentle with you, too respectful of your tender sensibilities. Shall we try it the other way and see?"

He pushed his fingers beneath her hair, forcing her head back. His mouth descended on hers, devouring in its heat, twisting, demanding a response. His tongue slipped past her defenses, invading her being, a foretaste of the greater invasion to come. Her swelling breasts were pressed to the rock-hard planes of his chest. The heat of his loins burned into her skin.

Did he expect her to submit spinelessly to being ravished? To bow her head to whatever punishment he decided to dole out? She would not. If it took every ounce of her strength she would best him. So she was spoiled? Then so was he. He was far too sure of himself, too accustomed to controlling what passed between them. From this moment let him look to himself. If he would give no quarter, then neither would she.

By slow degrees she ceased to fight him. Instead, she began to return his kiss with every sign of hunger. Her body became pliant, and she molded herself to him. Experimentally she moved her hips, sliding the silk that separated them back and forth against him. His sudden indrawn breath was her reward.

He drew back slightly, staring down into her eyes. And then they came together like duelists, seeking a weakness or an advantage. He loosened his hold, transferring his hands to her hips, drawing her tightly to the lower part of his body. Her hands, freed of restraint, crept up to smooth over his shoulders to the ridged muscles of his back before locking behind his head. Their mouths clung in savage exploration, a wild ravishing of lip and breast and thigh. Julia felt a fierce exultation rising within her, a singing madness in the blood that urged her to greater fury.

She trailed the sharp edges of her nails along the strong column of his neck and drove the taut peaks of her breasts into his chest. With fingers not quite so deft as usual, Rud pushed the small cap sleeves of her underdress from her shoulders, one after the other. As Julia extended her arms, allowing the underdress to fall about her feet, he lowered his head, trailing searing kisses from the hollow of her throat to the mound of her bared breast.

The settee was behind him. Rud lifted Julia with a dizzying swing. A few steps, and she felt the cool silk upholstery beneath her back. Then he was beside her, plundering her body with his mouth and hands as she reached out for him in a primitive instinct to grasp and hold.

A prickling sensation ran over her in waves and her skin seemed to glow with an internal heat. As he rose above her, she sought to guide his entry, welcoming the hard penetration. She closed her eyes tightly, her breath caught in her throat. He began to move and she surged upward, unwilling to lose contact, unable to contain the pleasure of the joining that rippled through her. She clutched the corded muscles of his arms, the rasp of his breathing an echo in her mind as they strove together, foes, combatants caught up in the blood lust of battle, sharing a ferocious joy in the struggle. Julia began to pant, turning her head from side to side. Her mind lost its grasp on her motives as she felt the onrush of pure sensation, an incredible, boundless expansion of ecstasy. It was so intense that a convulsive shudder raced along her nerves, leaving in its wake a voluptuous desire to encompass the man whose weight pressed her down, to forge him to her with the powerful bonds of passion.

Dazed, overwhelmed by her own emotions, Julia hardly knew when he left her. There was not room for both on the narrow settee. He knelt beside her, stroking her gold hair that spilled in a shining mass to the floor.

"Dear God," he breathed, and leaned to kiss her trembling eyelids and the vulnerable curves of her mouth.

Slowly she opened her eyes. Her expression was bleak as she stared for long moments into the deep, fathomless blue of his eyes. Then, with a weary shake of her head, she sat up. As unconscious of her nakedness as a pagan priestess, she got to her feet and walked away, leaving him on one knee there beside the settee.

A light tap fell on the sitting-room door. Julia looked up from the book in her lap. "Come in," she called.

Aunt Lucinda stepped into the room, closing the door behind her. "Ready, my dear?" she asked, then went on, "Yes, I can see you must be or you would not be reading.

How calm you are, to be sure. I am always in a transport of excitement before I set out on a journey."

"So am I," Julia said inviting Rud's aunt to sit down with a smiling gesture. "Only at the moment I am too tired to show it."

"I don't doubt it. Driving hither and yon with Rud, dancing attendance on his mother, seeing to your packing and his, all on top of your stint of nursing? Anyone would be exhausted."

The older woman's understanding was, as always, balm to Julia's spirits. "I will have plenty of time to rest when we are at sea—more time than I will know what to do with, no doubt. Let me thank you again for the box of books you are sending with us. As you can see, I could not resist dipping into them at once."

Aunt Lucinda reached to pat Julia's hand in absent approval. "I'm glad, but I find myself wishing you did not have to go just yet. I have so enjoyed your stay with us, especially at this time. Thaddeus and I feel that Rud could not have chosen better for a wife than you, my dear. We will miss both of you exceedingly."

Touched by the tribute, Julia said everything that was appropriate for both herself and Rud.

"There is another reason I wish it were possible for you to delay your departure," Aunt Lucinda went on. "I am worried about Rud. He does not seem himself to me, not at all. He never used to be so edgy and temperamental. And that bruise on his cheekbone when he was nearly well. I never understood exactly how that came about. I didn't like to pry, of course, but I could not help wondering if he had tried to get up too soon and fallen. He was so uncommunicative about it."

The accuracy of her aim with a chess piece had caused Rud no small amount of discomfiture. The bruise had been magnificent, even spreading to his eye. "I don't think you need worry. I promise you he is completely recovered. He is plagued with an occasional headache still, and he will always have an extra part in his hair from the scar, but he is as strong as ever."

Aunt Lucinda sighed. "It would be foolish not to take

your word, but I cannot be easy in my mind. I assure you he never used to be so dour. He was always of a serious turn, but he did not act as though he carried the weight of the world on his shoulders."

"He is a married man now," Julia said quietly.

"Oh, my dear! I never meant to suggest that there was any connection, truly I did not. No bridegroom could be more loving and affectionate than he is with you. It quite reminds me of how Thaddeus and I were many years ago. No, I would far rather suspect he has some secret trouble he does not wish to discuss, something to do with the *Sea Jade,* perhaps."

"I suppose it is possible," Julia said in a neutral tone. Though she had had more reason than Aunt Lucinda to notice Rud's moodiness, it was not a thing she could discuss with the other woman. The causes were many and varied; the responsibility of going forward with the expedition, the irritation of having to pander to his mother's wishes or risk exposure, the last-minute arrangements to satisfy himself that the *Sea Jade* would rendezvous with the *David* in Rio de Janeiro at the proper time, and last of all, his relationship with her. Add to these his headaches and the feeling that valuable time had slipped away while he was tied to his bed, and it was no wonder that Rud was not himself.

"Well, I'll not say any more. He is a grown man and knows his limitations, while I am a silly old woman who should have more to worry about. Only, you will keep an eye on him, won't you? I am certain you can persuade him to have a care of himself if anyone can."

"Of course I will," Julia promised, the warmth in her tone more for Aunt Lucinda's thwarted mother instincts than for the prospect of being Rud's appointed keeper.

"Ah! Silly old woman indeed," Rud's aunt exclaimed. "I was supposed to tell you to make sure your trunks are ready, for they will be coming for them at any moment. Also, Rud is with his uncle just now, but he said he will be ready to leave for the *David* as soon as you see the trunks taken away and come downstairs."

The words were hardly out of her mouth when a commotion was heard in the hallway outside. With a quick embrace and the assurance that she would see Julia downstairs before she left, Aunt Lucinda took herself out of the way. Julia hardly had time for more than a nod before she was surrounded by maids, footmen, and draymen. Signaling to Masters, who stood in the doorway, she pointed out the boxes and trunks gathered in one place and left the task of seeing them transferred to the vehicle outside to him. Moving through the bedchamber into the dressing room, Julia took up her bonnet of gray-and-black straw banded with black ribbon and set it on her hair. While she tied the strings beneath her chin, she surveyed her traveling costume of French twilled silk. Though well enough in itself, its gray-and-black severity did not suit a pale complexion. With a faint shrug, she touched the gold bee at her throat to be certain it was secure, then picked up her gloves and reticule and turned away.

A final check of their suite of rooms revealed nothing left behind. With a measured step, Julia followed a pair of footmen carrying the last box down the stairs.

There was no one in the drawing room or the downstairs sitting room. Rud was still closeted with his uncle, then. She did not wish to interrupt their farewells. The drawing room would be the best place to wait.

The windows of the long room looked out over a pleasant rose garden, Aunt Lucinda's special retreat. In the weeks since Julia had arrived in England, spring had advanced slowly into summer. Now the mossy green buds of the roses unfurled their petals in masses of red, pink, and white. Drawn forth by the warm sun, their fragrance was wafted into the drawing room through the open window. Julia inhaled the perfume as she moved into the window embrasure in order to look out, wondering if Aunt Lucinda had stepped outside for a few moments. Yes, there was Rud's aunt standing beside the ancient gardener. From their gestures they appeared to be discussing the weeding of a herbaceous border filled with iris and spicy carnations.

Dear Aunt Lucinda, Julia thought. The elderly woman's breeding and ingrained courtesy prevented her from inquiring too closely into the relationship between her nephew and the young woman he had married, but still she was sensitive enough to realize that all was not as it should be. It would have been a relief to confide in her and seek her advice if so many things—the security of the mission, the nature of the trouble, and Rud's likely reaction to the impulse—had not prevented it. It would also have been a shame to disabuse his aunt of her illusions. Aunt Lucinda could have little experience with which to judge the strange bond that tied Julia and Rud together. Julia herself did not pretend to understand it. Her anger with him for what she considered his deceit had died away. Without conscious intent, she had clamped a tight lid on her feelings since then. She had discovered the holocaust that could ensue and had no desire to repeat the experience. So much feeling could not be safe, not under the circumstances. The exact danger she would not allow herself to perceive, but she protected herself from it as best she could. When next Rud approached her, she had retreated behind a facade of cool reserve, responding dutifully but without enthusiasm. It was an attitude she managed, at great cost, to sustain. Not that it deterred Rud one whit. He seemed to recognize, without the necessity for words, that this was also a form of warfare. He continued to exercise his conjugal rights, retaliating for her passive acceptance in the most effective manner possible, with honeyed phrases and gentle, insistent caresses that made her bite the inside of her lips to prevent herself from crying out. Afterward Rud would sometimes raise himself on one elbow, staring down at her with an expression so bleak it nearly undermined her defenses. She learned to avert her face or lie with her eyes closed until he turned away. Once or twice she had sensed his anger, but for some reason beyond her understanding he never released his control over it. He would remove himself to the far side of the bed, lying with his back to her for long hours. Later, in the dark stillness of the night, he would turn half in sleep to draw her roughly to the curve of his body before settling into slumber.

Julia was so deep in thought that she did not hear the

door opening behind her. The first indication of others entering the room was the voice of Rud's uncle.

"I'm really sorry, my boy," he was saying, "that things between you and Julia had to work out as they have. Duty is a jealous mistress; it seldom allows happiness to those who serve her."

The abrupt gesture Rud made to silence Thaddeus Baxter was plain to Julia as she turned. Their voices had been low, almost confidential. In the brief instant of time she had in which to react, it seemed the best thing to do would be to pretend she had not understood, and hope the faint color in her cheeks would be attributed to excitement. Smiling a little, she started forward, saying, "At last! The trunks are loaded and I was beginning to wonder if I was going to have to come and drag you out of the library. We must go or the ship will sail without us."

"Highly unlikely," Uncle Thaddeus declared, his voice overloud. "The captain would not dream of raising anchor without my nephew aboard. He knows if he did he would find himself without a ship before he could blink an eye. Still, the rise and fall of the tide means money. It would be a pity if you had to wait another day, and it would not be the best thing to get off on the wrong foot with the man who is going to be your host at table for two months and more."

Before he had finished speaking, Aunt Lucinda had hurried in from the garden to join them. The goodbyes became general. Julia and Rud's aunt embraced, promising to write each other long letters, while Rud and his uncle contented themselves with a hearty handshake.

Then Rud was ushering Julia out of the house with an arm about her shoulders. The dray laden with their baggage was just pulling away down the drive. They stepped into the carriage, and with a final wave to the elderly couple standing on the steps, set off after the dray.

The *David* was a three-masted, square-rigged frigate built for commerce but armed for combat with twenty-four cannon. She was 148 feet long and could accommodate twenty-four passengers as well as two hundred tons of cargo. Her usual destination was around the horn to China. On the outward voyage she carried household goods of iron and steel, woolen cloth, Scotch whisky, Spanish wine, and a multitude of other small items. She returned laden with tea by the ton, with spices, opium, ivory, and lengths of silk and Indian mull. She roamed the seas, defying pirates, weather, and the gods of the deep. And before this voyage was over, Julia found herself thinking as they slipped their moorings and moved with the tide down the Thames, she would be carrying the most valuable cargo ever entrusted to her. She would be carrying Napoleon Bonaparte.

There was no sign of Marcel de Gruys among the passengers, nor had he appeared with Gourgaud and the others who came to see them off. Julia welcomed the news with relief and the fervent hope that the man had lost his taste for the venture. He was not dead; that much they had been able to discover. What had become of him was something of a mystery. Inquiries revealed that a physician had been summoned to him, then later he had been taken away from his lodgings in a fancy carriage. After that, nothing. Rather than explain the exact nature of his interest in de Gruys' whereabouts, either to the authorities or to Gourgaud, Rud had had no option except to let the matter drop.

Little occurred to relieve the tedium of long days at sea. One sunny day followed another. Julia slept, read, and sat on the deck watching the endless miles of ocean roll past. She saw little of the other passengers, though now and then one or another of the ladies would try to engage her in conversation. In some subtle way, perhaps through the ship's captain, it had become known that she and Rud were newly married, and so they were left alone except for the occasional company of M'sieu Robeaud. The three of them sometimes played cards together or took a turn about the deck. More often than not, M'sieu Robeaud kept to his cabin, plagued by an unrelenting seasickness and a general feeling of debilitation. It was thought wise, in any case, for that gentleman to keep his public appearances to a minimum. In his new beard and mustache he did not particularly look like the emperor, but there might be someone on board who would mark the resemblance, some who might look closely at his drab figure and be amazed if he did not appear so subdued after putting into port at St. Helena.

One afternoon while Rud was absent, called by special invitation to the cabin of the captain, and most of the other passengers were dressing for dinner, Julia strolled the deck with the mild-mannered Frenchman. A fine wind lifted her hair and fluttered her skirts about her ankles. Overhead the sails bellied full, while the sheets hummed and the pulleys creaked in accompaniment. As she passed, one or two of the deck hands glanced up, eying the way the wind molded her gown to her form. Julia, her attention on M'sieu Robeaud, did not notice. The quiet man seemed to be enjoying their walk so immensely that she felt a pang of guilt that she was a part of a scheme that would forever prevent him from enjoying sea breezes.

"When you are on St. Helena, M'sieu," she said in a low tone, "what will you do to amuse yourself?"

A smile flickered over the benign countenance of the man beside her. "For a time I shall simply play the emperor," he said. "It is a heady feeling to receive the deference, the bows and scrapings, accorded to one so highly placed."

"Yes, I am sure it must be," Julia said.

"That isn't all," Robeaud went on as if he had given much thought to the matter. "The food and wine will be excellent, and the comfort superior, or so I surmise. There have been tales of rats, mice, roaches, and fleas at Longwood, but these will be minor inconveniences to a man born a peasant like myself, I do assure you. I shall be upheld by the knowledge that I have served my emperor and my country. There will be cultivated men and women, such as Count and Countess Bertrand, and the Count and Countess de Montholon, whose very purpose it is to entertain me. I will have the services of a valet, any or all six of those in the household if I so desire, to keep me presentable. And if all else fails, I can always revert to being myself. I might indulge in a bit of French humor at the expense of the English. Or embark on the life of a farmer by cultivating a garden. That should astonish the English commander, should it not?"

"Of a certainty," Julia agreed, smiling at the idea of the great Napoleon grubbing in the soil with his graceful white hands. "You do not think you will be bored, then?"

He shook his head. "One hopes, of course, that Napoleon will have regained the throne of France before that state of affairs can come to pass. In any case, although I hesitate to remind you, Madame Thorpe, at the end of a year, two at the most, I shall be dead and buried."

"You are satisfied?" she insisted.

"Indeed, yes. I live only to serve the emperor, and my gratitude is boundless that in my final days I can be of use to him. Were you aware, madame, that my symptoms mimic those of Napoleon's father, who died with cancer of the stomach? That is not my complaint. Still, it seems like the hand of fate that I should have a similar disease. If I should die before the emperor comes to power, it will not seem unusual that I will have expired from a cause that might easily have been contracted by the emperor. Naturally I realize that Napoleon considered all these things before he chose me. Still, it appears to be the will of the almighty, does it not?"

It was an odd way of looking at the situation. Julia could only send him a small smile before looking away to hide the moisture in her eyes.

Rud's absence was an oddity. It was seldom that he left Julia alone. Day and night he stayed close to her side. If she sat in a deck chair reading, he sat next to her. If she walked the deck, she had the support of his arm. Descending to their cabin for an afternoon nap was tantamount to an invitation to make love. The slow, plunging rhythm of the ship, up and down, up and down, acted as an aphrodisiac. They spent hours lying in their bunk, rocking endlessly across the ocean, allowing the pulsating motion to lull them into sated somnolence.

Julia might have allowed herself to feel flattered at Rud's close attendance if she had not remembered too well his motives for it. At times she even suspected him of putting about the news of their recent marriage to ensure their privacy and make certain she was given little opportunity for female chatter that might betray their purpose. He never alluded to the possibility by word or deed, but still Julia could not forget the times in the past when he had done so in no uncertain terms.

Another possible reason for his preoccupation with her was his unaccustomed position as a passenger on the ship. Unable to stride the quarterdeck and shout orders at the crew, he found other ways to make use of his excess energy. When not below, he often propelled Julia to some point on the ship where he pointed out the mistakes made by the frigate's captain in close sailing, or his slackness in keeping the ship in trim. He thought nothing of rousting Julia out of bed in the first light of dawn to go above and cast a weather eye over the heavens or watch the sun rise over the sea, and it was not unusual for him to take a final tour of the deck in the dog watch before turning in for the night.

In the Canary Islands, they landed for fresh supplies of water and perishable foodstuffs. The passengers were encouraged to disembark in order to stretch their legs in the tropical atmosphere and to partake of the pale Canary wine, but were warned not to go much beyond the port. Within forty-eight hours they were again at sea, making their way with the wind behind them toward St. Helena.

They were three days out from the Cape Verde Islands when a sail was sighted. It was not the first, nor would it be the last, to hail into their view, yet it caused excitement among the crew and no small amount of consternation among the passengers.

The ship that came swiftly down upon them was identified by Rud as a felucca of Turkish design. It featured a bank of oars numbering more than twenty per side, and red, triangular lateen sails stepped to twin masts. On each side of the stem was an enormous painted eye which seemed to turn, ogling, in their direction as the ship passed them just out of the reach of their cannon.

"Part of the navy of the dey of Algiers," someone said.

"Bloody Barbary pirates," someone else declared bitterly. "You can safely wager those oars are being plied by Christian slaves with whip marks on their backs."

"Will they attack?" a woman asked fearfully.

The answer came from Rud. "They dare not brave our guns. If we were smaller, less well armed, it might be different."

A man in clerical garb drew himself up. "We should do something to free those poor souls in captivity if ours is the superior ship."

Another man snorted. "We are not a military vessel. Do you seriously suggest we endanger the lives of our women and children?"

"It goes against the grain," the cleric said unhappily, "to do nothing to stop this abominable practice of using free men as animal labor."

"Hard luck on them, but there's nothing I can do about it," the other man said, and he turned away, taking his wife by the arm.

Rud, standing silently at Julia's side, followed the felucca with his eyes until she was out of sight.

They landed at Jamestown harbor on the island of St. Helena on August 18, 1818, sixty-seven days after they had left England.

Chapter
Ten

It was hot and humid. A fine mist hung over the island like steam. It enveloped the *David*, muting the cries of the sea birds overhead and beading the surfaces of the furniture in the cabin with moisture. Standing at the open porthole, Julia could feel it upon her face. It blurred the lines of the island, making it appear less barren and rocky than it actually was.

It was possible, from where she stood, to see a large portion of St. Helena. The volcanic outcropping in the middle of the south Atlantic Ocean which served as the prison for the former emperor of the French was not large, only a little more than ten miles long and six miles wide. It rose above the bay where the ship was anchored in a series of crags strewn with gray lichen-covered rock and stands of prickly pear. On the higher elevations could be seen English gorse, brambles, and the dark green of pines and cedars. In the sprawling port of Jamestown, nestled in the narrow valley at the head of the bay, the umbrella-like branches of palm trees could be seen amid the brightness of bougainvillea.

The hovels and decaying mansions were in need of some form of camouflage, Julia thought, though nothing could hope to cover the stench of open sewers and rotting fish drifting seaward from the town. Closing the porthole would alleviate that problem, but with the heat of a tropical afternoon pressing in upon the ship the cabin would be stifling.

The click of the cabin door brought her head around. Rud entered, closing the door behind him. He surveyed her cool state of dishabille—she was wearing no more than a batiste peignoir—with a lifted brow. "Dressing, or undressing?" he inquired.

He was just returning from a tour of the island with the captain and one or two of the male passengers. The irritation Julia felt at being left behind, pent up on the ship, made her answer shortly. "What difference does it make?"

"I have a certain interest in the outcome," he drawled, tossing his beaver hat on a chest before sauntering toward her. "I don't like to miss any of the few opportunities offered to me."

"If you think I was waiting for you, you mistake the matter!"

"You disappoint me," he said, heaving a mock sigh as he reached to take up the ribbons of her peignoir, which she had left dangling untied for coolness. The batiste material of her wrapper was old and soft from many washings, yellowed to an écru shade, and so thin as to be transparent. She wore nothing underneath, neither chemise nor underdress, since she had not yet begun to dress for dinner.

"A pity," she answered, and snatched her shell-pink ribbons from his hard brown fingers.

His pensive gaze on her shapely form through the film of batiste, he said, "Now, I wonder how I might tempt you? Maybe my welcome would be warmer if I were to tell you how the matter of freeing your emperor is proceeding?"

"You have learned something?" she asked quickly, her hand going out to touch his arm in an unconscious gesture.

"On second thought," he mused, "the results might be better if I allowed you to persuade me to give up the information."

She drew back instantly. "You wouldn't!"

"Wouldn't I? Do you really expect me to refuse the prospect of something more from you than a tepid surrender? A kiss, freely given, should do for a start."

Julia hesitated, trying to decide if Rud was serious or merely having a joke at her expense. She assayed a smile. "You can't mean it. It isn't fair. How can you—you enjoy it knowing you had to bribe me? You may as well offer me money and be done with it!"

A warning glitter came into his eyes. "Oh, no," he said softly. "I wouldn't dream of insulting you."

He had stressed the last word. Was he saying that he felt insulted by her remark? Ridiculous. He could not be so sensitive. She glanced at him through her lashes. "Rud—" she began.

"I am waiting," he said, cutting her appeal short.

"I won't do it!" she flared.

"No? And I was so sure you did not want to miss the rescue of your idol, no matter the cost."

"You can't keep me from doing my part," she said, though her voice was far from positive even to her own ears.

"I can't keep you from trying, but I doubt you will want to rush in uninformed. You might jeopardize the emperor's plans so that more than a year's planning would go for naught."

He was right. What was more, he was going to get what he wanted, just as both he and she had known all along he must. She raised amber eyes filled with gold flecks of rage to his. "Damn you," she said through clenched teeth, then took the step that would bring her up against him.

She placed her hands lightly on his chest, smoothing them upward beneath the heavy faille lapels of his coat. Going on tiptoe, she linked her fingers behind his head, drawing it down. His mouth tasted of wine and his clothing held the smell of warm linen and the freshness of the southeast tradewinds that blew across the island. Faithful to her part of the bargain, Julia held nothing back. She moved her lips tantalizingly on his, allowing him unimpeded access to the curves of her body. His hands slid under the edges of her peignoir. She was drawn close, until she could feel the press of his shirt studs and watch fobs.

A trembling seemed to run through his strong frame, and suddenly she was caught so tight her ribs ached in protest and her bare feet left the floor. She grew light-headed for want of air while her lips burned with the scorching pressure of his. Then, just as abruptly, she was set from him. Rud held her for the instant it took for her to regain her breath, and then he stepped away.

"As much as I would like to carry this to its logical conclusion, I am afraid we don't have the time. We dine this evening with Sir Hudson Lowe."

The change was so drastic, so unexpected, that it was a long moment before Julia could force her brain to follow what Rud was saying. She was suspended in disbelief that he had not accepted her sacrifice, and in a growing suspicion that he had never meant to do so. "Sir Hudson Lowe, the British governor?" she inquired at last.

"Precisely."

"Why? For what purpose?" She clasped her hands together, striving to sound composed.

"He is Napoleon's keeper, and from all accounts a proud and petty man with a near mania concerning the safekeeping of his prisoner. He will expect us to pay our respects, especially as we are connected with the East India Company, which, you will remember, holds nominal control of the island. If we ignore him in favor of the emperor we may find ourselves refused permission to approach Napoleon, since the request for an audience must be routed through the governor's office."

"You have made this request?"

"Yes, in due form to the governor's secretary."

"I suppose you gave a reason?"

Rud nodded. "The same as all other good British subjects who have visited the emperor during this way-stop in their travels in the past few years—a desire to lay eyes on the Corsican monster who terrorized dear old England for so long."

"I see," Julia said, a frown drawing her brows together.

"That is what you meant by progress in freeing Napoleon?"

"It is. There has been no contact with the emperor, won't be any until the day of the audience. The rest you know, have known since New Orleans. Nothing has changed. The success of all we have worked for in the last few months depends on tonight."

"It will not be a pleasant evening," Julia commented with a sigh.

"No. I don't need to tell you, I think, that we must take care nothing is said to give the governor the idea that we have the slightest interest beyond mild curiosity in the man at Longwood."

Julia sent him a sharp glance, then swung away, presenting him with a superb view of the slim, tapering lines of her back. "Perhaps it would be safer if you went alone," she suggested. "You can always tell them I have a headache."

"I wouldn't think of it," he replied, a sardonic tone in his voice that managed also to be understanding. "I depend upon you to charm the gentleman into forgetting his responsibility to the crown. He should be well and truly enslaved before the soup plates are removed."

"Toward what end?" she queried, her voice wary at the unexpected compliment.

"None in particular. It will be best if Sir Hudson Lowe remembers us favorably should events not go as we plan."

She turned quickly to face him, her eyes wide. "Has something gone wrong? Are you keeping something from me?"

"Not at all," he answered, his blue gaze steady. "There is nothing like that. It's just that it is better to leave as little as possible to chance."

Despite his denial, Julia could not be easy in her mind. The difficulties of what they had set out to do loomed large now that they were on the island. The remoteness of Longwood, perched on a treeless plateau three and a half miles from Jamestown harbor, the strength of the garrison set to watch him, the presence of the commissioners of Austria, Prussia, and Russia, besides the British governor, all seemed insurmountable obstacles. The plan to drive in broad daylight with Napoleon sitting beside them down the single street the town possessed seemed suicidal.

At the dinner party, the sharp, almost wild eyes of Sir Hudson Lowe seemed to bore into Julia's skull, trying to read her thoughts. He stared at her with unsmiling attention, his reddish-brown brows drawn together, whenever she spoke. Nothing she could do, no deep breaths, no calming thoughts she could muster, would control the flush on her cheekbones. At any other time, the knowledge that she looked her best in black velvet would have given her confidence, but not on this night. There was too much at stake.

A portion of her problem was the fact that she was seated on the right hand of the British governor with no less a personage than the Russian commissioner, Count Alexander Antinovich Ramsey de Balmain, on her right. She knew without being told that the cultured, rather sleepy-looking nobleman was far more dangerous than Sir Hudson Lowe could ever be. Evidence of sharp intelligence and the intricate turnings of the mind of a diplomat shone in his dark, hypnotic eyes. Without difficulty, he followed his conversation with his partner, the wife of the commander of the army regiment stationed on the island, and still missed nothing of what was going on around him.

Also at the table was Captain Asbury of the *David* and his lady, a middle-aged couple who had enlivened the tedium of the voyage from England, and Lady Lowe's young stepdaughter, doubtless included as a balance for the Count de Balmain, who was a single man.

As guest of honor, due to his position as a relative of one of the most influential directors of the East India Company, Rud was placed on the right hand of his hostess with Charlotte, the quiet, almost invisible stepdaughter, beside him. Glancing now and then in that direction, Julia found buxom Lady Lowe an unusually animated woman. She reached out a number of times to touch Rud's sleeve, her high laughter pealing over the table. When she was not speaking, she was motioning for the footman to fill her glass. Between Rud and the drink, the poor captain on her left received scarcely so much as a nod. It was Sir Hudson Lowe who finally signaled for the turn of the table, the English custom of switching conversational partners from right to left halfway through the meal, at the same time making an obvious gesture to the footman to ignore his wife's signals for more wine. Lady Lowe, flushing beneath her rouge, looked ready to protest until Captain Asbury captured her attention with some comment.

Julia, sipping at the sour, watered-down liquid in her own glass, was unable to account for Lady Lowe's predilection for it. The vintages served on the *David* were far superior. Her father had always contended that giving bad wine to guests was a sign of parsimony, lack of discernment, or both. Slanting a glance at the thin, gray face of the governor of St. Helena, Julia wondered what manner of wine he allowed his noble prisoner, a man who had been emperor of the country where wine was considered as life blood.

There was a small disruption at that moment. One of the governor's secretaries, a subaltern in the gray and red of the Fifty-third Regiment, entered the room and placed a message on the table at their host's elbow. Sir Hudson Lowe read it and nodded dismissal.

Turning to the company with eyes blazing, he said, "Ladies and gentlemen, you will be pleased to know that the prisoner is still held secure. General Bonaparte has partaken of a light dinner and retired to his bed for an early night."

"My word, your excellency," the captain's wife exclaimed. "You must have a most efficient surveillance system."

"Quite. You will have noticed the semaphore posts set up about the island? These stations are utilized to keep me constantly informed of the slightest movement of my prisoner. This note in my hand tells me, for instance, that the general did not sit down to dinner, but was served a meal on a tray in his study. A short while later, the candle in the adjoining bedchamber was extinguished."

The captain's lady shivered. "I would not like to be so closely watched."

"The man's feelings do not weigh with me, madam. He is extremely dangerous. He escaped once from an island prison and was only rounded up again at great cost, in both money and lives. It is my responsibility to see that this does not happen again, one I take with the utmost seriousness."

"How the mighty have fallen," the woman murmured.

"Thank God," the governor said with a snort. "For my part, I say he can consider himself fortunate he is still alive. More than one ruler in recent years has suffered a crueler fate."

The captain's wife was silent, though more for the sake of good manners than from awe of the governor. Julia eyed the man at the head of the table with distaste. It had been rumored aboard ship that the troops assigned to guard the emperor had instructions to use any method they thought suitable to ascertain his presence within the old farmhouse known as Longwood, including peering in at the windows. The charge was almost certainly true, since there did not appear to be any other way the information in the message just delivered could have been obtained. She did not realize she had allowed the contempt she felt for such tactics to register on her expressive face until she caught the eyes of the Russian commissioner upon her. She was able to summon a vague smile without too much effort, but she was aware of the flicker of interest that made his gaze return to her again and again as the meal progressed.

It was with every appearance of reluctance that their hostess rose to lead the ladies from the dining room. "Don't linger too long over the port, gentlemen," she said, her arch smile growing a shade more caressing as it lingered on Rudyard Thorpe.

Julia, passing behind her husband's chair, lifted a brow in ironic communication as he glanced her way. In return she received a scowl.

The ladies, consoling themselves with coffee rather than strong wine, indulged in an hour of gossip and idle conversation. In exchange for news of the latest fads and swings in London fashion, the ladies of Plantation House regaled their guests with the scandals of the island, necessarily including many tidbits about the emperor. Lady Lowe contended that the great man was ill. It had been weeks, she said, since he had been seen outside the walls of Longwood—indeed, since any of the sentries could swear to having laid eyes on him. He not only had not appeared at the dinner table with the others of his retinue this evening, he had not done so for some time. Blankets had been placed over the windows of his bedchamber and study to keep out the light and drafts of air, a suicidal practice in the August heat, though it effectively kept anyone from seeing into the rooms. The general had refused the services of the British physicians, Stokoe and Arnott, declaring them to be useless, much preferring to allow his body to heal itself. There was hepatitis in Jamestown, and now and then a case of some tropic fever, but so far no one had any idea what ailed Bonaparte.

"For my part," Lady Lowe confided, "I am by no means certain the general retires to bed when his candle is doused. He is only fifty, after all, and I understand that some of his best maneuvers were performed between sunset and dawn, both military and amorous. Haven't the names of over a dozen of the most beautiful women in Europe been connected with him in the past decade? They say that Albine, the Countesse de Montholon, has been generous with her favors. Her daughter, born on the island, is named Napoleone. And then for a time there was the Balcombe chit—Betsy, she was called. He was quite taken with her, though she was barely out of the schoolroom. What her response was to the great warrior we may only guess, but she was in the habit of slipping through the lines of the sentries to visit him at odd hours. She was also allowed to ride his horses and even, on one occasion, to wear the famous mantle he wore at Marengo. If that isn't preference, I don't know what is!"

"Balcombe," the captain's wife mused. "I believe I

know the family. There was a William Balcombe who, it was whispered, was the natural son of the mad old man at Windsor Castle."

"Betsy Balcombe's father, my dear," Lady Howe said. "It is amazing to me that such a family could form an attachment for a man with so little breeding, but there it is. Betsy was coming and going at Longwood without so much as a by-your-leave, much less a permit. Hudson became suspicious and set a watch on the father, who was the purveyor of food and drink for the French. It was discovered that he was smuggling correspondence for the general, and that was that. They were sent back to England. I expect your ships passed in midocean. That being the case, it would not be surprising if Napoleon was now taking up where he left off with the Count de Montholon's accommodating wife."

"I liked Betsy," the stepdaughter offered. "She was always so gay and full of spirits. The men in the regiment could not resist her."

"Oh, I don't deny she was a great beauty, my dear Charlotte," Lady Lowe replied, "but I do say she would have been better for a bit more supervision. Whether she was the mistress of General Bonaparte or not, there can be little doubt that the taint of her years on St. Helena will follow her back to England. What kind of life can she have there with such notoriety attached to her name?"

Julia thought she detected a shading of wistful envy in the voice of the governor's wife. Did she regret that she had never been exposed to the temptation to become Napoleon's *chère amie*? With a shake of her head, she dismissed the thought as being unnecessarily feline. Still, she did not care for Sir Hudson Lowe's blowsy and overblown wife. Her contempt only deepened when she saw Lady Lowe remove a vial from her reticule and furtively tip the liquid contents into her coffee cup.

The gentlemen rejoined them in good time. The talk was general, concerning the voyage, the political situation in England, the Irish question, and the latest developments in the propulsion of ships with steam power. Julia, sitting to one side, exchanged a few remarks with Lady Lowe's stepdaughter, but otherwise remained in the background. Mindful of the importance of not saying the wrong thing here in the stronghold of the emperor's enemies, she chose the prudent course, which was to say as little as possible.

"Madame Thorpe, permit me to welcome you to St. Helena."

It was the Russian commissioner making his bow before her. Receiving her permission to take the chair next to her own, he continued. "It is always a pleasure to see a new face here in our enclosed society, especially such a charming one. Do you propose to tarry long?"

His manner was suave, his address polished. The Count de Balmain, in his dark, Slavic, and faintly mysterious fashion, was an attractive man. Smooth-shaven, he wore a tonic scented with bergamot. A white ribbon slashed the dark blue of his coat, and his chest glittered with orders and insignia.

Julia smiled. "Thank you. You are very kind, but my husband and I are en route to Rio de Janeiro. Our visit will last only as long as the *David* lingers in the harbor."

"Ah?" he said, a thoughtful look crossing his features. "It is possible that I, too, shall be returning to civilization soon."

"To Russia?" she inquired.

"Eventually one always returns to Mother Russia. Still, there is much of the world I have not seen. Rio de Janeiro, for instance."

It would be nonsense to think that the man before her was suggesting that he would make such a trip for her sake. She suspected some hidden meaning to his words, but could conceive of no reason for it. "I—understand that it is a lovely place in a beautiful country," she said with care.

He gave a slow nod, as if weighing her words. Casually his gaze moved to the gold bee, worn this evening on a fine chain so that it nestled between her breasts. "I realize, madame, that it is improper for me to comment on the ornament you are wearing, but it is quite unique. I don't remember seeing its like before."

"It belonged to my mother," Julia said with a small shrug.

"Does it have some special significance, I wonder? For instance, is it a queen bee, or does it, perhaps, have a stinger in its tail?"

Julia swung her head sharply to stare at him. "What do you mean?" she demanded in a low voice.

But his dark eyes were hooded, unreadable. "Forgive me, Madame Thorpe. That was a small *gaffe,* was it not? My English sometimes trips me up, just when I think I have it perfectly. Such a barbarous language. Now, French is entirely civilized, is it not?"

The Count de Balmain, on the last sentence, had slipped into the tongue he named. Julia had no more than an instant to decide if he was merely making a point, or presenting her with some form of test. She inclined her head in a deliberately gracious gesture. "It has been called the language of diplomacy," she answered, following his lead.

"It is spoken almost exclusively at St. Petersburg in Czar Alexander's court. The Russian emperor is a great admirer of things French, and of Napoleon."

"Indeed," Julia said, for want of anything better.

"Yes. I myself had heard so much of the man I was eager to come face to face with him at last, to speak with him. But alas!"

"Alas?"

"I have not set eyes on him in all the weary months of my office here. We exchange messages, no more. I watch for him with my telescope, as do we all, the commissioners of France, Austria, Prussia; Sir Hudson Lowe, the soldiers of the Fifty-third Regiment posted as sentries. And, from the flashes at his windows, I often think he watches us with his glass. But this is what we see of him, a flash, a movement, a shadow. I sometimes think that the man has become a mirage that we pretend to watch, and tell each other we see, because the alternative is unthinkable."

"I see," Julia answered. Her words fell into a pool of silence. Turning her head, she found that she and the count were the focus of attention for everyone in the room. Sir Hudson Lowe appeared stunned with disbelief that the despised French language was actually being spoken in his drawing room.

Vacant surprise gave Lady Lowe all the charm of a gaffed fish. Embarrassment held Captain Asbury ramrod-stiff, while his lady wore an expression of distress. Rud smiled, though there was an ominous tightness about his eyes. It was her husband who broke the silence.

"So you found someone to talk with in your native tongue, my dear? Now you can be happy." He turned from Julia to the governor. "You understand, your excellency, that my wife is an American Creole from the city of New Orleans. Her father's family, though resident for several generations in the new world, was from France. My wife is bilingual, and she also has an understanding of Spanish and a smattering of Latin and Greek."

"Ah," Sir Hudson Lowe commented with a slow nod, though his choleric color did not abate.

"I beg your pardon if I have offended," Julia said with as remorseful a smile as she could muster. "So thoughtless of me to go chattering away in a foreign tongue."

"No, no, the fault is mine, if fault there is," the count objected. "It was I who spoke first. Madame Thorpe was merely being polite by answering in kind."

"I do wish I could speak more fluently," the captain's wife said, her voice shaded with defiance. "One was taught the rudiments, of course, as a child, but there has been so little chance to use it, with the Continent in an uproar these two decades and more."

The count leaned forward. "It seems, then, that the emperor, who would have enjoyed seeing the English become a French-speaking people, is to blame that you are all not proficient in the language!"

Acknowledging chuckles and trills of feminine laughter ran through the room, easing the tension. Sir Hudson Lowe did not so much as smile. In the face of his silent displeasure, it was not long before the gathering began to break up and the guests to take their leave.

The governor's own personal carriage, one of the few on the island, transported Julia and Rud, with the captain and his wife, back to the ship. The presence of the coachman on the box above the open barouche inhibited conversation until they were safely aboard the *David*. Once there, the ladies enjoyed a pleasant half hour of rending the evening apart over a final glass of superior wine. At last Rud rose to his feet. Julia followed his example, though her legs felt like lead. The time had come when she must be alone with her husband.

In the cabin, Rud began to undress, stripping off his coat and untying his cravat. Julia put down her reticule of black net and her gloves, and reached up to take the headpiece of black velvet and upstanding ribbons from her hair. They proceeded in silence, each aiding the other. Rud helped with her buttons, and Julia put his coat and shirt studs away so that he would not have to squeeze past her to reach the trunk or the washstand in the small space.

His broad back was to her when he finally spoke. "Was the count so fascinating that you lost your head this evening, or did you deliberately set out to make the governor suspicious?"

Julia was not certain she liked the phrasing of the question, but she tried to answer as honestly as possible. "Neither. When the count spoke to me I had the feeling it was in the nature of a challenge. Anyone who takes the time to listen to me can tell that French is my mother tongue. It seemed to me that it would be just as incriminating to pretend ignorance as to speak it. I had no idea the Russian commissioner intended to make a public display—not that it would have made any difference, for I did not realize Sir Hudson Lowe was so sensitive."

"He is not only sensitive, he is almost insanely prejudiced. In addition, he has little liking for the aristocratic Count de Balmain. Please strive to keep that in mind next time, and confine your conversation to the ladies of the company."

Julia drew a deep breath. "Very well," she said distinctly. "I will undertake to do that, if you will accept a word of advice from me. You will be better employed if you would turn your attention to the gentlemen. No man, least of all one bordering on insanity, likes to see another paying particular attention to his wife under his very nose. Of course," she went on sweetly, "the flirtation might have a certain value if the purpose is to draw the governor's notice away from your interest in Napoleon. Otherwise, it seems to me that you are unnecessarily endangering the emperor's chances of escape."

"That is ridiculous," he said, swinging around sharply.

"No more ridiculous than what you had to say of the Count de Balmain!"

"The cases are entirely different!"

"Are they? I fail to see it!"

"You will find out when Sir Hudson Lowe refuses to issue the permits necessary to get us past the squadron of men and the sentries guarding Napoleon," Rud grated. Stepping out of his breeches, he slung them in the direction of the trunk and climbed into the extra-wide bunk.

If she had been more certain of her ground Julia would have retaliated. Instead, she preferred to affect disdain for his opinion. Following his actions almost exactly, she flung off her underdress and got into bed.

The bunk was not wide enough for them to share it without touching. They lay in angry discomfort side by side. The boat rocked gently on the tide. Somewhere in the room a fly buzzed, blundering into the walls, aimless and clumsy.

"You forgot to snuff out the candle," Rud said after a moment.

"You always do that," Julia replied, refusing to look at the taper in its holder on the washstand.

"That's because I always get into bed last."

"And that," she answered, "is because you sleep on the outside."

With elaborate calm he said, "This time, I am on the inside."

"In my place," Julia agreed in the patient tone one used with the simpleminded.

Rud came up on one elbow. "Are you going to snuff the candle or not?"

"It will burn itself out eventually."

"This may come as a surprise to you, but this ship does not carry an inexhaustible supply," Rud said, shifting as his forearm came in contact with the softness of her breast.

A corner of Julia's mouth twitched. "Then when they are all gone you can sleep in the dark as you please."

The wavering candlelight gave a soft sheen to her skin, highlighting the curves of her naked form, while leaving the hollows in mysterious shadow. A reluctant smile rose in his eyes as he let his gaze travel over her. "It's possible sleeping wasn't all I had in mind."

Their glances met. Somewhere inside her Julia was aware of a sense of unfurling, of the release of tightly held distress. "I can't think of anything else," she answered, her eyes wide with shining innocence, "that can't be done just as well by the light of a candle."

Chapter Eleven

*There was no need to worry after all. The precious per-*mits were granted on the day before the *David* was due to sail. There were three of them, one for Rud, one for Julia, and one for M'sieu Robeaud. Since Lady Lowe had ordered the governor's carriage for a round of afternoon visits and no other was available, they proposed to make the three-and-a-half-mile journey to Longwood by supply wagon. The consignment of food and drink provided by Lord and Lady Holland had been thoroughly gone over by the governor and his minions to be certain it contained no concealed messages. It could now be delivered to the emperor. With a wagon on hand to transport it, it was felt that to demand the use of some other vehicle would call unnecessary attention to their trip.

Julia knew a qualm or two at the thought of having to tell Napoleon Bonaparte, a man who had ridden in golden carriages of state, that he must escape on the hard board seat of a dray wagon, but it could not be helped, and might even be to the good. Such conveyances were a common sight on the island, and were less likely to attract notice than a carriage bowling along in a cloud of dust.

In the launch which took them from the ship anchored in the roadstead to the quay, Julia held her hands tightly clasped in her lap, a lawn handkerchief pressed between her damp palms. At last. At last the day had arrived, the hour, the moment when Napoleon would be freed. So intense was her excitement that she could scarcely contain it. The effort to do so left her unnaturally stiff and straight in her seat. Once she exchanged a glance with M'sieu Robeaud. He smiled and gave her a slight nod, as if to say that everything was going to be all right. In truth, it did appear to be so. He sat composedly on the seat in a full beard and mustache, wearing the latest thing in fashions for men—a frock coat, a pair of pantaloons which fastened beneath his boots, and a wide-brimmed felt hat. In that garb, he had scant resemblance to the famous figure portrayed in so many paintings in a cocked hat, tailed coat, breeches and boots, and ankle-length cloak. If only the same miracle could be made to take place when they started out on the return journey to the ship!

The road rose as it left the port of Jamestown, twisting past the governor's mansion, Plantation House. It turned to skirt the edge of the property overgrown with tamarind, banyan, oak, and willow, known as The Briars, where William Balcombe had lived with his daughter, Betsy. From there it climbed up to the treeless, barren plateau crowned by the renovated farmhouse called Longwood.

The building had been chosen for its inaccessibility and for the lack of cover around it. Its isolation was thought to be extremely suitable. Of a single story only, it was built in the shape of a truncated letter T with two small rooms in each wing. Behind it were a few outbuildings which had been adapted for a kitchen, servants' quarters, and housing for the other members of the emperor's entourage. A sentry in a gray uniform, looped back with gold lace to show red revers, stood at the end of the drive, while another was stationed at the entrance doors.

Rud presented their permits to the first sentry. After a careful examination, and a reminder that the time limit of an hour had been set on their visit, they were allowed to pass. The second sentry ignored them, permitting them to step unannounced into the small antechamber at the front of the house.

Inside, Longwood was no more prepossessing than outside. The walls were covered with tarred canvas, and the carpet on the floor had been tracked over by muddied feet so many times the pattern had been obliterated, worn down to the backing. The draperies at the windows were sun-faded and musty with mildew. The few chairs sitting about the room were crude, obviously handmade on the island. A desk of the same general style held pride of place in the center of the room; an inkstand and a single pewter candlestick occupied its blank surface.

As they stood undecided just inside the door, a man hurried into the room. "My apologies for keeping you waiting," he said. "I am the grand marshal of the emperor Napoleon, Count Henri-Gratien Bertrand. May I be of service?"

The count was not an excitable man. He appraised M'sieu Robeaud, a man he had known well in better days, without the flicker of an eyelid. As Julia raised her hand in a deliberate gesture to the gold bee at her throat, he observed the movement closely but gave no visible sign that it had significance for him. Outside the door, open to the chance of a breeze stirring in the August heat, the sentry shifted his position with a rasping noise on the grit-covered steps.

Rud greeted the count with ceremony and gave their names. "We assume that Sir Hudson Lowe's secretary informed you of our request to see the emperor? We would be greatly honored if he would agree to grant us a brief audience."

"Yes, we have been apprised of your coming," Count Bertrand said, his gaze sliding past them to the broad gray back beyond the doorway, well within earshot. "I must inform you, however, that the emperor has been indisposed for several days. I will inquire if he will receive you, but I can promise nothing. I am sure that, should he consent, you will keep his indisposition in mind and cut short your visit at the least sign of fatigue on his part?"

"Naturally," Rud agreed.

"Very good. If you will pass into the salon and be seated, I will endeavor to see that your wait is a short one."

Penetrating deeper into the house, Julia was assailed by the distinct odor of mice. Beneath the settee, on which she

213

gingerly seated herself, was a scattering of what had the look of stuffing material from the piece of Directoire-style furniture, torn from it, no doubt, by rodents. As the footsteps of the count died away and the room grew quiet, they could hear plainly the gnawing of what could only be a large rat in the ceiling above them.

In this room, some effort had been made toward a civilized manner of living. The chairs and tables had the polished finish and styling of a fine cabinetmaker, the carpet looked to have been added at the time of Napoleon's occupation of the house, and the walls were papered. And yet, all, including the window hangings, appeared to have been chosen at random without the least attempt to correlate either color or design. Since Napoleon had brought little with him in the way of household goods, Julia could only assume the English were responsible for the resulting hodgepodge. The fact that the wallpaper was peeling and the draperies as mildewed as those in the antechamber only emphasized the appalling conditions the former emperor of the French was forced to endure.

Julia thought with amazed contempt of the splendors of Plantation House, of the thick, jewel-hued carpets, the beautiful draperies embellished with braid and fringe, cord and tassels, the brilliant chandeliers and polished mirrors, and the exquisite bibelots scattered about. Her mind ran on to the grandeur of Versailles and Malmaison, famous for their marble floors, gilded furnishings, gold plate, and vaulted ceilings painted with representations of gods and goddesses and emblems of fruitfulness and love.

There was the possibility that Napoleon might, in the first years of his confinement, have preferred this rat-infested squalor in the hope that reports of it in England would cause a public outcry, forcing the allied commissioners to change his place of exile. At Elba, close enough to Europe to permit frequent visits from his family, he might have been content to await a summons to him from the French nation instead of plotting escape. There was every reason to suppose that the countries which held him prisoner here in such a manner had brought the prospect of more war upon themselves by their harsh attitudes and treatment.

Count Bertrand permitted himself a smile as he entered the salon once more. With a polite bow, he said, "The emperor will receive you in his study. Follow me, if you please."

They came to their feet, galvanized by a sudden, breathtaking rush of expectancy. After all the planning, the expenditure, the weary months of travel and of waiting, they were at last to enter into the presence of the emperor, and to close ranks with him in this great endeavor.

The grand marshal, Count Bertrand, drew himself up in military precision outside the door of the study. Head high, he turned the knob and pushed into the room. "Captain Rudyard Thorpe, Madame Thorpe née Dupré, and Eugène François Robeaud!" he intoned.

The light was dim inside the study, a condition caused by the blankets covering the windows. There was little furniture in the room, only a large table with a fairly comfortable chair behind it. A brace of candles stood on the makeshift desk, posing a constant threat to the papers piled around it and the books stacked higher than a man's head on all sides. Books filled the corners of the room and, without benefit of shelving, lined the walls in terraced rows. Mathematics, geometry, history, law, poetry, novels, Latin classics, Greek plays, books in French and Italian and English, and in the ancient languages; all were well thumbed, and some were ragged and dog-eared like the veterans of military campaigns.

The Emperor Napoleon stood beside the desk with his feet firmly planted and his hands clasped behind his back. He was dressed in his uniform tunic of dark green, with orders, and white breeches tucked into black knee boots. Of average height for a European male, perhaps five inches under Rud's imposing six feet, he looked fit and hale, not at all like an invalid. His torso was the muscular one of a horseman and a soldier, with none of the corpulence attributed to him by the English press. His chestnut hair, though receding slightly from his high forehead, was carefully brushed, with a single lock falling forward on his brow. His features were strong, with a classic Roman nose and firmly molded mouth, though the latter was almost concealed by a growth of beard, doubtless the reason for his close confinement of the last few weeks. But it was his eyes, gray-blue and piercing under heavy brows, which drew attention. They burned with the strength of his will and the impatient and consuming fire of his intelligence.

The two gentlemen bowed, Julia sank into a deep curtsy, and then Napoleon, breaking his regal pose, came toward them.

"Delighted, madame," the emperor said, and taking her hand, carried it to his lips. "Captain Thorpe, a pleasure! Ah, and my friend Robeaud!"

Turning to the Frenchman, he opened his arms wide and clasped Robeaud to him like a brother. Stepping back, he surveyed the other man. A grimace crossed his face as he noted the loose-fitting coat, the pantaloons. "Is this what you have brought me to wear? *Ma foi,* the sacrifices of dignity one must make!"

Seen together, the men were astonishingly alike, and yet unlike. Robeaud, some ten years younger than the emperor, had the more unlined face. It was even possible that, feature by feature, he was the more handsome of the two, though his teeth were not nearly so good, so white or even, as the emperor's, and his was the shorter, fuller figure. Still, it was in matters of the spirit that they differed most. Robeaud had the quiescent but willing air of the soldier awaiting orders, combined with an impression of melancholy, while the man facing him exuded purpose and certainty coupled with the indefinable air of command. There was one other difference. The emperor's eyes were gray-blue; Robeaud's were hazel-brown.

With unsteady fingers Julia reached up to unfasten the gold bee. When the emperor's attention was free once more, she stepped forward, extending the small piece of jewelry on the palm of her hand.

Napoleon Bonaparte picked it up, glancing at her with a smile in his eyes before he held the bee to the light to examine it. His lips also curved upward as with ceremony he returned the bee to Julia. "There was never any doubt of your identity from the moment I saw my good Robeaud. I am amazed to find him so little changed in these four long years since last we met. Nonetheless, I am happy to see this small token you bring. It is a symbol of supreme loyalty, something of which I stand in great need at this time. I understand your father died on the voyage from America. Accept if you will my most sincere condolences. It is a thousand pities. When I asked him to come I had great hopes. I could have used such a one at my side in the days ahead."

Julia murmured some few words of gratitude before the emperor continued, his soft tone becoming brisk once more.

"As you have complied with my request in this small matter of the bee, may I hope that the remainder of my instructions have been carried out as faithfully?"

"They have," Julia replied, her chest filled with pride that she could make such an affirmation. "The East Indiaman, the *David,* rests in the harbor, as you must have seen with your glass, waiting to transport you to Rio de Janeiro. There, my husband's ship, the *Sea Jade,* stands ready to carry you to Malta."

"Ah," the emperor exclaimed, turning to Rud. "You are the American sea captain I specified, then?"

"British-American," Rud answered, inclining his head.

"British?" Napoleon drew himself up, stiff with displeasure. "I requested a ship of American registry."

"The *Sea Jade* is so registered, your majesty," Rud replied.

Julia, recognizing an undercurrent of hardness in his tone, slanted a quick glance at him.

"It is an armed vessel?" the emperor demanded.

"Yes, your majesty."

"And you, yourself, do you stand ready to resist boarding by a British vessel?"

"If it should prove necessary, your majesty."

"Very well, then. I do not like it, but it cannot be helped. One must always be flexible."

They were interrupted at that moment by a footman in green-and-gold livery who entered with two chairs. Robeaud at once turned his back to the man, moving with an air of intense interest to inspect a volume in the pile of books on his right. It was a sensible precaution, especially for the man whose safety depended on his impersonation of the emperor going undetected. Only a chosen few must know of the exchange. It would not do for the entire household, comprising above thirty serving people, to be privy to the secret. If that were the case, the whole island would soon know.

"Now we may be comfortable," Count Bertrand said as he pointed out where the chairs were to be placed. "Or as comfortable as it is possible to be among so many volumes. You must forgive the confusion. The roof of the library gave way the other day, and we could not let the books be spoiled by rain."

The idle chatter ceased the instant the door closed behind the footman. The grand marshal cleared his throat. "I do not like to rush you, your majesty, but it seems to me the sooner this business is done, the better."

"You are right, my dear Bertrand. Come, Robeaud, I can give you what instruction I must while we exchange our apparel. If it is somewhat sparse by your lights, you need not worry. The excuse of illness has been carefully prepared, and should give you time to become comfortable once more in your role. You will have Count Bertrand at your hand, and also the Count and Countess de Montholon, to offer you support."

At the door to the next room, which was presumably his bedchamber, Napoleon paused. "Captain, Madame Thorpe, you will forgive me, I hope. We shall have much time to become better acquainted in the next few weeks. During my absence, Count Bertrand will be your host. He has, I believe, ordered what passes with us as an English tea."

They were served tarts filled with fruit, buns glazed with sugar or frosted with chocolate and then sprinkled with slivered almonds, and cakes filled with cream or lemon-flavored gel. Julia could not eat. She toyed with a demitasse of strong coffee, her nerves tightly strung in anticipation of the ordeal which still lay in front of them.

Her thoughts turned to her father, the pride and joy he would have felt in this moment if he had lived. How fragile a thing was life, more fragile than the tiny china cup in her hand. It required very little to put an end to hopes, dreams, and ambitions.

Before the coffee had grown cold in her cup, the door burst open. A woman in the vicinity of forty years of age, with blond hair and a raddled complexion only partially concealed by paint, strode into the room. Behind her came a man, expostulating at every step.

"You cannot do this, my dear," he was saying. "I positively forbid it. You will make him angry."

"What do I care for his anger if he is leaving us?" the woman cried.

Count Bertrand got to his feet with alacrity and moved to close the door. "My dear Albine," he said. "This is unseemly. Would you spoil everything?"

"I saw the man who was supposed to come from my window. I changed my gown and waited for the summons, waited for the honor of the last goodbye. Do not mouth to me of spoiling the great man's plans! If he can have so little consideration of what is due to me, and my husband, then why should I have consideration for him?"

"Madame!" Count Bertrand exclaimed.

"My dear," her husband, the Count de Montholon, pleaded.

The door into the adjoining bedchamber swung open. The emperor, attired in pantaloons, linen shirt, and cravat, and just shrugging into his snuff-colored frock coat with pewter buttons and velvet lapels, emerged. "What is this noise?" he demanded. "Silence at once!"

"Your majesty," the Countess de Montholon said piteously.

"Albine, it is you. I should have known. You have come to say your farewell. Very well. Let it be brief. Let all our farewells be brief."

The woman would have flown into his arms. Instead, he grasped her hand, saluting it. Turning to her husband, he gave him the Gallic embrace, then did the same with Count Bertrand. "My friends, we have gone over what

219

must be done many times. There is no need to repeat it. I commend my friend Robeaud to you. You will be to him, you must be to him, as you have been to me. He will have need of your aid, much need, but he will appreciate it, as I have appreciated your companionship and loyalty in these dark years. I regret that I must leave you behind now, but I ask you to have faith that I will not let you linger here one moment longer than necessary. Until we meet again—"

Taking up the hat Robeaud had left on his chair, Napoleon moved at once to the door. At that moment M'sieu Robeaud emerged from the bedchamber, dressed in the emperor's somewhat snug uniform. It sat so ill upon him, compared to the way Napoleon had worn it, that Julia felt a pang of dismay. She knew that the emperor's valet, Marchand, could be depended upon to rectify the fit, but the quiet man she had come to know so well aboard ship had so much the look of a forlorn, costumed figure after a masquerade that tears rose into her throat. On impulse, she ran to him and flung her arms about his neck.

"There," he said gently, patting her shoulder. "Do not distress yourself, *ma chère*. I am content."

Julia knew that it was so, and yet it hurt to smile and turn and leave him. Her vision was blurred as she joined Rud and the emperor and passed with them out the door.

Exercising the right and privilege of a monarch, Napoleon took the lead, striding swiftly before them. Julia caught her bottom lip in her teeth, reluctant to speak. One did not correct an emperor with impunity.

"M'sieu Robeaud?" she called, as loudly as she dared.

He gave no sign that he heard. They were passing now from the salon into the antechamber. In a moment they would be within sight of the sentry. The man on duty could not be blamed if he thought it odd, even suspicious, that a gentleman supposed to be of no particular importance should precede a lady out of the door.

"M'sieu!" she said again, then with a harried look in Rud's direction, she ran forward and caught the arm of

220

Napoleon Bonaparte. By setting her heels, she halted his progress.

He swung on her in amazed anger, then caught the appeal in her amber eyes and her quick nod in the direction of the sentry. The emperor smiled, and with a flourish of the broad-brimmed hat in his hand, indicated that they would continue at a more moderate pace together.

They passed the first sentry without incident, the emperor choosing that moment of emergence into the outside world to clamp his hat upon his head. Strolling composedly, they moved down the walk, drawing farther and farther from the house. The second sentry nodded and gave them a good afternoon. While Napoleon escorted Julia to the far side of the wagon and helped her to climb in over the wheel, Rud exchanged a comment or two with the man on duty. When Julia and the emperor were settled, he took the whip from its holder, touched it to his hat brim in farewell, and mounted to the driver's seat.

There had been no time to mention to the emperor that he would be expected to make his escape in a dray wagon. Julia almost expected to hear him refuse to lower his dignity so much. But no, he occupied his portion of the seat as if he had never known any other form of transportation.

During their absence within the house, the wagon had been unloaded. The comfortable, obscuring bulk of crates and barrels was gone. As Rud gave his horses the office to start and they rattled away down the drive, Julia felt as though dozens of eyes were riveted upon her back. The feeling did not subside until they had reached the roadway and rounded a wide curve, leaving Longwood behind them on its hill.

Even then she could not entirely relax, nor, judging from the stiff way in which they sat their seats, could the men on either side of her. Sir Hudson Lowe's semaphore posts stood about the island like giant sentinels, enormous cyclopean monsters with one red eye glittering in the rays of the setting sun. Julia stared at each one as they wheeled past. Was it blinking out a message of Napoleon's escape?

Would soldiers suddenly appear on the road before them? The signal that Boney had escaped was reputed to be a blue flag in addition to the signals, or so the island gossip said. No blue flag flapped in the trade wind, but this did not ease Julia's mind. The gossips could be wrong.

The streets of Jamestown were hot and crowded, and yet no one, it seemed, had anything to do except sit on the side of the road and watch wagons roll by.

Soldiers. They stood on the quay, a pair of them in regimental uniform, their backs to the town as they stared out at the *David* at anchor. As the wagon came to a halt they turned and started toward it, their faces serious.

"Your pardon, sir, but are you Captain Rudyard Thorpe?"

Rud answered in the affirmative.

"We have permits to visit with friends aboard the ship on which you are sailing. We are told that the launch tied up here at the quay is at your disposal, awaiting your return. We wondered—that is—we would like to request permission to make the trip out to the ship with you, if it would not be an inconvenience, sir."

There was more than enough room in the launch, even with the seamen who had been assigned to man the oars. Lack of room could not be used as an excuse to deny the two soldiers a place. There seemed, in fact, no reasonable grounds for refusing them. Rud had only a brief moment to form an answer.

"Certainly," he replied, "if you don't mind taking the forward seat. My wife cannot bear sea spray in her face, and my friend here is susceptible to seasickness if he has to endure the greater movement in the prow."

"We aren't choosy," the soldier replied with a grin, only barely suppressing a salute. "Thank you, sir."

It was as good a compromise as any. Facing forward, they would not be able to spend the short passage studying the emperor. With any luck they would be off to find their friends the instant their feet touched the deck of the *David*.

Julia, settling herself upon her own hard boat seat, allowed a small sigh to escape her lips. Rud, as slight as the sound was, glanced at her, his eyes darkening with concern at the paleness of her face. Uncaring of the others, he reached out and drew her against him, absorbing the shock of the incoming waves as they crossed them.

Events turned out much as expected. By the time Julia stood on the deck of the *David* the two young soldiers had vanished. Rud went below at once with the emperor to show him the way to M'sieu Robeaud's cabin. He would remain closeted with him for at least an hour, putting him in possession of the facts, bringing him up to date on matters going forward in London, and giving him a thorough grounding in the layout of the ship and the passengers he should recognize. Then Rud must return to Plantation House, where he would be expected to give a thorough report of everything that had, supposedly, passed between the emperor and his party.

Julia made her way alone to her cabin. Her head ached with a steady throb from the strain of the past few hours, and she felt a heaviness within herself so debilitating that she could hardly put one foot in front of the other. She should have been exhilarated, delirious with joy at the success of their mission. Instead, she only felt deathly tired. Her one desire was to shut herself away from prying eyes and weep.

The *David* sailed on the morning tide. Since Rud was once more with the emperor, Julia stood by herself at the rail, watching the sunburned island of St. Helena grow smaller with distance. Lost in her own thoughts, it was some time before she became aware of the man who moved to stand beside her. It was only when he spoke that she turned her attention in his direction.

"A miserable place," the Count de Balmain said. "I am sure that, after only a few days, you are as happy as I to see the last of it."

"You!" she said, and was at once aware of the inanity of the word.

"Even so. I told you I would be traveling to Rio, did I not?"

"I never dreamed that you meant it," she said frankly.

"It was, I must confess, a somewhat sudden move." As he spoke he lifted the telescope he held in his hand to his eye. From this distance Longwood, desolate upon its plateau, could just be seen. The searching eye on his glass turned in that direction. "I understand you were admitted into the presence of the emperor yesterday afternoon," the count continued.

"That is correct."

"How I envy you," he said, bringing the telescope down and closing it with a snap.

"Perhaps when you return you will have such an opportunity." Julia did not look at him, but turned to stare out to sea so that the frame of her gray straw bonnet hid her face.

"Shall I return? I wonder. I am of the opinion that there is nothing on the island of interest anymore."

An enigmatic shading in his voice sent alarm coursing along Julia's veins. She turned her head sharply. "What?"

A smile lit his dark eyes as they met hers. "I mean, of course, since you are not staying," he replied.

Julia was not convinced, but it would not do to pay too much heed to his odd statement. "That is not a polite thing to say to a married woman. In any case, I rather thought you found Lady Lowe's stepdaughter something more than interesting."

"You are most observant," he said, his gaze narrowing, "and also most intelligent."

"And quite unsusceptible to flattery," she answered, laughing. But despite their banter, there was tension between them. It was an uncomfortable feeling, one she had no wish to prolong. As soon as she could without seeming abrupt or in flight from him, Julia left him and returned to her cabin.

Contrary to her expectation, Count Alexander de Balmain did not prove a matter for concern during the eighteen hundred miles of the voyage to the coast of South America. For the first few days her free time was given over to the alteration of Robeaud's wardrobe to fit the emperor. The pantaloons had to be taken in at the waist and lengthened considerably. This last was not so difficult; the necessity had been foreseen and provision had been made for it by the London tailor who had made the clothing. Still, it was a trying period. The emperor was more than a little particular as to fit, and Rud was not the most skilled wielder of a measuring tape.

No sooner had this task been accomplished than they began to run into bad weather. The squalls of rain and wind were enough to make her keep to her cabin, but she also fell victim, for the first time in all their traveling, to the malaise and nausea of seasickness. She was able to keep nothing but a little water and dry toast down, and she was overpoweringly sensitive to every odor that wafted about the ship. Her nerves were on edge and her temper uncertain. She came to hate the interminable motion of the frigate as it plowed on and on over the ocean. It seemed their voyaging would never end, and it did not help to know that when they reached Rio they must turn about and make the long sea trek back toward Europe.

Rud was kindness itself during this period, but he could not seem to understand that all she wanted was to be left alone to lie as quiet and as still as possible. She did not want vinegar in water, his sovereign remedy for what ailed her, nor did she want beef broth, coffee, tea, or chocolate.

"Please," she said, swallowing against the bile at the back of her throat caused by the mere mention of such things. "I don't want anything."

"You must have something, some form of nourishment. If you go on in this way your body will become parched and will burn itself up. I am going to bring you broth and sea biscuits, and sit here until you take at least a little of them."

"I will throw up," she warned, "if I don't throw whatever you bring at your head first!"

"All right, then," he said, his tone laced with something suspiciously like laughter. "A glass of lemonade?"

"I couldn't," she said with a shudder.

"You can, if you sip it slowly."

"Oh, very well," she said with a sigh, "but if it makes me sick, don't say I didn't warn you."

Rud sat on the edge of the bunk, staring down at her.

"Julia," he said slowly, "are you certain seasickness is your problem?"

"What do you mean?" She refused to look at him, watching through lowered eyelids as her fingers pleated the sheet.

"Are you certain you are not troubled by morning sickness as well?"

"What makes you ask that?" she asked, striving for a light tone.

"Little things, little changes in your body that I have begun to notice. You must have seen them too."

"If I have, which I don't admit," she said quickly, "would it matter to you?"

He was so long in answering that her eyelids swept up, and she caught him off guard. A shadow lay in his eyes as he stared unseeingly at his hands, and there was a gray line about his mouth. "Matter?" he said. "That's a strange way to put it."

"Ours has been a strange marriage."

The flick of a wry smile across his mouth signaled his agreement; still, he made no attempt to answer her question.

She turned away. "I was right then. A child was no part of your plans."

"That isn't true. It would be extremely stupid to overlook the possibility under the circumstances, don't you think? A child is the natural consequence of the kind of activity which has been our chief amusement in these past weeks."

"But it would not make you happy to learn you are to be a father, all the same. Why?"

"I will undertake to tell you if you will answer me this, in all honesty. Are—would you be happy?"

She wanted to cry out, to rail at him for thinking that she had the least reason for happiness in the prospect. She was a woman far from her home, without friends or family, dependent on her husband for every bit of food and stitch of clothing. And such a husband—a man who had taken advantage of her weakness to force her into a loveless marriage, and then used deceit to persuade her into his bed. Now, as the consequence of that act she was probably going to have a child. Her illness was aggravated unbearably by motion of the ship, and all she could look forward to was months more of the same. Where in all that was there reason for happiness?

"You see?" Rud said when she did not reply. "It is harder than it seems. We have the habit of reserve, you and I. Just as in our more tender moments you never quite give all of yourself to me, I cannot open my mind to you. The reason in your case is fear, I think. My reasons may be different, but they are just as compelling. Don't!" he said as she raised her hand to her eyes. "Don't torture yourself with wondering and worrying. It will be time enough to tell you how I feel about a child, and about other things, when our babe is born."

Leaning over her, he pressed a kiss to her forehead and then left the cabin. He sent the lemonade to her by a steward, but it was far into the night before he returned. He woke her by stumbling about the cabin, trying to undress in the dark. His clumsiness was explained when he fell into the bunk beside her. He was thoroughly, soddenly, asleep the instant his head touched the pillow. His breath reeked of brandy fumes.

The sun was shining on the day that the *David* hove into view of the blue, conical mountain the seamen called Sugar Loaf. The weather was delightful, fresh and warm, just coasting into the tropical spring season of this southern hemisphere. The deep-blue waters of the Atlantic Ocean faded into turquoise as they sailed into Guanabara Bay. The waves of the bay washed like liquid aquamarine onto the white beaches of the city known as Rio de Janeiro, "River of January." It was there, within view of the city, that they saw the most beautiful sight of all, the sharp, clean lines of the Baltimore clipper *Sea Jade,* sitting at anchor.

They were not able to make a long stay in the Portuguese city. Napoleon, understandably, was anxious to transfer from the British-owned East Indiaman to the *Sea Jade.* For him, the pleasure of treading dry land was outweighed by the danger of recognition by some chance-met member of the French colony resident in the city. Many of these included his former officers and members of his court and cabinet. As much as he would have liked to see them, he was not yet ready to make public his miraculous resurrection from the living death of St. Helena. Though they had scanned the seas day after day since leaving Jamestown, there had been no sight of British warships in pursuit, the dreaded sign that the masquerade had been discovered. With Dame Fortune smiling on them in such a manner, it seemed best not to test her favor any more than necessary.

Julia felt certain Rud was just as anxious to go aboard the other vessel, taking his place on his own quarterdeck once more. Regardless, he stood by while she made her farewells to the other passengers, including the sardonically smiling Count de Balmain, and then accompanied her into Rio without protest.

In the sprawling South American town, they hired a small carriage, pulled by a ribbon-bedecked horse, to take them about. Julia, suddenly ravenous, insisted on stopping at a fruit stall and laying in a supply of the least perishable items to take onto the ship. From there they went to a small café, where, oblivious of the staring patrons who were not used to the presence of ladies in such places, they feasted on the hot, spicy, highly seasoned fare Julia craved. It was delicious beyond imagining, so different from the bland food served up by the English chef aboard the *David*.

They visited a flower market and an ancient church, and strolled through one of the many small squares that made pockets here and there in the town. By the time they returned to the bay, the *Sea Jade*'s first mate, Jeremy Free, had seen to the moving of their baggage and even escorted the gentleman who was traveling with them aboard the Baltimore clipper. He had been placed in the cabin occupied on the journey to England by M'sieu Robeaud and Julia's father. There was no occasion this time for the first mate to be displaced; Julia's belongings had been put in the captain's cabin. There was nothing left for her and the captain to do but enjoy a bath in Rud's own copper tub,

228

prepared to just the right temperature by his steward and valet, and go to bed.

The passing of twenty-four hours found them far from land. With a spanking wind behind them they were, in the words of the old salts, clipping the tops from the waves. There was little except ocean between them and England, allowing them to make time in spite of the fall of darkness. It was dinnertime, but how much food one was able to consume in the dining saloon under the circumstances was more a question of skill than appetite.

Julia sat laughing over their difficulties with Rud, the emperor, Jeremy Free, and Second Mate O'Toole when the door swung open. Expecting only the steward with another course from the galley, Julia did not look up until Rud, facing the door, pushed back his chair and got to his feet.

"De Gruys," he said, his voice cold. "What in hell are you doing here?"

It was indeed Marcel de Gruys. In a coat of mustard yellow with brass buttons the size of saucers worn over gray-and-white pantaloons, he sauntered toward a vacant place at the table. "First you sail from London without me," he complained, "and now you neglect to call me to dinner. What next will I suffer at your hands?"

"Hold it right there," Rud ordered.

"Who is this man in the incredible coat?" Napoleon demanded. "From where does he come?"

"Your majesty! I did not recognize you," de Gruys said mendaciously as he made the emperor a graceful leg from where he stood in the center of the room.

"You have not made an answer to the questions of either Captain Thorpe or myself," the emperor pointed out, his voice hard.

"Permit me to introduce myself—since no one else seems likely to perform that office. I am Marcel de Gruys, lately of New Orleans, a member of the expedition which set out so many months ago to effect your removal from your English prison. Ill health forced me to remain behind in London, where I would have languished waiting for news if M'sieu Free had not kindly authorized my passage aboard this ship to the rendezvous at Rio de Janeiro."

"I'm sorry, Rud," Jeremy Free said. "He said if I left him behind he would go directly to Lord Bathurst. I would have mentioned his presence on board earlier, but he has become such a fixture I'm afraid it slipped my mind."

That Marcel could dare to be there in the room, smiling and smirking and pretending innocence, was beyond Julia's comprehension or belief. Did he think that his disguise had not been penetrated on the night Rud was shot? Did he think that because no complaint had been lodged against him no one was aware of his perfidy?

"I understand, Mr. Free," Rud was saying. "However, you will inform the helmsman that we will be putting back into Rio, and chart a new course accordingly."

"Wait," Marcel exclaimed as Jeremy got to his feet. "Are you certain that is wise? I am, as I hinted to M'sieu Free, something of a chatterbox. Will the emperor wish to have the news that he is at large bandied about so soon?"

Napoleon Bonaparte rose. "You have a price, I suppose, M'sieu de Gruys, for remaining silent?"

"But naturally, your majesty! I will be as silent as death as long as I am allowed to remain with you to the end of your great adventure."

The emperor directed a sharp look at De Gruys before turning to Rud. "What do you have to say of this man's conduct? Why are you so determined to leave him behind?"

"He—it is a personal matter, your majesty," Rud replied at length.

"Not a question of loyalty?"

"No, your majesty."

"One sees that he is unscrupulous. The question one must ask is, does he pose a threat?"

"Yes, he does!" Julia said, her voice ringing loud in the room filled with males. She thought she saw a hint of censure in the emperor's gray-blue eyes, but she rushed on, undaunted. "He is a criminal three times over, guilty of attempted rape, and on a separate occasion, of attempted kidnapping and attempted murder!"

230

Rud's jaw tightened at this public exposure of Marcel's criminal intentions so obviously directed toward his wife.

It was Napoleon who spoke at last. "All these crimes attempted only? He cannot be so formidable a villain, then."

"He was unlucky, that is all. And yet, it shows how far he is willing to go."

"Your majesty, I protest!" de Gruys said.

Napoleon ignored him, staring at Julia with a considering look in his eyes. "The best compromise, one that would save everyone much time and trouble, would be to hang him."

"The most sensible thing I've heard all night," O'Toole said in approval.

"Your majesty!" de Gruys said, his voice issuing from his throat as a croak.

"We cannot do that," Julia said, her wide gaze fastened on the emperor's impassive face.

"Why not? You contend this man is untrustworthy. The good captain does not want him aboard. We are all reluctant to lose the time it will take to return him to Rio, even if we could trust him to remain silent."

"You can, your majesty! I would not speak a word. It was no more than an idle threat I spoke, made to assure me a place on the ship!" De Gruys looked from Julia to the emperor, his face greenish-white in the light of the overhead lantern.

Julia turned to Rud, a sense of chill moving over her. This could not be happening. It was impossible that a man's life could depend on her next words. Rud seemed not to notice her appeal. His brow furrowed in concentration, he stared at Napoleon, as if searching for the motive for his extraordinary suggestion.

Julia swung back to the emperor. "To hang him for our own convenience would be barbaric. We cannot take the law into our own hands."

"An interesting point. As ruler of France, I formulated laws. I crowned myself emperor, the final authority for hundreds of thousands of people. My words, my ideas, became the law. Since this power was self-appointed, can it have been wrested from me as was my throne and my country? Could it not be that I am still, here and now, the law?"

Julia's amber eyes met his without evasion. "If you believe that, then I am willing to abide by your decision on the fate of this man."

"Julia!" Marcel cried. "How can you be so bitter? I never meant to hurt you." Seeing she had no attention to spare him, he turned to the emperor, dropping to one knee in supplication. "Your majesty—please—"

Napoleon glanced at him and then away. Lips curling with disdain, he said, "For such a one we interrupt our dinner? Enough. Let him stay, as long as he keeps to himself. Since he has been taking his meals in his cabin to avoid us since last evening let him continue. I see no need for Madame Thorpe to be offended by the sight of him."

Marcel did not wait for any further dismissal. Jumping to his feet, he made a jerky bow and quitted the room. Julia caught the look of virulent rage and burning humiliation he cast back over his shoulder just before the door closed behind him.

One fair day blended with the next as the ship pressed northeastward, skirting the coast of South America. The winds were favorable, the skies edged with cumulus clouds like high-piled cotton wool. The water sparkled in the sunlight, stretching ahead of them to the far horizon. It was hard not to entertain the notion that the ship could, and would, sail on and on without stopping over glittering seas stretching to infinity.

Such ideas were common to Julia in these days. The discomfort which she had blamed on the ship's motion had not abated, despite the fine weather. As the second month passed without the appearance of her usual courses, she was forced to face the fact that, as Rud had suggested and she had feared, her problem was not seasickness. She was *enceinte*. She was indeed going to have a child.

Although there was a certain fascination in the idea of having a small baby to hold and to love, she was also filled with a vast depression of the spirit. She had never been a timid person, but still she was conscious always now, of a nameless unease and fell prey to the gloomiest of fancies. The tension aboard the ship, caused by the brooding presence of Marcel, affected her strongly. Rud, finding that his absence had encouraged slackness among the crew and a lessening of his standards in the maintenance of his ship, was busy utilizing the perfect days to remedy matters. Julia was left much to her own devices. It sometimes seemed, as she strolled the decks, that Marcel was everywhere, watching her with eyes which made her feel undressed, talking in spiteful asides to the one man on the ship willing to associate with him, the spindly-legged, jaundiced ship's surgeon, Dr. Hastings.

Napoleon Bonaparte, when he was available, proved a more than adequate refuge from Marcel's constant observation. That gentleman took care to stay out of the emperor's way. Julia could not tell whether Napoleon realized the position she was in, but he often invited her to stroll the decks with him. As he walked beside her, with his hands clasped behind his back, their discussions ranged from theology to the theory of navigation, from philosophy to women's dress. He was interested in all things and well informed about most. Excellent company, he had a droll wit when he troubled himself to exercise it, and a fund of anecdotes concerning the famous of Europe that kept Julia spellbound for hours. He seemed to have no great opinion of the intelligence of women in general, holding that the Turks, who banished females to the harem, had the correct approach to the sex, and yet at no time was she aware of condescension toward her in the subject or wording of his discourse. On occasion, she was made to feel that the emperor found her attractive, but he was always most punctilious in his attentions, whether they were in company or alone, whether Rud was in evidence on the quarterdeck or not.

One of the many things they had in common was the enjoyment of the ritual of the nightly bath. Rud's steward was kept busy shifting the copper tub back and forth from one cabin to the other. Julia, in order to avoid too great

233

a confusion in the galley with the heating of water while dinner was being prepared, arranged to make her own ablutions in the late afternoon. This had the extra advantage of allowing her to spend as long as she desired relaxing in the warm, scented water.

Julia was engaged in this luxurious pastime one afternoon when Rud stepped into the cabin.

"So this is where you disappeared to; I might have known."

"You might," she answered, "if you had troubled yourself to notice what I have been doing lately."

"My dear Julia, have I been neglecting you?" he asked.

The tone of his voice made her wary. She glanced at him, catching a familiar gleam in his sea-blue eyes.

As they neared the equator the weather had turned hot and sultry. Rud wore no coat and had discarded his cravat and studs, and his linen shirt flapped open to the waist. Staying constantly on deck had deepened the bronze of his skin, making his teeth startlingly white by contrast. Through the open front of his shirt, she could see that his chest had also taken on a darker hue. It was not unexpected, considering that she had often seen his shirt decorating a pile of rope at midday.

"I would not say I was neglected precisely," she answered at last.

The movement of the ship turned Julia's bathtub into a small tidal ocean. The water washed back and forth, rising to her neck and then receding, leaving her breasts like gleaming high-peaked islands each time it retreated. The phenomenon seemed to fascinate Rud. He studied it intently as he unfastened his cuffs and stripped off his shirt.

"I rather thought the emperor was keeping you tolerably amused," he said almost at random.

"Yes, tolerably," she said without enthusiasm.

"Then it is not a lack of conversation that is the cause of your complaint?"

Julia began to wish she had never spoken, but she would not back down. "No."

"I thought not. I have noticed Jeremy playing at piquet
234

with you on several occasions when he was off duty, so I surmise it is not companionship you require?"

"Apparently not," she answered, squeezing water from her bath cloth along the turnings of her arm. From the corner of her eye she watched as Rud sat down on the bunk and began to remove his boots.

"What else could you need?" he mused. "Something only I can supply? Lessons in how to sail a ship, maybe?"

"I think not," she said with a shake of her head that set the curls piled high on her head to dancing. "I am heartily sick of ships and of sailing."

"I don't doubt it, my dear Julia," he said, "but you have been heartily sick of everything here lately, haven't you? Tell me, how do you feel now, at this moment?"

"Well enough," she said with a slight shrug. "My stomach hasn't refused anything in nearly a week. I can't answer for it if we have fried fish again."

Advancing toward her, he knelt beside the tub. He reached out, drawing a line with his fingertip down the deep valley between her breasts. "Has it been so bad?" he asked quietly.

"I have survived," she answered, trying for a light tone of voice.

"Yes, and grown more beautiful with each passing day, more desirable than I can bear, though I have tried to spare you."

It was true, he had. His consideration had caused Julia surprise and gratitude, but it had also caused her to wonder if she was losing her attractiveness for him. "I know," she answered him, and drew in her breath as his hand slid beneath the water, smoothing down over the satin flatness of her abdomen to the indentation of her waist, and then rising upward once more to cup the swelling fullness of her breast.

"This sweet, ripe perfection is more than I can withstand. I need you as I need food and drink. You are my dearest reward and my chief torment, and you will be, I think, my greatest and most dreaded punishment."

He gave her no chance to question him. He molded his

235

mouth to hers in an aching kiss as his hands gently caressed her in the silken water, moving along the length of her thighs, slipping between them. His kiss deepened, his tongue probing in gentle ravishment.

Julia felt her heartbeat begin to quicken. Deep within, she felt a spreading urge to abandonment. Lifting her arms, she slid them around his neck, drawing his head down to increase the pressure of his lips as she moved her own against his.

He shifted his position, sliding his arms beneath her. With a strong upward surge, he drew her to her feet. Reaching for a towel, he wrapped it around her, and then with slow intimacy dried each curve and crevice, each slope and turn of her body, before lifting her into the bunk. They moved together in trembling ecstasy, their warm breath mingling as parted lips clung. Her body, soft, cool, and moist with the freshness of lavender soap, came against his hard, sun-warmed maleness tasting slightly of sea salt. They were in no hurry. With tender exploration they stretched rapture to the breaking point. When their senses could stand no more without spilling into madness, he raised himself and pressed into her, moving deeper with slow insistence. The heat and expanding pressure sent radiating waves of sensuous delight through her. For long moments he was still. She stirred, and he began an almost imperceptible movement that became an easy, undemanding rhythm. Pleasure coursed over her in a series of tiny shocks that made her clutch at his arms with her breath burning in her throat. Entranced, she let her eyelashes flutter upward. Her dark amber eyes met his gaze of deepest blue in an exchange of wondrous pleasure that was tinged also with a painful emotion, held close in the heart, that neither could nor would admit.

In a measured cadence as ancient as the sea around them, they plumbed the fathomless depth of sensual enchantment. The loving transport went on and on until they were caught in a quickening tide of passion that washed over them, leaving them at last in spent and breathless content.

Her hair had been loosened from its pins. Rud smoothed

it back from her face, straightening the shining, wild silk tangles. "Julia," he whispered, and pressed his lips to the fragile skin of her eyelids. With deep-drawn breath he held her close, his grip tightening slowly as if afraid that if he let her go she would be torn from him.

"Rud? What is it?" she asked, smoothing her fingers over the muscles of his shoulders.

"Nothing," he said, but his voice was husky and it was a long time before his hold relaxed.

The weather continued hot, one brassy day following another. The sun came up in pink and rose, stood straight overhead at noon, and set in rose and pink. The ship's crew, citing the old proverb concerning a red sky, battened down for a storm that never came. The deck of the ship shimmered with heat from sunrise to sunset, and the cracks between the planking bubbled with melting pitch. Below decks, the cabins were like ovens. The only bearable place on the entire ship was the canvas shelter Rud had rigged for Julia on the deck.

At night, heat lightning played around the horizon, tantalizing them with thoughts of cooling rain. None fell in their path, though banks of dark clouds loomed up, passing over the ship. Their wake foamed in the dark hours with the yellow-green glow of phosphorescence. The peculiar, ghostly light gleamed now and then from a leaping fish or in the crest of a wave. Once the entire ship flamed with the eerie orange dancing light of St. Elmo's fire playing over the masts and spars.

The seamen began to talk in low voices of ominous signs and portents, and of ill-fated voyages they had heard mentioned in waterfront taverns and saloons. A vast unease settled over the ship. Everyone on board began to scan the skies and con the featureless horizon a dozen times a day.

It was a morning like countless others. Julia was breakfasting in the dining saloon with Rud, taking advantage of the comparative coolness of the new dawn. It was the only time of day when hot coffee was actually enjoyable. She was just pouring the last drop from the coffee pot into her cup when Second Mate O'Toole entered the room, stepping over the threshold of the door, which was blocked open for coolness.

"Morning, captain, Madam Julia. Jeremy said I was to tell you, sir, that the barometer has fallen two more points. There's a whopping great cloud coming up out of the southeast, I might add."

Rud nodded. "Everything secured in readiness?"

"Aye, sir."

"Good. Had breakfast? You don't want to be caught in the middle of a high wind without something under your belt."

"I've eaten in a manner of speaking, sir. Coffee and a biscuit at the railing. I expect I'd better be getting topside now. If I don't watch that cloud no telling what it's liable to do."

Julia smiled after the departing Irishman before turning to Rud. "You think we are in for a storm?"

"There's every indication of it," he answered. "Don't worry. The *Sea Jade* can ride it out. If we are hit by it, I want you to go to the cabin and get into the bunk. Less chance of you being hurt that way."

Julia agreed, warmed by his concern. Taking up her cup, she sipped at her coffee, trying to remember if there was anything important that she needed to put away in her cabin. Her brushes and scent box, possibly. That was all.

Footsteps, the unmistakable tread of the emperor, echoed in the companionway. She looked up in time to see Napoleon pause to see if they were inside, then step into the room. His hair was ruffled, as if he had been on deck, and a frown creased his high forehead.

"Captain," he said, "I must speak to you concerning a matter of importance."

"Shall I go?" Julia asked. She was already on her feet, having slipped out of her chair in order to make the expected obeisance to the emperor. Now she glanced from one man to the other.

"That will not be necessary," Napoleon replied. "The matter can scarcely be kept a secret."

"In what way may I be of service, your majesty?" Rud inquired courteously.

"According to my calculations, the ship changed course as much as four and twenty hours ago. If she keeps her present direction, she will not land at the Canary Islands as is the usual case."

"No, your majesty."

"I fail to see the reason in that. You have need of fresh water, fresh food."

Julia, like the emperor, waited for Rud's reply. She never doubted for an instant that he had good reason for his decision; still, she wondered at the hard expression that suddenly entered his eyes.

"Shall I tell you?"

The question came from Marcel, lounging in the open door. Without waiting for an answer he strolled forward with his arms crossed over his chest. He made the emperor an insultingly shallow bow, his lips twisted in a sarcastic smile tinged with triumph.

"Ma foi!" Napoleon exclaimed. "What is the meaning of this sneaking about listening and interrupting private conversations?"

"I mean at the moment to inform you of what you wish to know, what you must surely have guessed. You are not being taken to Malta. This ship is set on a course for the West Indies. There, in the pleasant surroundings of the group of British-held islands called the Bahamas, a new, healthier, and more comfortable prison has been prepared for you."

"This cannot be true!" the emperor declared, his head thrown back and his lips tight.

"I assure you it is. Public opinion in England, in that land of fair play, is such that a decision was made to make your exile more pleasant. Due to your many sympathizers who were known to be plotting your escape, it was thought unwise to make public the change of location. It might serve to encourage an attack en route during the transfer from St. Helena to the Bahamas. Under such conditions you could easily be killed, and who would accept the word of the British government that it was not deliberate murder? The British Admiralty is well aware that you hoped to use the conditions you were enduring at Longwood as a lever to prize yourself off your island. To be reincarcerated in yet another tropical paradise was no part of your plans, however. If you knew of the removal you might resist. Physical force, which could result in your injury, was to be avoided at all costs. This was the state of affairs when correspondence was intercepted from St. Helena which set out your brilliant plan of escape."

Napoleon turned with slow dignity from Marcel to Rud. "Do you deny the allegation, Captain Thorpe?"

"No, I do not, your majesty."

Julia clenched her hands into fists, pressing them to her abdomen. With wide, burning eyes she stared at Rud. His words conceded his guilt, and yet, seeing him standing so calm and straight before them, she could not make herself believe it.

"Our fine Captain Thorpe was ideally placed to be of service. A hero of the battle of Waterloo, a sea captain with American connections, owner of a ship conveniently registered in the United States—who could be a better choice to infiltrate this plot? All he had to do was present himself in the right place at the right time to be invited into the conspiracy, though doubtless he would have taken more drastic steps if they had proved necessary."

Outside, the wind was rising, the motion of the ship taking on a new rhythm. The lantern above the table swung back and forth with an increasing tempo. They did not notice.

"It is incredible!" the emperor declared, smacking the table with the flat of his hand. "That I should have been betrayed so easily surpasses my belief. How do you know these things?"

"Ah, you would like to see my credentials? I wondered when you would begin to be curious as to my part. I have the honor to be an agent for the Royal House of Bourbon and of Louis XVIII, who is now master of France. His regime and the government of Great Britain, now the coziest of allies, engage in lengthy exchanges of information concerning the man, yourself in fact, who is the greatest threat to them. The English were most frank about their activities. Naturally the king of France and his ministers did not divulge all their secrets—my own identity and purpose, for example."

"A Bourbon agent—" Napoleon murmured, then abruptly exploded in rage. "A traitorous, sniveling little dungheap bastard of a Bourbon agent!"

Marcel grew flustered and his eyes burned bright with hatred. Still, he held to his temper. "Traitor? Now, that is too strong a term. My loyalty lies with France, not with its ex-emperor. I am merely doing my duty to my country, just as Captain Thorpe was undoubtedly doing his when he went through the ceremony of marriage with Mademoiselle Julia Dupré. If we both manage to find some modicum of enjoyment in the performance of our obligations, that is our good fortune."

Julia drew in her breath in an inarticulate sound of distress. That aspect of the situation had not occurred to her. Now it struck her with a pain so great her mind sought to escape it by the cessation of all feeling, all thought.

"Your duty?" the emperor exclaimed in heavy sarcasm. "I fail to see that you have accomplished anything. You seem to have left it all to Captain Thorpe."

"Not entirely. There was the matter of M'sieu Dupré. I had to take care of his removal in Havana myself. Unfortunately for him, he received information there of a Bourbon agent who had been sent to New Orleans. The identity of this man was unknown, but it would not have been long before the old man put two and two together. This I could not allow."

"You killed my father," Julia whispered. She accepted the fact without question. There had been two men hovering over his fallen figure that night, however. Who had acted with Marcel? Hastings, the ship's surgeon, had also gone ashore, she thought.

Before she could voice the accusation, Marcel went on

with barely a glance in her direction. "It was necessary for the sake of my mission."

On the last word, he unfolded his arms. Flicking aside his coat, he drew a pistol from his belt. No ordinary weapon, the pistol had four silver-chased barrels fused together and attached to a stock carrying a single hammer.

Rud made an abortive move, coming up short as Marcel turned the pistol in his direction.

"Careful," Marcel cautioned. "You are valuable as a sailing master for this ship, but you are by no means indispensable. Perhaps I should warn you that this pistol was crafted especially for me on the order of King Louis by a Prussian gunsmith. It is capable of firing four shots without reloading, and is equipped with an extremely fragile trigger that responds to the slightest touch."

"You spoke of a mission," Napoleon said, drawing Marcel's attention back to himself. At the sight of the weapon he had regained the steely control of the soldier he had been for the better part of his life.

"Yes. The king and his court have discovered what an unpleasant thing it is to be forced to flee for the border of France for the sake of their lives. They wish never to be faced with that necessity again."

"Bah! They are stupid aristocrats who have forgotten nothing and learned nothing! Do they not yet understand that their security depends on the responsiveness of their government to the needs of the people?"

"I think not," Marcel said tightly. "They are firmly convinced that their safety depends on the certain knowledge that you will never set foot in France again. This can only be assured by your death. And that is my mission!"

The explosion that followed on his last word sent waves of concussion around the room. Through the acrid blue curtain of gunpowder smoke, Julia saw Napoleon reel backward, clutching his chest. He crashed to the floor and lay still.

"Hold!" Marcel shouted as Julia started toward the fallen man and Rud surged around the end of the table. At the same time Marcel, with his left hand, twisted the barrel of his unusual pistol, making it ready to discharge once more. "Hold it right there, Captain Thorpe, or I finish the job I started on a foggy night in London. Julia, come here to me. Napoleon Bonaparte has no further need for your services, or those of any woman. I said, come here! Unless you would enjoy seeing me put a period to the life of the good captain?"

Julia dragged her gaze from the great bloody hole in the center of the emperor's breast. Could any man sustain such a wound and live? It did not seem possible. A suffocating wave of grief and rage rose into her throat, and she swallowed hard on the hurtful pressure of tears, her hands gripping each other with paralyzing numbness.

"Julia, now!" Marcel rapped, his voice rising.

Julia glanced at Rud, but his gaze was fastened on the pistol in Marcel's hand, his every nerve strained in anticipation of a chance to disarm him. Slowly, inch by reluctant inch, Julia moved around the long table. Her mind numb with shocked disbelief, she could see no alternative except to do as she was ordered.

As she neared Marcel, he reached out, grasping her wrist. With a jerk he pulled her against his side, encircling her waist with his arm. "Now," he said, "the two of us will retire to my cabin. If you, Captain Thorpe, care anything for the safety of this woman, you will set a course for the Canary Islands. Do not try to take her from me or thwart me in any way, or, regardless of my enjoyment of her, I will put a ball between her beautiful eyes. If you do exactly as I say, I may return her to you when I go aboard the ship awaiting me at Tenerife. I cannot, of course, guarantee her condition."

The ship lurched as though buffeted by a giant's hand. Even there, below decks, they could hear the whine of the wind in the rigging above them. Lightning flashed, followed by the roll of thunder. Marcel's arm tightened cruelly about Julia's ribs as he sought to keep his balance.

"There is no need for this," Rud said, his voice grim. "Release her, and I will give you my word as a gentleman to set you down wherever you wish to go, and leave you unmolested until you reach your destination."

Marcel gave a harsh laugh. "Will you indeed? Your offer is generous, but I must decline. You have had the pleasure of our Julia's company long enough. Now it is my turn. I have suffered a great deal of pain and humiliation on her account, and it is time she was made to answer for it. I quite look forward to the next few days alone with her. If you want to communicate with me, you may do so by way of Dr. Hastings. Otherwise, I would prefer not to be disturbed!"

Step by step he forced her back with him toward the door. Julia flicked a look at the gun in his hand. It was shaking slightly with his excitement and, she thought, his anticipation. What would happen if she struck at it? Regardless of what occurred or what he did to her, she could not go meekly to the punishment he intended to mete out to her. Before the thought was completed, before she had even begun to examine the consequences, the act was done. With all her might, she drove her fist up under Marcel's wrist.

The weapon went off. Simultaneously, there was a tinkling crash, and the lantern in the ceiling spun on its chain, scattering broken glass in a wide arc. Marcel swung his fist at Julia, catching her a ringing blow on the side of the head. Even as she fell, she saw Jeremy Free appear in the doorway.

"Back! Get back!" Marcel screamed. A third shot blasted through the dining room.

Rud lunged, and there was the sound of a scrambling struggle, then more men were pouring through the doorway. Ranting and cursing, Marcel was disarmed. With blood streaming from his nose and one eye fast closing, he was led away to be locked in his cabin. Eventually he would be taken to England and tried for murder. Napoleon, it was discovered, still lived, but there was another charge that would be laid at his door—the death of first mate of the American-registered Baltimore clipper *Sea Jade,* Mr. Jeremy Free.

They picked up the emperor and carried him to his cabin. There he was left to Julia's care, for the storm was

245

upon them and the captain and every hand were needed on deck.

The ship's surgeon offered his services, but Julia, mindful of her suspicions and his overeager interest, refused to let him in the cabin where Napoleon Bonaparte lay. With the help of the steward, she cut away the emperor's coat and shirt. At the full sight of the injury thus exposed, she felt a sinking hopelessness. Still, she could not give up. She folded thick pads of linen and tied them in place. After a time the bleeding seemed to ease, but she was reminded wrenchingly of her father's death under similar conditions so many months before.

The tempest outside the vessel grew more violent. Lightning forked in brilliant streaks across a sky that was as dark as night. Thunder exploded around them like a thousand cannon, while rain lashed the ship in windblown sheets. The *Sea Jade* rose and fell valiantly, dipping her bow into the waves that rolled toward her, washing over her decks and swirling into the scuppers. Now and then came a ringing crack as a sail was torn away, but for the most part the brave ship held her own, riding the storm as Rud had promised.

Julia sent the steward away to see to the body of the first mate while she stayed with the emperor. When she was not sitting beside his bunk, she stood at the porthole staring out at the gray sky, gray water, and gray wind-driven spray. She did not think; that exercise was much too painful. Still, she could not prevent the images that formed in her mind's eye, images of her and Rud together, walking the deck, talking, making love. They filled her with impotent, raging anguish. She felt debased, as though her body and its response had been manipulated for Rud's treacherous purpose. How could he have used her so? Their marriage had been nothing but a farce and a sham from beginning to end. A shabby trick, nothing more. She should have known. There had been more than one indication that all was not as it should be. His failure to mention his service in the British army, his attempt to conceal his wealth, the ease with which he had arranged for the *David* to sail to St. Helena, his mother's odd pity, even his uncle's strange words on the day they had sailed, all pointed toward concerted deception. With the advantage of hindsight, the reason for all of it seemed transparently clear. She must have been a fool not to have seen. A blind, stupid, fool!

"Madame—"

The word was a whisper of sound, but still Julia caught it. Turning, she moved with quick steps to the bunk where Napoleon lay. "Yes, your majesty?" she said, leaning over him.

"A little water—"

Julia poured water from a carafe left standing on the floor. Raising his head, she held the cup to the emperor's lips. He gave a weak nod when he was finished, and she took the cup away.

"My thanks." He breathed with a shallow movement of his chest, as if a great weight rested over his heart.

"Is there anything I can do for you, your majesty?" Julia inquired softly.

"No, madame. I think there is nothing—anyone can do. Strange. I never meant—for it to end this way."

"I am sorry there is no priest, no one to say a prayer for your soul except myself."

"There is no need. I did not require religious trappings for my living—why should I have them for my dying?" He gave a wintery twitch of the lips that might have passed for a smile. "It will be said—when Robeaud passes —that I—that I recanted. Too much to expect of him—to die unshriven for my sake. Poor man—they will poke and pull at his body—searching for the source of greatness. Such surprises they will find—such mysteries. How, one wonders, will they explain them—"

His short laugh turned to a cough. As a red-tinged froth appeared on his lips Julia reached for a wet cloth, passing it over his mouth.

"Merci," the emperor whispered.

"Your majesty?"

"Speak."

"Do I understand that you do not wish it to be known

that you made your escape, even if—" She could not complete the question. There was no need.

"The Emperor Napoleon will die a martyr's death—the victim of the British—on St. Helena. A man called Robeaud will be buried at sea. I refuse—to give de Gruys the honor of having caused my death. He is a madman— let him be—so revealed if he should claim the credit."

"It will be as you say," she promised, her throat tight with tears. "You must speak no more just now. Conserve your strength, if you will, your majesty."

"For what?" he inquired, coughing again. "Tell me, was the lunatic de Gruys—secured?"

"He was, your majesty." In the distance, from his cabin across the way, she could hear the Frenchman shouting to be released. He had been calling at intervals for the past half hour, apparently afraid the ship would sink while he was locked in his cabin.

"A Bourbon agent—" the emperor said, the words no more than a thread of sound. "I knew—we should have— hanged him."

He did not speak again. His breathing took on a slow rattling sound. It grew fainter, stopped. Within a quarter of an hour of his last words, Julia, using a mirror, could find no sign that he still lived. With trembling fingers she closed his staring eyes. For long moments she stood gazing down at the strong, composed features. So many hopes and dreams had ceased to be with the death of the man on the bunk. Large dreams of empire, and small dreams— such as her own return to a plantation in Louisiana known as Beau Bocage. She had never found the right moment to approach the emperor about her father's overgenerous contribution to the Bonapartist cause. Too late. It had always been too late. She should have known.

Tearless, composed, she let herself out of the cabin. Someone had to be informed. The burden of being the only one to know of the passing of Napoleon Bonaparte was too great to be borne alone. With an unsteady gait from the rolling ship, she made her way forward to the companionway. Clinging to the handrail, she climbed steadily upward.

The wind struck her like a lash as she stepped out onto the deck. It tore at her hair, sending her pins spinning away into nothing. It flattened her gown against her, then billowed and burrowed underneath as if it would strip it off over her head. The door behind her crashed back and forth on its hinges, and she had to let go of the door frame, stumbling a few steps away, to keep it from crushing her fingers. As the ship plunged into the breaking seas, only a lifeline, strung across the deck, kept her from losing her footing. Straining for balance, she looked around for Rud and caught sight of him upon the quarter-deck. He saw her at the same time and pointed with a definite gesture back toward the companionway, yelling something that she could not quite catch as it was torn from his lips by the wind.

And then above them came the cry from a lookout in the crosstrees. "Wave!" he bellowed, pointing forward. "Giant wave!"

Swinging toward the bow, Julia saw it. Towering a hundred feet into the air above them, hurtling toward them faster than a runaway carriage, it was a green-black wall of water. No mere storm-blown swell was this; it was a monstrous thing such as sea legends are made of. There was no hope of fighting it, no chance of mere men surviving by the use of muscles and knowledge. It was so mountainous, so gigantic, no man could hold the wheel or cling to the rigging in the face of its awesome power. There was only one chance for safety, and that was within the buoyant hull of the wooden ship.

"Get below!" Rud shouted. "Every man below! All hands below decks!"

Suddenly there was a man beside her. "For God's sake, Julia me darling, get below!" O'Toole said, sweeping her with one long arm back toward the companionway. He half supported, half lifted her down the steps. No sooner had they cleared them than other seamen came pounding down the short stairway. Julia flung a look back over her shoulder, but it was too dark to make out faces, to tell who was among the men already below and who was still on deck. Farther down the corridor, she saw Marcel out-

249

lined in lamplight in the doorway of his cabin. Dr. Hastings stood beside him, the tool he had used to force the door in his hand. The two men stared in total incomprehension at the sudden rush of men below decks. Panic leaped to Marcel's face, and he stepped back inside his cabin and slammed the door.

At the captain's cabin, O'Toole paused. "Inside," he said, giving her a small push. "Get yourself a pillow, hold it over your head, and lie down flat on the floor."

Julia held back, her hand on the doorjamb. "What about you and Rud?" she asked.

He did not have time to answer. The ship turned on end, bow first, plummeting downward as though it was falling into a great black hole. They had reached the trough of the monster wave. There was a roaring sound, and Julia lost her footing. She felt herself hurled forward, sliding, slipping down into dark space. She slammed into a bulkhead. Bright light exploded behind her eyes, and in her ears was the shifting, grinding sound of creaking timbers. A tremendous crash came overhead as the weight of tons of water poured down upon the *Sea Jade*. Water swirled around Julia, drenching her to the skin. A wave of pain, as enormous in its way as the mountain of water crushing them, trying to drown them, washed over her. She closed her eyes, slipping mercifully into the wet darkness.

"Julia! Julia!"

There was an urgency in the sound of her name that demanded an answer. She opened her eyes and was surprised to find that she could see, though the light was dim. There was a heavy weight across her legs, and the salt water that nearly covered her splashed into her eyes and mouth, making her cough. She could hear someone moaning, a faint sound above the noise of wind and rain, and hear also the ominous gurgling and sloshing of water in a confined space. Beneath her, the ship was still buoyant, but it moved with a heavy, sluggish roll that could mean only one thing.

"Julia!"

It was Rud, leaning over her as he spoke her name.

His face was pale and water trickled down his face, turning red as it ran into the raw graze across his chin. With more haste than care, he dragged aside the body of the seaman which pinned her to the floor, then raised her to a sitting position out of the rising water.

"Are you all right? Can you walk?"

"I think so," she answered, though her voice sounded weak in her own ears, and she spoiled the brave effect by setting her teeth on her bottom lip as she was torn by a gripping agony deep in her belly.

He did not wait for more, but scooped her into his arms and turned toward the shattered opening above the companionway.

The damage above decks was incredible. The foremast was torn out of the planking like an uprooted tree, the mainmast had broken in half and fallen, dragging its sheets and sails over the side, while the mizzenmast had been stripped to the bare pole. Where the bow had been was a gaping hole, huge beyond hope of repair. They were taking water at such a rate that the ship had already settled until there was less than two feet of freeboard between the water and the ship's railing.

With the passing of the wave, the storm had begun to die away, though the wind still tore at the crippled ship and the rain splattered onto the sluggishly rolling deck.

Carrying Julia, Rud picked his way through the debris scattered over the deck to get to the clear port side. There O'Toole waited in the ship's longboat with two other men, both injured from the look of them, stretched out in the bottom of the boat.

At the sight of Rud and Julia, a grin of relief broke over O'Toole's face. "That's the ticket, sir! Bring her aboard," he called, releasing one hand from the rope which held the longboat to the *Sea Jade* in order to steady Rud as he stepped into the craft.

Rud settled Julia in the stern, hurriedly drawing a piece of canvas over her as protection from the wind and pouring rain, then he turned away, leaping back to the deck of the ship.

"Captain! Where are you going?" O'Toole shouted.

"There may be others below!"

"Don't be daft, sir! The water's rising so fast anybody still below will be drowned by now. You've done all you can, saving Madam Julia and these other chaps. Let it go!"

As if to lend weight to the second mate's words, at that moment the bow of the ship settled so that the decks were awash. There came a rending sound as of a bulkhead bursting below, and spray shot from the open maw of the companionway.

"Come on, sir! We have got to pull away, or she'll suck us down with her!" O'Toole's voice changed, deepening. "I know you hate to leave her, sir, but you've got a wife to think of now, and you are the only navigator among us."

Rud gave a nod and stepped back into the longboat. O'Toole cast off, and then took one oar while Rud took the other. They pulled strongly away from the dying ship. At a safe distance they shipped their oars and rested, letting the boat drift in the wind as they watched the mizzenmast sink beneath the waves.

"Look," one of the sailors cried, hanging on the gunwale as he pointed away to the left. "Is that a man?"

O'Toole squinted against the driving rain. "It's a hatch cover, that much I can make out."

"I thought I saw something move on it," the seaman insisted.

"We can find out," Rud said, and set his back into the oar. But though they tried with all their sinews to reach the hatch cover, they could not. In the turbulent waves, the wind and rain, the piece of flotsam eluded them. Each time it was sighted, it seemed to be farther away than the last. Finally they lost sight of it altogether and were forced to the conclusion that it had broken up in the heavy swells.

For Julia, what followed was a nightmare of pain and blood. Lying in the bottom of the longboat with rain falling in her face and a wounded man on either side, her sore and battered body gave up the child she was carrying. Weak from the ordeal, she grew feverish during the night, and as the dawn broke on a clear sky the next morning, the heat of her skin rivaled that of the tropical sun that burned down upon them. At some time during that first night, one of the sailors died of his injuries and was passed gently overboard. On the third morning the other succumbed to the fluid trapped in his lungs. Julia, Rud, and O'Toole were alone in the longboat without provisions, and with only a bailing tin half full of rainwater between them. By sunrise of the fifth morning the last of the water was gone. The day grew hot. Julia, her mind moving in and out of consciousness, was protected from the worst rays of the sun by the canvas boat cover. She lay staring at nothing, her mind blank and uncaring, protected by nature from the terrible shocks she had sustained. Her face was drawn, revealing the well-defined bone structure, and already she was thin to emaciation.

So great was her detachment that she gave no sign of understanding when O'Toole straightened from his oar to whisper through cracked lips, "Sail. Sail away."

Rud turned his head. He stared at the ship, his eyes narrowing to slits, before he gave a slow nod. "It's a ship, all right."

"Then we be saved, sir. Julia, me darling, we're saved!" O'Toole croaked.

"Yes, at least our lives," Rud answered in a tone so flat and without emotion that Julia turned her eyes in his direction. Something in the slump of his proud shoulders and in the dull expression of his eyes touched her with dread.

O'Toole swung his head to gaze across the water at the ship once more. Impelled by the sudden still hopelessness, so like Rud's, that gripped him, Julia raised herself slowly to one elbow, clinging to the gunwale.

The ship veering in their direction, bearing down upon their small craft, had a high prow painted with enormous eyes on either side, twin banks of oars, and a pair of red lateen sails. From her stern flew a flag bearing the crescent of Islam. It was a Turkish felucca.

Part Two

```
┌─────────────────┐
│                 │
│    Chapter      │
│                 │
│    Thirteen     │
│                 │
└─────────────────┘
```

More than a hundred men thronged the decks of the felucca. They were a wild, fierce-looking crew with pistols and knives in their belts, and each with long, curved saber at his side. Black-bearded and dark, they watched with hard grins as Julia, Rud, and O'Toole were brought aboard.

From among them stepped a man more villainous-looking than the rest. His dress, his bearing, and the deference paid to him identified him as the captain of the vessel. He put a question to them in what was doubtless the Turkish tongue.

"I am sorry," Rud said. "I don't follow you."

The captain switched to a corrupt Spanish. Julia stared at him, understanding that he wished to know their names and circumstances, and yet unable to force her numb mind to answer. It was all she could do to remain on her feet, even with the support of the Moorish seamen on either side who held her arms in a cruel grip. Rud shook his head.

With a curse, the captain phrased his request in French.

"I am Bayezid Reis, captain of this ship. You are my prisoners which I claim by right of the sea in the name of my illustrious master, the dey of Algiers. If you value your lives you will make no attempt to escape. You will identify yourselves and tell me how you came to be adrift in a small boat."

Rud obliged him by supplying the information. To this Bayezid Reis gave a satisfied nod. "I thought as much. I have had word of your tall ship more than once. I am sorry to lose such a prize, but that is the will of Allah. Tell me, this woman who is with you," he went on without so much as a glance in Julia's direction. "She is, perhaps, the wedded chattel of one of you?"

Rud hesitated for no longer than the flicker of an eyelid. "Would that it were so," he said with a timbre of regret in his voice. "She is unwed."

"Ah," the captain said, smoothing his beard. "She is older than most maidens, but wondrous fair even in her present state, and it is said the women of Frankistan ripen late. It may be that I have captured a prize worthy of further inspection."

Julia flung a look at Rud. His face was stony, but his eyes seemed to burn with the blue fire of sapphires.

"It may be true, what you say, captain," Rud answered, "for the woman is a great lady in her own country. Her sire, who is now dead, was possessed of vast lands, and counted his horses, cattle, and slaves in the hundreds. He was friend to the great ruler Napoleon, whose fame must surely have reached Algeria. She wears at her throat the token symbol of his reign."

Bayezid Reis gave a wise nod. "If that is so, the prize may be greater than I dreamed. And yourself?"

Julia's husband appeared to have as little use for modesty in connection with his own rank. "I was the captain of the brave ship struck down and sent to the bottom of the ocean by the great wave. This man beside me was my second officer."

"Indeed? If it is so, my master the dey may have use for you. His navy is his pride, his strong right arm which brings glory and tribute, one he ever seeks to strengthen. But if you lie—"

The threat hung in the air, a palpable thing, heavy with the sound of quick but difficult death. Bayezid Reis made a gesture with one hand, giving an order in Turkish. The men supporting Julia came to attention and half-led, half-dragged her away.

Behind her, Rud made an abrupt movement as though to prevent the rough handling, then stood still. "Take care. She has been ill."

There came the cracking sound of a sharp blow as the pirate captain struck Rud across the face. "Be still, Christian dog! I need no one to tell me how to handle slaves. Take them below. We have wasted enough time on such puny merchandise. Like as not the female will be shark bait before morning."

At the sound of a scuffle, Julia looked back to see Rud at the captain's throat with his guards clinging like monkeys to his arms, while O'Toole was the center of a second melee. As he was hurried below deck, she heard behind her the sodden sound of blows and the hoarse voice of Bayezid Reis ringing out. "Forty lashes with the kurbash for both of them! They need a lesson in how a slave should act. They will learn it, or else!"

Julia was taken to a small, airless cubicle bare of furnishings except for a pile of rags in one corner. The seamen gave her a push in the direction of the makeshift bed. She fell to her knees. With a remark that had a ring as ribald as it was scathing, the two men turned and left her. She heard the grate of a key in the lock.

Slowly, she lowered herself onto the rags, sitting with her back against the bulkhead and her head resting on the wood. She closed her eyes. The ship got under way once more. Time crept past. At the sound of approaching footsteps, she came alert, her nerves tingling with dread.

The door opened to reveal Bayezid Reis. Behind him was a man in the long flowing robes of an Arab, with a turban wrapped about his head. His copper-colored skin was drawn tight across his cheekbones, crinkling into a thousand tiny wrinkles around his eyes, while his beard was sprinkled with gray. In his eyes was mirrored only an impersonal curiosity.

"Stand up," the pirate captain ordered.

Julia understood what he said. She recognized the wisdom of obeying, also, and yet there seemed a great distance between her mind and her will. She stared at him with fevered eyes that appeared enormous in her thin face.

Striding to her, Bayezid Reis reached down to catch her arms and drag her to her feet. He turned her back to the Arab, who with skillful fingers began to strip the buttons of her gown from their holes.

Weakly, Julia struggled, her heart beginning a frantic beat. She knew beyond all doubt that she could not bear to be taken in lust so soon after the miscarriage. She would surely bleed to death.

"Peace, unfortunate lady," the Arab said, his voice soothing in purest Castilian Spanish. "We mean you no harm. This which comes to you is necessary for an exact evaluation of your worth."

Her senses swam and her eyesight grew dim. In some dark recess of her mind, she felt her knees buckle and knew when they laid her naked upon the makeshift bed. She felt the touch of the Arab's hands pressing the bruised flesh of her right side, over her ribs, passing over her in swift examination, including a careful probing of internal intimacy. She understood when he called for water to wash the bloodstains from her thighs, knew his gentle ministrations. A soft and sooty ball of some unknown substance was pushed into her mouth and a beaker of tart juice held to her lips.

"Swallow, my lady," the Arab said. "This is precious musk which will stimulate the life force within you, warming you to living."

His words were true. In a short while she felt strength returning. When she opened her eyes she was alone in the cabin with the Arab physician. The captain had gone. The man who knelt on the floor beside her looked into her eyes, searching deep. At last he gave a slow nod.

"It is well," he said. "Attend to me for the sake of your life and your future. You are not a virgin."

Julia shook her head, mesmerized by the dark, burning eyes above her.

"It lowers your value. Still, you have hair which, when cleansed and rubbed with unguents, will shine like the morning sun. You have the eyes of a sorceress fit to destroy men's souls or lead them to search for the treasure therein. Your body has the grace of a gazelle, it is a poem of tender symmetry. When fed with rich food, bathed and tended by slaves, your skin will glow like pearls and your breasts will be like mounds of warm snow. I see this plainly. There are not fifty maidens in all Islam of your coloring, and of that number, not five who can match you. In such rare beauty great men will accept a small flaw. Failing that, others will pay handsomely for the honor of possession of so novel a woman."

Julia did not know how to answer such praise. She said nothing, waiting for the reason for it, waiting for the purpose she could sense in the Arab's manner. It was not long in coming.

"There is one thing more I must put to you, O daughter of the moon. As a physician I am aware that you have conceived and that your body has rejected the seed. Think well before you answer what I must ask you, for it will determine your fate. No Mussulman may take to himself a woman who has been wed for fear of committing the great sin of adultery, endangering his immortal soul and his hopes of paradise. If you have had a husband, then you must be sold as a mere drudge or consigned to the owner of a brothel which caters to infidels. In either case, the reward of Bayezid Reis would be small. He might think it scarcely worth the expense of bringing you back to health."

The implication was plain. If she could not declare herself unfettered by matrimonial ties, then the Turkish captain might decide to be rid of her as not worth the investment he must make in her care. Was this why Rud had denied her? Had he foreseen, with his small knowledge of Islamic customs acquired in Mediterranean ports, the present situation? In the press of the moment, Julia could not decide whether she should be grateful to him. If she answered truthfully, as she would have without the Arab's guidance, she would no longer need to live with grief, painful anger, and humiliation. But the power of the musk circulating in her system was pervasive. She wanted to live. Regardless of where she lived or in what condition, she must protect the fire of her life and keep it burning. She would shelter the flame until such time as it could leap high, feed it on dreams of vengeance and visions of final freedom from all the specters of her past. She would not blame herself for what had happened. Despite a deep-seated feeling that she must be somehow at fault, she knew she was not. Remorse and self-pity were useless emotions. What she needed now was strength.

"No," she said slowly. "I have never been a wife. For a short time I had a lover, but he died when our ship sank, and is forever lost to me."

They put ashore under cover of night as though there were something not quite legal about landing white captives in the bright light of day. Julia, who had been lost for what seemed like weeks on end in a drugged state, half sleeping, half waking, had no idea what country they had reached. From the smell of dust, dung, charcoal smoke, and spices which wafted toward them on the night wind, she could only surmise that they were somewhere on the continent of Africa.

Bundled in a woolen barracan with a veil over her face and leather sandals on her feet, Julia was led from the ship and pushed into a curtained litter. An order was shouted and the litter was picked up and borne quickly away. Peering through a slit in the striped cotton curtains, Julia could see armed guards walking on either side. From the ship she had just left emerged a winding line of men —captured sailors, no doubt. The chains on their wrists and ankles made a clinking sound in the quiet. Bowed by the weight of their fetters, made featureless by the moonless night, they had the look of shuffling beasts without intelligence or personal identity. If Rud and O'Toole were among them, she could not tell, though she watched until they were lost from sight.

It was a jostling ride through narrow streets, Now and then she caught the tinkling of bells or the wailing sound of music like a dirge in a minor key. Men in robes or covered by the heavy folds of a burnoose, men black, brown, and white, shouldered past the litter. All appeared empty of feeling, their features honed by wind and weather and hardship to a cruel edge. Julia pulled the curtains tight after a time and huddled back against the cushions.

They entered a gate and crossed the open space of a courtyard before plunging down the dark labyrinth of a tunnel. Here they were forced to wait before entering a second courtyard. At last the curtains of the litter were parted. The Arabian physician, called Ismael, handed Julia out. She was conducted into a small, dark chamber where an enormously fat Turk with a beardless chin waited. She had heard of eunuchs before, but this was the first one she had ever beheld. He said something to her that she did not understand, and she glanced instinctively at the Arab.

"This man is Abdullah. You will place your hands to your forehead, as I have shown you, and bow to him as a sign of respect. It will be to your advantage to smile upon him also, for he is the keeper of the harem of the dey of Algiers and has great influence, something you will need if you are accepted."

"If I am accepted? You mean, if I become a member of the harem of the dey?"

"It is impertinent of you to ask. When your fate is decided it will be made known to you. Go with Abdullah Effendi now and do as you are bid, having no will other than that of your master and of Allah. Do this according to my instructions and all will be well."

There was a stern note in the Arab's voice, but beneath it Julia could detect a trace of compassion and concern. She had had no contact on the Algerian ship except with this man. He had given her drugs which had helped to mend her spirit and her body. Though Julia realized that his purpose had little to do with her as a person, she thought he was not as indifferent as he would like to appear to what became of her. For that, and for his aid, she was grateful. She sought to express it in the only way possible.

"I will do as you say, O healer of wounded souls. May there be peace with you."

Julia followed Abdullah the eunuch through endless branching passages. They paused at last before a doorway that the huge man opened with a large and ornate gold key which dangled with several others at his waist. They passed through, and Abdullah locked it behind them.

She was aware at once of the fragrance of perfume. It hung in the air like a pall, a combination of all the scents in the world, it seemed; rose, orange blossom, lilac, musk, patchouli, bergamot, frankincense, and jasmine. They stood in a hallway lit at intervals by brass oil lamps with fat bellies and twin spouts. At the end of it was an arched opening leading to a garden. From that direction came the sound of a fountain playing into a pool and the sleepy cooing of doves disturbed in their rest.

Turning to Julia, Abdullah indicated a door on her right. She followed behind the eunuch, pushing through the curtain that closed off the doorway, and found herself in an enormous bathing chamber. Two Numidian slave girls came forward at their entrance and salaamed deeply to Abdullah. He gave terse, detailed instructions in Turkish, then stalked away as if he considered the task he had just performed to be beneath him.

With much giggling and exclamations at her yellowing bruises, the slave girls undressed Julia and then removed the trousers and short tunics they wore. Smiling, they urged her into the steaming water which filled a small tiled pool in the center of the room. After much consultation among themselves, they chose a soft soap scented with the damask rose, and with their hands filled with this gel-like substance, stepped into the pool after Julia, advancing upon her.

Julia knew a moment of panic. She did not trust the mischievous look of anticipation in the girls' eyes. Then she lifted her head. There was little she could do to protect herself. The water was wonderfully hot and silken. Her skin, chafed by the woolen material of the robe she had worn and clogged with the accumulated grime of weeks, had begun to itch frantically. Let them do their worst. It would be worth it to be clean again.

They soaped her hair again and again. Their quick,

slim hands scrubbed, massaged, and kneaded, cleansing her with a thoroughness that seemed to indicate that they considered her defiled in some way and in need of purification. Satisfied at last, they wrapped her in a gigantic bath sheet and escorted her from the hot bath into a second chamber, where a pool of clear, tepid water awaited. There they rinsed away the last vestiges of soap and allowed her body temperature to return to normal. From there she was taken to yet another room set about with long marble tables. When she lay full length upon one table, one of the slave girls combed the tangles from her hair and rubbed it dry, coaxing it into soft waves and curling the ends about her fingers. The other smoothed precious oils over Julia's body, oils with a base scent of roses. This was followed by a gentle, soothing massage. Taking up a pumice stone, they removed the rough skin from her feet, elbows, and knees. While she feasted on a confection made of almonds and honey and washed it down with the refreshing juice of pomegranates, her fingernails and toenails were shaped, then buffed to a gloss. A bit of oil was smoothed over her lips where they were still dry and peeling at the edges. A touch on her brows and lashes, and they were done.

Next, a barracan of transparent, rose-colored Samarkand silk was brought forth and draped around her. A veil of a slightly darker hue was placed over her face. Julia glanced down at herself, dismay flitting through her mind. Her body was clearly visible through the silk. As pleasant as it was to be arrayed in color instead of black or the heavy woolen garment given to her on the ship, she could not believe this was what all women of the Turkish empire wore. The Numidian girls had been more decently covered. It could not be denied that the slave girls had chosen wisely, however. The rose silk was the perfect complement for her coloring. Through its gauzy folds, her skin gleamed like living marble and the pink tips of her breasts were as dark as rubies, while her bruises were minimized. She was by no means certain what was going to happen to her, but she had the uneasy suspicion that she was being prepared to be put on display. She had not expected it so soon, despite the words of Ismael, the physician. *If you are chosen—*

The Arab had explained to her that as a captive of a ship of the Algerian navy, she would be inspected by a representative of the dey to see if she was suitable for the royal harem. The honor of being so chosen was great, but she must not expect it. It had been some time since a woman had been added to the harem; the dey was an aging ruler who had turned to the pleasures of the mind in recent years. Still, it was rumored that an edict had gone out from the palace to all slave dealers to be watchful for females of unusual or extraordinary attraction. If she was not accepted, she would be taken to a slave dealer, who would arrange for discreet viewing by a larger clientele. There were over five hundred houses in Algiers alone owned by men of enough substance to gratify their desires for novelty in the way of bedmates, five hundred prisons which could swallow her up. The irony was that though all five hundred could stare at will at her body, none could see her unveiled face except the slave dealers and the man who bought her. How many times must she be prepared and paraded before she was finally bought? How many indignities would she have to endure?

The slave girls arranged the barracan around her, straightening the folds, draping them with so much precision it was almost as if they expected her to have her portrait painted. That done, they stepped back and salaamed deeply before effacing themselves, moving to stand against the wall. Their obeisance was not toward Julia, however, but toward a pierced screen set into the wall directly in front of her. Alerted, Julia caught a whisper of sound coming from behind the screen. A flush rose in a wave of heat to her forehead. She was being watched. On the other side of the screen there was a man staring at her with appraising eyes. It had been easy enough to consider the idea, but now that it was actually happening she wanted nothing so much as to run and hide. Only by clenching her teeth tightly, staring straight ahead, and holding her arms rigid at her sides was she able to subdue the impulse.

There was more than one person in concealment, she realized, as she heard a deep voice speak and the answer come in another quieter tone. They were discussing her, like a mare or a heifer up for auction, she thought as another wave of color spread over her. The man was the Arab physician, she was almost certain. The other was a stranger, but one used to command.

"You will turn about."

Julia obeyed the order as one in a dream, turning stiffly and without grace or attempt to please.

"Have you any accomplishments?"

Julia hesitated, at a loss. "Of what kind, effendi?" she inquired at last. "I can do many things."

"Do you sing, or play the dulcimer?"

"My voice is fair only. I have never played the dulcimer, but I have some skill on the pianoforte."

"These other accomplishments, what among them might be of use in distracting a man from his cares?" the disembodied voice asked.

"I can ride and shoot—"

"Useless, if not an idle boast for which you deserve to be punished."

Julia searched her mind. Running her tongue over her lips, she said, "I have some skill with games of chance, and I was accustomed to playing chess with my father before his death."

"Do you dance?"

"Why, yes," Julia began, then recognized that the man on the other side of the screen could not possibly mean the kind of dancing executed by western women upon a ballroom floor.

"That much is in your favor."

Behind the screen the second man murmured something, and the first spoke again. "It is said you are acquainted with Napoleon Bonaparte of great fame, and that you bear his token. Are you his kinswoman, perhaps?"

"No, effendi. My father was his follower."

"But you have spoken to him face to face, unveiled, as is the Frankistani custom?"

266

"Yes, effendi."

"I wish to see this token."

Julia put her hand to her throat, where the bee had rested for many a day. It was not there. "I don't have it. It was removed with my other clothing."

An order was snapped, and one of the slave girls bowed and hurried away. She returned with the gold bee on the palm of her hand. Bowing once more, she passed it through the screen.

Julia stilled herself for the loss of the bee. She had lost so much else, so much she would not let herself think about it. What was one small jewel more?

"Curious," the man behind the screen said. "Most curious. Why a bee, I wonder? Eagles, falcons, lions, dragons; these I understand. But why a bee?"

Julia moistened her lips. "In ancient times it was thought that the supreme ruler of a beehive was an emperor who served for the good of his subject bees, while they in turn brought their bounty to him in the natural order of things. I have heard my father say that this is the reason, effendi, though I cannot be sure of it." There was no answer. After a moment Julia went on, "The bee is dear to me, effendi. May—might I be permitted to keep it?"

The assent was careless, offhand, as though the speaker had weightier matters to consider. With the press of tears in her throat, Julia accepted her brooch from the hand of the slave girl who plucked it from through the design in the screen. She curled her fingers so tightly around it that the wings cut into her palms.

There came a rustle of clothing, as though the men on the other side of the screen had risen. Dread moved through Julia, though she could not have said whether its cause was fear that she would be rejected or alarm that the decision might be in her favor.

"Conduct her to a chamber in the harem," came the pronouncement. "See that she lacks for nothing."

Julia had thought that she was in the harem. She discovered her mistake as she was given back into the custody of Abdullah. She traversed with him miles of corridors before they came at last to a great Arabesque door of cedar inlaid with ivory and guarded by a pair of Ethiopian eunuchs as black as Hades itself.

Once more Abdullah used a key at his belt. They entered an enormous chamber with a vaulted ceiling. Closed and shuttered against the night, it was dimly lit by brass lanterns. Low divans piled high with silken cushions were set here and there, with small tables of ebony and ivory holding fruit and sweetmeats before them. Faintly through the gloom could be seen walls covered with vivid tiles in geometric designs. Rugs, soft and glowing with color, covered the polished marble floor. In one corner was a small grove of orange trees planted in tubs, and attached to their branches by small gold chains were a number of jewel-colored birds.

From this communal room branched several hallways, each lined with curtained door openings. Abdullah led her down the hall farthest from the entrance. Choosing a doorway halfway down the hall, he whipped back the curtain, heavy with metal beads that clattered with every movement, and indicated with a jerk of his head that she was to enter. Remembering the admonition of the Arab physician, Julia inclined her head in a formal bow and obeyed.

The chamber was not large, but it boasted a window casement fitted with an ornate iron grill through which filtered a cool night breeze. There was a sleeping couch against one wall, and on the other, a carved chest redolent of cedar. These things Julia saw by holding back the curtain at the door after Abdullah's footsteps had faded back down the hall. Though a lamp hung on a chain from the ceiling, it had not been lighted. The only illumination came from the starshine filling the garden beyond her window and the faint glow of the lantern at the entrance to the hallway.

She let the curtain fall to with a noisy clacking sound. There seemed nothing to do except seek her couch. She slipped out of the barracan and draped the silk garment over the chest. After an instant of indecision, she gave up all thought of a nightgown. Even if she could find one in the semidarkness, she was not certain she wanted such a thing. She had lain for too many days aboard the ship in the same day gown. As long as she was away from prying eyes, she found she enjoyed the lack of confinement. The low couch had a satin coverlet that would be cool and soothing to the skin.

Julia was certain she would lie sleepless in such strange surroundings. So much had happened that she needed to sort out in her mind. She should make plans, decide what she was going to do, make some plan of escape. But her brain mocked such exercise. Escape? How? She was locked away behind thick doors with guards posted night and day. Beyond the harem stretched the unknown corridors of the palace, where she would quickly become lost without a guide, even if she wasn't stopped by the ranks of guards at every door and gate. And outside the palace lay the streets of the city, where a woman would be at the mercy of men like jackals. Then, if she got so far, how was she to find a ship to carry her to America or England? Who would dare to take a harem slave of the dey of Algiers aboard unauthorized, even if she had the money to pay for her passage?

No, she must not think of such things, not yet. Later, perhaps, when she was better prepared. For now, she was a slave. She must, for the sake of survival, have no will except that of her master. Her future would be planned for her. She would be told what she must do.

In the meantime, a current of air circulated through the room, passing lightly over her bare arms and making the beads on the curtains rattle gently. She could hear the dry clatter of palm-tree fronds, a sound with much the same calming properties as slow, persistent rain. The couch beneath her was softer by far than her rag bed on the ship. Clean, wrapped in comfort and the scent of roses, she drifted into sleep.

Chapter
Fourteen

Julia was awakened by the clash of the bead curtain
being thrown violently open. Bright light streamed into
the room. It was noticeably warmer than it had been the
night before. From the garden beyond the window came
the cheerful cries of birds, and something more, the
chatter of feminine voices.

Memory returned with a rush. Julia raised herself,
turning toward the doorway. In the opening stood a
woman with her hands propped on her hips and her face
twisted with fury. She was Circassian, Julia thought,
having heard much of the breed. From the Caucasian
mountains, her hair was silver-blond, and her blue eyes
were set at a slant in her face. Her cheekbones were high,
and her mouth was formed of sharp, chiseled angles
which gave her a cruel look. Perhaps two or three years
older than Julia, she was not quite so tall. Her shape was
lithe and muscular, marred only by a slight heaviness in
the thighs and ankles.

Her eyes raked over Julia's form beneath the satin
coverlet. A spate of furious Turkish fell from her lips.

"I'm sorry, I don't understand you," Julia said, first
in French and then in Spanish.

"Faugh!" the woman exclaimed and whirled from the
room.

Julia sat up on the couch. Before her feet could touch
the floor, a serving woman entered. She carried a small
270

round table upon which was set a morning repast of fried lamb, wheat cakes, fresh figs, and candied apricots, with hot mint tea to drink. There were also a bowl of hot water and a small linen towel. While Julia bathed her face and hands and turned her attention to this meal, the woman moved to the cedar chest. From its depths she drew a pair of aqua cotton-gauze pantaloons, and a loose, embroidered blouse in turquoise silk that tied beneath the breasts. These she laid out for Julia, adding a pair of velvet slippers embroidered across their turned-up toes. The servant folded the rose barracan and put it away with gestures which seemed to indicate that such a flowing garment and its matching veil would not be needed within the harem.

When Julia had eaten and donned the set of clothing, the woman made pushing motions in the direction of the communal chamber. Though reluctant to leave the safety of her room, Julia followed her suggestion.

This morning, the main room was light and airy. The solid blinds had been thrown open, giving free access to the sunlit garden. Women were everywhere. They reclined upon the divans, sat upon cushions thrown upon the floor, strolled about, passing in and out of the garden and stopping to feed the live birds on the branches of the orange trees and croon to them in soft voices. The smell of food hung on the air. Serving girls scurried here and there with traylike tables laden with all manner of food and drink. Near the top of the vaulted ceiling hung a pall of smoke from the perfume censers sitting at intervals about the room.

It seemed to Julia that among the women was represented every nation under the sun. There were coal-black Ethiopian women with skin that gleamed like ebony, Egyptian women with eyes outlined in kohl and thin lips, Syrians with pouting lips and long noses, dusky-skinned Turkish and Indian women with hair that reached to their knees. Tiny, pale-skinned beauties with slit eyes from the Far East stood beside savage-looking women from the Mongolian steppes. There was a sultry Italian beauty, a Macedonian Greek goddess, and a Navarran with auburn in her brown tresses. Though they each wore some version of the costume given to Julia, no two wore precisely the same color. Some wore small turbans, while others wore soft velvet caps hung with long silken tassels, or woven fillets to hold back their hair. Shimmering with gold and silver embroidery, with silk braiding and metallic fringes, and gleaming with gold and silver jewelry, they were like gaudy-plumaged birds themselves. The sound they made as they laughed and talked among themselves was not unlike that of a foraging flock. There were nearly two hundred. One and all ceased speaking and turned to stare as Julia advanced into the room.

From their midst rose the Circassian woman who had visited Julia earlier. She beckoned imperiously to the auburn-haired Navarran. Followed by the woman, the fair-haired Circassian approached Julia with a swift, insolent stride. At arm's length she stopped and spoke. The Navarran, obviously brought forth as a translator, hurried into speech.

"Mariyah, named for the beautiful concubine of Mohammed, demands to know who you are, by whose will you have come among us, and why."

"As for who I am, I am Julia. I have come among you because I was chosen by the dey, and I expect the purpose was the same as that for which all of you were chosen."

The two women held a brief consultation, then the Navarran spoke again. "You lie. Though several women have been sent as gifts to the harem of the dey, the mighty and illustrious ruler of Algiers has not troubled to choose a woman for himself since he chose Mariyah more than a decade past. Mariyah was the last woman sought as a vessel for his spilled seed, and that happened nearly three years ago. Have the loins of the dey grown suddenly youthful at the sight of your skinny form? Such a thing cannot be. It is ludicrous that you could stir him to desire, aged as you are, when a nubile and tender virgin has failed to make his ardor rise."

"That may be," Julia said, flushing a little. "I only know I was captured by Bayezid Reis and brought here."

"You are a spy, installed by Abdullah to report on our

discontent, to tell him who escapes into opium dreams and who indulges in the vices of Sappho."

"That is not true," Julia declared.

"We say it is! What other explanation is there?"

Turning to the other women, Mariyah began to harangue them. Vehement in her denunciation of the traitor she professed to believe Julia to be, she worked herself to a fever pitch, shouting and shaking her fist, throwing her hair back behind her shoulders with a righteous toss of her head. There were sullen murmurs from the women around her. They began to edge closer, darting looks of venom in Julia's direction. Handicapped by her inability to communicate with them, Julia could only put her case to the Navarran woman.

An ugly feeling grew in the room. There were shouts from among the crowd of women that Julia took for threats or recommendations for violent reprisals. Surely, Julia thought, if they believed she was Abdullah's tool they would not harm her for fear of angering him. They pressed closer and closer around Mariyah and Julia. The perfume of their bodies, heated by their emotions, became a rank and suffocating miasma. A hand reached out and tweaked at her hair. Another pinched her forearm, twisting the flesh. Julia lurched forward as she was pushed from behind. Spinning around, she set herself to strike out at her attackers, but she could not tell which in the press of women had touched her.

She was jostled and shoved now from both sides. Her hair was given a harder yank. Her blouse was snatched from her shoulder, exposing a breast. She flailed out, catching an arm there, a sly face there, but her foes were too many. Pinching, pulling, scratching, they came at her with vicious, smiling faces.

Abruptly there came a high-pitched scream from the rear of the crowd. Another rang out, followed by the shrill shouting of eunuchs and the whistle of the rhinoceros-hide whip known as the kurbash. Like magic, the women parted, leaving Julia standing alone, disheveled, her clothes torn and blood trickling from the scratches on her arms.

Facing her across the room was Abdullah, with a kurbash in his hand. With slow and cold enmity, he allowed his gaze to move over the women. Certain they were properly cowed before his mastery, he gestured for the two guards to return to their posts. With ponderous steps, he moved down the room toward Julia.

"What is the meaning of this disturbance?" he asked in a voice thin and high for his enormous bulk.

Julia ran her tongue over her lips, searching her mind for Spanish phrases. Before she had time to speak, Mariyah began a rapid explanation. Abdullah gave a slow nod and made a brief movement of his hand that stopped her words as though they had been sliced off with a knife. As he swung back toward Julia, the light gleamed in the red-orange jacinth in his turban and slid over the scimitar he wore in a scabbard at his side. Julia had no way of knowing what lies the woman had told, but lies they must have been to bring that look of bestial rage to Abdullah's black, close-spaced eyes. A cold, sick feeling moved in the pit of her stomach as he stumbled toward her on small feet ridiculous in their yellow slippers with upturned toes. She watched in paralyzed disbelief as his arm moved, swinging upward, the kurbash arching its limber length before it began its whistling, downward slash.

"Enough!"

The cry came from the first corridor branching from the common room. It was neither loud nor harsh, but it carried with it a final and unquestionable authority.

Abdullah nearly fell on his face, so great was the effort he put forth to stop the descent of the kurbash. With staring eyes, he turned to face the elderly woman who came toward them with a stately tread. He bent himself almost double with the depth of his salaam. Since the woman had spoken in Spanish, he answered in the same tongue, though he had not deigned to share his knowledge of it with Julia the evening before. "O beloved and most high lady," the eunuch said. "What is your will?"

"I stand as witness that this newest addition to the harem is without guilt. She has been vilely slandered by Mariyah out of jealous spite. She did not call you a fat, sexless pig, most deadly of insults, nor did she in any way incite the unwarranted attack upon herself. That also was Mariyah's work. Having placed these facts before you, I now give you leave to take what steps you may consider necessary to restore order and ensure justice."

"You are all-seeing and all-knowing, my Lady Fatima! What say you to ten lashes with the kurbash for this one who seeks to cause strife in the harem?"

The Lady Fatima inclined her head in assent. Abdullah clapped his hands and the guards appeared once more. An order was given, and they advanced upon Mariyah.

White to the lips, the woman began to protest, turning to Abdullah with words that had the sound of pleading. He did not relent. Julia stared, horrified, as the guards stripped Mariyah naked and threw her down across a large fat cushion. They grasped her wrists and ankles, holding her still. Abdullah strutted forward, sending the kurbash whipping through the air once, twice. Then, with a mighty effort, he brought it slashing down upon the woman's shoulders.

It was possible to cut the flesh from the bones with a kurbash; it was also possible to do no more than bring welts to the skin. The latter was Abdullah's choice. Mariyah did not cry out at the first blow, though it left her shoulders red-striped. She took the second lash, the third, each spaced evenly down her back. As the whip cut across her waist, she gave a grunt. With the next blow a shriek came from her throat. She began to writhe, jerking her legs and arms, a scream gurgling in her throat. Mercilessly, Abdullah brought the kurbash down across her buttocks, her thighs, and to the backs of her knees. When the tenth lash was laid on and he stopped, beads of sweat stood on his face, trickling to the point of his chin. He stood back, surveying his handiwork for a moment. Mariyah's flesh was not broken, but her body was marked with ten fiery red ridges of pain, and her head lolled on her neck as she sobbed brokenly into the pillow.

Abdullah gave a nod. The eunuch guards released the woman, salaamed, and went about their duties. Abdullah turned, making his obeisance to the Lady Fatima. "The deed is done," he intoned.

"It is well," the Lady Fatima replied, and she dismissed him with a brief wave of her hand.

The instant Abdullah's broad back was out of sight, the other women of the harem crowded about Mariyah. She was lifted and carried off down the second corridor to the right.

Julia watched them bear the woman away, her mind filled with distress. Aboard the Algerian felucca, Bayezid Reis had ordered forty lashes of the kurbash for Rud and O'Toole. Had they been administered? She did not know. In her weak state, shut away in her tiny cubicle, she had been set apart from the rest of the ship, with the exception of the Arab physician. She hated Rudyard Thorpe, she told herself, despised him for his betrayal, and yet she cringed at the thought of such punishment being visited upon his broad, muscular back. Forty lashes, and no one to care if the skin was marred by scars. How had he and O'Toole survived? Had they?

Behind her, the Lady Fatima spoke. "The others will care for Mariyah. If it pleases you, I would be most honored to have you accompany me to my humble quarters."

Though it was phrased as a request, Julia did not make the mistake of refusing the invitation. "The honor is mine," she replied, and followed behind the woman and her maid.

The apartment of the Lady Fatima consisted of three magnificent rooms opening out onto a private garden. Unlike the relative bareness of the other chambers of the harem, these were filled with a multitude of articles, the accumulation of a lifetime. There were the usual couches, piled high with cushions, and tiled walls. In addition, there were carved wooden screens, and arabesque window and door openings draped with damask, cloth-of-gold, and silver lace. Brass lamps chased with gold hung from the ceiling and stood upon intricately wrought stands, gold and silver vessels were clustered here and there for water, juice, oil, and ointments. There were carved chests of

276

sandalwood and ivory in sizes from the merest trinket box to enormous wardrobes higher than Julia's head. And there was the treasure—enormous tapestries sewn with gold and silver thread as well as many-hued silk, ivory elephants with gold-tipped tusks, alabaster drinking vessels and perfume jars, enamelware trays and bowls with gold and silver rims and flowing designs of birds, camels, and stylized flowers, peacocks in bronze, and statuettes of green and pink jade. In the corners were bales of silks and brocades and bundles of carpets. Scattered over a low table, as though the lady had been disturbed while counting over them, were fabulous gemstones—emeralds, diamonds, opals, pigeon's-blood rubies, jacinths, amethysts, aquamarines, and smooth, shining pearls. It was a trove of jewels fit for a king's ransom, or a queen's safety.

The serving woman moved unhurriedly to put away the gems. Her mistress seated herself upon a divan and indicated a satin cushion nearby for Julia that would place her on a slightly lower level. The older woman gave an order, probably for refreshments, then turned to Julia.

"You are bewildered," she said. "You have found yourself the object of malice for no apparent reason. You have been reviled, attacked, hurt, caught in a maelstrom of events you do not understand."

"This is so," Julia answered as the woman paused expectantly.

"It is well for you to know why you are the target of such enmity. I, the first and only surviving wife of the grand and illustrious dey of Algiers, will make the reasons known to you. Ten years ago, at the age of fourteen, Mariyah was chosen to warm the bed of the dey. She was tender and young then, and for a time she was able to fan the embers of his dying ardor. Then the times when she was called to his bed grew further and further apart. The dey of Algiers is not a young man. He nears his seventy-fourth year. The last time he sent for Mariyah was during the moon of Ramadan over three years ago. Still, in that time he has sent forth for no one else, and since Mariyah was the last to feel the thrust of his desire she has been, from that time, the reigning favorite. Having held the position for so long, both by her own efforts and by default, she now believes she has a right to it. She has forgotten that she was raised so high only by the will of her lord the dey. Your arrival was a severe shock to her. She feared that you would usurp her place. She decided to do away with you before you became a threat, or at least make you so aware of her power that you would not dare try to supplant her among the other women, regardless of the status you attained elsewhere."

Julia signified her understanding. "I have not yet expressed my gratitude for your kind intervention, O great lady."

"Do not thank me, my child. I am not immune to the soul wrenchings of jealousy. You gave me the opportunity to see a sentence carried out that I have long wished to order, that of watching stripes laid on the back of that she-dog Mariyah. Though my position as first wife of the dey cannot be taken from me, I have seen myself replaced in his affections many times. The dey married his permitted three other women, one of whom died in childbirth, one of whom was beheaded for passing letters to a former love, and one of whom went mad in the confinement of the harem and was returned to her father in her own country. There have been concubines without number, women who were favored for a night or a week, a month, or, less often, for a year. And yet none of their number has given me so much humiliation, none has deliberately made me feel so old and ugly, as Mariyah. Such a thing need not have been. In a harem there are always envy, greed, and jealous feelings. And yet there is also companionship, cooperation, and much aid and comfort from one woman to another. This is necessary because all know that the happiness and continuation of their lives depends on the whim of a single man. But I go on too much. These things you will discover for yourself in the weeks to come."

The serving woman appeared with tiny cups of thick, sweet Turkish coffee, a dish of figs, a platter of almond cakes, and a fresh blouse to replace Julia's, which had been torn by the women. Except for the grounds, which settled to the bottom of the cup, the coffee was not a great deal different from the brew Julia had known from childhood in New Orleans. She drank it with relish while the servant fussed over her scratches, cleaning them and applying a soothing salve to the deepest nail gouges before helping her into the blouse of aqua silk.

"Eat, my child," the Lady Fatima said. "You are much too thin to tempt a Mussulman. They like round curves on their women, and soft thighs to support their hard masculinity." Her expression grew thoughtful. "However, often an older man will be appalled at climbing to the top of such a mountain of flesh."

An old man of seventy-four, toothless no doubt, stooped, fumbling. Julia swallowed hard upon the sickness at the back of her throat.

"Do not be distressed," the Lady Fatima said, noting her repugnance. "The dey is not a well man. If he is capable of mounting so much as his horse, then my spies have misinformed me and should have their tongues torn out. He likes the company of women and values them for their tenderness and sensitivity as well as enjoying their beauty, but he cannot bear petty meanness or stupidity— hence Mariyah's banishment once he was unable to possess her. Occasionally he sends for me for the sake of conversation. Still, though he values what he is pleased to call my wisdom, we have long since plumbed the depths of each other's minds, and can no longer look forward to the thrill of discovery."

Julia said nothing, her mind busy with what she had been told, sifting through it for the hidden meaning she was sure was there. Was the other woman trying to tell her she had nothing to fear, or was she saying she would be expected to do mental acrobatics to amuse the dey? Something tugged at her memory, something at variance with what Lady Fatima had told her. She could not drag it to the full focus of her attention, however.

The Lady Fatima paused while she took up a fig and peeled it with care. She popped fruit into her mouth, dipped her fingers into a water bowl, and dried them on a linen cloth. Abruptly, she said, "You were not chosen by the dey."

Julia looked up quickly from her coffee cup. The memory she had unsuccessfully sought now presented itself. Two men behind a screen discussing her as though she were not there. One had been Ismael, the physician; the other had not sounded aged, far from it. "I see," she answered with a slight lift of her chin. "Then who did send me here?"

"For me to answer that, you must first understand something of the situation here. Algeria is a vassal state of the Ottoman Turkish Empire. The dey is nominated to his high position by the officers of the Turkish militia, the Janissaries, and he must divide his allegiance between them and the sultan of Constantinople. The throne is his for life. However, if he is stupid, if he displeases either faction, his life may not be long. By this you may judge the wisdom and diplomacy of the present dey, who has held the office for more than a quarter of a century. Mehemet Dey has been well loved and much respected, but he has made a great mistake in the man whom he has selected to support as his heir. Like all men who gain great power, he wishes to pass it to those of his own blood—in this case, Kemal, his grandson. At present he is directing all his energies toward this end. He ignores the fact that this young man is unworthy, that he is weak, unprincipled, and forever at the mercy of his emotions. The dey cannot be brought to see that there are other men more capable ready to hand. For instance, his own nephew, Ali Pasha."

"Forgive me," Julia said, when the woman paused. "I assume the grandson, Kemal, is also your grandson?"

"Not so. Kemal is the grandson of the dey's second wife, the woman who died in childbirth. Her son, born on that occasion, lived to sire another as fat and as greedy as both himself and his mother. If the woman had not stuffed herself until she was as round as a barrel, she might not have died. The son was also a glutton. One feast of Ramadan he consumed the better part of a whole sheep by himself. His intestines burst and he died, though not before he had gotten a son off a poor flattened slip of a slave girl. No, never say such a worthless one is a relation of mine. My children, a magnificent son and a daughter more beautiful than the moon, died in a cholera epidemic with many others in the harem. I do not champion Ali Pasha because he is of my blood either, for he is not. He is the eldest son of the only brother of the dey, a man felled by an assassin's knife. I champion him because I enjoy the intrigue, the flexing of my scant power, but most of all because he has shown himself possessed of those virtues necessary for a ruler—strength of character, an ability to inspire and lead men, and a sense of justice. If you could know him, an impossibility now that you have entered the confines of the harem, I believe you, too, would come to admire him."

"Perhaps I would," Julia agreed. "And yet, if he is all you say he is, surely he will bring himself to the attention of the Janissaries."

"Of course, but will that be enough? The will of the dey is strong not only because he is an honored ruler, but because of the love the people, and the men of the military, have for him. When he is dead they will wish to show their love and respect, and how better to do so than to follow his will and nominate Kemal as the new dey?"

"What can be done to prevent it?"

"Several things. Kemal could be exposed as the greedy fool that he is, and those nearest the dey can sing the praises of Ali Pasha. It is for this last purpose that you were chosen."

"You overwhelm me," Julia said. "I see no reason for Mehemet Dey to take an interest in me, much less come to value me to the point of listening to my counsel."

"I think you underestimate yourself. We have had good reports of you from Ismael the physician."

"I see," Julia said for lack of anything better.

"Do you? I would like to think so, for it would go far in proving Ismael right. The Arab physician, you understand, is a friend of Ali Pasha, and there is binding loyalty between them. He had occasion to travel to the

Canary Islands, there to meet a colleague who had important information to impart to him concerning the many fevers which ravage the northern coast of Africa. He took passage on the ship of Bayezid Reis, the ship which took you and your two male companions aboard. Despite your illness and the hardship through which you had passed, he was impressed with your beauty and intelligence. He knew that Ali Pasha had toyed with the idea of introducing a new favorite into his uncle's harem, had even sent out a request for unusual women in his uncle's name, but despaired of a mere physical attraction with which to snare his interest. He was intrigued by an intimation that you had known and spoken to Napoleon of France, for he knew that this man exercises a great fascination on the mind of Mehemet Dey. For these reasons, he did his utmost to heal you and assure that you would be granted an audience. So it came to pass that you were observed in your bath, and while draped and veiled, viewed by Ali Pasha. Other than an excess of modesty and pride, he had no fault to find with you."

"And so I was brought into the harem?"

The Lady Fatima inclined her head. "In due time, when you are prepared, you shall be brought to the attention of the dey, and it shall be your duty and your delight to become his consort of the mind—and all else that he may desire."

Julia, remembering Mariyah writhing under the strokes of the kurbash, recognized that there could be but one answer. "I shall do my best to be worthy of your faith and goodness."

The preparation of which the Lady Fatima had spoken included, among other things, the learning of two new languages, Moorish and Turkish. Moorish was the common language of Algiers, used in the marketplace and with the servants within the palace. Constantinople was still the heart of Islam, however, and all Moors with any pretensions to breeding or education spoke Turkish fluently. In addition, Turkish was the language employed at court and, most important, that preferred by the dey.

To make certain that Julia learned the two allied tongues as quickly as possible, an older member of the harem, a Turkish woman in her mid-thirties of ample proportions and affable disposition, was sent to be Julia's companion and share her bedchamber. Called Jawharah, she was an indefatigable talker. She was, in addition, an endless fountain of information concerning the harem, the palace, the town, and all the people who dwelled therein. Since she related all this in the two basic tongues of the Barbary Coast, Julia, with her penchant for languages, soon began to be able to understand what was going on around her and to make herself understood.

She was not surprised to discover that Mariyah was her bitter enemy. Against all logic, she blamed Julia for her beating, and whispered in corners that it was obvious that what she had suspected was true: Julia was Abdullah's spy. She had among her followers the more discontented and desperately bored of the women. Though they never dared openly attack Julia again, they made her the butt of dozens of malicious tricks. Scorpions found their way into her slippers. A pet monkey was shut up in her chest for hours, fouling and jumbling the clothing allotted to her. Walking in the garden, she was jostled into the fish pool and came up with her hair dripping green slime. On one occasion she became ill after eating a salad of palm hearts, and thereafter the woman who served the wife of the dey also served Julia.

Julia was not without her own group of followers. At first for the sake of the Lady Fatima, and then for herself alone, well over half of the women of the harem were ranged on the side of the new favorite. Though Julia had not yet been seen by the dey, this was how she was known. Her name they changed to Jullanar, after a queen in one of their favorite and most quoted books, the *Arabian Nights*. Though they did not know how or why it had come about, every woman in the harem realized that she was being made ready for the delectation of the dey, and each pitied or envied Jullanar according to her nature.

Winter came. The blinds of the harem were closed

against the coolness and blowing rain. Charcoal braziers glowed red in the center of every room. Lessons continued for Julia. She was taught how to bow to the dey, when to kiss his hand or the hem of his garment, how to ask permission to speak or to leave him, when and where to sit in his presence, making certain her head was never higher than his. There were even, should the need arise, instructions in how to enter his bed. One entered humbly from the foot, progressing toward the head by degrees and only with proper encouragement.

Jawharah, a woman of many parts, expounded to Julia on a wide range of subjects. As their friendship deepened and she grew more intimate in her discourse, she revealed to Julia that she had been sold by her father at the age of thirteen to a slave dealer who had come to her native village. The caravan in which she had been traveling toward Constantinople had been attacked. The brigands had carried the female slaves out into the wasteland, where they had raped and left them. The slave dealer had tracked down his merchandise, but finding it already damaged, he had turned the girls over to the camel drivers for the remainder of the journey. At Constantinople he had purchased the services of a physician of a certain skill who, with simple surgery, had made them new, almost impenetrable maidenheads. Lo, they were virgin once more.

Jawharah had then been sold to a rich, aged merchant. She had become his favorite concubine, having learned a few tricks from the camel drivers which served to whet his jaded appetite. Then one day, on her way to the bathhouse, she had cast her eyes upon a young and lusty soldier. Straightaway she had discovered within herself a talent for deception. Messages were passed, and one day while visiting the bazaar, she had lost herself from her serving woman and bodyguard. She enjoyed such good sport with her soldier that another time she had bribed the attendant at the bathhouse to engage her serving woman in conversation while she slipped out a side entrance. This subterfuge did not work more than once.

On the second try she was caught and her master was informed of her conduct. The merchant wielded the kurbash himself, Jawharah said, reminiscently rubbing her broad beam, and then he had sold her to the owner of a brothel.

"I suppose I was lucky he did not have me strangled, for my soldier was found dead next morning. At the brothel I was kept for special clients, men past their prime whose interest had begun to sag. My success in this area, and the gusto with which I performed, became widely known. Now, the dey of Algiers has ever been more ready to admire the beauty of a woman than to use it. For proof of my words, look about you. This is a childless harem. Granted, the dey is not a young man. Still, there are many such as he who become fathers. There has never been a large number of children to his credit, not even when I came here nearly twenty years ago. The babes sired by Mehemet Dey were conceived before he came to sit upon the throne. Six children! A paltry number when compared to the accomplishment of the sultan of Constantinople, who has planted over three hundred in the wombs of his harem. Of the six of the dey, only one reached manhood, and such a one! The dey's son was himself able to get only one child, this Kemal. They tell me the fat grandson of the dey is interested in women not at all, preferring pretty young boys. But I was telling you how I came to the palace, was I not? When Mehemet Dey came to the throne there was a brief period when he felt it important to secure his line after the cholera epidemic. The slave traders were informed of his problem, and eventually they came to me. I was then only seventeen. I received yet another maidenhead, a comical little fiction, since it was my skill that was my main attraction. Was I supposed to have brought it with me from another life, imbibed it with my mother's milk? No matter. I enjoyed a brief popularity with the dey, and then he conceived a dislike for the artificiality of the proceedings, or perhaps I was too demanding of the exalted one's strength." Jawharah gave a gusty sigh. "I was relegated to obscurity—and abstinence. The last, my dear, is the most difficult of all to bear, as you will discover."

Although the nominal purpose of Jawharah's rambling story was to acquaint Julia with her life, it soon became apparent that there was a much more subtle reason behind it. As the woman grew more garrulous, Julia began to suspect that Jawharah had been ordered to impart to the new favorite the secrets of her skill. The suspicion became a certainty when one afternoon she and Jawharah, with one or two of the more favored women of their faction, were escorted to a small chamber outside the harem. Its only article of furniture was a single divan. It had no windows, though set into one side was a pierced wooden screen giving access to the next room. There was no light once the door had been closed behind them. The only illumination came through the screen from a lamp burning in the next chamber. Seated on the divan, they were able to see without hindrance through the screen into the lighted room.

At first, there was nothing to observe except a serving girl setting out sweetmeats and mint tea before a rather commonplace damask-draped couch. The girl went away and all was quiet.

A man entered, dressed in the garb of a soldier. Removing his clothing, he lay down upon the couch. If he was aware of the women behind the screen, he gave no sign. Certainly the females of the harem made not a sound as they devoured him with glistening eyes. The door into the inner room opened, and a woman stepped inside. As she moved, smiling, toward the man on the couch, Jawharah caught Julia's wide-eyed look and smiled at her in the dimness.

The woman began to disrobe. She was not a serving girl, that much was obvious from the richness of her barracan and the cosmetics that highlighted her face, bringing the eyes and rich red mouth into prominence. She was Moorish, Julia thought, and in all probability she was a courtesan from one of the houses near the harbor. The removal of her clothing revealed breasts that had been rouged to subtly alter their shape and color so that they resembled ripe pomegranates. Her black hair was long, looped back from her face by a fillet of pearls which narrowed to hold a single teardrop in the center of her forehead. Elsewhere, she was smooth-shaven, without a single hair to mar the perfection of her skin. Smiling at the soldier like a cat surveying a bowl of cream, she took the initiative. No doubt she was an expert at her art; at least it appeared she must be from the enjoyment of the soldier in her performance.

Julia grew warm with embarrassment. She would have liked to leap to her feet and flee the room, but outside the door stood the ever-present guard. She would not be allowed to make her way alone back through the palace to the harem. She would have to wait for the others.

Leaning close, Jawharah spoke in her ear. "Watch and learn, Jullanar."

Julia sent her a small smile. She found herself thinking of the convent school she had attended as a young girl. Her existence now, surrounded by females, was similar to the way it had been then. And yet different, oh so different! What would the good nuns have to say if they could see her now? What would her aunts and cousins think? Would they understand that she had no choice?

She did not sleep well that night. For long hours she tossed and turned upon her couch. When at last she found oblivion, she dreamed of Rud. Once more she was in his arms. His lips were warm on her mouth and throat. He whispered in her ear as they moved together, their bodies joined. And then she was alone, listening to his footsteps as he walked away from her. She awoke with tears streaming from the corners of her eyes.

Staring into the dark of the midnight hour, she admitted to herself that in at least one particular Jawharah was right. Celibacy was not going to be easy.

When she had first come to the harem she had been amazed that any woman would risk death in order to conduct a liaison with a lover from behind its high walls. After months of such a life, she was no longer so ready to condemn them as fools. What was life behind the curtain of purdah except a living death? No wonder the women were fat and vain and vindictive. They had nothing else to do except eat and care for their looks and plot among themselves to relieve the numbing boredom. An excursion such as the one they had indulged in the evening before could only heighten their sense of being cut off from life. Certainly there were interests they could pursue. Some of the women did needlework, made tapestry, painted portraits of each other and scenes remembered from the times before they were shut away behind walls as the plaything of a man who had outgrown such toys. Still, it was such a waste of lives, of emotions and intelligence. No, it was no wonder they courted danger. The excitement of it proved they were alive. Snatching at brief moments of happiness had to be better than wasting away and discovering one day that their lives were over and done. Wasn't the risk of death better than the solution of one woman who, discovering that menopause was upon her and knowing she would never have a child, had hanged herself in her cubicle, and been found dangling from the brass lamp chain by a silk scarf?

The bright sun of morning brought a lightening of her mood. The winter was turning into spring. The blinds could be thrown open once more, and it was possible to enjoy the garden. Jawharah, perhaps disturbed by Julia's wakefulness, rose earlier than was her usual habit. She ordered their breakfast served in a warm corner of the garden where peach trees in blossom were espaliered against the stone wall.

"You are pensive this day," the woman said to Julia when they were settled. "Perhaps you think of your lover?"

It had been impossible to keep secret from the Turkish woman the fact that she was not a virgin, though Julia had steadfastly refused to give the name of the man, saying only that he was dead. Julia smiled and shook her head in answer now.

"It would not be unusual. Last evening brought back many memories for me." Jawharah sighed, then went on. "Are you homesick, then, pining for news of people you have known? If so, then you may be glad to hear that one of the men who was captured with you has prospered."

Julia took a wheat cake from the plate before them. Breaking it into pieces, she scattered the crumbs for the iridescent gray doves and the brilliant and lordly peacocks which had come to investigate their repast. Was it a coincidence that Jawharah had mentioned a lover and one of the men she had been captured with in practically the same breath?

"Oh?"

" 'Twas the Frankistani captain of your ship which sank. He was made an officer under Bayezid Reis and has become greatly respected. With his knowledge of ships, he modified the sails and rigging of the Algerian felucca so that it flew like the wind. In recognition of his skill, Bayezid Reis allowed him to command the ship during battle. Between them, they have captured many prizes, though curiously all of them are French. So many Frenchmen have been brought as slaves for the dey that the French consul here in Algiers has protested, demanding to know if the dey has launched an undeclared war against his country. Mehemet Dey was so pleased with the efforts of the slave captain that he sent a personal commendation to the man, and requested that he be transferred to his personal service. Though reluctant, Bayezid Reis had no choice except to agree. Since that time, this man has occupied himself in improving the remaining ships of the dey's navy. He has also proposed building a new ship for the Exalted One's greater glory. The dey has agreed, and now the slave has no labor except to see that the ship is completed. Already they say that the ship is touched with *baraka,* the magic of the jinn, so that it will skim along on air like the flying horse made famous by Scheherazade."

"Indeed?" Julia said. "It must be a miraculous ship, then."

"This is so, and it will be captained by no ordinary man, but by Ali Pasha, the nephew of the dey himself. 'Tis said the infidel slave who gave the ship its magic has become the friend of Ali Pasha, and is seen everywhere with him. They ride, they hunt, and Ali Pasha has even been known to invite the unbeliever to partake of meals with him in his private *gulphor,* or visiting chamber, where important guests are received. It may be that soon your countryman will be invited to become a Mussulman and be no longer a slave."

"It is good," Julia said, her careful words in the unfamiliar language giving away nothing of the feeling that burgeoned inside her. She had not allowed herself to think too much of what might have been happening to Rud and O'Toole. Once, when she had traversed the corridors of the palace with the Lady Fatima on their way to the library of the dey, she had glanced out a window to see a long line of slaves pulling an enormous block of marble toward a ship in the harbor. The slaves had been scrawny caricatures of men with long hair and beards, and wasted, muscle-corded bodies. A rusty iron band had been clamped about their waists, with chains attached, running to bands about their ankles. Their backs had been masses of scars overlaid with fresh red stripes from the kurbash in the hand of the overseer who stood to one side. The marble quarry called the Sepulcher of Dry Bones was the fate of large numbers of Christians sold into slavery. It was more dreaded than the galleys, since, as suggested by its name, few returned from there.

"Have you nothing more to say? I thought you would be happy."

"I am, of course," she said, smiling a little, but not too much. "But what of the other man, whose name was O'Toole? Have you no news of him?"

"My informant thought he was set to manning an oar in Bayezid Reis' ship. It may be, however, that his fortune has improved along with that of his friend. Such can happen sometimes when a man achieves a degree of influence."

"Still, they remain slaves, both of them?"

Jawharah nodded. "No doubt it is their kismet, just as it is ours to languish here in luxury."

Julia thanked the other woman for taking the time to learn about her companions in disaster. Picking up her coffee cup, she let her gaze rest on the pink petals of shattered blossoms that lay upon the mosaic-tiled walk before them. Kismet. She had tried to find content in the oriental concept of fatalism. At times she seemed to succeed. At others, her very soul rose up in protest at bowing to what was, in Islam, a male idea of fate that served admirably to keep women, slaves, and the poor satisfied with their lot. In her country fate was female; Lady Luck, Dame Good Fortune. It could be good or bad or fickle, but more than anything else, it could change. Oh, how much she wished for a change!

Chapter Fifteen

"Come, Jullanar, put on your veil and your barracan. Mehemet Dey is holding court, and we are invited to view the audience. Hurry, for you know how impatient is the Lady Fatima, and we do not want to be left behind!"

Jawharah lifted up the lid of the clothing chest and tossed a barracan of cream-colored silk edged in gold embroidery in a Greek-key design to Julia, along with a cream-colored veil. For herself, she drew out purple raiment. To Julia's eyes, it made the other woman look like a vat of wine, but since Muslims did not foul their lips with such a drink, she supposed Jawharah would have no such association. Throwing the book she was reading aside, she took up the barracan, settling the semitransparent folds around her. The veil she fastened across her face, holding it in place by the simple expedient of pinning it, with her gold bee, to the gold fillet which held her hair in place. The bee rested on her temple for an unusual effect that had been much exclaimed over by the other women.

This was not the first audience she had been privileged to attend. She had been taken to view the court by the Lady Fatima once before, but the grand vizer had been presiding and there had been little of interest taking place. The matters brought before the court had been simple cases of petty theft and disputes over property. Judging from the tone of Jawharah's voice, today would be different.

292

Leaving the harem, the ladies carried in their hands ornate painted fans shaped like teardrops with curved tails and with long, silk-tasseled fly whisks attached. The audience chamber, at the top of five flights of winding stairs, would be far from cool. Flanked by guards, they hurried along through endless passageways and up curving steps from one level to another, climbing ever higher. They passed through a maze of richly appointed rooms and entered at last a small, grille-enclosed balcony above the audience chamber that was not unlike a box at the theater.

The room below was dim, lit only by a series of small windows set high in the walls and covered by iron grilles of the same pattern as the one that concealed their viewing balcony. Perfume censers allowed a soft haze of smoke to drift upward, further obscuring their sight. They saw first the flash of jewels and the sheen of fine fabrics before they could make out the faces of the resplendent Moors and Turks. The blond hair and rich dress of Mamelukes made themselves apparent before the shining ebony skin of Ethiopian slaves could be made out.

Facing this throng, squatting upon a cushioned divan like an American Indian before his campfire, was the dey of Algiers. He sat upright with his back stiff and his wrists resting on his knees. He was dressed in a jacket of peacock brocade slashed to reveal an apricot undergarment, which in turn parted to show orange silk pantaloons. The turban on his head was of muslin encircled by a blue sash. Dark, all-seeing eyes were set in his stern face. His beard was long and white, curling down his chest. At his side protruded the handle of a golden scimitar, its scabbard set with a blaze of jewels that flung their rainbows of light through the gloom to dance upon the silk and satin clothing of the courtiers.

No sooner had they seated themselves on the divans set for their comfort than the harsh sound of a man's scream rang out. Julia started, swinging to look at Jawharah.

"There is no need for alarm, I think," the woman said. "It appears that a man has been sentenced to have his

293

right hand cut off for theft. Since a good Muslim uses his left hand for all bodily functions, leaving his right, pure and clean, with which to feed himself, it is a terrible punishment, though not an extraordinary one."

Julia could not restrain a shudder. She stared at the implacable face of the old man sitting on the dais in the room beneath her, the first time she had ever seen the man who was her master, with something like dread in her eyes.

When the struggling criminal had been led out, another man stepped forward. He bowed and kissed the hand of the dey. "The French consul," Jawharah whispered.

Julia nodded, her gaze fastened on the tailored coat of dark blue he wore with straight-legged pantaloons and polished half-boots. She was able to follow much of what passed between the representative of France and the dey of Algiers. The Frenchman, as Jawharah had said, was incensed at the attacks of the Algerian navy upon the ships of his country. The dey commiserated with him, while blandly denying any knowledge of the incidents, placing the blame on the Barbary pirates, whom he insisted were a faction beyond his control. The consul, unable to call him a liar to his face without endangering continued diplomatic relations between the two countries, made veiled threats of war. The dey deplored the possibility with courtly gestures and protestations of friendship.

Losing interest in the flowery, hard-to-follow phrases, Julia allowed her attention to drift to the men ranged about the chamber once more. Abruptly she gave a strangled gasp, sitting forward on the edge of her seat.

"What is it, Jullanar?" the Lady Fatima asked sharply.

It was a moment before Julia could find her tongue. "That man, there beside the Mameluke in bronze silk."

"The Frankistani?"

"Yes, that's the one."

"It is said he was found by Bayezid Reis floating in the sea, clinging to a few scraps of wood after a shipwreck. He had upon him papers which identified him as a man of importance connected in some way with the king of France. Therefore, when he was brought into port, word of his capture was brought to the French consul, who then paid a substantial ransom for his release. It was, according to all accounts, a profitable transaction both for Bayezid Reis and for the coffers of the dey. This man, in exchange for a promise of free range of the ship and other privileges, is said to have informed Bayezid Reis of the presence in the waters where he was found of a boat containing three other Christians, one of them a woman who would make an admirable harem slave."

As Julia listened to the expressionless voice of the older woman, she stared at the familiar face of the man below, her lips curling. "Marcel de Gruys," she said, without realizing that she had spoken the name aloud.

"Yes, I believe that is how he is called," the Lady Fatima answered composedly.

"I wonder why he has not left Algiers?"

"Who can say? He is employed at the moment by the consulate. Perhaps they see a way to use his influence with the king of France to inform him of the dangers in these waters to French shipping? Or possibly, since he is such an opportunist, he sees some other profit to be made from staying. He has been seen lately in the company of Kemal. One wonders if the grandson of the dey grows tired of waiting for the throne to be vacated and begins to treat with those who might have reason to have a grudge against the present ruler of Algiers."

Jawharah nodded as the Lady Fatima finished speaking. Leaning across Julia, she said, "It would also be of interest to know if Ali Pasha is aware of this possible alliance between the French consul and Kemal." She paused, then grimaced as she tilted her head toward a man just entering the chamber below them. "Speak of an afreet and you hear the whip of his pinions!"

"Kemal?" Julia asked.

"None other," Jawharah replied.

He was a stout beast of a man, fatter even than Abdullah, although his corpulence had the hard look of congealed lard. His muslin turban was adorned by an enormous ruby, which supported a trio of aigrette plumes that nodded at his very movement. His beard, reaching nearly to his small, cruel eyes, was frizzed into a bush, and the ends of his mustache curled into ringlets. He wore a tunic of lilac silk fastened down the front with gold-braid frogs and slashed to reveal an undergarment of cloth-of-gold. His pantaloons were composed of yard upon yard of billowing rose satin. Rings covered his stubby fingers, while a number of pearl and ruby brooches had been pinned to his rotund chest. On either side of him walked a beautiful boy of perhaps fourteen or fifteen years dressed in identical garments with the exception of the turban. Being Christian, they were denied this Muslim headpiece and wore instead linen headscarfs held in place by rolled silk ropes.

At a gesture from the dey a cushion was brought forth and placed on a slightly lower level than the older man's dais. Kemal saluted the hand of his grandfather and with an effort lowered himself to the floor to take the place of honor. One of his boys seated himself at his feet, while the other stood to one side plying a fan of ostrich plumes. By leaning forward, Mehemet Dey could converse with his grandson, and he did so despite the growing anger of the French consul at being virtually ignored.

"What can be his purpose in coming here?" Jawharah asked.

"Only to show his interest in the governing process and to remind those present that it is the will of his grandfather that he be raised one step higher when Allah, whose name be exalted, condescends to remove Mehemet Dey to paradise."

Julia barely heard the question or its reply. With a cold feeling in the pit of her stomach, she watched in disbelief as Kemal and Marcel de Gruys acknowledged each other across the width of the audience chamber.

When the court came to an end, the three women left the viewing balcony and descended a flight of stairs to bring them to the level of the audience chamber. Trailing their guards, they traversed a series of rooms and started down a long hallway which led toward yet more stairs. Catching sight of a group of men ahead of them, they lowered their eyes and adjusted their veils, preparing to brush past them. As they drew even, the guards came to a halt. A voice spoke.

"Well met, my wife Fatima."

Glancing up, they beheld the dey. The Lady Fatima salaamed deeply, and Julia and Jawharah copied the obeisance exactly. "Well met, indeed, O Prince of the Faithful and Dispenser of Justice," his wife declared. "I kiss the ground before your feet. My heart rejoices to see you so well."

A smile lit the ascetic face of the dey. "Your beauty does not wane, nor does your dignity, O Fatima, daughter of the desert. It is always a pleasure to greet you when you have long been from my sight. You have the rare ability to make me believe you mean your honeyed phrases."

"May my tongue wither if I ever speak other than the truth in your hearing, my master."

The dey accepted the declaration with a slight inclination of his head. "It is said you have taken a protégée, a young woman whom you have caused to be taught all you know of the ways of men and the world," he said, never once glancing in Julia's direction. "It is rumored that she is an apt pupil such as must reflect honor upon her mentor."

"By the will of Allah, this is true, O Ruler of the Age."

"And is it true also that this incomparable one, who may stimulate a man's mental powers as well as his physical senses, has sat at the feet of the ruler of the west known as Napoleon?"

"Verily it is so, master of my heart."

"It comes to me that I would give myself the pleasure of gazing upon such a paragon," the dey said, looking only at his wife. "I request that you will order all that she may be made ready to await my command this evening."

"It shall be done, even as the least of your desires, my master."

A signal granted them the permission to pass on. When they were alone once more in the harem, Jawharah cried out in exultation. "It is as has been set forth in the

Arabian Nights. He has loved her from hearing her qualities described, for sometimes the ear loves before the eye!"

"He is intrigued," the Lady Fatima agreed in a dry tone. "How could he not be when I have had her virtues extolled to him without ceasing? But it will be the task of Jullanar to make him love her. If she succeeds she may count herself most fortunate among women." Turning, the first wife of the dey left them without a backward glance.

The preparations for the long-awaited summons began in the late afternoon. Once more Julia underwent the ritual of the bath. Jawharah accompanied her, and while Julia was tended by the slave girls, the woman kept up a running commentary of advice and admonition. Once more the scent of damask roses filled the air. It was soaped into her hair and steeped into her body by the hot water, and then, following the tepid pool, it was massaged into her skin in the form of scented oil. Julia thought that never in her life had she been so clean from crown to heel, never had her skin been such smooth perfection, never her brows so perfectly arched, her hair so luxuriant, like a gold curtain falling past her waist, or her almond-shaped nails so rosily immaculate. Even her teeth had been cleaned and her breath freshened with crushed mint.

Her costume, chosen by the Lady Fatima for the occasion, included a short blouse and pantaloons of emerald silk covered by a barracan of softest mint green edged with gold braiding. With it went a small, close-fitting cap of emerald velvet braided in gold, and a veil of amber silk that matched her eyes.

Returning to the common room of the harem, she ran the gauntlet of spiteful comments and vicious stares. "You have made yourself ready for nothing," Mariyah called out in a voice made shrill with hate and ill-will. "He will forget you as soon as you have left his sight!"

As night fell and stars began to appear in the black arch above the garden, it looked for a time as if Mariyah had the right of it. No summons came, though the time of the evening repast came and went. Since it was thought that the dey might wish her to partake of his dinner with him, she did not dare eat for fear of offending him by being unable to grant his wish. She grew so weak from hunger that she felt faintly sick, or at least that was the excuse she gave herself for the illness that hovered at the back of her throat. She did not like to admit that it was fear that had unsettled her. Despite the months she had spent in the harem, she could not understand the convoluted oriental mind. She could not come to terms with people who accepted the total control of their lives and happiness as though it were a God-given right. It was demoralizing to realize that around her were any number of persons who could smile on her one moment and order her whipped, tortured, or killed the next, all without an apparent qualm. She could not bring herself to trust them, and yet she had no choice. She was in their hands.

A serving woman pushed through the curtain of her chamber with its clashing beads. Julia turned from the window casement. The woman bowed low. "Abdullah awaits," she said.

The time had come. A flush of mingled alarm and triumph mounted to Julia's face. Still, it was with firm steps and a high head that she followed the woman into the communal chamber. As an indication of her sudden change in status, Abdullah salaamed as she came into view. Jawharah, having taken her meal with the others in order not to tempt Julia's will too much, now came forward with a happy smile to straighten Julia's veil and place the folds of her barracan more perfectly about her. "Allah go with you," the woman whispered. "And for my sake, smile!" Though Julia looked around for the Lady Fatima, she was nowhere in sight. Making an effort to follow Jawharah's sound advice, she moved beside Abdullah from the room.

Once more they traversed the endless hallways of the palace. They crossed moonlit courtyards where purple shadows stirred and whispered beneath the colonnades. It was that that there were more than a thousand rooms in the palace, and of that number, fully half opened out onto either a courtyard or a garden to provide the cool circulation of air. Of the doors of these many chambers, Julia thought several hundred must have guards posted before them, enormous turbaned figures with curved scimitars in their belts, standing like painted statues in the dim corridors.

At last they approached a massive door of carved cedar. It was guarded by sentries, who came to attention and drew their weapons at the sound of footsteps. Recognizing Abdullah, they relaxed, their eyes passing over Julia as if she were invisible.

Beyond the huge doors was a great vaulted hall, its spangled floor sweeping to a broad-based marble stair with a gold balustrade. At intervals up the staircase were candelabra of spiraled silver holding slim, steadily burning tapers. From the top of the stairs, the same candelabra could be seen stretching down a long marble hallway, the numbers of candles they held multiplying into the hundreds.

The guarded doors of the dey's private chambers were opened by a dwarf who could barely reach the handle. There were several such small people about the palace, for they were considered to have *baraka,* or good magic, by the Turks. This particular little man was called Basim, and his influence with the dey was reputed to be great. He was a Moor and wore Muslim dress, had an Egyptian-style beard, and had the saddest eyes Julia had ever seen in a human face.

Basim dismissed Abdullah with a bow faintly ironic in its deep respect, then closed the door upon the eunuch. "If you will come this way," he said to Julia, and started off at a swift pace, not even looking back to see that she followed.

The dey sat directly underneath the light of a glowing double-spouted lamp. A large volume was open across his knees. He looked up as Julia entered behind Basim. She salaamed. He closed the book and extended his hand for her to kiss.

"You may serve us, Basim," the dey said, and he

touched a velvet pillow beside his divan to signify his wish that Julia seat herself.

The dwarf brought forth a table and set it with all manner of rich dishes. As the covers were removed, an appetizing steam rose which caused Julia's mouth to water. Swallowing, she looked away, trying to appear unconcerned.

"You may go," the dey told Basim when he had finished. As the door closed behind the dwarf, a small silence fell. Julia glanced at the dey to find him smiling with kindliness upon her, and also with a hint of understanding.

"Will you remove your veil, or must I be treated like a stranger who has no right to view your face?"

Julia complied with his wish, striving to give the gesture the smiling grace that she had been taught.

"How are you called?" Mehemet Dey inquired.

"I have been given the name of Jullanar, effendi," she answered.

"You have great beauty, Jullanar, to rival that of Kobah, the evening star. Since you have come to me in the waning of my days, I shall call you by that most precious name."

"It shall be as you wish, O Great Ruler." The flattering title of respect did not come easily to Julia's lips. She tried to think of it as being much like the title of "sir" tacked onto each sentence uttered to a superior officer by a soldier or a sailor; a formality, nothing more. She hoped she would be able to remember to add it when she spoke.

A faintly cynical expression crossed his face at her reply, but he did not comment. "Will you remove your outer garment also, or is it too cool?"

Despite the sea breeze lifting the thin curtains at the windows, the night was far from cool. Julia recognized the suggestion for what it was, exquisite politeness designed to give her an excuse to retain her barracan if removing it would embarrass her, and also a subtle hint that he had no intent to ravish her upon the spot. Taking advantage of such an excuse would have been cowardly. She slipped the garment from her shoulders and placed it to one side.

Receiving permission, Julia poured mint tea and presented it to the dey. He accepted it graciously, then with a sparkle in his eyes, signaled his wish that she serve herself also, joining him in the meal rather than waiting until he had finished. As she complied, Julia flung him a look of interest. He was not at all the flint-hard monarch she had expected after witnessing his summary justice that afternoon. He had a sense of humor and a quick, intuitive understanding. In addition, there was a sensitivity lying in his dark eyes that was at variance with everything she had heard or been led to expect.

"You do not ask permission to speak," he said, bearing her inspection with equanimity. "Do you have no conversation, then, with which to amuse me?"

He spoke without looking at her, but Julia did not make the mistake of thinking that he was unaware of her start of surprise.

"Certainly, effendi," she said, carefully choosing her words in the elegant Turkish of the court. "I thought only that you might like to enjoy your meal without disturbance."

"I was under the impression that the Frankistani of a certain class believe that conversation is an aid to digestion."

"It is so, effendi. Are you interested in the customs of the Frankistani?"

"I will allow that I have a certain curiosity. It may even be that such knowledge would be of use to me should our dealings with the west increase." He gave a nod. "You may speak to me of your people."

"To begin with, the people whom you call the Frankistani belong to many nations that are as different from each other as an Arab is different from a Tartar. My own country is young in years, but it is large and will grow greater as time passes. It is called America."

"Ah, yes. We have had some experience of Americans on the Barbary Coast."

He was referring, of course, to the contretemps between the United States and the Barbary state of Tripoli. In the early part of the century, the Barbary Pirates had captured the U.S.S. *Philadelphia* with her officers and three hundred crewmen. The United States marines, in an effort to free the men and retrieve the ship, had landed at the capital of Tripoli. Much of the town had been destroyed and the ship burned, since it could not be saved. A few men had been rescued, but most had languished as slaves until the end of the war in 1805. Julia hesitated, wondering if, in spite of the term the dey had used to describe the people of the west, he was better informed concerning it than she had first believed. His next words confirmed it.

"But knowledge of this sort I can acquire elsewhere. Tell me where you lived, and how. I understand your father was a man of property who kept many slaves?"

His request was not a difficult one to grant. As she talked, Julia saw him smile more than once and shake his head a number of times in disbelief. He appeared to find the customs of courtship and marriage extremely puzzling.

"The young woman is allowed to speak to the man she is to marry, to decide for herself if she wishes the marriage?"

"As long as the suitor is deemed acceptable by her parents, yes. There may be some cases where pressure is brought to bear upon the girl if the match is particularly advantageous, but usually the parents of the couple wish for their happiness and abide by their choice."

"And you are quite certain this is the only marriage the young man is allowed, in all his life?"

"For those of my faith, this is so, effendi. Only death can dissolve the marriage. However, there is another religion which allows a marriage to be terminated in the case of adultery or great dishonor. This happens very rarely."

"What if the man and woman discover they dislike each other? What if there is no heir?"

"It cannot be helped, effendi."

"What if there is a great surplus of females due to the ravages of war among the men of your country?"

"The women must remain spinsters, effendi."

"This is not sensible. We arrange matters better in Islam. A Muslim may have four wives. In this way, all women are given the protection of a man. In addition, if one wife is barren, there is always the chance of an heir with another."

"That only holds true if it is the woman's fault that there is no child. If the man is at fault, then he has in his harem four or more barren women with wasted lives, instead of only one," Julia said.

"That is unimportant."

"I'm sure it is, to the Muslim husband!"

He stared at her, his eyes dark with mingled anger and amazement, as if he had reached out to pet a kitten and it had slashed him with its claws.

Realizing what she had done, Julia flushed. "I crave pardon, O Ruler of the Time. I meant no disrespect." She hardly dared look at him, but sat waiting for him to raise his voice for Basim to turn her over to Abdullah for punishment.

He did not do so. "The women would be taken care of, kept from harm, served, fed, wrapped in luxury," he said at last. "They would have security from poverty or injury. What more can they want?"

Julia pressed her lips together, reluctant to antagonize him further.

"Well?"

"Freedom. They could want freedom. The right to come and go as they pleased without having to answer to a guard, like prisoners, effendi."

"The guard is there for their protection."

"Then why does he have the right to punish them, O illustrious dey?"

"Order must be maintained."

"No doubt, given the frayed tempers and overwrought nerves of the women, caused by their confinement—effendi."

304

"A high emotional state is natural to women," he declared.

"How can you presume to judge, never having seen women outside of purdah, O Prince of the Faithful?"

"Are they so different in your country, then?"

Julia could not, in all honesty, answer that question with an unqualified affirmative. "Some are," she temporized, "but some are not, primarily because they are just as confined by their husbands, their children, and their duties as are the ladies of your harem."

He nodded slowly. "This is the fate of women. Why should it distress them? Why can they not accept it and be calm and happy?"

"While it may be their fate to bear children, it is not the nature of any human being or animal to accept confinement calmly and happily. It doesn't matter whether confinement is effected by ornate iron grilles or by the tentacles of laws made by men."

"Is this why you have never married, then? Because you feared to lose your freedom?"

This was dangerous ground. Julia made her answer with care. "Not entirely, for I realize that it is possible for a woman to fashion her own freedom, even within the limitations of marriage. I was happy with my father, making a home for him, caring for our people, and I had found no man with whom I was willing to live, no man whose children I was willing to bear."

"And when your father died, did nothing change?"

It was an effort for Julia, thinking of the child she had lost, to bring her thoughts to bear. "There was not an immediate change," she denied, carefully blanking images of Rud aboard the *Sea Jade* from her memory. "I continued the journey my father and I had begun, spoke to Napoleon on St. Helena as he wished. Much would have been altered when I returned to New Orleans, however. I suppose I would have gone to live with relatives, or sought refuge in marriage if I could have found a man who would take a dowerless bride."

"Ah, yes, the Emperor Napoleon," the dey said, losing

interest in her background as she had hoped he would at the mention of this man in whom he had expressed an interest. "I have followed the career of this ruler with much closeness. You spoke at length with him, I think."

"Yes, that was my good fortune, O Ruler of the Age," she answered, remembering to use his title once more. It did not seem wise to disappoint the dey in this particular. If she was to discuss the emperor with any degree of believability, she must admit to a lengthy acquaintance and hope that it would be assumed it had taken place during the visit to St. Helena. What a claim she might have had to his attention if she could have revealed the true events of Napoleon's last days! That could not be, even to assure herself of the place as favorite. History, the emperor had been fond of saying, was a lie agreed upon. It had been his will that history show he died a martyr upon the island of St. Helena. This was to be his final victory against the hated English, and she could not, would not, jeopardize it.

"Great men are a rarity. They occur seldom, perhaps no more than one or two in every century."

"This is so, effendi," Julia said in formal agreement.

"I would have been honored to have conversed with this man who commanded great armies, deploying them with greater skill than any man since Alexander the Macedonian, a man who demanded other kings to pay him homage, and yet one who was able to govern with the cunning and wisdom of Solomon the Wise, son of David. Since I cannot speak to him I would have you tell me what you can."

They talked deeply and long. Julia drew upon the opinions and thoughts revealed to her in the days when she and Napoleon Bonaparte had strolled the decks of a flying ship, and the times when she had, at the emperor's request, sat writing down his views while he paced up and down before her. She managed to make satisfactory answers to most of the questions put by the dey. She had not realized herself the extent and range of the subjects which she had discussed with Napoleon. History had been almost a mania with him. The great military campaigns of ancient times had been as familiar to him as his own. He knew of the lives, times, and contributions of the Greek and Roman philosophers. Law had been another fascination. He had considered that his Napoleonic Code would stand as the most lasting memorial of his reign in France. In it he had ended for all time the practice of great estates being passed to a single, firstborn heir, and he had made it impossible for a widow and her children to be disinherited, providing for fair and equal succession to property. But science had been his greatest love, and he had often said that if he had not been forced into the traditional life of a soldier he would have liked to devote his life to an exploration of that branch of knowledge.

The dey shook his head when they came at last to an end of Julia's memories. "To have accomplished so much in such a short time! He must have been an indefatigable worker."

"Indeed he was, effendi. He seldom slept more than four or five hours in a night. He was up at dawn and worked well into the dark hours. Sometimes he would rise at three in the morning, summon his secretary, and dictate until first light."

"Ah, such industry fatigues me merely to think of it. I will seek my couch now, Kobah, my bringer of delight. You have given me great pleasure such as I would repeat another day. You will await my summons on the morrow."

"It shall be as you desire, O illustrious dey," she replied.

A bell was rung for Basim, and a short time later Julia found herself back in her chamber in the harem. As she laid herself down upon her couch alone, she gave a trembling sigh of weariness, and of gratitude that the ordeal was behind her. She would not think about tomorrow, or the next day, or all the days that must follow.

Chapter

Sixteen

The hot winds of summer swirled about the palace, making uncomfortable eddies in the suffocating heat, stirring up the smells of hot stone, decay, and camel dung. They evaporated the water in fountains of the gardens, withered the roses, lilies, and tuberoses, set the palms to a constant dry rattling, and made the flies swarm. They blew up sudden squalls of rain that fell hissing on the hot stone floors of the courts and gardens. Gradually, they died away, leaving the dull lethargy of autumn.

Except on the occasions when the dey bestirred himself to go hunting for wild boar and desert lions, Julia dined in his presence and spent several hours each evening at his side. Much of the time they talked, the dey finding amusement in her opinions and ideas. Julia sometimes thought it was as though a pet monkey had been trained to speak. Often as the elderly man listened he would caress her hair, running the silken strands through his dry fingers, or he would toy with her hands, taking pleasure from her presence beside him without attending to what she said. At times they played chess, a nerve-wracking occupation for Julia since she had been warned that she must never defeat the dey, though she still had to give a good enough accounting of herself so that he did not become bored with the game. One day, inadvertently, she left a bishop standing so that his king was placed in check. She saw her mistake the moment it was done, but

308

she could not correct it without drawing attention to the error. With wide eyes, she stared at him, hoping he would not notice. It was a futile hope.

"Ah!" he cried, clapping his hands to his knees, his bright black eyes searching the board for some route of escape. The silence drew out between them. "Kobah!" he exclaimed, and reaching across the board, placed his hands on her shoulders and drew her toward him. His lips touched hers in a light, dry kiss. "Star of great beauty, I accept with gratitude the gift of your trust, for I now have the satisfaction of knowing you do not fear me!"

It was true. Though she did not like to kindle his anger, Julia was no longer frightened that he would wreak some terrible vengeance upon her for disagreeing with him. She thought that he enjoyed their arguments, though he never quite lost the look of surprise when she failed to applaud his pronouncements. She often witnessed harsh judgments when he held court, which he commanded her to attend so that they might later discuss the cases. Nevertheless, she had come to the conclusion that he was not a cruel man. Like the Emperor Napoleon, he considered that quick and severe punishment acted as a deterrent to crime. He believed in the example set to warn a convicted felon's fellows. If an innocent man was sometimes caught in the net of the law, it could not be helped. A single man did not count. The object was the greatest good for the largest number.

The dey wanted to remove Julia from the harem and place her in private apartments with her own retinue of servants. On the advice of the Lady Fatima, Julia pleaded to be allowed to remain with the other women. She was just as happy herself not to be so honored. There was no way of knowing how long the interest of the dey would last. He might grow bored with her within a week or a month. She might only begin to be settled in the private apartments before she would be sent ignominiously back to the common room. So far removed from the harem, she would not be able to enjoy the company of Jawharah as often as she would like. During the daylight hours, when the dey was involved with the business of ruling

Algeria, she would be left to her own devices. There could be only so much time spent in eating, bathing, and dressing. What would she do then to entertain herself and keep her servants busy?

Reluctantly, the dey had acceded to her wishes. Foiled of conferring his recognition and sign of favor upon her in one way, he simply chose another. He inundated her with gifts. Her chamber bid fair to becoming as crowded with beautiful and precious things as the cave of the fortunate Ali Baba—or the apartments of the Lady Fatima. So many jewels were presented to her, so many rich fabrics draped about her, that she began to suspect that Mehemet Dey would not be displeased if it became reputed in the city that he had taken more than a mental joy of his new white harem slave.

Slowly it came to Julia's notice that she was being treated to an ever increasing degree of deference. The women of the harem, especially those who had slighted her before, began to make gestures of friendship, complimenting her appearance and soliciting her opinion on everything from the weather to the change of a hair style. Even Mariyah ceased to be openly harassing, withdrawing into sullen resentment. Servants in all parts of the palace smiled upon her and moved with quickness to do her bidding. Basim the dwarf began to confer with her as an equal, explaining the likes and dislikes of their master and enlisting her aid in persuading him to have a care for his health. In the corridors of the palace, the courtiers and hangers-on always moved at once from her path, then stood watching her progress from the corners of sly, inquisitive eyes. In this manner she realized that she had become the favorite of the dey in actuality as well as in name.

It was Jawharah who confirmed this transition for her, however. The Turkish woman claimed that the rank of the Lady of the Gold Bee was acknowledged not only in the palace, but also in the town. There, her beauty, her beneficial effect upon Mehemet Dey, the fact that she did not always bow meekly to his will, and his great indulgence of her were known as well. In zestful recognition of what they saw as his infatuation, she had begun to be known in the streets of Algiers as Jullanar, the Keeper of the Honey.

The only person who refused to acknowledge Julia's improved status was the Lady Fatima. The wife of the dey retreated behind a cold hauteur, leaving Julia to the unwelcome suspicion that she was jealous even of the woman she herself had helped to rise in the affections of the dey.

Regardless of the woman's attitude, Julia was ever mindful of the duty she owed to her and Ali Pasha, and of her promise to further the cause of the dey's nephew. This last she did to the best of her ability. She did not fall into the error of criticizing Kemal; she praised him, but with a doubtful, even fastidious, look in her eyes. Greatly daring, she hinted on one occasion that the emperor of France had distrusted men of Kemal's sexual preference. Ali Pasha she did not extol, though she was brought grudgingly to concede, after her first sight of him in the audience chamber, that he did bear some slight resemblance to Mehemet Dey, her master. He was just such a desert hawk as the dey must have been in his youth, with hooked nose, black beard, dark, shining eyes, and the hard, muscular body of a horseman.

Making this small contribution to the cause of Ali Pasha troubled her not at all. The more she saw of him, the more convinced she became that he was the rightful heir to the throne of Algiers. Conversely, the more she saw of Kemal and his pretty following, the less willing she was to see him take his grandfather's place.

In vain did she look for Rud in the audience on court days at the side of the man who was rumored to be his friend. He never appeared. Once in a great while, like some dim, far-off echo of a time long past, news of the comings and goings of the ship he had helped to build and launch was heard. Whether he stood at the helm or lay rotting somewhere at the bottom of the sea she did not know. She told herself she did not care, that her interest was mere idle curiosity or the impulse to rejoice that he was so powerless. If she longed to see him, it was because she wanted to witness his humiliation. Seeing him might ease the torment she still felt at the way she had been used. In the cool autumn nights, as she allowed her mind to linger on the weeks and months they had spent at the house at Berkeley Square and aboard both the *David* and the *Sea Jade,* the muscles of her stomach tightened slowly with cramp and she lay with clenched fists staring wide-eyed into the dark.

Her second winter in Algiers closed around Julia. Following a trip to the harbor with Kemal, during which the two of them were caught in a sudden cold rainstorm, Mehemet Dey became ill with pneumonia. Though he conquered the disease, it took much of his precious strength. At Julia's suggestion, while he was convalescing he delegated a portion of his duties to Kemal and a portion to Ali Pasha. This division so enraged his grandson that Kemal stormed into his sleeping chamber trailing perfume and ribbons, and there enacted a scene of such shrill tragedy that Mehemet Dey was visibly repulsed. He sent his grandson away with words of anger so forbidding that Kemal did not dare approach him for a month.

Sulking, nursing his injured dignity, Kemal neglected the duties given him. The different manner in which Ali Pasha carried out his appointed tasks was marked. Making quick, capable decisions, the nephew of the dey yet reported each of his actions to his uncle for approval. His attitude was respectful without being obsequious, an expression of the esteem in which he held the aging ruler.

Returning to the harem one night following an evening with the dey in which he had praised Ali Pasha, Julia reflected on how much she had accomplished. Given a little more time, it appeared likely that Mehemet Dey would support his nephew as his successor. She could not take all the credit for the change. Kemal, in his fawning sycophancy and his childish sullens, had done little to bolster his own prospects.

Bidding Abdullah goodnight at the door, she stepped into the communal chamber of the harem. As on the night she had arrived, it was dark; the solid blinds were closed and the room was lit only by the hallway lanterns. Even the brazier in the center of the room had lost its red glow, though it still gave forth a faint, radiating warmth. Treading her careful way across the room between the low divans and dozens of small tables, Julia glanced around uneasily. There was a strangeness in the air this night, an odd feeling she could not quite define.

Abruptly she came to a halt. A shadow moved upon the wall near the head of the hall leading to her sleeping chamber, a shadow that was not her own. For long moments she stood still, inspecting the dimness around her with narrowed eyes. Seldom left alone for an instant from morning until night, she felt at the moment as isolated as if she had stepped into a deserted house echoing with loneliness.

The shadow moved again, a fluctuation of light and darkness. It undulated with a stately slowness, like a heavy curtain moving in a draft. Suddenly she realized the source of the shadow. One of the tall blinds which led into the garden was not quite closed. The night wind through the aperture was causing the lanterns to flare.

Releasing her breath in a long sigh, Julia started toward the opening. As she reached for the handle of the door, the heavy panel swung wider. A woman wrapped in a burnoose slipped through the opening.

Julia stepped back, disbelief making her face blank. To be caught outside the harem after dark had fallen would be to invite the sternest punishment. If not the kurbash, then the bastinado, the long thick rod applied to the soles of the bare feet, a method of chastisement which could leave the culprit crippled for life. If examination proved that the purpose of the nighttime outing had been for carnal reasons, then death by strangulation was the preferred method of correction. To understand why anyone would risk so much was one thing; to discover them actually doing it was something entirely different.

The woman was Mariyah. Face pale, eyes dilated with shock, she stared at Julia. Then her pointed chin came up.

"You are late coming from the bed of the dey." She sneered. "Odd, you do not look tired."

Julia recognized the ploy for what it was, an attempt

to put her on the defensive. She knew that she should raise her voice at once, summon Abdullah, wake the harem, draw witnesses to the scene. She could not. She had no wish to be the cause of such a terrible punishment being inflicted on anyone, much less another woman. "Strange," she said. "I feel so tired, so exhausted and sleepy, that I can barely see. Since you have gotten up out of your bed to shut this open door, I will allow you to complete the task. We must inform Abdullah of it tomorrow. Obviously the latch is defective."

Turning, Julia continued on her way. At the branching of the hall, she glanced back. Mariyah stood staring after her, a look of open contempt in her slanting, catlike eyes.

"You should have screamed, called the guard!" the Lady Fatima exclaimed when next morning Julia told her of the incident.

"I could not be the cause of Mariyah being whipped—or worse—a second time."

"Foolish girl! Do you think she would have spared you? Never!"

"It doesn't matter," Julia said, a stubborn look closing over her face.

"Of course it matters. Do you have some romantic idea that she was indulging in a lover's tryst in a moonlit garden? Not Mariyah. Besides the fact that she prefers the embraces of her slave girl, she would not be so foolhardy for the sake of a moment's gratification. I fear a much more dangerous reason."

"Dangerous? In what way?"

"She has a brother who is a Mameluke and a member of the palace guard. When the dey departs this earth, may Allah postpone the inevitable moment, the loyalty of these guards, or lack of it, could well determine who is to be the next to sit upon the royal divan of Algiers. A man who has been throttled in his bed cannot possibly succeed. You see?"

Suppressing a shudder, Julia signified her understanding. If she lived all her life in the palace she would never grow accustomed to the casual manner in which pain and death were discussed. "Perhaps if Mariyah were questioned?"

The Lady Fatima shook her head, her mouth grim. "It is too late. She would only deny ever leaving her bed and produce testimony to prove it. She would end by making you appear vindictive and power-hungry, something which might cause the dey to look upon you with disfavor. No, we cannot risk it. We must be glad we have been put on our guard. Ali Pasha must be informed. Steps must be taken to counter the threat this stupid little she-dog poses to our plans."

"I am sorry," Julia said. "I did not realize the seriousness of the situation."

"I doubt very much that you are aware of it yet. Tell me, Jullanar, most favored of the dey. What do you think will become of you and the other women of the harem when the dey dies?"

"Become of us?" Julia repeated, ignoring as best she could the bite of the other woman's sarcasm.

"What do you think you will do when your master is gone and the new dey requires your places in the harem for his women? Where will you go? Did you think you would stay on? I can tell you, that is not the way of purdah. As the wife of Mehemet Dey, I will be allowed to take my possessions, the gifts presented to me, and leave. If I still had a family, I would return to them a rich widow. If I had borne a son who had lived, I could have remained in the palace, an honored and respected member of the court. I did not. This being so, I will be free to buy a house and a few slaves to see to my comfort, and live out my life without fear, peddling my gifts for the means of my subsistence. This is the fate of a wife. What think you becomes of a mere concubine?"

"I have no idea," Julia answered with slow composure.

"Your fate rests in the hands of the new dey. If he is the kind of man who has little use for women, he can with impunity have all your throats slit and dump your bodies in the desert. He can tie you in sacks and toss you into the sea, a means of disposal chosen by a past sultan of Constantinople. If he does not choose to dispose of valuable merchandise in this way, he can turn you over to the slave traders, though with so many thrown onto the market at once, and those far from their first youth, the return to him would be small. Very likely, most would be bought as menial servants or as fodder for the brothels near the harbor. It is possible that he may consider the best thing to be done, from an economical point of view, would be to turn you out onto the streets to beg or accept the dubious charity of the men of the town. The most likely prospect, however, is that he will find it convenient to reward the Janissaries or his own military followers who may bring him to power. What better gift could he give them than the free use of the flowers of the old dey's harem?"

"You can't mean what you are saying!"

"I can. I do. Despite your new position and the great largess you have received, you are a chattel, a thing. You do not belong to yourself, nor does the clothing you wear or those valuables which clutter your chamber. All belongs to the dey, whoever he may be."

Julia lowered her gaze to the toe of the Lady Fatima's slipper, which tapped the floor in a measured cadence. It could not be denied that the woman was deriving a large amount of pleasure from the things she was saying. There could be little doubt also that they were true. "Is there nothing that can be done?"

"Your one chance of avoiding the fate reserved for the rest of the harem is to win the gratitude of Ali Pasha by the fervor with which you press his claim to the throne. Already he values you. He has instructed me to tell you that he commends the effort you have made thus far in his behalf. And yet I, who have some experience in these matters, warn you. You cannot depend on the gratitude of princes. Unless you render Ali Pasha some great and signal service, you will be forgotten in the fight to take the throne and in the exultation of victory."

"I shall endeavor to remember, O honored wife of the dey."

The Lady Fatima smiled her satisfaction at Julia's apparent humility. "Before you go, there is one thing more.

I do not like the way my husband has clung to his couch since his illness. I find the slowness with which he regains his strength highly suspect. Has it not struck you so?"

"He is no longer young, and his illness was not minor—" Julia began, only to be interrupted.

"Even so, it is not in his nature to have so small a store of strength or to show so little interest in what is happening around him. I fear his illness is being, shall we say, prolonged."

"Perhaps he is only recruiting his strength for the spring?"

"Do not be obtuse!" the Lady Fatima exclaimed angrily. "I do not mean that I suspect Mehemet Dey of malingering. Must I shatter your innocence yet again? What I suspect is that a slow poison is being administered by someone in his household, minute doses which would not immediately affect the slave whose duty it is to test his food, or cause great affect upon an otherwise healthy man. It would not be the first time such a thing has happened, nor, I daresay, the last."

"I suppose it is possible," Julia said.

"By all the jinn!" the Lady Fatima swore. "Of course it is possible, even probable. It is a good thing Mehemet Dey has more than one woman to look after his needs!"

Julia inclined her head. "I will instruct Basim to be vigilant."

"No doubt the dwarf is aware of the danger. Still, it will not hurt to make it known to him that others are aware of it also, and of his duty."

The Lady Fatima was correct, Julia found when she broached the subject to Basim. He bowed himself nearly in half, like a child's stuffed toy. "Most gracious one," he said. "You do me great honor to bring your fears for our master to me. I too have been troubled by the effendi's lack of strength. This morning I sent to the kitchens an order, in the name of the exalted ruler of Algiers, that every person who prepares a dish must partake of it before it can be brought before the dey. Already the underling who prepares sherbet, one of the effendi's favorite dishes, writhes on his pallet. The effect upon him was so great compared to that upon our master, or his food taster, that it must be accepted Mehemet Dey has been receiving increasing amounts of this poison for an extended period of time."

"Has the man confessed the name of the person who bade him administer the poison?"

"No, fair mistress. His faculties are disordered and he speaks only gibberish when he speaks at all. It appears that he will be dead by nightfall. In any case, it is doubtful if he ever knew any other than a go-between, perhaps some guard or slave in the pay of the man who would profit most from the deed."

Basim carefully avoided her gaze. Still, they both knew the name of the man of whom they spoke. "Is there nothing that can be done to prove the guilt of this man and put an end to his plotting?"

"Not yet," Basim answered, his spaniel eyes dark with an expression that was by no means gentle. "The time is not yet."

Following that incident, the health of the dey improved, though his color remained yellow. Julia feared that his mind was affected also, for often he would sit staring for long moments at nothing, and when brought to himself could not be made to realize that time had passed since last he had spoken. He became more and more dependent on his advisers, his grand vizier, his grandson, the captain of the Janissaries, for decisions. More than once, he allowed Julia, concealed behind a curtain, to listen when he entertained male guests in his private *gulphor*. Afterward he asked her opinion of their discussion. What was particularly disturbing was the frequency with which he agreed with, and acted upon, her conclusions.

One summer afternoon, Julia prepared the hookah, lit it, and passed the mouthpiece to Mehemet Dey. Taking up her fan, she leaned back swatting at a buzzing fly, then plying the painted paper vigorously against the sultry heat. She knew that when she stopped she would feel hotter than ever, but it could not be helped. She had to stir the air in some way in order to breathe.

The dey, seated above her on his divan, seemed not to

feel the suffocating warmness. He sat holding to the stem of the hookah as if he had forgotten what to do with it. Abruptly, he spoke. "Did the great emperor of the west, Napoleon, believe in kismet?"

"I am not sure, O Ruler of the Age. I think, like all humans who cannot know the will of Allah, that sometimes he did, and sometimes he did not. He spoke often of destiny, and yet another time he said that the higher he reached, the less free will he had. He felt all his life that he had been destined for a great goal, and that until he reached it he was invulnerable, unassailable. Still, he feared that when destiny had accomplished its purpose with him, then anything, even a fly, would suffice to destroy him."

"Ah," Mehemet Dey said, nodding slowly, "I also, I also. And did he think as he sat on the island of St. Helena that his destiny was done?"

It was a moment before Julia could answer. "I do not think he could admit such a thing to himself, Mehemet Effendi. But I believe that it was—is—so."

He inclined his head in a slow nod of understanding and gave a great sigh. "Kobah, star of joy, bring your dulcimer and play to me until I sleep, that hearing your sweet music I may forget the pain of knowing that my destiny also is run."

Playing the dulcimer was an accomplishment that Julia had acquired as the months had fled past. Now she did as she had been bid, drawing from the strings a haunting melody tinged with sadness. For no reason she could think of, she had to stop now and then to dry the tears that crept slowly down her face.

By slow degrees Mehemet Dey regained his old strength, and with it threw off his morose moodiness. As the heat of summer began to lose its grip, he bestirred himself to plan a hunting party. Julia, who seldom left his side now, was to go. The prospect of leaving the palace and the hot, dusty, stench-filled streets of the city was an excitement almost beyond bearing. For nearly two long years, she had been penned up like a prisoner. With the exception of one or two brief forays into the bazaars with the dey, she had not left the turrets and towers of the palace. She longed for a breath of fresh air untainted by the omnipresent perfume censers, or the smell of the foul drains of the palace and the open sanitation in the hovels of the city that crowded up to its walls, smells which the burning perfume was designed to cover. She wanted the sun on her face and the wind in her hair. She wanted new sights, new sounds and experiences. Most of all, she longed for the illusion, however brief, of freedom.

The hunting ground of the great lions sought by the dey were in the foothills of the Atlas Mountains some two hundred miles from Algiers. It was to be reached by a caravan traveling in easy stages. They left the gates of the city before daybreak in a winding cavalcade of two hundred camels. With them went the nobles of the court, including both Kemal and Ali Pasha. They were mounted on fleet Umaniyan beasts, while lesser breeds carried the brilliant-colored pavilions, the rugs and cushions and furniture so essential for comfort, and also the food and cooking utensils, and the slaves which would use both to provide the feasts the court of the dey would expect whether in a banquet hall or a desert bivouac. Even fully loaded, the camels could travel seventy to eighty miles per day.

They camped the first night in a jewel-green oasis. Julia was tired from the unaccustomed exercise, of trying to keep her place in the curtained palanquin aboard her camel. Lulled also by the soporific effect of pure air deep in her lungs, she retired early to her couch and slept dreamlessly. With the morning, she allowed herself to be dressed in the long, black, hooded garment with a slit for the eyes which was considered proper wear for a woman among many men. Thus attired, she stepped outside the tent.

The scene was one of purposeful activity as the drivers called and cursed at their camels, and the beasts groaned with a completely understandable disinclination to be burdened on such a fine morning. The air was cool, tainted only by the smoke of breakfast fires. The date palms lifted their crowned heads in a gentle wind high overhead. The light was so clear, hovering there at the edge of dawn, that the blue tent of the dey stood out crisp and clear, while the ensign that flew above it appeared touched with silver.

Two men left a distant tent on the edge of the oasis and started toward the pavilion of the dey. Both were dressed in the tunics, full pantaloons, long cloaks, and soft, supple, knee-high boots of Algerian Muslims. One wore a turban bound with a sash; the head of the other was covered by a scarf held in place by rolled rope. Both were bearded, both tall, though one topped the other by at least two inches. In the hands of the pair were long rifles, which they carried with the ease of thoughtless familiarity. As they drew nearer, Julia recognized the shorter of the two men, he who wore the turban of a noble. It was Ali Pasha. The other she did not place at once, though some instinct made her follow him with her eyes.

The two men came on, walking easily. Julia knew that she should draw modestly back within the tent, but she did not. She held her ground, and as the men drew nearer, she saw the leap of recognition in the black eyes of the nephew of the dey, caught the hard gleam of his interest before he averted his gaze.

She glanced once more toward the other man, then went still. There was red in his beard. His face was weatherbeaten, his sun-bronzed skin drawn tightly over the bones. Beneath thick brows, his eyes glittered like blue glass. He did not smile. His gaze swept over her as if she were not there, and then he and Ali Pasha passed on, talking in low voices between themselves. The desert wind, grown suddenly cold, lifted their cloaks, fluttering the soft wool about their ankles.

As they reached the edge of the encampment, the first orange shaft of sunlight struck the tents. Prayer rugs went down as Muslims faced Mecca for their morning prayers. Ali Pasha, for all his nobility, knelt with the others, placing his rug beside that of a lowly camel driver.

Only slaves stood in waiting quiet for the ritual to be over. Among them was the tall, dark man who had strode at the side of the nephew of the dey. Now he stood still, his hard blue stare fixed on the soft haze of the foothills in the distance. Beneath the headdress and the Moorish clothing, beneath the beard and the visage with the look of refined steel touched to copper by the rising sun, there was a white Christian slave. His name was Rudyard Thorpe.

$\boxed{\begin{array}{c} Chapter \\ Seventeen \end{array}}$

*O*n *the morning of the third day a pride of lions was*
sighted by the far-ranging scouts. Since they were located
at no great distance from the caravan, Julia begged to be
allowed to ride beside the dey. Her motives were obscure,
even to herself. She hated the idea of being left behind
in the camp to while away the time within the stifling felt
walls of her tent. She wanted to be where there was movement and, yes, even an element of danger. The fact that
the man she had identified as Rud might make one of the
party was also a compelling reason. Mehemet Dey, seeing
her request as a compliment, was delighted to give his
permission and made many references to the uniqueness of
his groom before they set out. There was an even dozen in
the party which finally rode from the camp. Included
were Julia and the dey, Basim, two other gentlemen of
the court, three scouts, Kemal with one of his young
male companions, and Ali Pasha with the Christian slave
who had become his friend.

The country was rough and rocky, covered with thorn-
brush and fleshy spiked aloes. Scaly lizards sunned themselves upon every outcropping of rocks, while in the cool
shadows scorpions lay in wait with curled tails.

The lions had made their lair in a narrow, winding
gully made impassable by thorn scrub. As they drew near,
a great black-maned beast could be seen standing on a
boulder at the head of the ravine. Tawny, magnificent, he

watched them come for long seconds before leaping out of sight.

"The king refuses us an audience," the dey said in a whimsical tone. "I wonder if he will sally forth to defend his domain against invaders?"

The three scouts and the noblemen began to beat their way along the high ridges skirting the gully. They raised dust and sent the sound of falling rocks echoing through the foothills, but did not flush the quarry.

The wind died away. The sun beat down, turning the stone enclosure at the mouth of the ravine into a caldron. Ali Pasha and Rud discussed the possibility of finding other game, and, soon after, the hawklike nephew of the dey urged his camel from among them and was soon lost to sight, following the other beaters. Basim drew the camels of Julia and Mehemet Dey to one side, into the slender shade provided by a thorn-covered hillock. Kemal dismounted, petulantly demanding a ground cover to be spread for him to seat himself upon.

The fat grandson of the dey had taken his place, sitting on the ground in the shade cast by the body of his follower, when there came a crashing noise from the gully. An instant later, a golden lioness erupted from the thorn thickets. With her teeth drawn back and a rumbling in her throat, she launched herself at Kemal.

She moved with incredible swiftness, a rippling river of strength and fury. Kemal tried to rise, tried to free his scimitar, a high, feminine shriek coming from his throat. The young boy behind him threw down the fly whisk he held in his hand and took to his heels. The dey, after a frozen moment, reached for the rifle he had placed at rest across his knees. But even if he might be able to stop the beast with the one shot in his ancient musket, Julia saw that he would never be able to raise the piece to his shoulder in time. Before it was halfway there, the lioness would be at Kemal's throat. Even in the horror of the moment, she knew a brief flare of gladness. With one leap, the golden lioness would do what she and Basim had not been able to accomplish. She would assure the safety of the dey and make their rest easier.

Then came the crashing roar of a rifle. The lioness somersaulted, shuddered, and was still. In disbelief, Julia swung toward the direction from which the shot had come. Rud stood wreathed in the blue-black smoke of burning gunpowder with his rifle still nestled to his cheek. For an instant he met her gaze with a look of bitter irony, and then he brought his gun down, moving toward the fallen beast.

"There is no deity but Allah," the dey intoned in accents of wonder.

"Imbecile! You might have killed me with your shot," Kemal screamed at Rud, the paleness of fright giving way to a flush of embarrassed rage that it had been necessary for a slave to preserve his life.

"Is it meet that you accept the return of your life to you with so little gratitude?" the dey demanded, swinging on his grandson. "Would you have preferred to be torn by the fangs and claws of the lioness at your feet? You have felt the hot breath of death. Give thanks that your time was not yet come!"

While Mehemet Dey spoke, Kemal had regained control of himself. Making an extreme effort, he reached out with the toe of one exquisitely embroidered boot to spurn the carcass of the lioness. As the body twitched, he drew back with a curse and a black frown. At that moment Ali Pasha came into view. The small eyes of Kemal narrowed in a look of sudden cunning as he followed the progress of the other man down the slope of the ravine. "You have much wisdom, my grandfather," he said in a hushed voice, "and I admit my fault. Give to me of your knowledge of animals, however, and tell me why this beast, who should have slunk away at our approach, chose to charge me with death in her eyes. Could it be she was driven from yonder gully with murderous intent?"

A great stillness came upon the dey. The old man did not speak, however, until Ali Pasha had reached them and, surveying the scene with quick comprehension, brought his camel to a halt. "What say you, Ali Pasha?" the dey of Algiers inquired then. "Did you by accident or design turn the lioness upon Kemal as he has suggested?"

"He does me too much honor, O Mighty Ruler of the Age," Ali Pasha answered easily. "I fear it is not in my power to direct the creatures of the desert to attack one man and not another. And even if I could, I must surely have had the foresight to tell my friend Rudyard to be slower with his gun so as not to spoil my evil plans."

"I am not the only target here," Kemal said with a sidelong glance at his grandfather. "Explain, if you can, why else the lioness attacked if you did not drive her toward us."

"That is easily done. She had with her in the ravine a pair of cubs three-quarters grown. She thought with her great heart to protect them, and at the same time, show them the true face of courage. It is the female of the species who bares her fangs and rushes forward only when there is something worthwhile to be gained by the effort."

"I suppose you can produce these cubs as evidence?" Kemal demanded.

"Certainly, if you will mount your camel and come into the ravine with me."

Kemal blanched. "That—will not be necessary," he muttered at last.

"It is done then," the dey said, his lips tight and his eyes stern as they rested on his grandson. "We must give thanks to Ali Pasha for reminding us of a great truth. That done, it will be time to turn our thoughts to how best we may reward the man who stopped the terrible advance of the mother of lions."

Scowling, Kemal did not reply. Ali Pasha waited politely for his uncle's pleasure. Rud, his rifle lowered at his side, stood back. For a few moments his stance had been taut and watchful as Ali Pasha was accused; now he deliberately effaced himself.

Smiling faintly, the dey turned to Julia, seated in her palanquin behind parted curtains. "Jullanar, O moon of my constant delight, as one above these petty quarrels and the excessive pride of manhood, what think you would be a suitable recompense for the slave who has saved the life of my grandson?"

Julia gazed down at the dead lioness. The tawny pelt

glinted in the sun, though already stinging blue flies were beginning to gather. It was as though an accomplice in a dangerous but necessary mission had been struck down. The female lion was dead. Napoleon, Jeremy Free, her father, all were brought to naught, while base men like Marcel and Kemal flourished, always escaping death by a hair's breadth. What had Rudyard Thorpe done that he should receive a reward? He had infiltrated the Bonapartist movement with lies and trickery. He had deceived her, used her to further his base schemes, and made of her a convenient receptacle for his lust. Because of him, she had lost her father, her child, her patrimony. She had been enslaved, forced to live with daily fear of humiliation and the knowledge that her body was not her own but could be disposed of at the will of the man she was forced to call master. What irony that she was asked to choose a reward for the man who was the cause of all this.

The camels stirred and groaned in ill-humored impatience at being kept standing. Out on the desert, a dust devil rose, whirled madly, then died away.

The range of what she might heap upon Rud's head was limitless. Jewels, riches, fine horses and riding camels, a body slave to do his menial tasks, weapons, advancement in the service of the dey, or even the greatest gift of all, his freedom; anything was possible. She had only to let fall the words and it was his.

"Jullanar, you have permission to speak," the dey said gently.

"Forgive me, O Glorious Ruler," she said. "It is a matter which requires great thought."

Did Rud stir, awaiting her decision? Did his eyes search her face, pleading with her to be generous? No, he stood back, his face impassive, set in the look of blank acceptance worn as a protection by all slaves. Did he realize that she had the power to set him free? He must. He had taken on too much of the protective coloring of the Moorish society around him, its clothing and its language, to be ignorant of its customs and privileges.

She drew a deep breath. "That the Christian slave was

able to kill the lioness was certainly the will of Allah. It was He who guided his hand and eye. Also, the deed was done with little prospect of personal danger. A reward, then, must be based on the ability of the man with firearms, rather than on extraordinary valor. This being so, I think that a jewel from your body, Mehemet Effendi, will suffice."

"You are as wise as you are beautiful, Jullanar. It shall be done as you say."

Kemal made a slight sound in his throat, as though he had started to speak and thought better of it. Glancing at him, Julia saw the purple of fury engorging his round face. Not until that moment did she realize that by valuing the service Rud had performed so low, she had also placed the worth of Kemal's life on the same level. He would not readily forgive her for such an insult.

But even as she watched, a smile spread across his oily face. "And I will add to this jewel, in token of my appreciation to the Christian slave, a jewel of my own, a blond Circassian female whom I recently purchased. She was one of a set of male and female twins which the slave trader would not sell separately. The girl is not particularly intelligent, but she is young, only fifteen, and her physical attributes are perfect. These, after all, are what is important."

Julia had no trouble recognizing the trend of his remarks. They were a deliberate slur, first upon her age, and second upon her attractiveness, with a hint that she substituted mental allure for physical appeal. This was certainly his meaning, Julia told herself. Still, she could not forget that Marcel de Gruys, who knew only too well the relationship between herself and Ali Pasha's companion, had been seen in the company of Kemal.

If the dey noticed this byplay between Julia and his grandson, he gave no sign. Calling Rud to him, he presented him with a magnificent emerald ring and many courtly phrases of gratitude. Equally polite, Rud accepted the jewel with polished gratitude. He did not permit his infidel gaze to touch even the garments of the favorite of the dey.

The hunt went on for a week more. Julia did not leave her tent to follow the dey again. Pleading the heat and dust, she lay upon her divan. Depression, black and wearisome, gripped her. Sometimes she was happy that she had been able to even the score with Rud. She exulted that she had destroyed the prospect of freedom for him, just as he had destroyed it for her. At other times she was haunted by his masklike acceptance of the destruction of his hopes. It troubled her that a man who had been so commanding must now bow to the will of others. Her thoughts dwelled on this image much more than she wished. It fostered memories of the times they had shared, and of the events they had witnessed together, memories she had kept pushed into the dark corners of her mind for the sake of her sanity. They pressed forward now, filled with sound and color and smells, as though they had happened only the day before instead of years ago.

Nerves on edge, she would rise from her divan to pace the floor and snap at the serving women. It was all she could do in the evening to pay the necessary respect to the dey, though at the same time she watched him anxiously, torn by a gnawing doubt of what would become of her when he died and the new dey ascended the throne.

On her return to the harem, Julia found that her sleeping chamber had been ransacked, her clothing had been slashed with a knife, and everything of value she had been given that she had not taken with her had been stolen. Abdullah was abject in his apologies. The chambers of the other women had been searched, but had turned up exactly nothing. The eunuch guards who had been on duty the night it happened had been beaten, to no avail. It was as if a jinni had sifted like smoke into the room, wreaked his havoc, and moved what he wished by magic from the harem.

The jinn were often blamed for the small accidents and playful tricks for which no one wanted to accept the responsibility. Practical jokes, many of them with a malicious tinge, were a favorite recreation among the women. Julia was not so foolish as to believe that the attack upon her had anything to do with either one. The obvious person to suspect of the devastation was Mariyah. No doubt she had smuggled the items of value out into the garden to the man she had met before. But why? Was he a lover who demanded payment? That hardly seemed likely. Mariyah might be involved with Kemal as the Lady Fatima had suggested, but even so, the trinkets she had taken would not be enough to finance a rebellion, would not equal even a thousandth part of the wealth already at Kemal's command. It could be, however, that Mariyah could see the frailty of Mehemet Dey as well as any and, knowing the uncertainty of the fate which might lie in store for her and the other women, had made a sizable investment in the future. With a small amount of wealth, and the aid of Kemal, she might persuade kismet to be kind.

Though Julia might suspect Mariyah, there was no way of proving her guilt. Julia was too proud to mention the incident to the dey; he might think that she expected him to replace the valuables that had been stolen. This she meant to avoid at all costs.

Such reticence did not serve.

"Jullanar, dove of my heart, my Kobah," he addressed her when they had been back in the palace for the better part of a week. "You are far from a chatterer at the best of times, but still, you have been more than ordinarily silent since our return. Can it be that you mourn the loss of the riches I have bestowed upon you, and yearn for their return? I would not have you unhappy. Would copies of what you have lost make you content?"

Julia shook her head, trying to smile. "You are all goodness and mercy, effendi. Still, some things are irreplaceable."

"I must agree, light of my life, my Kobah, for no one could take your place. You have brought me more joy than I deserve. I kiss your lips and I am young again, like a boy with his first maiden. My mind leaps where my body cannot follow. This saddens my soul, but it also gladdens my heart, for I am free to love you as I would a daughter in my own image, with pride and sympathy, and a great wish that I could arrange your happiness. If you

330

had come to me as a child, I could have passed you through my wife's shift in the rite of adoption practiced by the desert tribes, and then arranged for you a great marriage which would bring you many fine sons and a long life of honor and comfort. It was not to be. That being so, I have arranged as best I can for your safety. Hear me now, star to my waning moon. If death should overtake me, you must trust Basim. He has been instructed to have a care for you in the turmoil which must follow. With Allah's will and his great *baraka,* he will keep you from harm."

His voice grew lower, faltered. Julia put out her hand unbidden to touch his arm. It trembled beneath her fingers, and, though the day was fine, not at all warm, there was a sheen of perspiration on the parchment-colored face of the dey of Algiers. He had not been really well since their return from the hunt, another reason Julia had not wanted to distress him with her problems. She thought the heat, the dust, the exertion and the excitement, had been too much for him.

"Are you all right, Mehemet Effendi? Shall I fetch you anything, water or the juice of pomegranates?"

"No, no," he whispered. "Only stay beside me, and remember well what I said to you of Basim."

"In this as in all things, I am your slave," Julia replied, and felt only the truth of the words instead of their shame.

Once she had seen Rud, he seemed to be everywhere she looked. He appeared in the audience chamber beside Ali Pasha numerous times, more than once in the same press of courtiers as Marcel de Gruys. Despite her fears of a confrontation, the two men ignored each other. They might have been strangers from their outward demeanor. One morning she saw the man who was her husband from the window of the dey's apartments, making his way toward the harbor. Later in the same day he crossed a courtyard ahead of her as she moved along a narrow passage, and it occurred to her to wonder if he had taken up residence within the palace itself. Perhaps he was staying as a guest of Ali Pasha in one of the more remote sections, where the distant relatives and officers of the Janissaries were housed? If that were so, no doubt the Circassian slave girl with which Kemal had presented him shared his rooms. A fifteen-year-old girl. One so young could be molded, taught to defer to his judgment in all things, instructed in the best way to please him, indoctrinated with the idea that her one purpose in life was to anticipate his needs. Julia wished him joy of her! She hoped the girl was able to sing and dance and play the dulcimer or to—to stand on her head. If she could not, a young girl of small intelligence would bore him out of his mind within a month. And serve him right!

In her absorption, Julia did not notice when Abdullah, serving as her escort, dropped behind her to speak to a eunuch on guard before a doorway. She was alone as she stepped out into the bright sunlight of the courtyard. She came to a halt, allowing her eyes to adjust after the gloom of the passage. A breeze wafted through the barren court, and automatically she reached up to hold her face veil in place, touching the gold bee on her temple to see that it was secure.

The scrape of a booted foot on the stone flooring made her glance to the right. Rud stood under a colonnade not three steps from where she stood. There was an arrested look on his face, as if he doubted his own eyesight. Slowly he began to move toward her.

Fear seized Julia. It was madness for him to approach her. If he were seen it could mean nothing but death, as instantaneous as a scimitar thrust, or as slow and torturous as being impaled on a steel hook and hung from the palace walls.

If Rud realized the consequences, he intended to ignore them. His expression had hardened to one of determination. The look in his eyes made Julia suddenly aware of the transparency of her barracan and the inadequacy of her harem dress, which left her midsection bare.

"You are looking well for an old man's darling."

The shock of the English words rippled over her. Before she could recover, her ears caught a sound from the hallway behind her that made the flesh on the back of her neck creep. It was the rasp of a scimitar being drawn from its scabbard.

Abdullah appeared like a large, dark shadow at her side. "What did the infidel say to you?" he demanded.

Julia held her voice steady with an effort. "He saw me alone, unguarded, and thought I might be in distress. He asked if he could be of service to me in any way."

Her choice of words placed a portion of the blame for the encounter upon the shoulders of her guard, Abdullah himself. The implication did not escape the eunuch. "You swear by the most holy name?" he asked, his high-pitched voice shaded with suspicion. And yet the mere asking of the question was an indication that he was willing to accept her answer.

"I so swear," Julia said.

For the briefest flicker of time, she raised her clear gaze to Rud's eyes, and saw in their deep-blue depths the knowledge that if she desired she could end his life then and there in agony.

Abdullah grunted. "Pass then, Christian dog, and never again let your infidel's gaze fall upon so much as the shadow of the most precious treasure of the dey of Algiers."

"Jullanar! Jullanar! Awake, my dove, you must awake!"

Julia opened her eyes. The gray light of dawn was seeping into the room, though it was not yet strong enough to bring color to the objects around her. Jawharah leaned over her with her dull-brown hair streaming over her shoulders and her face rumpled from sleep.

"What is it?"

"A message. You must go to the dey," Jawharah said, her voice laced with caution and a strange excitement verging on dread.

"He is not—dead?"

"Not yet. He is asking for you. You must hurry."

"Yes," Julia said, her voice catching in her throat. "Yes."

The sleeping chamber of the dey was filled with people. Julia recognized Ismael the physician and several others of the same ilk. Kemal was there with a pair of his companions. The grand vizier, the captain of the Janissaries, and a number of the court nobles spoke in whispers in a corner. There was no sign of Ali Pasha.

Basim led her straight to the head of the couch on which Mehemet Dey lay. He pushed aside the tasseled bedcurtains to make a place for her. As she knelt, he stood at her shoulder.

"Mehemet Dey, Ruler of the Time," the dwarf intoned. "Your slave Jullanar, whom you call Kobah, awaits your recognition."

Slowly the eyes of the dey opened. They were unfocused, the color already fading, Julia saw, as he turned his head in search of her face. He made a slight movement of his right hand, and Julia reached to take the hot, dry claw in her gentle fingers. The rasp of the elderly man's breathing was loud and labored. His grip tightened a fraction as he gathered himself for a final effort. His tongue crept out to moisten his lips.

"Kobah, bringer of delight," he said, his voice a husky thread of sound. "I waited for you. Close my eyes with your cool hands, kiss me, and speed me to paradise."

The instant the breathing stopped and the thin chest was still, a clamor broke out around the bed. Kemal tore his clothing, slapped his own face, pulled at his beard, and began to weep, calling upon Allah to witness his grief. The commander of the Janissaries left the room with hasty strides. Slaves, hidden until now in the shadows, came forth with tears streaming down their faces to view the calm and lifeless face of their master.

Basim touched Julia's shoulders. In a low voice he said, "It will be best if you return to the harem now. There is much that I must do here. When the time is right, I will come for you."

Julia nodded, getting to her feet with difficulty. As she left the room, she heard Kemal issuing orders while the grand vizier addressed him with the title so recently given to the dead man.

Abdullah had escorted her to the royal apartments. He had not remained at his post outside the door, delegating the responsibility to his second in command, a friendly, outgoing man whose soul had been unscarred by the mutilation which made him a eunuch. He had often shepherded Julia to and from the dey's apartments, and was not above exchanging a few friendly comments on the way. As Julia walked beside him now, she reached up to unpin the bee which held her veil. When they were beyond the hearing of the guards outside the great cedar door, she stopped and, staring straight ahead, said, "My friend, would you do a service for me, and perhaps also for yourself?"

"I have ever been a slave to beauty, O Keeper of the Honey."

"It may be that if you will take this bee and present it to Ali Pasha with the news that the dey is dead, you will receive a prize worthy of the risk."

He stood beside her in silence for so long that Julia grew afraid he meant to refuse. If he did, the consequences to herself would be unthinkable, for surely Kemal, with ample time to group his forces and spread his bribes, would become the next ruler in fact as well as in name. Already he resented her influence and suspected her loyalty to Ali Pasha. If he could prove that she had acted against his interests, his retaliation would be swift and cruel.

The eunuch held out his hand. "It is meet," he said as he accepted the bee. "I hear and I obey, not for the sake of the prize, but because you ask it who have never looked at me with scorn but always smiled upon me. And because I have not always been as I am now, but was once such a hawk among men as Ali Pasha."

The moment she stepped into the common room of the harem, a serving girl approached her. "The Lady Fatima requires your presence," she whispered, her face pale. Turning, she scurried in the direction of the woman's apartments.

The reason for the girl's distress was not hard to discover. The senior wife of the late dey of Algiers was in a towering rage. She whirled on Julia as she entered and made her obeisance.

"The rumor has come to me that the dey is ill, in extremity perhaps, and that he sent for you."

"This is so, O relict of Mehemet Dey, the greatest ruler of his time."

Slowly the woman's hand went to her throat. "The relict. You do not mean—"

"Mehemet Dey sups tonight in paradise."

"You were with him when he died? They sent for you, and not for me?"

"It is so, by the wish of your husband and my master."

"Why? Why was I not informed? I was his wife. I had the right to be with him in his last moments, to bid him farewell. Why was I kept from him? Why?" Her face twisted in grief and rage, the Lady Fatima began to stride about the room. She pulled at her hair, dragging it down over her face. She tore rents in her clothing and clawed at her arms. Tears spurted from her eyes, but her face was congested with such a variety of emotions it was impossible to tell what caused them.

"I am sorry, my Lady Fatima. I did not think. I only obeyed the order that was brought to me."

"You lie!" the woman screamed, fast whipping herself into a frenzy. "You kept the messengers from me. You wanted him to yourself, wanted his last thoughts to be of you. He would not have done this to me. Though it is many years since we were last man and wife, he would not have dealt me this insult for the sake of the position I hold, if for nothing more. I know he would not!"

It would have been too cruel to insist that there had been no message, that no thought of his wife had crossed the mind of the dey as he lay dying. "I swear I did nothing to intercept the message, though I cannot say what others may have done. The fact remains that it is over. We must now decide what we are to do."

"We? We? You expect me to care now what becomes of you, to include you in the plans to be made, when you have given me such a mortal blow? Get from my sight! Now, before I call the guards and have the skin flayed from your bones. Get out, I say! Get out!"

The woman could not be reached in her present state. There was nothing to do except obey. Still, Julia realized that Lady Fatima's threat showed plainly that she did not believe Julia was at fault—else there would have been no threat, merely a command. The fact that her husband had not sent for her was at the bottom of her senseless rage.

The day begun so early crept forward. As the dread news spread through the harem, crying and wailing was heard. There was much rending of garments and tales told over and over of each woman's moment in the sun of the dey's smile. But behind it all lurked the hysteria of fear. In corners the women whispered of the fate of other harems. They patted and hugged each other for comfort, clinging together in small groups. In every pair of wide and staring eyes there lurked the question: What is going to happen to us now? Only Mariyah seemed immune to the prevailing despair. She did not say so aloud, but the contempt with which she looked upon the others made it apparent that she did not fear she would share their fate.

Set apart from them by the preference shown for her, Julia watched the women with pity. Why did it have to be this way? she wondered in distress. Why did the death of one man make these women who had been pampered and cosseted, dressed in the costliest of fabrics and fed the richest of foods, suddenly useless? It was as if they had no value within themselves, as if their worth depended on their attachment to that one man. Surely there were tasks they could perform, services of some kind they could render about the palace to earn their bread. After keeping them mewed up in useless luxury for years, it was bestial to simply push them out. And for what? Kemal's beautiful young men? Or would Ali Pasha install his wives and other women here only to have the same tragedy repeated a few years hence?

Toward the evening of the first day, the news came of fighting in the city. Out in the garden, the acrid smell of smoke was strong, and cinders drifted down upon their upturned faces. From far away they could hear a noise like the buzzing of locusts, accompanied by the rattle of gunfire. To their strained ears it seemed the sounds came ever nearer.

No one slept. Conflicting reports, brought on the palace grapevine maintained by the servants, kept the women in a state of confused uproar. The city was burning, the palace would be next; they would all be charred in their beds. Kemal had taken the throne with the blessing of the Janissaries. The army had pinned Ali Pasha and his followers in a cul-de-sac in the city, and were slowly massacring them all. No, it was Ali Pasha who had been the choice of the Janissaries. He had the aid of a naval vessel in the harbor which, if he desired, could turn the palace into a pile of rubble if Kemal did not surrender. Already the French consulate had been shelled because of a French adviser with Kemal who had promised the backing of France. With the grand vizier and a group of the court nobles, Kemal was leading the loyal palace guards in a pitched battle. False. Kemal was cowering in his private apartments, making plans with his young men for an escape route in the eventuality of defeat. In the meantime, he had kept the palace guards to defend him while graciously allowing the court nobles and their hired minions to fight Ali Pasha. No, he was sitting upon the dais issuing orders, as though he had no doubt of the outcome of the fighting. One of these orders, it was said, called for the arrest of Basim the dwarf. The charge against him? Administering a tasteless poison to the dey, his master, in a handful of dried dates. Was the rumor true? It must be, for though a day and night had passed since Mehemet Dey had closed his eyes in death, Basim still had not come.

By midmorning of the second day, the Lady Fatima had collected her belongings and quitted the harem. She made no farewells, leaving women she had known for more than thirty years without a backward glance. She had majesty, the widow of the dey. But Julia, seeing the villainous-looking soldiers who had come to escort her dare to exchange smug glances behind the woman's back, wondered how she would fare without the protection of her illustrious husband.

The harem was visited by a second soldier's escort. A pair of men bearing the insignia of officers of the Janissaries presented themselves at the carved door shortly after the departure of the Lady Fatima. It was a measure of the uncertainty of the times that they were treated courteously and permitted to speak to Abdullah instead of being attacked by the guards on either side of the door.

Julia, lying alone in her chamber, did not see them. It was Jawharah who hastened to her with the tale. The soldiers had asked for the blond Frankistani woman. Mariyah, the only fair-haired woman present in the common room, had stepped forward. She was not Frankistani; still, after a moment or two of communication with Abdullah, she was allowed to leave with the Janissaries.

There had been such an air of hurry and secrecy about the proceedings that no one had had time to consider or raise a protest. Few had noticed the token one of the Janissaries had shown to Abdullah.

"I saw it," Jawharah said. "With my own eyes I saw and recognized what the man held, and I came at once to tell you, Jullanar. I swear by the sacred name that the ornament which rested on the hand of the soldier was a brooch of gold formed in the shape of a bee, your bee, my dove."

"You are certain they were Janissaries?" Julia asked.

"Indeed yes," Jawharah said with the echo of a coquettish smile. "I once knew such badges of rank well."

"It may be it is true that the Janissaries have chosen Ali Pasha."

"It may be," Jawharah agreed, more to encourage the thoughtfulness she saw in Julia's face than because she could see evidence to support such a belief.

If it was true, then Ali Pasha, in recognition for her warning, had sent the Janissaries for her to lead her to safety. Perhaps Mariyah had grown tired of waiting for Kemal to fulfill his promise. It was even possible that she had identified herself as the blond Frankistani at first in an honest expectation that the escort was for her. Discovering her mistake, she had persuaded Abdullah in some manner to let her take Julia's place. How? Had Abdullah been her accomplice in the arrangement of her meetings in the garden? It would certainly explain the ease with which they were conducted. Or was it simpler than that? Had the Turkish eunuch some outside knowledge of the way the fighting was going? Had he seen that Kemal would be his new master, and trimmed his sails accordingly, favoring one who might be thought to have some influence with the grandson of the old dey?

The issue could not have been settled yet, or Ali Pasha would not have been able to send his men.

What would Mariyah do when the deception was exposed? Would she try to brazen it out? Would she shed contrite tears and plead a terrible mistake? Or did she intend to try for an escape before the time when she must face Ali Pasha? What would Ali Pasha do? Would he consider that his debt was paid by the attempt to rescue her? Would he command the soldiers to try again to infiltrate the palace for her sake? There was one other possibility: that he would not discover the substitution of the wrong woman until it was too late.

Chapter Eighteen

The doors to the harem crashed open. Abdullah en-
tered, followed by what appeared to be his entire command of eunuch guards, marching in a double row. There
was a shrill outcry from the women as the body of men
penetrated into the common room, and then quiet. Abso-
lute stillness.

Abdullah pushed his thumbs into his scabbard sash.
Standing with his feet wide apart, he said, "You will each
of you gather the personal belongings you brought with
you to the harem of Mehemet Dey, leaving behind all
jewelry, ornaments, furnishings, carpets, and clothing
given by the Illustrious One. You may each have one
change of raiment, and one only. When you have made
your bundles you will each return here to the common
room and form a line. Make haste! Those who are not
ready when I give the command to leave must carry only
what they have in their hands."

As he spoke, the eunuchs spread down the sides of the
room. Each had his scimitar, a jeweled dagger in his belt,
and a kurbash in his hand. There was no exit from the
room, either into the garden or to the chambers, except
through these formidable lines.

Jawharah, seated beside Julia upon a divan, reached to
squeeze her hand. "The time has come," she said. "Our
fate is upon us." All around them there was now a rising

crescendo of sound as women protested and questioned this edict.

"Silence!" Abdullah roared, slashing the air with his kurbash. "Silence! And hear me well. We will proceed from here with order and swiftness. Anyone who lags, or fails to heed this warning, will live to regret it."

The women were instantly quiet again, though they sat unmoving, as if stunned. Slowly Julia rose to her feet. Placing her hands together, she made a ceremonial bow. "We hear and obey, effendi," she said. "But as you hope for the mercy of Allah, whose name be exalted, in the afterlife, will you not extend mercy to us and tell us what is to be our destiny so we may fortify our spirits to face it with dignity?"

"Jullanar, Keeper of the Honey," he sneered, "you go to a hive where many robber bees wait, ready to strip your comb bare and steal away the sweetness which has been protected so long. It is the wish of Kemal Dey that you, and all these other fat and lazy slugs called by the name of women, be taken to the barracks, there to provide amusement for the men who have so ably defended against the pretender, Ali Pasha."

It was a sentence to rough and continual misuse at best, and at worse to death from repeated rape. As at all desperate tidings, the women did not weep or wail, but accepted it with white-faced numbness. Like those in the possession of an afreet, they moved to gather their belongings, returning to the common room with their pathetic bundles.

Flanked by the double row of eunuchs, they marched from the harem. For some it was the first time they had been beyond its walls for five, ten, even fifteen years. They walked the corridors with a fearful shrinking, starting at every shadow and noise, huddling within themselves and trying to stay close to each other.

As Julia walked, she listened. From far away she could hear the sound of rapid gunfire and an occasional explosion like the landing of some far-flung cannon ball. If it had not been for Abdullah's calm imperturbability, she would have sworn that at least a portion of the sounds came from within the walls of the palace itself. Kemal's seat upon the throne was none too firm, if she was right. It made little difference to the women of the harem. Kemal, the despiser of women and lover of boys, had reigned long enough to seal their doom.

The barracks were empty. Julia had the pleasure of seeing Abdullah disconcerted. The women smiled at each other in unconcealed relief at this respite, however brief. Staring around at the signs of hasty departure, the equipment chests left open, the empty weapon racks, the scattered sleeping mats lying on the floor, Julia felt a rise of hope. It looked as though there had been an unexpected call to arms, perhaps a surprise attack mounted against Kemal's defenses. Pray God, or even Allah, God by another name, that it was so. Let Ali Pasha be triumphant!

Abdullah hurried away, leaving them under guard. The women looked around them at the huge, open room, at the plain tall columns which supported the ceiling, and the windows lining the walls for air. One by one, they sagged down upon the sleeping mats, resting their backs against the walls beneath the windows. Jawharah chose a prayer-rug-covered mat near one of the central columns, and taking Julia's arm, steered her in that direction. "We may as well be comfortable," she said.

"What do you think is happening?" Julia asked quietly when they had settled down, leaning against the column.

Jawharah shrugged. "Who can say? It is not something which we can alter. For now, we must look to ourselves, and give praise to Allah for His mercy."

"You can't be serious?"

"You think not? Then you cannot have considered. If that swine Kemal had not been kept frantically busy in the last few hours, if he had not seen the need to assure the loyalty of the palace troops, then he might have bethought himself of some more dramatic way to be rid of us. A favorite means of disposal for men, as you know, is to impale them through the chest and leave them hanging in agony as from a meat hook. It is possible for women to be impaled for sport also, my dove, though not through

343

the chest. Some decadent rulers have discovered that the skin of women makes a fine leather, especially suitable for binding books and for marvelous money and tobacco pouches. Drowning, fighting the sack whose opening has been sewn shut, is a most final disposition of a woman, as in their way are the waterfront brothels where women are chained in their stalls. If maltreatment does not shorten their lives, disease will as they service customers to their last breath. Do not doubt that such a monster of cruelty as Kemal would seek to make himself remembered with an act equal to these of which I speak, or that he would lose the opportunity to accommodate his sadistic nature."

"And how is this any different?" Julia asked with a bitter gesture around them.

"For you, I am not sure it is. Like the honey that they have named you, you are too desirable; you will attract many. If you are lucky, one will be stronger than the rest, or higher in authority, so as to keep the others from you. For myself, I expect no such problem. Except for the purest accident of discoverance, you may be sure I will keep out of the way as much as possible until I see a man who is old and ugly enough that he hesitates to press himself forward with younger, more lusty men. Such a man may relish that which is freely given rather than what he must take by force. He may be so wise as to welcome comfort and skill upon his sleeping mat, rather than spread-eagled pleasure or a sharp tussle that contents no one."

"I have always known that you were wise in your own way," Julia said. "Now I have proof of it."

"We shall see. There can be no harm in the attempt. If my plan succeeds I may count myself more fortunate than the next women who occupy the harem, poor creatures who will beget an heir from Kemal with very little help from him. It may be that I will consider myself luckier than I have been in some time. I was never meant for a celibate existence, especially knowing as I do a wider, more varied style of life."

When Abdullah returned to the barracks, his face was streaked with runnels of perspiration, and his satin tunic ripped and dirty. He did not linger, but snapped an order which made the eunuchs feel for their weapons and start at a quick trot from the barracks. Only a handful of men were left to guard the two hundred women. Since these had weapons, and the women none, it was enough.

Time dragged. There was water to be had in clay cooling pots hanging from the ceiling, but food there was none. They had not eaten since morning, and as the shadows began to fall, bellies began to growl. Terror died away, ousted by the imperative demands of the body. With the thinning of their guard, some even dared to complain and ask in querulous voices when they would be fed.

The breezes of evening brought the faint sound of cheering. Moving to the window, Julia stood listening, trying to hear whose name was being cried in the courtyard and streets of the city. She could not tell; she could only surmise that as in all conflicts, one army had been victorious, one had gone down in defeat. Regardless of the outcome, men must rest, seek a place to lick their wounds and sleep. Soon the victors would turn toward the barracks. Whether they were the men of Kemal or of Ali Pasha made little difference to the women who waited to receive them.

Shadows began to gather in the room, but no one came to light the lanterns. Then as Julia stood straining to hear, she caught the rumble of voices. Loud, boisterous, they came nearer.

The doors of the barracks were thrown open to slam against the wall. A captain of the Janissaries strode into the open room and stopped, his hands on his hips. Behind him crowded a second man, and a third. More poured in at the doorway, pushing against those who had halted at the sight of the frightened huddles of women.

"I heard, but I did not believe. Truly the dey is a generous man who values the well-being of his followers!"

"The leavings of the old dey," a man behind him growled.

"But long unused, from all accounts," another jeered. "They should be ready."

"Not as ready as I!" came yet another voice from farther back in the crowd.

Grins appeared on bearded faces. Slowly the men in front inched forward, pushed by their fellows behind, as more and more struggled to see the prizes that awaited. They fanned out, closing the women into a circle like wolves surrounding sheep. They brought with them the fetid stench of sweat and blood and high-pitched excitement. Lust, and a cruel enjoyment of the helplessness of the harem, glittered in their eyes.

The women struggled to their feet, clinging to each other, moving into a tight cluster in an instinctive act of self-preservation. Some began to cry and moan. Others stared, white-faced, with wide, unbelieving eyes at the advancing men. Jawharah caught Julia's arm, drawing her to the dense-packed center of the group.

Abruptly the circle broke and the men closed in. Women screamed as they were pulled down to the sleeping mats. Scratching, biting, shrieking, they fought. It availed them nothing. There were too many hard hands, and arms and legs bulging with muscles. Their barracans were torn to shreds, their protecting veils ripped away and thrown aside. Eager fingers grasped, wrenching at their pantaloons, baring their white, quivering flesh. Arms and legs were pinned, while brief fights broke out and arguments flared over who would be first, second, third, fourth. Shouts, grunts, the thud of flesh upon flesh filled the room, while yet more women were jerked from the small knot that was left.

Plumb, overblown Jawharah shielded Julia with her bulk from the front, while her back was protected by a center column. Ruthlessly, the larger woman pressed other females into the grasping, clawing hands. But even her covering form could not protect Julia for long. As their numbers dwindled, Julia became more and more exposed. In a peculiar way, Julia could not be sorry. Though she appreciated the concern that caused Jawharah to wish to protect her, she felt like a coward sheltering

346

behind her when all around her other women were going down to violation.

"The Keeper of the Honey!"

The cry went up as a man caught sight of Julia's soft golden tresses. Soldiers turned, their glazed eyes avid for this creature whose legendary beauty and wisdom had made her the favorite of the old dey. Jawharah was seized and thrown into a sprawling heap. Moist, meaty hands reached out, yanking Julia off her feet so that she fell to her knees. Immediately she was thrown onto her back. Her veil was wrenched away. With her teeth tightly clenched to keep from crying out, Julia heaved and kicked. She tried to claw with her nails until the vicious weight of men's hands clamped her arms out straight, pressing on her elbows. Her knees were pulled apart. She was pushed this way and that as her barracan was ripped from her. Her soul cringed at the rough exploration, the kneading and pinching of her body. They knelt upon her bright hair spilling over the floor, causing tears of pain to spring to her eyes, as they fumbled to expose her milk-white skin.

At her feet, a man's voice with the sound of the captain of the Janissaries was heard. "The pick of the lot," he grated in strained tones. "I command first entry."

Without waiting for a reply, he began to tear at the sash which held the scabbard of his scimitar.

"And then I," said the man who had recognized Julia. Other voices chorused, one after the other. They were drowned only by the sound of a gunshot reverberating through the room.

Activity ceased as the men fresh from the heat of battle dived and rolled in instant reaction to the sound. They scrambled for weapons before they looked up to search for danger. The captain of the Janissaries whirled, facing the detail of men who stood with smoking rifles in the doorway. Striding forward, he shouted in goaded frustration, "What is the meaning of this?"

"The women of the harem of the dey were sent here on the orders of the pretender, Kemal, whom you so gallantly

347

defeated. It is not the wish of the new dey of Algiers, Ali Pasha of illustrious name, that these women be abused!"

That voice. It belonged to Rud. Julia, with the weight gone from her arms and legs, levered herself to a sitting position. Drawing the tattered edges of her bodice together over her breasts, she reached as automatically as any Turkish or Moorish woman for her veil. Hope hovered in her mind, but she would not allow herself to trust to it, especially with the captain of the Janissaries standing over her with his hands on his hips, blocking her view.

"He cannot take them away, not now, when the men have tasted of the meal set before them. They deserve some reward; none could please them more than this."

"If any woman wants to stay after such rough wooing as she has received, then she may," Rud snapped. "Otherwise, they come with me."

It was a tense moment. The number of soldiers was large, and the detail in the doorway small. Only the might invested in the office of the dey kept the red-eyed Janissaries from committing murder on the spot. No one moved. The sound of gasping breathing and small, ragged moans filled the strained quiet. Slowly Julia gathered her bruised and trembling legs beneath her and pushed to her feet. She stumbled to where Jawharah lay, and catching her arm, helped her to stand. No one spoke, no one put out a hand to help or stop them as they threaded their way among the stiff figures of the men. Another woman staggered after them, and yet another, each trailing bits of clothing like apparitions newly risen from the grave.

As Julia stepped to Rud's side, he reached out a hand and caught her wrist, drawing her close against him. The detail moved aside, allowing the other females of the harem to pass between them out the doors. When the last woman had quitted the room, Rud gave a short nod. A man stepped forth from the detail and presented a fat purse to the captain of the Janissaries. "Accept this with the compliments of Ali Dey, along with his assurances that the women of the brothels of Algiers will serve you better than these sheltered creatures who have been snatched from you."

"It may be so," the captain said, his hot gaze terrible as it scorched the woman at Rud's side, "but their taste cannot be as sweet."

Rud's voice rang with the hardness of steel as he answered, "Without doubt—still, they can be taken with no fear of stinging."

When they reached the doors of the harem, Rud drew Julia to one side while the other women passed through. His fingers pressed into the flesh of her upper arms as though he meant never to let her go. The lanterns in the corridor had not been tended for some time, and they flickered low. Still, even in that indifferent light Julia thought she could see a shadow of concern in his eyes, and something more, a fierce gladness that sent the warm blood coursing through her veins.

"I will tell Ismael the physician to make ready for those who have need of him," he said, his tone abrupt.

"There may be some who must avail themselves of his services," Julia said, her gold-flecked eyes searching his dark, bearded face for signs of injury, of pain past or present, and of change. "For myself, I have taken no hurt. This much I owe to your timely intervention, for which I give praise. May I know how you came so opportunely?"

"A blond woman was brought to the quarters of Ali Pasha and left there while the battle for the throne of Algiers was fought outside the palace gates. The final engagements were brief but bloody. In the past two days I have spent much time at the side of Ali Pasha and was there at the last pitched fight. I went with him back to his quarters, where he intended to remove the signs of the fray before he appeared in public to accept the fealty of the nobles. Learning of the woman's continued presence, he had her brought before him so he could thank her for the part she had played in his great victory. It may be the woman thought that since no one had seen the unveiled face of the Keeper of the Honey, she could pass herself off as you. She was mistaken. Under persuasion, she revealed what she had done and where you could be found. I do not think she will try such a masquerade again."

Julia suppressed a shiver at the grimness of his voice. For the sake of her own peace of mind she did not inquire what had been done with Mariyah. "I am grateful for your quickness and also for the mercy of Ali Pasha, now Ali Dey, in sparing the women. My—my indebtedness would be boundless if I only knew what was going to happen to us now."

Rud hesitated, looking away as though he wished to hide the expression that burned in his sea-blue eyes. "That is a question you must put to the dey himself. He has requested that I bring you before him in as short a time as possible so that he may honor you. If you are certain you have taken no injury, I will wait for you here while you make yourself ready."

There could be no arguing. The state of her nerves, the feeling she had that she had been touched by something unclean, her reunion with her husband, were of no moment to the dey. With Jawharah's help, Julia threw off her torn clothing and cleansed herself as well as she might with a bowl of water. She then donned a bodice and pantaloons of cloth-of-gold with a barracan of pale-yellow silk banded with cloth-of-gold thrown over it. For her face was a yellow veil. Jawharah wanted to weave pearls into her hair, but there was time for no more than the quick application of a brush. With the burnished strands spread upon her shoulders like a golden mantle, Julia hurried back to Rud.

Surrounded by the smoky glare of lanterns, Ali Dey sat with folded legs upon the richly draped divan of the deys of Algiers. His sashed turban was pinned with an enormous ruby. His wrists rested on his knees in a relaxed pose. His hawklike face was creased in a slight smile, but in his eyes was a hard and fearful watchfulness.

Rud approached, kissed the extended hand, spoke a few quiet words. Only then did the new dey allow his gaze to travel to Julia, alone and unrecognized in the center of the room.

"Come forward, Jullanar, O Keeper of the Honey," he said, his gaze probing, admiring.

With her head held high, Julia obeyed. She steeled

herself to ignore the curious and malignant stares, the sibilant whispers of the men that crowded the room behind her. Her lips touched the hem of Ali Dey's garment, then she stood back with her bearing stiff and straight, her gaze downcast.

"You have served me well, Jullanar. I honor you for all you have done to further my cause. In acknowledgment of my appreciation, I present to you this small token, with the hope that it brings you as much pleasure and good fortune as this other jewel which has become your symbol, and which I return to you, your gold bee."

The gift of the new dey of Algiers was a magnificent yellow diamond the size of an egg yolk. Set as a pendant, it hung from a fine gold chain. With unsteady fingers, Julia took the jewel from the hands of the man who served as the new grand vizier and passed the chain over her head. The brilliant stone settled between her breasts, drawing all eyes to its flashing light. The gold bee she pinned in its old place between her temple and cheekbone. It clung, a loved and familiar weight, to her veil.

"Your generosity is exceeded only by your kindness, O Illustrious Ruler of the Time," she murmured, salaaming once more. "That this evening you stayed the harsh command of Kemal, the false dey, will make your name ever one for praise among women. It is not often that strength and ability are so well wedded to honor and mercy as in your exalted self."

Ali Dey flicked Rud a sardonic glance. The thought shafted through Julia's mind that perhaps her husband had exceeded his authority in the matter of rescuing the harem from the soldiers' clutches. She did not falter, however. Now that deed was made public, the dey could not rescind it without being made to appear both incapable of making a firm decision and unable to control his followers.

"It only remains," Julia continued, "for you to make known to us, the women of the harem of the old dey, what you have chosen for our fate."

"This matter has vexed me sorely," Ali Dey answered, his tone dry. "It would be incestuous conduct for me to retain the women presently in the harem, the women of my uncle, who stand as aunts to me. Moreover, there might be strife with my own wives and women. While I see no difficulty in overcoming the objections if I should so choose, I have no wish for discord in my household at this time. On the other hand, these women are not equipped to fend for themselves. It appears they must have either husbands or masters."

"You are as wise as Solomon, the son of David," Julia intoned.

He lifted a brow in an indication that he accepted her flattery with reservations and a certain admiration for her daring. At the same time, his eyes wandered over her, lingering for the space of a heartbeat in the area of her girdle. Beside Julia, Rud stirred, placing his hand on the hilt of his scimitar. Ali Dey looked at the Englishman and smiled, raising his hand to his dark beard with a look of regret at the back of his eyes. "Have you a suggestion to make, O Keeper of the Honey?"

A rustle ran around the room at this unheard-of honor to a woman of publicly asking her counsel. Julia felt a flush rise to her face, though her composure remained even. "There is a possibility, effendi, though I fear it may cost you a small portion of that which is traditionally the spoil of the new ruler."

"I am not surprised. Still, you may speak."

"If every woman were permitted to keep the valuables which have been presented to her during her sojourn in the harem, then this wealth might constitute for each an acceptable dowry. With this in their favor, then might not husbands be found for many?"

"It is possible," the dey agreed, nodding.

"Then for those who do not find someone willing to wed them, this property could be sold. With the money, they might eke out some form of free existence, or else it could be invested with a merchant who might be willing to guarantee a small monthly stipend."

"For the other women, your proposal merits some consideration," Ali Dey said. He paused, as if reluctant to continue, slanting a brooding glance at Rud from under his eyebrows. Then he gave himself a small shake. "I find, however, that in your case I can undertake no such arrangement. This is due to the essential fact that I have already committed myself as to your disposal."

A coldness moved over Julia. For a moment her voice failed her, then she whispered, "May—may I know how I am to be placed?"

"The Englishman beside you has been of great service to me. His knowledge of ships and gunnery has proved invaluable. This afternoon before the palace gates, he fended injury and death from my back no less than a half dozen times. What could I refuse such a stalwart companion? How could I reward him? I offered riches, jewels, position, the great boon of becoming a Mussulman. This last he accepted along with the freedom that necessarily accompanies such an honor, but all others he refused, asking only one thing more of me. He requested for his use and enjoyment the white Christian slave of the old dey known as Jullanar, the Keeper of the Honey. I did not deny him."

Julia swung to stare at Rud. She was stunned, and yet a slow anger ate like acid into her heart. By his request, he had denied her the prospect of freedom as surely as she had ever denied it to him that day in the aftermath of the lion hunt. Moreover, he had seen to it that she was enslaved to him for his "use and enjoyment." The passionate gratitude she had felt at his intervention in the barracks, the warmth she had known at his concern, evaporated as if they had never been. She would not let him use her for his own ends again. Never again.

"I won't!" she declared, forgetting the submissiveness proper for such a place, forgetting that one never defied so powerful a figure as the dey, even if one were a man. "I will not be his slave! I will never endure such a thing! Never—"

The fatal word "again" was not spoken. While she raved, Rud inclined his head to the dey, and receiving his dismissal, turned and swept Julia up into his arms. His lips came down, warm through her thin silk veil, smothering what she would have said to reveal their prior knowledge of each other. The hard, punishing force of his kiss restored a measure of sanity. The shock of recognition, of distant familiarity brought forcefully to the present, robbed her of breath. She did not protest, but lay stiff and unyielding against his chest as, to the accompaniment of masculine laughter and congratulations, Rud strode swiftly from the audience chamber.

"You may put me down now," Julia said when they were well away from the court.

"Only if I have your promise that you will say or do nothing that will put both our necks in a strangler's cord."

"I hope I have more sense than that," she answered with a lift of her chin.

"So do I!"

"You are still alive, aren't you?" she replied, her tone tart in its defensiveness. "If I had spoken at any time in this past two years of our marriage vows, you would have been a dead man, crushed like an ant for the danger you might have posed to the immortal soul of Mehemet Dey."

"So I would. I have often wondered why you held your tongue. Not, of course, that I believe there was any danger of the dey committing the physical sin of adultery with you. The palace grapevine is too all-knowing and accurate for that."

"The thought was in his heart, if not within his loins, so it is much the same."

"But it is the loins that matters, isn't it? I wonder what you would have done if he had offered to marry you?"

"Agreed, no doubt, and prayed that Allah and God between them could see that as a slave I had no choice. Bigamy would have been a more acceptable sin to have on my conscience than the murder of my husband," she answered, her voice cold.

Abruptly he came to a halt and set her on her feet. "And your conscience was your only concern, I suppose?" he said.

She flung a quick glance at him in the dimness of the stretching corridor, seeing like a dream long remembered his dark brows drawn together over his dark-blue eyes,

354

the sun-bronzed skin of his face and the firm lines of his mouth. She allowed her gaze to slip to one side, passing over his shoulder. "What else should there be?"

A sound escaped him like the grunt at a half-expected blow. "What else indeed? Come, we cannot talk here. Let us go to my quarters."

At the door of rooms which must assuredly have been equal only to those given to the dey's personal guard, they were met by a soldier on duty. "Your pardon, effendi," the man said, bowing low. "Your effects have been transferred to the quarters formerly occupied by our illustrious ruler Ali Dey. There has been a great scurrying hither and yon between the different apartments, but all should be in readiness."

"I know nothing of this," Rud said.

"It was the order of Ali Dey, our new master, may his line prosper and his reign and his life be long!"

As Rud signified his agreement with such sentiments, Julia thought of Kemal, whose reign had been cut short. What had become of the grandson of Mehemet Dey? As she and Rud retraced their steps to a more exalted section of the palace, she put the question to him.

"No one can say with any degree of certainty," he answered. "Even now, men are still searching the dark corners of this stone-and-marble pile for him. He was never seen in the forefront of the fighting. It is said he made his escape during the last assault, with a number of his followers, and has gone into hiding in the city. No matter. He will be ferreted out and dealt with as he deserves."

"And how is that?"

"With whatever severity may be needed to see that he poisons no more old men, and sends no more women to the barracks."

The harshness in his voice was new, something acquired in this cruel land. With a shiver, Julia drew her thoughts away, turning them deliberately toward more domestic matters. What, she wondered, would the wives of Ali Pasha, now Ali Dey, think when they discovered the harem of the old dey still in residence? Would the women share the quarters for a time, or would the displaced females be sent to occupy some of the unused cubicles about the palace? Purdah, the protection of the curtain, was no longer important now that their master was dead. It could not shame him to have other men look upon their faces. But why was she exercising her brain with such problems? It was no concern of hers. Her place had already been decided.

There were no guards before the doors which led into the former apartments of the new dey. Rud pushed the door open, stepped aside for Julia to enter, then closed the heavy panels behind them. A squeal of piercing loudness rent the air. From the direction of the *gulphor* erupted a plump blond girl. Face wreathed in smiles, she ran toward Rud.

This was obviously the Circassian slave presented to Rud by Kemal for the boon of saving his life. Though she was of the same nationality as Mariyah, she could not have been more different. Her hair was the brownish-gold of desert sand. Her face was round and broad, and her dark Mongolian eyes were tilted upward, as were the corners of her generous mouth. There were creases of laughter in her ivory cheeks, and dimples in her elbows. All in all, she was beautifully designed to appeal to the average Turk or Moor, but somewhat embonpoint for western tastes. It was also plain from the puppylike devotion with which she came forward to greet Rud that she did not dislike her change of masters.

She came to an abrupt halt as she saw Julia. Her face dissolved into a mask of woe. She salaamed to Rud, an obvious inquiry in her eyes.

Rud caught Julia's hand. "Julia, may I make known to you my slave girl, Isabel. She had another name, but it was nigh unpronounceable. Isabel, this is Julia—Jullanar. You will serve her with as much joy and willingness as you have served me."

"Yes, effendi," the girl said, bowing low once more to Rud, but apportioning Julia a genuflection a great deal less respectful. "There is a meal ready for your comfort, my master. And soon the bath will be of the correct temperature for your enjoyment." The girl smiled, a shade of her enthusiasm returning to her face. "These rooms have their own bath, effendi, of a great richness and convenience."

"Good," Rud answered. "I will call you when we are ready to be served."

From the arrested look on the girl's face, Julia wondered if she was accustomed to sharing Rud's meals. It occurred to her to wonder what else of his she shared. Although her type might not appeal to the vast majority of Englishmen, Rud had taken on so much of the style and mannerism of his captors that he might also have adopted their version of feminine beauty.

Julia had no time to consider the matter as thoroughly as she might have wished. Dismissing the other girl, Rud placed his hand on Julia's elbow and propelled her into a large sleeping chamber. There was a solid door closing the chamber off from the others, rather than a curtain as in the harem; Rud closed it deliberately behind him.

"We are going to talk," he reminded her, his voice grim.

Julia pulled away from him the instant they were out of sight. Keeping her voice low, she said, "What of your slave girl?"

"You may say what you please. Even if she could hear us, or if she would listen, she speaks no English."

"If she would listen?" Julia scoffed. "Of course she would. Doesn't everyone in this misbegotten place, most of them without shame or the thought of it?"

"So you don't like it here? I was beginning to think you were well suited in your position." He moved easily to pour a cup of water for himself from the gold carafe on a table beside the curtained couch.

"What do you mean?" Julia demanded, astonishment as much as wrath in her amber eyes.

"There you were, the darling of the dey, queening it over the harem, your every whim granted, your every wish fulfilled, petted, pampered—"

"—Enslaved, at the constant beck and call of an old man," Julia interjected. "Playing endless games of chess, struggling not to win, hardly daring to open my mouth for fear of displeasing—"

"Lavished with praise and compliments, your opinions sought and considered with care, your recommendations acted upon—"

"Oh, yes," she exclaimed, snatching her veil aside as it pressed against her lips, preventing her from speaking as quickly as her sense of outrage demanded. "And walking a tight line between the opposing factions, committed to aiding Ali Pasha while realizing it was against the natural inclinations of the man I must call master to favor him, afraid one day I would go too far and be accused of disloyalty."

"With the power to alter people's lives—"

"Knowing all the time that I could not alter my own! And then, when finally the time came that I might have won freedom and realized a small amount of riches with which to find my way back to my old life, what happens? Once more I am enslaved, a thing to be owned, used, and enjoyed by a man I heartily despise!"

"Would you rather have become the odalisque of Ali Dey? Would you? I assure you that is what would have happened."

"I don't believe it," she threw at him. "He promised to allow the women their valuables, to let them find husbands or a new life as best they could."

"He promised the take the idea into consideration only. It is possible that some of the older women, those with little value, he will set free. But though I admire him as a soldier and a leader, he is still of the east. To him, a woman is a piece of property, one he would no more allow to go free than a good horse or a fine camel. It would be a piece of stupidity, for not only would he lose her value, but some other man would take her and make her his chattel the moment his back was turned. There is no such thing as freedom for a woman here, just as there is no such thing as a fine mare without an owner."

"I am not a mare!" Julia pointed out.

"No," he agreed, "though deny, if you can, that Ali Dey would have liked to put you through your paces."

"But he did not. He gave me to you!"

"Yes, damn you! Am I supposed to apologize because I asked for you? Because I thought you would prefer to be the woman of a man of your own race, someone who speaks your native language, someone who is, incidentally, your husband?" He set the gold drinking cup he held down with such force that the metal rang.

"Certainly, why not?" Julia cried, flinging up her hands. "Why would I not be overjoyed to find myself once more in the power of a man who is guilty of treason and murder and deceit? How could I possibly object to being conferred upon such a man as his slave?"

He paled beneath the deep brown of his features. "I murdered no one, nor ever intended to. As for treachery, show me where it lies. I was an Englishman under orders from my government to infiltrate the plot to free Napoleon Bonaparte and use his plan of escape to transfer him to a more secure and less restrictive and unhealthy prison. It was not part of my orders, or of my government's proposed course of action, to cause his death. I am sorry that it happened, but I will not have the responsibility for it put upon my shoulders. I swear that what I have spoken is the truth. I performed my duty to my country, nothing more."

"Duty? Ha! A feeble excuse for doing what your heart must tell you was wrong."

"Your heart may tell you so; mine does not. Napoleon may have begun his reign with the best of intentions, and I will admit he accomplished much. He ended the Terror, brought order out of chaos, and unified France. But at what cost? Like all men who attain unlimited power, he was corrupted by its lack of limit. He was a great man, but because he was great, should Russia and Britain have meekly agreed to become French vassals? No. I do not regret doing my best to defeat the emperor on the field of battle at Waterloo, nor do I regret what small part I played in preventing him from being set loose once more upon the unsuspecting world."

"In fact you, and also your country, are glad he is dead?"

"There may be those in England who will not be sorry to learn they need never fear him again; I refuse to be counted among them. Moreover, I will remind you that it was France, itself, that killed him."

"Very well," Julia said. "You will not admit to being a murderer or a traitor, but I defy you to deny that you used deceit to worm your way into the Bonapartists' group, and also into my bed!"

A strange expression flitted across his face as he stared at her flushed face and the lush, gleaming curves of her form through the gauzy barracan she wore. Almost casually, he moved closer, reaching out to pick up the yellow diamond presented to her by the new dey, letting his hard fingers rest in the soft valley between her breasts. "To the first charge I must plead guilty, but my reasons for marrying you were more complicated. Despite the arrangement outlined with your father and the other Bonapartists, it was always my intention to travel to St. Helena in order to consult with Sir Hudson Lowe concerning the transfer of his prisoner. Taking you as a wife was a convenient excuse. However, I could just as easily have pleaded a business assignment for the East India Company, since my uncle and the company were both cooperating fully with the British government. The truth is, I was attracted to you. I had come to admire your beauty, your gallant courage—even your fanatic loyalty to your emperor. And I felt responsible for you. My actions would deprive you of all hope of regaining your heritage. With your father dead you would have no place to go, no way to live. What could I do except give you the protection of my name?"

Julia was still for an instant, then she said, "Very noble, but you need not have forced me to consummate this charitable marriage."

"Forced, Julia?" he queried, his head coming up. "I used no force with you, though it cost me dear. I came near to ravishing you a dozen times over, but would not. Deny that if you can."

"You tricked me!"

"For a purpose I have explained before and see no need of repeating. I took you at last, against my most honorable intentions, for the same reason that I asked for you as my slave. Because I could not resist you, because then as now I wanted you with every fiber of my being. Between that time and this there are other similarities," he went on, dropping the jewel and sliding his hand to cup the fullness of her breast. "Then, as now, I had to bring you away from an encounter with the brutal side of men's nature. This time, however, I don't believe you are much affected."

Julia shifted so that his hand fell away. "No," she answered, "I have become used to surviving."

"So have I," he returned, reaching for her once more. "But I have never grown used to being without you. I wonder if you are still as you were before, unwilling?"

Julia placed her hands on his chest. "More so now than ever."

"So you think. I prefer to put it to the test. Especially since in this case I need not heed your tender sensibilities."

With an abrupt movement, he circled her waist with his arm, dragging her against the hard planes of his chest. As she gasped, throwing her head back, he pushed his fingers through her hair, twining them in its shining mass. His mouth came down upon hers with burning pressure. She felt the soft wiriness of his beard caressing the sensitive surface about her lips with something like pleasurable surprise, and then all thought and feeling dissolved in an enormous surge of rage. She bit, kicked, and scratched, twisting and turning. Though tears started in the corners of her eyes, she did not care if her hair was torn from the roots or her bones crushed. She wanted only to be free. In a desperate effort to make it so, she pitted her strength against him. Once, twice, she broke his grip on one hand or one wrist; still she could not free both, could not escape the steely confinement of his arms. At the instant when she felt her strength begin to ebb away, he bent to place his arm under her knees and lift her onto the couch.

Immediately, his body covered her, stilling movement, constricting her breathing. The bruises caused by the soldiers on her arms and ankles throbbed. She panted with a rasping, labored breathing as helpless tears began to track slowly from the corners of her eyes, and across her temples into her hair.

"Julia, Julia," Rud breathed, his eyes dark with pain as he stared down at her. "Why do you make it so hard? I would have asked for my wife to be returned to me, if I only could. Forgive me if I have caused you pain. I will take the hurt away if you will let me. And if you will, O moon of infinite longing, perhaps my own will depart."

English did not lend itself to such phrases. It was Moorish which slid sweet and caressing from the tongue, expressing as much in its soft intonation as in the words themselves. Almost against her will, Julia felt the hard knot of anguish somewhere in the region of her heart begin to dissolve.

"I have yearned for you, O purest of pleasures, as the Muslims for the moon of Ramadan which ends a month of fasting with a feast. My fast has lasted more than two long years. Must my hunger for you ever go unappeased?"

A shiver ran over Julia, half reaction, half a response to the tenderness of his voice. Against her will, she recognized the truth in his words. "How can I take comfort from someone who has brought me so much grief?" she whispered.

"I have brought you no grief, Julia. You brought it to yourself when you left your safe woman's place in New Orleans. But knowing it would come, would you have stayed behind and missed all else as well as the grief?"

Missed the excitement of the Bonaparte cause, the wonders of sailing the seas, missed coming face to face with Napoleon, or knowing that wise man Mehemet Dey? Through her mind ran, unbidden, the singing joy of the love she had made with Rud once, an endless age ago, somewhere between Rio de Janeiro and the equator, a gentle, unending possession. Slowly, she shook her head.

"Then what use is there in repining? This moment is ours. We are promised no other." His eyes burned with the blue fire of his desire, and yet they were watchful as he lowered his head to take her lips.

Warm, tentative, his kiss offered no more and no less than the solace he had suggested. And yet there was a faint trembling in his arms, as though he held himself in check by only the most stringent effort of will. He touched his mouth to her eyelids, following the salt path of her tears, tracing the curving of her cheek and chin back to her moist, parted lips.

He shifted his weight from her. As she made no move to leave him, or to evade his caresses, he smoothed the palm of his hand down the tender turning of her neck to her shoulder. Curve by curve, he traced the outlines of her body like a poor man assuring himself that the valuable coin he has lost has been found again. If her barracan hindered him, he gave no sign, but lowered his head to press his lips to the curves of her breast through its sheer transparency.

Julia put her hand on the corded woolen scarf which covered his head. Her skin felt branded where his lips had touched, and beneath the depression of fading anger which weighted her, she knew a quickening.

"Forgive and be merciful, Julia, as you were merciful that day in the courtyard when you lied to save me. Don't force me to take you against your will; for I must have you though I regret it all my days."

Forgive? Hadn't she done that, given him her benediction with a lie on that day of which he spoke? What need had she to deny it now? *I would have asked for my wife to be returned to me if only I could—* Curiously, she believed him. His pride was of that caliber. Once an action was taken he would not disavow it.

She drew a deep breath of air into her lungs, then let it out in a slow sigh with the last vestiges of her bitter anger. Her movements deliberate, she removed the woolen scarf and pushed her fingers through the crisp waves of his hair. "Love me, then," she whispered, "for I have been so alone."

With patient hands and many small caresses, he removed her barracan and beaded bodice, and unfastened her girdle. While he undressed, she kicked her slippers off and slipped from her pantaloons. His chest was like sculptured mahogany, a strange contrast still to the paleness of his lower limbs, though there was wooden hardness there also. His long hair and curling beard gave him an odd aspect, at once foreign and familiar, pagan and Christian, an aspect unchanged by the silvery words with which he wooed her as they lay upon the couch.

"Your hair has captured the bright glory of the sun and stolen the most fragrant perfumes of Araby," he said as he buried his face in the silken mass. "Your skin shimmers like pearls from the depths of the ocean, and yet it is soft and welcoming. Breasts like sweet, sun-warmed melons tempt my lips, and I am enthralled by the smooth planes, the gentle roundness and gilded shadows of belly and thighs." Where his fancy wandered, his hands followed. "Will I feel your sting, O Keeper of the Honey," he whispered, "if I borrow a taste of your sweet nectar?"

On a crest of wanton tenderness, he entered her. With a wild and measureless rhythm, they moved together, scaling thunderous heights of pleasure. Clasped breast to breast, they soared into a soft darkness exploding with unbearable wonder.

Chapter Nineteen

"*Baraka*," *Rud whispered as, still molded together, they* lay with panting breath. He drew the hair from across her face and placed a kiss between her eyes, and they were quiet until their frantic heartbeats steadied.

"Hungry?" Rud asked after a time.

Was she hungry? She had taken only a few dates and a handful of almonds since a light breakfast more than fourteen hours ago. "I could eat," she replied, her tone droll.

Rud stirred, then heaved himself up. Pulling on his pantaloons, he called for Isabel. When she came, he gave the order for food to be served. With downcast eyes and a sorrowful countenance, the girl appeared not to notice Julia upon the couch, covered only by Rud's woolen cloak. She accepted the command without apparent reluctance and went away to do his bidding.

With her going, a sense of strain invaded the room. Julia found herself unable to raise her eyes from the fastening of the cloak that lay across her. She smoothed the wool beneath her fingers. "What—what will happen now?" she asked at last.

"If you mean with us, we will eat, bathe, and sleep, letting tomorrow take care of itself. If you speak of the new regime, let us hope that Kemal will be captured so that Ali Dey can rule in peace. He is a young and vigorous leader who, if he is allowed to do it, can steer his country out of the dark ages into the nineteenth century."

"And if Kemal is not captured?"

"More fighting, a divided country, an uneasy rule and broken sleep for Ali Dey."

"And you? What will you do?"

"What I have been doing all along. I will act as military adviser and nonpartisan observer for Ali until such time as he no longer has need of my services and will grant me leave to return to England."

At the bleak tone of his voice, Julia looked up at last. "They say you improved the ships of the Algerian navy and designed a ship of magical swiftness which, when I saw it from the palace window, had the look to me of a Baltimore clipper. Doesn't it trouble you that these innovations may be used against England and her allies?"

"It does," he admitted, moving to the window casement of the chamber, which looked out onto the inevitable garden. There was nothing to be seen in the darkness, but he breathed deep of the night air. "It does, despite the fact that the improvements I made still leave the Algerian ships considerably inferior to British shipping. As for the Baltimore clipper design, so far none has sailed her other than myself, and for reasons that may or may not be obvious, I have concentrated on England's ancient enemy across the channel. What weakens France must strengthen England. In addition, it has come to my attention that the French consul here is attempting to solidify the French position in Africa by the installation of puppet rulers such as Kemal, a situation that would be unacceptable to England. Tripoli and Morocco, as well as Algiers, are targets."

"I have not seen Marcel for some time," Julia said, remembering Jawharah's hints that he might be involved in this conspiracy.

"No, it appears he may have made a voyage to France for instructions on how to proceed in this part of the world. I'm sure he did not expect the old dey to die in his absence. It is said he expects to return with money to buy troops. If he had been on hand to succor Kemal in these last days, the battle this morning might have gone differently. Kemal was a fool to go forward without his presence."

Julia sat up. The woolen cloak slipped down into her lap, but she did not notice. "That is one of several hints I have heard expressed that the journey of Mehemet Dey to paradise was hastened by poison. Do you think it is true?"

"It would not be surprising. It is a common practice in the east for succession to the throne to be cleared by what we would call drastic means."

"It is rumored that Basim, the dwarf who served the old dey, was arrested for the crime of putting poisoned dates before his master. This I cannot believe. His loyalty to the dey was unquestionable; he certainly had no liking for Kemal. Doesn't it seem to you that Kemal must have had him arrested as a scapegoat?"

"That is always a possibility," Rud replied, turning at the intensity of her tone to stare at her with a query in his eyes.

"Basim was kind to me, more solicitous of my feelings than he was required to be. I am sure he would never harm anything, much less the man he served and loved. He enjoyed his position in his own way, the prestige and power that went with it, and he was proud that Mehemet Dey considered him not only the source of much good magic, but a trusted friend and confidant. It is ridiculous to think he would endanger all this for the sake of mere money, even if he could have brought himself to do the deed. Isn't there something you can do to help him?"

"It's possible that I could speak to Ali, if it means so much to you. You realize it may be too late?"

"Yes, I know," she whispered.

It was only later, when a steaming platter of rice and lamb had been set before them, that she remembered Basim had once held the key to her escape. Did he still have it in his hand? Did it matter?

While they ate, Julia and Rud talked, closing a few of the gaps in their knowledge of each other, and the things that had happened to each of them, in the past years. It was difficult at first, like trying against natural reticence to reveal one's private self to a stranger, though toward the end of the meal it came easier.

Rud dipped his hands into the perfumed water of the bowl set between them and dried his fingers on a linen cloth. Gathering his feet under him, he pushed away from the low table laden with food scraps and stood. He stretched hugely, looking down at Julia with a smile. He put out his hand. "To the bath now, with a handmaiden in attendance," he said. "I choose you, O Jullanar of the golden hair."

"Handmaiden?" Julia asked with a lifted brow.

"I am inviting you to share my bath," he explained patiently. "Of course, if you would rather wait until I am done and more water is heated—"

The prospect of a bath sounded like heaven. This was one more thing there had been no time to enjoy before the audience with Ali Dey. "I suppose you will want me to scrub you?"

"A charming notion, not at all what I am accustomed to."

"Not even from your precious Isabel?"

"I had to deny her that pleasure, since I prefer a little more water in my tub and a little less maiden."

"Most men are not so choosy."

"Most men are not married to a vixen who once knifed an importunate suitor."

"Does she truly have no attraction for you?" Julia persisted.

"I am not a seducer of girls of fifteen, an age nearly young enough to be my daughter. Why do you ask—unless you are jealous?"

"Jealous? I?" She scrambled to her feet unaided. Elaborately casual, she looked around for her pantaloons and bodice and pulled them on, fastening the girdle with an unnecessarily firm jerk.

"Logically, you have no reason to be, but I find that with you logic does not always serve. Why are you doing that? You are just going to undress again."

"Am I? Yes, of course," she answered herself, and at

once began to do so. "Have you really not had a woman since our last night aboard the *Sea Jade?*"

"There are few opportunities offered to a slave, especially one who spends most of his time at sea."

"There was Isabel," Julia pointed out.

"She does not excite me, being at once reminiscent of you in her coloring, and yet a constant reminder of how far all women fall below the standard you set in beauty of face and form."

In the act of flinging his cloak around her nakedness, Julia turned to stare at him. "Rud," she began uncertainly.

Reaching out, he drew the edges of the cloak together under her chin. "Come now, doesn't such flattery deserve at least a back scrubbing?" he teased, and smiled as he saw disappointment replace the doubt in her face.

The hot scented water was languorously soothing. In the large, pool-like tub, there was more than enough room for Julia and Rud together. She washed his back with a loofah sponge and a great deal of vigor. He scrubbed hers with tender care, though he seemed much concerned in searching for a secure hold to keep her soap-slippery body from eluding his grasp. At the same time, he complained loudly that her twisting and turning did not help. The result of such play was inevitable. Though of an experimental nature, it was also extremely satisfying, helped along by the buoyancy of the water, and the lighthearted glee with which they approached it.

That night, naked in Rud's arms beneath a woolen coverlet lined with silk, Julia slept as she had not in countless ages of time. Toward dawn, she was awakened to passion once more, coming straight from oblivion to the swift, escalating beat of devouring possession. In the sated aftermath she slept once more, and she did not awake until the sun had reached its zenith overhead.

She opened her eyes. The chamber in which she lay had ocher-colored walls, decorated about the door openings and window casement with tiles. The polished marble floors were covered with rugs and animal skins. One of the skins was the tawny pelt of a lioness. In the garden beyond the window, birds called, and she could hear the cooing of doves. It was cool in the room, but not unbearably so. There was only one thing wrong. She was alone on the couch. The place beside her had long lost its warmth. Rud had been gone for some time.

Rising, Julia donned the clothing she had worn the night before, since she lacked any other. She combed her hair with her fingers as best she might, and left the sleeping chamber in search of Isabel.

She found the girl in a small back room of the apartments beyond the empty servants' quarters. She was crouched over a charcoal fire which burned in an ovenlike embrasure in the wall. She was surrounded by a collection of pots and bowls from which rose a dozen savory aromas.

At the sight of Julia, Isabel leaped to her feet. "My Lady Jullanar! You should have summoned me."

Her round face was puffy, as if she had been crying, and yet if she bore Julia a grudge, it did not show on her tear-stained countenance. The title of respect with which she had addressed Julia came naturally to her lips. Julia was forced to wonder if it was an indication of the span of years that separated her from the young girl, or the results of Rud's instructions.

"Perhaps I will another time, if you don't mind," Julia answered. "For now, could I have a few cakes and fruit as a morning repast?"

"You must have more than that, my lady. If you will return to the *gulphor* of the master, I will bring an array of dishes to tempt your palate."

"You are most kind," Julia answered.

Isabel slanted a quick look over the costume Julia wore. "Your box from the harem of the old dey has arrived. If you would care to see it, it is in the *gulphor*. Later, after you have eaten, I will call another servant to help me place it where you would wish."

"Thank you." Julia recognized from the girl's manner that she would not appreciate an offer of assistance. Until now, Isabel had considered Rud's household her own province. This was not the time to challenge it. Julia did as had been suggested.

The afternoon advanced by slow degrees, and still Rud

did not return. Isabel, when applied to, merely shook her head with a look of surprise in her eyes, amazed that Julia could even expect that Rud might confide his intentions to a mere slave girl. With stolid acceptance of the vagaries of males, Isabel busied herself preparing for her master's homecoming.

Julia had no such outlet for her energy. After she had changed her gold costume for one of turquoise, she had nothing to do except sit and examine her bruises and think of the day and night behind her and what had happened.

Clouds gathered overhead at dusk. A northwesterly wind began to blow, bringing with it the salt smell of the sea and the acrid darkness of old smoke from yesterday's burned-out buildings. Donning a burnoose, Julia walked out into the garden. With her head thrown back, she stood staring up at the sky. High above were vultures riding the currents of wind, searching for carrion. They seemed to linger above the palace. Julia permitted herself to wonder what had become of the bodies of Mehemet Dev and the men who had been killed the day before.

The paths here in the garden of this new set of rooms were of stone, not mosaic. The fountain, though there was grace in its carved stone basin, did not work. The pool into which it fell was barely half full of water. Beneath the scummed surface, the water lilies were dormant, the fish hidden under the floating islands of fallen leaves. Rain, the remorseless, chill, gray rain of winter, drove her back inside.

The lamps had been lighted against the sudden onslaught of darkness that came with the pouring rain. Julia was sitting in the yellow glow of one which swung from the ceiling, trying to read, when a knock fell on the entrance door. Isabel, hurriedly adjusting her veil and muttering something under her breath about the need of a male attendant, ran to open the panels.

At the sight of the person the girl ushered into the *gulphor,* Julia sprang to her feet. "Basim," she cried, her voice ringing with gladness.

"My Lady Jullanar," he said, salaaming profoundly, though his face remained solemn. "I trust I see you well?"

"Yes," she answered without hesitation. "And you?"

A grimace crossed his features, and he flicked a disparaging look at his feet. Only then did Julia notice that beneath his baggy pantaloons, which nearly touched the floor, his feet were bound. "I do not walk so well as yet," Basim said, "but I will live."

"The bastinado?" she whispered.

"It was thought prudent to wring a confession from me, one way or another. They failed to succeed only because their time ran out. I did not come here to enlist your sympathy by my complaints, however. I came to present myself to you as your lowliest servant for as long as you have need of me and Allah wills."

"There is no need, Basim. I did not ask that you be freed from prison only to have you become a slave to me."

"There is every need, fair mistress. To see to your safety and happiness was a task laid upon me by my master, Mehemet Dey. I could not shirk it even if I wished, which I do not. For the freeing of my poor self from prison, I owe you much devotion, and I am sworn both to myself and to Reuben Effendi to protect you."

"As you will then, Basim. It may be that I will have need of protection. But who is this Reuben of whom you speak?"

"Reuben is the new Muslim name chosen by the one who was known as Rudyard. The rites which have made him one of the faithful are over. You are no longer the slave of a slave, but the property of a free man."

Rud a Muslim. She could not blame him for converting to the faith of his captors. She had been in Islam long enough to know that conversion was his only chance of gaining his freedom. The change was not such a great one, after all; the Allah of the Mussulman and the God of the Christian were the same, only the prophets were different. What would the effect be? That would depend on Rud. Beneath his robes and Moorish trappings, he was still an Englishman. Or was he? After the passage of so much time she could not say.

"I see," Julia said slowly. "Why has he not returned here? Why has he sent you and not come himself?"

"He may not lie with a woman now for many weeks. To remove himself from temptation, and at the same time serve his friend and master Ali Dey, he has put to sea on a voyage of great importance."

"Put to sea? He is already gone?"

"Even so, my lady."

"He could have come to tell me himself and to say goodbye," she said, her voice tight with what she recognized, and deplored, as disappointment.

"It was not permitted. Reuben Effendi appointed me his spokesman and entrusted to me a purse of dinars for the purchase of food and other comforts, and also a letter and a package for you."

"A letter? Why didn't you say so?" She reached for it, almost snatching it from his small hand. Reading it brought no comfort. It said little more than Basim had been able to tell her. It instructed her to see to Isabel, to trust to Basim to purchase food and drink from the vendors who came daily to the back gates of the palace, and to take care of herself. No date was given for his return. It was signed only with his initial.

As Julia and Basim spoke, Isabel had crept nearer and nearer. Julia knew she could banish the girl, drive her away with a few sharp words. At the sight of her round brown eyes filled with woe, however, she did not have the heart. Instead, she read the note aloud, translating the English phrases as she went for the girl's benefit. With a small sob, Isabel turned and stumbled from the room. Julia stared after her, shaking her head, before turning her attention to the package which had accompanied the note. Her fingers trembled slightly as she drew back the paper to reveal a small, beautifully worked knife of damascened steel. Its hilt was of gold encrusted with precious stones. The scabbard which held it was not of such fine workmanship as the blade itself, but it brought a smile to Julia's lips. Made of burnished Cordovan leather, it bore a design of flowers, leaves, and scrolls set around an open oval. In the center of the oval was depicted a honey bee poised to sting.

She stood staring at the knife for long moments until Basim once more drew her attention to himself. "It is well that we are alone, for there is a serious matter that I must put to you, O fair one."

"Speak on, Basim," she said, absently caressing with her thumb the rubies, diamonds, and sapphires which bejeweled the knife.

"You know that my master, Mehemet Dey, may his soul take joy in paradise, did not mean for you to be enslaved again. By a foul plot his wishes were set aside. It is well that your new master pleases you—still, I can do no more than attempt to carry out the last command of my old master before I surrender my will to you, bright mistress. I have the means of effecting your removal. Safely hidden away where only I can find it is wealth enough to secure your safe passage to the land whence you came, or else to establish you here like a princess in a great house with many servants. Before I can act you must tell me what is your wish."

Julia stared at him, her eyes searching the waiting solemnity of his face. Basim made what he was suggesting sound certain, and yet she was not fool enough to think that she would be allowed to leave so easily. No matter how magnanimous the new dey, he would not like to let any form of riches slip from his grasp, especially for the use of a slave girl. The property that had belonged to Mehemet Dey he would regard as his own, regardless of a dying man's wish. He would consider it theft if it was removed against his will. If they were caught, the penalty for this crime would be severe. Could she permit Basim to risk so much for her sake?

There was one other important consideration. Rud was no longer a slave, but neither was he entirely free. After what had happened between them, could she go and leave him behind?

"I don't know, Basim. I must consider," she said after a time.

This answer the dwarf accepted without the least sign

of displeasure. "There can be no harm in that," was his formal reply. Salaaming, he left her.

Ali Dey, perhaps as a gesture of honor toward Rud, perhaps as a recompense for sending him from Julia, directed a covey of servants to the apartments occupied by Julia. They included a cook and two serving women, all three of middle-age and a monumental ugliness. A pair of eunuchs was posted outside the door as continual guards. Julia, weighing the idea that they may have been suggested by Rud, considered sending them away. She dismissed the idea reluctantly. It would not do to insult the new dey, if by chance the gift of protection had been his alone.

Julia, though careful not to act as if she meant to try to supplant Isabel, began slowly to make her influence felt. Her first move was a cleaning campaign. She did not criticize the Circassian girl's housekeeping ability, or even those of the former occupants, in order to obtain the removal of the accumulated grime of centuries. She only hinted that the men of Frankistan were repelled by filth and odors, regardless of dim lights and perfume censers. Isabel, ashamed she had not realized this important fact, entered into the proceedings with a will, sweeping the other serving women with her. Basim, with the threat of a curse backed by his magic, was able to persuade the eunuch guards to lend their assistance.

Gray swags of spider webs were swept from the vaulted ceiling, and wads of caked dirt raked from the corners of the rooms. The brass necessary chamber vessels were washed and scalded instead of merely emptied. Scrubbing the dust and soot from the walls brought forth in places brilliant-hued mosaic murals as beautiful as they were lascivious. A number of these were found in the bath. Here also they attacked with soap and water, rubbing the tiled surfaces with sand to free them of their ancient layer of scum before treating the mildew that abounded with quicklime and lemon juice. The introduction of a cat into the kitchen considerably lessened the rodent and insect life. Further, on pain of strict punishment for failure, Julia required that all who touched food wash their hands, and wash and scald each dish after each use. Tiring of explaining the reasoning for these last measures, Julia fell back on her first strategy—the necessity of pleasing Rud, plus obeying an ancient tribal law of both her own and Rud's people. This Isabel, Basim, and the others found easy to understand. They obeyed the edicts scrupulously thereafter.

Chests, tables, couches, rugs; all were arranged and rearranged. New bed curtains were needed, Julia found, and one of the divans in the *gulphor* could use a replacement for its cover. For the moment, however, she was satisfied with the inside of the rooms. Next, they must tackle the garden. The tiredness caused by the physical labor, as much of it as the others allowed her to do, helped her to fall asleep at night.

In the course of the upheaval, Julia grew close to the women of the household. She made friends of the serving women and the cook, learning in the periods when they sat down to rest where each woman came from and how she had come to be a slave in the palace. Gradually, they lost their awe in her presence and began to chatter as naturally as the cooks and housemaids, the laundresses and nannies she had known on her father's plantation so many years ago. This process of shared work and conversation had one other benefit also. Led by Basim, all concerned turned to Julia for orders and instruction. Slowly she came to be looked upon as the mistress. Painlessly, almost without the girl noticing, Isabel was set aside and her place taken by the elder slave, the bedmate of Reuben Effendi.

The installation of a cook in the kitchen had the effect of freeing Isabel from her main task. With little else to occupy her, she began to seek Julia out, forgetting that they had been in some sense rivals and treating her like a friend or older sister. As the days passed, Julia learned more of the girl's background. With her twin brother, she had been stolen during a slave raid and brought, after a long and weary journey, to Algiers. They had been bought within hours of their arrival by Kemal. Isabel had been separated at once from her brother. Since that time, she had known nothing except a brief stay in his quarters before being transferred to Rud's old rooms. She was, therefore, intensely curious about the palace, the harem, the new dey, and the style of life led by those close to the throne.

"Is the harem larger than these apartments, the rooms given to Reuben Effendi?" she asked, her eyes gleaming.

"Much larger," Julia answered, pressing her lips together to keep from smiling.

"Is the garden more extensive?"

Julia described the lush, verdant promenade allotted to the women of the dey in detail.

"A pool large enough for a hundred women to bathe in during the heat of summer. It must be magnificent! Were there peacocks?"

Yes, there were peacocks. And turtledoves. And all manner of songbirds.

"It is said the jewelry of the wife of the old dey, Fatima, filled a half dozen coffers. Can such a thing be true?"

"She certainly had jewels, how many I cannot say."

"They speak of a single ruby nearly as large as the fabled gem worn in the turban of the great chan of Tartary—"

"All things are possible," Julia quoted with a smile, reaching for a date from the fruit stand beside her.

"To be the wife of the dey would be a wondrous thing. A woman need never worry again. Do you regret that Mehemet Dey never asked you to marry him?"

"No," Julia said wih a quick shake of her head. She was happy she had never had to make the choice of telling the truth or committing bigamy. Despite what she had said to Rud, she would have willingly risked her soul before she would have condemned him to death.

"I would have wanted to kill myself when he died without speaking the words that would have made me his wife," Isabel said with youthful extravagance. "I most certainly would have expired with fright if I had been taken to the barracks afterward. Were you frightened, Jullanar?"

"I was frightened," Julia admitted, her golden gaze clouding as she looked away.

"Forgive me! I should have my tongue torn out with red-hot pincers for reminding you. All is well now. Reuben Effendi rescued you and brought you here where you are safe." As if the aftermath of that rescue hovered in the girl's mind, she went on. "They say you never shared the bed of Mehemet Dey. Do you suppose that is why he did not marry you?"

"I cannot say, in all truth. He was not a young man, nor a well one."

"Do you regret that he was incapable? Would you not have fared better if he had been as young and virile as Ali Dey?"

"Who can tell? Ali Dey might not like blond women."

"Oh, do not say so!" Isabel cried, raising her hands to clutch at her golden-sand curls. "Never say such a thing!"

The girl's antics banished Julia's momentary mood of darkness. She sent her a quick amused glance. "I understand the dey already has the four wives allotted to him."

"One is sickly, a poor skinny thing of no spirit," the Circassian girl said at once. "She is a Thracian, with sallow skin and muddy brown hair. She may die. Or, since she is childless, the dey might come to think it would be a good idea to divorce her."

"And you belonging to someone else," Julia commiserated with gentle mockery.

"Yes," Isabel said on a great sigh, then brightened. "But I still have my virginity."

Julia nearly choked on the date pit. "That is—lucky," she said when she could speak.

The girl agreed complacently. "At first I thought of slitting my own throat, because first Kemal scorned me and gave me away to a lowly slave, and then the slave, Reuben Effendi, also did not desire me. Now I see that our master had you in his eyes, blinding him to my beauty. I perceive it is my kismet to remain a pure maiden until such time as I will be taken by a great man."

If this was the fantasy with which the girl consoled
378

herself, Julia would do nothing to destroy it. "I see," she said with a grave nod. "No doubt it is so."

Another time Isabel, bringing a cushion and sitting at Julia's feet, began, "Did you enjoy sharing the couch of Reuben Effendi?"

"Why do you ask?" Julia hedged. She could not seem to get over being surprised at the outspokenness of the women of the east. No subject was sacred to them, no question too personal to venture.

"A first, when I knew he had taken you under his blanket to slake his lust, I felt slighted and even envious of your closeness, as I have said before. At the same time, I was glad."

"Because it allowed you to remain a virgin?" Julia asked, with a shade of gentle irony.

Isabel's smooth pink mouth curved into a smile also. "Not entirely. I was glad I need not worry anymore about such a frightening thing coming to me."

"I see."

"No, no! It is not being with a man that causes my knees to quake and my throat to close so tightly I cannot speak. It is Reuben Effendi!"

"What do you mean?" Julia frowned a little as she searched the girl's round face.

"He is not like other men, my Lady Jullanar. At least, not like the men I knew when I was a girl at home in my village. He is of the Frankistani, his body broader and taller than that of a Moor or a Turk, or even of the men of my own people. Surely he has more strength in his loins than a young girl like myself can support. Also, he never beat me or raised his voice in anger, showing always a control of his temper that cannot be natural. His skin is pale beneath his clothing, and unpleasant to see where the sun has not touched it, and the peculiar sea-blue color of his eyes must surely have been stolen from an afreet."

Julia pursed her lips. "You do not find him handsome?"

"Yes, as a statue is handsome, or a god, and yet strange beyond knowing."

"He is only a man," Julia replied, "with a man's need for love and comfort and the nearness of a woman." She spoke instinctively, without deep thought, and yet the truth of her words spread through her like a balm. Had she not, in her own way, been as impressionable about Rud as Isabel? For too long she had viewed him as a monster; like Isabel's afreet, a devil who used people and betrayed them without feeling or conscience. That was not true.

"He loves like other men, then?" Isabel insisted.

"It seems so."

"And you enjoyed it?"

"Yes," Julia answered, her eyes like twin pools of stillness. "Yes, I did."

It was a dull rainy winter. Little enlivened the gloom. Forbidden to view the audiences of the dey by simple lack of an invitation, tired of reading, needlework, and house-keeping, Julia's temper grew short. She snapped at everyone. Isabel's unremitting chatter began to grate on her nerves, as did Basim's eternal deference and air of patient waiting for her as yet unmade decision. Her nights, now that the chore of cleaning was done, were disturbed. The brief rekindling of old ardor, the awakening of dormant impulses, had upset her. Far better to have remained as she was, in the dreary habit of abstinence. In addition, there was the smell of smoke on the night wind again as fighting broke out here and there in the town. The search for Kemal continued without success. Men were arrested in their dozens and disappeared into the torture rooms of the palace; still, no one could produce the grandson of Mehemet Dey.

The lack of security kept the court and the city in a turmoil, making Ali Dey more harsh in his judgments, more unyielding in his leadership than he might otherwise have been. Snubs were administered to older men intent on advising the inexperienced ruler. Others, such as the commander of the Janissaries and a number of the court nobles, were slighted or ignored. Soon the odor of malcontent drifted about the palace corridors.

In such a situation, any small change of routine was

greeted with relief; a major incident could bring euphoria. The note from Jawharah was a major incident.

What made the missive outstanding was not so much the news it contained, though Julia was ecstatic to learn that her friend from the harem had married a dealer in rugs and was pleased with her situation. It was the promise inherent in the last sentence which caused such excitement. "I will be happy," Jawharah had written, "to have you visit me." Until her gaze had alighted upon that last phrase, it had not occurred to Julia that the purdah imposed upon her as Rud's woman was not as strict as that which kept the harem of the dey from viewing the world and being viewed by it. It was actually possible, with the permission of her master, for her to go into the city. Since Rud was not present to say her nay, she would go. There was, for excuse, the matter of the bedcurtains and the new cover for the divan. There were the souks and bazaars to be explored, sights to behold and friends to meet, a world of novelty to relieve her boredom. She would go at once!

It was a day bright with the promise of spring. The pale-yellow rays of the sun struck down into the narrow streets where already the tread of countless feet and the hooves of laden donkeys and camels was stirring the drying mud into dust. The mild day had brought a great influx of customers into the bazaar. High-caste Moors jostled elbows with villainous-looking Turkish sailors and mean-visaged wharf rats, swaggering soldiers with fair-skinned Mamelukes in silks and satins. Arab porters abounded, clamoring after everyone who had the look of prosperity. Once Julia was afforded the memorable opportunity of seeing a majestic Tuareg, most lordly of the desert tribes, perched upon the back of his milk-white camel with his handsome, light-skinned face covered by his mask, almost like a veil. Tuaregs were known as the masked men; it had been whispered in the harem that men of this lineage, though calling themselves Mohammedan, ate what they liked, drank what they pleased, including spirits, and prayed when they felt the need. Their women were treated with honor and respect, going for the most part unveiled, allowed to dance and sing and converse before other men, and have a say in the decisions that concerned them. More wondrous than anything else, the lines of inheritance within the tribe were traced through the distaff, surely a most realistic practice.

The major inconveniences of whining beggars and importuning porters were kept from Julia by the presence of Basim. Carrying a vicious kurbash, he strode beside her litter, while flanking her on either side were the pair of eunuch guards with scimitars at their sides. She was able to enjoy the sights and marvelous smells of the market without worrying that her purchases or her small bag of dinars might be snatched from her.

On this occasion Isabel, who was suffering the cramps of menses, had been left behind. Another time, Julia vowed to bring the girl and descend together with her upon the public baths. Then they might meet other women of their own kind, trusted women and concubines of the great merchants of the city.

Jawharah lived in a section of the city neither very poor nor very rich. The house of her husband, situated above his shop where fabulous rugs from all over the orient were displayed, was comfortable without being pretentious. Jawharah, her broad face beaming with pleasure at the sight of Julia, gave orders that her entourage were to be served refreshments in the kitchen. That taken care of, she led the way to the sun-warmed roof of their private apartments. Seated on cushions placed so they could overlook the comings and goings in the street below, holding glasses of hot, syrupy mint tea in their hands, the two women caught up on what had happened since they had last met.

"Are you happy?" Julia asked when she had laughed through the comical story Jawharah made of how her rug dealer had come to the palace, pointed at her, and commanded her to come with him.

"Beyond my wildest hopes. My man is kind, prudent, and lusty. What more can I ask? Ah, well, he could also be young and rich," she answered her own question with a shrug, "but one cannot have everything."

"No," Julia agreed solemnly.

"What is that dangerous-looking ornament you wear at your waist, my dove? Have you taken to going armed like a eunuch guard?"

"What? My knife? It was a gift."

"May I see?" The other took the small dagger in her hand as Julia passed it over. She weighed it for balance, then gave it what appeared to be a casual flip. It flew straight to a pomegranate in a bowl on a table before them and stood quivering in its orange-brown skin.

"Marvelous," Julia cried, retrieving the blade.

"It is a comforting trick to know," Jawharah agreed. "One I learned some time ago from a camel driver. Shall I teach you?"

"If you can."

"Of course, if you will undertake first to tell me how you came by such a pretty trinket, and what has happened to you since last we parted in the harem."

Julia's tale did not take long. When she had finished, Jawharah shook her head slowly, a look of pity on her face. "So. Your man became a Muslim. It was a brave thing, at his age. Did it hurt him much?"

"Hurt him?" An arrested expression entered Julia's eyes. She had been about to fling the knife in imitation of the other woman. Now she was still.

"You do not know? He did not return to have you care for him? I know you said he went away to sea at once, but I thought surely—"

"What do you mean?" Julia asked, her brows drawing together in an anxious frown.

"Jullanar!" the other woman exclaimed. "Did you not know that, unlike Christian men, Muslims are circumcised?"

Circumcised. Despite the fact that in the harem there had been much talk of the difference between circumcised and uncircumcised males, and the bit of surgery required to effect the transformation, she had not realized, had not applied the knowledge to Rud. "So that is why he went away," she exclaimed.

"One of the reasons," Jawharah pointed out. "If Basim said he was sent by the dey, then that also must be so."

"Why didn't he tell me?"

"Who can say? You must put the question to him when you see him again."

"Will it—affect—anything, change him in any way?"

"It should not," Jawharah said, beginning to smile, "but that too you must wait until your man returns to discover."

Julia nodded, her own lips curving in a rueful, answering smile, and then meeting the other woman's eyes, she bit her lips, trying not to laugh. The ordeal could not have been funny for Rud; it must have been extremely painful, in fact. Still, she could not help it. In this particular custom the tables were turned, and it was men who suffered an indignity to this section of their anatomy. The silvery trill of the women's laughter rose, floating freely toward the gentle blue sky.

Chapter
Twenty

*O*n the day that Rud's ship sailed back into the harbor, Julia, with Isabel and Basim, was in the bazaar. The palace grapevine had failed her. When she had set out, she had had no idea that he was expected, or that his vessel was approaching the harbor. There had been no particular need that day to be satisfied; she was only bored and in need of mental stimulation. The sun had grown hot in the past weeks, bringing forth smells both pleasant and unpleasant in the narrow streets. The scent of spices and perfumes, the aromas of roasting meats, baking bread flaps, and frying fat, vied heroically with the smells of dung and of offal from the flyblown butcher shops.

Overcome by the odors, the women turned homeward, bypassing the public baths. It was as they were traversing the streets near the harbor that Julia saw the tall mast of the clipper-style ship standing above the rooftops. She cried out excitedly to Basim, who prodded the bearers of the curtain-enclosed litter to greater speed.

Rud was nowhere in sight when they entered the *gulphor*. Disappointment at not finding him there left Isabel unnaturally quiet. Footsteps dragging, she turned in the direction of her own small cubicle, while Julia, dragging the black robe she wore in public off over her head, stepped into the main sleeping chamber.

As she fought herself free of the suffocating folds and

385

shook out her hair, she heard a small sound like an indrawn breath. She went still, turning toward the sound. Rud stood at the open window. The reflected light slanting across his face gave him a pale and terrible look of grief.

"Rud," Julia cried, a lilt of welcome in her voice as she started toward him.

The flush of sudden anger suffused his face. He reached out and caught her arms, giving her a shake. "Where have you been?" he demanded. "I thought you had gone."

An instant later, he crushed her against him, his mouth hard on hers and his hands making themselves familiar once more with the soft roundness of her body. His breathing ragged, he turned to the couch and drew her down. He removed her clothing with rough, uncaring haste, flinging it with his own into a corner of the room. His need was great, but so was her own, rising in a heady and dizzying wave to her brain. They pressed together in swift urgency, melting into each other in a desperation of desire. They plumbed the depths of being with an abrupt downward plunge like a dream of falling, a descent that brought them finally to rest in each others' arms. It had been a passage of frightening intensity but one that reaffirmed the pleasure of being alive. They lay for long moments while their heartbeats slowed and the perspiration dewing their skin dried, and then they began again more slowly, savoring the closeness, basking in tactile sensation combined with the certain knowledge that nothing could or would prevent them from arriving at the same intense moment of pleasure once more.

Later, with her head resting on Rud's arm, and her eyes closed, Julia allowed the corners of her mouth to curl upward. Nothing had changed; everything was the same.

"What are you smiling about?" Rud asked, his voice lazy with content.

"Nothing," she denied, then her eyes flew open. "Are— are you all right?"

He stared at her a moment before comprehension dawned. One brow shot up. "Why? Any complaints?"

"No, but are you certain?" she insisted.

"I am perfectly fine—now."

"I am serious," she said, distrusting his wry grin.

"So am I," he answered, moving closer to nuzzle the rose-jasmine-scented curve of her cheek.

Satisfied, she abandoned the quest for another. "Did you really think I was gone?"

"What else was I to think?" he asked, the teasing note dying out of his voice. "I returned to find the rooms empty, changed beyond recognition with new furnishing, and none of the old ones in the same place as when I left. Mosaics were on walls I thought had been nothing but stone, and in the kitchen were a trio of the ugliest women I ever beheld, and strangers to boot, who fled screaming at the sight of a male. As if any but a blind man on a dark night could find the heart to rape them!"

"Would it have mattered?" she asked, ignoring his attempt at humor, waiting, oddly breathless, for his answer.

"Matter? After the trouble I have been to establishing you here? If you had put me to the effort of finding you again, I would have wrung your neck the minute I laid eyes on you!"

That was not precisely the answer she had been seeking. The depth of her disappointment left her querulous.

"Instead of which, you bedded me the minute you saw me."

"A much more satisfactory proceeding, now that I think about it," he said.

Julia slanted him a quelling look. "I expect we had better get up before Isabel comes searching for you."

His chest moved in a soundless grunt. "Has she missed her lord and master too?"

"Too?" Julia inquired. "What makes you think I missed you?"

"I don't know. The fervor of your welcome?"

"Conceit!" she declared. "You couldn't tell your own fervor from mine."

"Could I not?"

"No. I see now where Isabel got her strange ideas."

"What kind of ideas?" he asked, ready to be amused.

"That you were like a god. No doubt you planted the impression in her mind yourself."

Rud raised one eyelid. "A charming girl," he murmured.

"I am happy you think so. You need not preen yourself unduly, however. She also thinks you have eyes like an afreet, and would be frightened out of her wits if you chanced to summon her to your couch."

Rud heaved himself to one elbow. "Is that so. Well, she need not worry."

"Oh, I don't believe she is worrying," Julia said, laughter beginning to dance in her amber-gold eyes. "She is happy in her virginity, and awaits only the day when she will be called upon to give it away to the great man who will be her kismet."

"A great man, huh?"

Julia gave a decided nod. "Preferably a Moor or a Turk."

"She has someone definite in mind?"

The interest in his tone made Julia uneasy. "You would not mind, would you?"

"No, not if I thought she would be happy," he answered. "I can hardly take a slave girl back with me to England, if by some remote chance I have the opportunity to go. Nevertheless, she is my responsibility and must be provided for in some manner."

He had mentioned the return to England of his own accord; he had no thought of becoming a Muslim for life, no idea of taking a second wife, or a third or fourth, as allowed by the overgenerous Islamic Code. Reassured, Julia said slowly, "I don't think Isabel would object to entering the harem of Ali Dey."

"You would see her go there, after your experience in the harem of another dey?" he asked, a brooding look in his eyes.

"Ali Dey is a young man, and as Isabel told me, one of his wives is sickly. It is a sad but opportune fact. In any case, there is as much security for a woman there as in any place in Islam. You pointed that out to me yourself."

He did not answer as he absently drew his fingertip

down the valley between her breasts, then began to circle one mound like a climber seeking the top of a mountain. He drew in his breath for a moment, and Julia thought he intended to put a question of importance to her. Instead, he lowered his head to her breast and let her feel the warm flick of his tongue.

"Isabel will be waiting, and Basim," she reminded him again, her voice not quite steady.

He did not raise his head. "Let them wait."

The mission which Ali Dey had entrusted to Rud had been a diplomatic voyage to Morocco and Tripoli. The purpose had been to warn them of the French threat along the North African coast, and to urge a coalition to combat it. The response had been polite interest, many expressions of condolence to Ali Dey for the loss of his uncle, congratulations on his succession to the honors of the august relative, and little else. Gifts of great magnificence had been tendered in recognition of the change in rulership, and Rud had dutifully presented them to Ali Dey. He could not, however, present the assurance that the nearest neighbors of Algeria stood with them against the might of France.

In spite of this setback, with Rud's return, the rule of the new dey became more temperate. The indiscriminate arrests stopped, and the nobles and other court officials were soothed and permitted to regain their former influence. This meant that they were able once more to turn their attention to squabbling among themselves and jockeying for the position of adviser to the throne. It did them little good. The place belonged to Rud, by virtue of some odd alchemy between the two men of a kind that arises sometimes between human beings, a brotherhood spanning the differences of race, birth, culture, and creed. Often in the late hours of the night, Ali Dey would seek Rud out in his apartments, and sitting crosslegged on a divan in his *gulphor,* discuss the events of the day. In these times they dispensed with formality of titles and obeisance, speaking not as ruler to adviser, but as one friend to another.

Usually Julia was called upon to serve some form of refreshment to the two men, or to set out water pipes. In the beginning, she sometimes stayed in discreet quiet listening to the men talk of politics, but also of hunting and the terrible glory of war, of the beauty of horses and the grace of ships, of the wonder of poetry such as that of the Persian, Omar Khayyam, and of the timeless grandeur of the stars which guide both ships of the sea and ships of the desert. Occasionally, as they talked, the dark, considering gaze of the dey would drift to where Julia sat, her face and form concealed by barracan and veil. A frown would crease his brow and his eyes would narrow as if he would penetrate the flimsy defenses which kept him from feasting his fill of her beauty. The black glances he sent Rud at these times sent alarm coursing down Julia's spine, and she soon learned to rouse one of the serving women to serve them, or to place their food and drink before them and withdraw immediately to the sleeping chamber.

One night she found Isabel in the kitchen when she went to give the order for sweetmeats and mint tea. Greatly daring, she suggested to the girl that she might don veil and barracan and personally serve the dey of Algiers. The flush which suffused Isabel's face was enough to show Julia that the girl had hoped for such an order. Assuming a stately air that went well with her size, she bore the prepared tray into the *gulphor*.

She returned pale and trembling with excitement, and with actual gooseflesh on her arms. The Illustrious One had actually looked at her with his black and flashing eyes, had probed with them through her barracan to the generous curves it covered. He had even been heard to inquire of Reuben Effendi the particulars of his ownership of such beauty. The compliments he had made to his host indicated extraordinary interest, so much, in fact, that there was scarce any way their master could refuse to present her to Ali Dey without giving offense.

Her joy was so transparent, her hopes so elevated, that Julia knew a pang of distress, afraid nothing would come of the incident. Rud's reaction was quite otherwise.

He slammed into the sleeping chamber and stalked toward Julia as she lay upon the couch. "What in hell do you mean, throwing Isabel at Ali's head like that? Are you trying to get rid of her? Is that what you want?"

"No, not exactly," Julia answered, sitting up. "You said yourself she needed to be settled."

"She is only fifteen. There's no hurry—unless you are so jealous you don't count the cost to her of getting her out of your hair."

"That's a terrible thing to say!" Julia cried, bouncing to her feet.

"What is so terrible about the truth? You have been at me ever since I came back to do something about her. I should have known two women under the same roof would not work!"

"Don't be ridiculous! I was only trying to help Isabel. She may be no more than fifteen, but by the standards of this part of the world, and her own, she is a woman. She will be much better off where she will be treated like one instead of staying with you as some sort of childish pet for your amusement!"

"You are jealous," he said, staring at her with deep-blue eyes.

Julia felt like slapping him, or screaming at the top of her lungs. Instead, she said through her teeth, "I am not jealous. Isabel and I never have a cross word."

"Because she is afraid of you. She holds you in such awe she hardly dares speak to you."

"Have you taken leave of your senses? She is never quiet, except when you are here, and then she is silent only because she has been taught that lordly males require it."

"That was not the way I heard it."

A suspicion flitted across Julia's mind, but she hardly dared give it credit. "The way you heard it? From whom?"

"From Isabel herself."

Julia's brow cleared. "I think I begin to see," she said slowly. Skirting the couch, she moved to the window casement, letting the soft night breeze fan her heated forehead.

"What are you talking about?"

"Suppose, Rud, that you were a Moor, and quite without any English notions of the tender sensibilities of young girls. Suppose you had two slave girls, one of whom—pleased you, while the other, though attractive in her own way, did not. And suppose further that there was discord between the two women, minor disturbances which upset your household and put your favorite into a temper. What would you be inclined to do about it, if you were a man of the east, a Circassian, perhaps?"

"If you are trying to make me say that I would get rid of the cause of the disturbance, the other woman, then I will remind you that I am not a Moor."

"No, I realize that, but I don't think Isabel does."

Scowling, Rud made no immediate reply. After a time, he walked to where she stood beside the window. Finally, he said, "You are trying to say that Isabel may be manufacturing a disturbance in order to encourage me to do something about her?"

"I think it quite probable, having learned a little something of the way her mind works. She would not want to tender you the insult, you realize, of asking you point-blank to let her go. For then you would lose what the Arab women in the harem called *izzat*, or face, and it would be made to appear also that she had no feeling for you, which would not be true. She respects you and is grateful for your chivalrous attitude toward her, though she does not entirely understand it. These things being true, she still requires more."

"Women!" he exclaimed, a single word that was both a curse and a prayer. A wry smile curved his mouth as he turned to face her. "Julia, my love, I suppose if you are right I must see what can be done. But if you are not right, I will be back to discover why you went to such lengths to deny that you were jealous."

Julia could only swing her head to stare at him and breathe a silent entreaty to whatever gods there might be that she was right.

What Rud said to Isabel, Julia did not hear and had no

way of knowing. The girl was subdued for several days and had trouble meeting Julia's eyes, although she wore also an air of quiet satisfaction. This mood soon wore away to one of high anxiety, and Isabel, forgetful of the wrong she had done Julia, began to seek her out once more, plying her with questions. The scope of her curiosity was wide, encompassing everything from the etiquette of the harem and the bedchamber to best ways to please a man. Julia answered as best she could.

Exactly a week after the climactic visit of Ali Dey, a messenger presented himself at the door with a note for Julia. It was from Rud, who had been on duty in the audience chamber all morning. It instructed her to make Isabel ready to transfer to the harem of the Illustrious Ruler of Algiers.

Within the hour, the master of the harem waited outside the door. This post was no longer held by Abdullah. The Turkish eunuch had been demoted and imprisoned at the time of Kemal's defeat. His second in command served now at this high post, the same man who had taken Julia's message to Ali Pasha long months before. They exchanged a smile and a few words; still, this did not keep Julia from being attacked by sudden apprehension.

As Isabel stood ready to go, Julia put her arms around the young girl. "Are you certain this is what you want?" she asked, her voice tight with worry. "It is not too late to change your mind."

The look of amazement Isabel gave her told plainly how preposterous the suggestion was. The girl's dark eyes shone with anticipation, and her few meager belongings had been tied into a bundle for nearly four days.

"Don't weep for me, Jullanar," she said, seeming suddenly older than her years. "All will be well. Armed with what you have told me, I will turn the dey about my finger. He shall be my slave, instead of I his. I shall have magnificent jewels and fabrics of an exceeding richness to drape about my body. I shall wax and grow fat, presenting many sons to my husband, sons which shall provide my comfort in my old age. I wish I knew your future could be has happy as mine, for I owe to you my most profound gratitude. Without you I could not have achieved this, the desire of my heart."

Julia prepared for Rud's homecoming that evening with some misgivings. She expected his mood to be somber, if not downright surly. That being so, she gave instructions that Basim and the serving women set out their evening meal and then retire to their quarters. She would be better able to deal with his doubts and recriminations without an audience.

She need not have bothered to assure such privacy. Rud did not mention Isabel until they had nearly finished eating, and then in a manner more casual than not.

"Was Isabel happy to leave us today?" he asked, surveying the golden fruit platter for a suitable dessert to top off his meal.

"Deliriously so," Julia answered.

"Ali jumped at the opportunity of taking her into his harem. He has the means now to support many more women than he has yet discovered. When I left him, he was excited as a bridegroom at the prospect of what awaited him tonight."

Julia glanced up. "So soon?"

"He did not want her trained—yet. Interesting, the things the Turks teach the women of their harems—or didn't you find it so?"

"Yes, very," Julia answered, her eyelids lowered as she watched Rud select a fig and pop it into his mouth.

"If I were the dey, or the sultan of Constantinople, how do you suppose I would go about persuading my slave girl to demonstrate what she had learned?"

Julia pretended to consider. "I expect you would simply issue a command."

"Very well. Demonstrate!" he commanded.

"Everything?" she inquired, slanting him an amber glance.

"Everything!"

"I hear and obey," she answered in a voice as subdued as she could make it. "Have I your permission to leave the room first?"

394

With a gesture consciously, or perhaps unconsciously, regal, he gave his consent.

Retreating to their sleeping chamber, Julia threw open the clothing chest. From its depths she drew a barracan that she had purchased in the bazaar. Of a curiously woven transparent silk, half-gray, half-gold, it was weighted at the armholes and around the floating hem with gold and silver beads. Chuckling to herself, she divested herself of her bodice and pantaloons and released her hair from her fillet so that it fell unimpeded to below her hips. Lifting the barracan, she settled it around her. It molded itself softly over the peaks of her breasts and swirled about her ankles. As she moved, the silk rippled with gold and gray shadows, a fascinating interplay of brightness and darkness. Through the shimmering material, her shape gleamed pale and more nudely inviting than total nakedness.

Leaving the chamber, she picked up a dulcimer, also purchased in the bazaar. Carrying it like a shield before her, she returned to the *gulphor*.

Rud glanced up as she entered. His eyes widened a fraction, and he followed her with an intently searching gaze, but said nothing.

Seating herself like a tailor on the divan across from him, Julia placed the dulcimer across her lap and began to play, choosing a plaintive melody in a minor key. Monotonous and unending, it was designed to be played as an aid to digestion during a meal. A quarter of an hour dragged by. Julia heard Rud move restively on his couch, but she did not look up. Her hair drifted over her shoulder, partially screening her lovely, absorbed face. Her breasts rose and fell with her steady, even breathing, causing dancing shadows of gold and gray to play across them.

"Enough," Rud growled at last. "I am sure you play that blasted instrument well, but is that all you were taught?"

Julia raised innocent, gold-flecked eyes. "I could dance for you, but there is no music."

"And a good thing too!"

Setting aside the dulcimer, she allowed her wrists to lie on her parted knees while she knitted her brow in a frown of concentration. "Did you have something else in mind? Let me think. Ah, I know."

Uncurling lithely from the divan, Julia started toward him. Her movements were fluid, marked with deliberate, feline grace. With some difficulty, Rud lifted his gaze to her face. What he saw there caused a wary look to come into his eyes. Already resting on one elbow, he pushed himself to a sitting position.

Julia placed one knee beside him on the couch. Her hands went to his shoulders. Holding his eyes with her own, she let her fingers slide to the fastening of his tunic. With a few competent movements, she stripped it from him. The sash that held his scimitar followed, and then his pantaloons. Trailing her nails across his chest, she lowered her head so that her fair fell silkenly across his lap and her lips were a warm fraction of an inch from his mouth. And then she whispered, "I may have been given to you as your slave, but I do not perform on command!"

Stiffening her arms, she pushed against his chest, sending him onto his back on the couch as she whirled and started from the room. She got no more than a few feet. She was caught and swung around. For long moments Rud stared down at her flushed and mutinous face, registering the hurt that lingered at the back of her eyes.

Abruptly, he gave a nod. "I was wrong," he said. "I am sorry, O dearest of my dreams."

His unexpected understanding brought a rise of slow tears. With a rush, Julia went into his arms, clinging to him while she hid her face in his neck. "So am I," she murmured.

Sighing, Rud kissed her hair, smoothing his hands down the long, silken curtain. Bending, he lifted her and carried her from the *gulphor* into the sleeping chamber. Much later, in the warm spring night laden with the scent of flowers and the cries of insects, came a sleepy voice: "Go to sleep, Madam Thorpe. If you will not perform on my command, will you at least stop on it?"

A soft laugh was his answer. In the space of a moment, his own low-pitched laughter blended with hers, a sound of shared joy in the night.

The pink fingers of dawn crept into the chamber. Slowly, carefully, Julia slipped from the couch and walked to the window. She rested her forearms on the casement, shivering a little at early-morning coolness of the stone. The garden outside was touched with an opalescent light, the heads of flowers and patches of grass shining with dew. In the quiet could be heard the soothing tinkle of water in the fountain, which Basim had repaired. It was a restful scene, and yet, like the stale air enclosed within the walled garden, it was a dull, stifling peace.

Another dawn, another day in Algiers. All was not the same, however. She was not the same. There was something which should, which must, be faced. She loved Rud. She had fallen in love with the man who was her husband, Captain Rudyard Thorpe, Reuben Effendi. It was a ridiculous thing to do; she was under no illusions on that score. One fine day their adventure would finally be over and they would be allowed to go home. Her attraction for him would fade. He would no longer desire her. His reason for wedding her would be done, completed at last after their beginning in New Orleans three, yes, three whole years ago now. Oh, she did not think he would cast her off penniless. There would be a ticket to New Orleans, an allowance of some form, a monthly or yearly stipend which would salve his conscience and keep her from the workhouse or the cruel charity of relatives. She could expect little more; she did not want even that much.

Would he divorce her? It would cause a scandal, require special dispensation from the church. Still, he must, if he wanted his freedom, if he ever desired to take a woman of his own country, England, to wife. Rud must have planned originally on an annulment when his marriage to her had served its purpose. That was before his lust had overcome his scruples. No, perhaps she was being unjust. Rud was not an insensitive man. There was every probability that he would hold to his marriage vows, regardless of his own wishes. The question was, would she accept the sacrifice? No, she would not. To love a man who did not love her would never be enough.

Pride. It could be a strong ally, and as strong an enemy.

The rustle of the bedclothes behind her told her that Rud was no longer asleep. His voice reached her, the words dropping like stones in the thick, somber quiet. "I forgot to tell you last night, Julia. The man on St. Helena is dead."

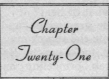

Chapter
Twenty-One

Jawharah reached for a peach from a silver platter. It was the fourth she had taken in the half hour Julia had been sitting with her.

"Truly, I know I should not," the woman said, giving a rueful grimace as she caught Julia's eye. "But I am so hungry now that I am eating for two. Ah, Julia, to think of a child at my age. It is a miracle! I am blessed among women. Sometimes my joy is so great I cannot bear it, and must cry to confuse the evil jinn who hate happiness."

This delightful news had been the reason for a summons to Julia to visit. Having already said everything that was appropriate for such an occasion, Julia now asked, "And your husband, what does he think?"

"His pride is great, though he says little. He walks taller, and smiles often. His first wife, long dead, gave him a son, who is now married and has children who will be older than this babe. My first child. A year ago, who would have dared predict such a thing? It is passing strange, the way life treats us, is it not?"

Julia could only agree, sharing the woman's wonder with a smile.

"I often think of the other women of the harem, and wonder how they fare," Jawharah went on. "It is as if I had two hundred sisters, some dear, some not so dear, and yet all of my blood."

"I hear news of them now and then," Julia replied. "I understand a few, a very few, were married like yourself. A dozen or so became servants in the palace, primarily in the nursery of Ali Dey."

"And Mariyah, what of her?"

"According to the grapevine—and you may judge for yourself how accurate the report may be—she was sold to a slave trader who took her to Beirut. There she was bought by an Arab princeling and disappeared into purdah."

One after another, names were mentioned. This woman had been sold to Constantinople, that one to Tripoli, to Tartary, or even to far-off Cathay. A few were to be seen in the houses of prostitution about the harbor, where they appeared resigned to their lot, if not content. In each case, Ali Dey, true to his word, had allowed the women to keep the valuables given to them by the old dey. Though he had not precisely set them free in the way Julia had envisioned, his disposition of the women had been humane in the eyes of Islam and had gone far to correct the earlier impression he had made of being less than a moderate ruler.

Jawharah shook her head. "Of them all, I fear you and I have come out best. We have both been accepted by men we can respect and, in the recesses of our hearts, even love."

Julia turned her gaze to the wise eyes of her friend. "Is it so obvious?" she asked after a moment.

"It isn't obvious at all. You do not look as happy as such knowledge should make you. At the same time, you no longer seem barren of feeling. I see in you a new grace, though not the harmony of content. Tell me if I am wrong."

"No, you are not wrong. I love the man called Reuben. The only difficulty is that my love is not returned. Speak to me in your wisdom, my friend, and tell me how to make a man love me."

The other woman sighed and tossed her peach pit over the parapet which surrounded the roof on which they sat. There came a yelled curse from the street below; it had struck someone. Jawharah ignored it. Licking her fingers free of juice, she said, "This problem is an ancient one. Some would say you must hold yourself ready to be of service to your lord at all times, assuring clean clothing to soothe his body and good food to fill his stomach. Certainly a man must appreciate such attention to his comfort, but his mother did as much for him, and you do not wish to be regarded with the same sort of fondness as the woman who bore him. Then, there are those who hint that the gratification of his physical desire is paramount. Still, cannot that be provided by any woman of the streets? Others expound on the necessity of engaging a man's mind, of appealing to his intelligence, but love is not a product of the brain alone, any more than it is of the stomach or the loins. Must a woman strain to satisfy every particular, then? No, I think not. A man loves a woman not for what she does, or even for what she is, but for the way she appears in his own eyes. Therefore, a man cannot be made to love a woman; he either does, or does not."

For long moments Julia was silent. At last she asked, "Under unusual circumstances, could he not love without being aware of it, without admitting it even to himself? I am sure this is so, for I did not recognize what I felt for Reuben until a short time ago."

"All things are possible," Jawharah said, "if it be the will of Allah, whose name be exalted."

Julia interpreted this to mean that Jawharah did not think so in truth, but would not deny Julia the comfort of thinking it might be possible. She smiled and changed the subject.

They fanned themselves against the summer heat, and switched at flies attracted to the bowl of sticky peaches. In a desultory manner, they spoke of many things—the weather, childbirth, Isabel the Circassian and the ease with which she had settled into the harem of Ali Dey.

In time, Jawharah said, "I have heard that on an island in the sea, the great ruler who presented the gift of the bee to your mother has died. This news came to you also?"

"Yes, I heard it."

"You are saddened by the death of this man, it may be?"

"Greatly saddened," Julia replied, thinking of Eugène Robeaud and his gentle courage. She prayed that his suffering had not been more than he could bear, and that he had not come to regret his sacrifice. Had M'sieu Robeaud and the others ever realized what had happened to Napoleon Bonaparte? How long had it been before they had recognized that there would be no return to power, no restoration of the emperor's glorious reign? What must it have been like on that hot, sea-washed island when hope was gone, and still the impostor lingered, preventing the release of Napoleon's entourage? Were they loyal to Robeaud? Did they stay? Or did they leave him to die alone?

"Do not look so, my dove," Jawharah exclaimed. "Sorrow passes as surely as night passes into day. Joy returns as does the sun."

Impulsively, Julia reached out to touch the other woman's hand. "You have been a true friend to me, Jawharah," she said. "I would have been lost without you."

"And I would have been lost without your bravery in speaking to Ali Dey for the women of the harem. How you ever dared I cannot imagine."

"He is not such a formidable man."

"Perhaps not, to a beautiful young woman," Jawharah returned.

"What you are hinting had nothing to do with his agreeing to what I asked."

The other woman glanced at Julia, at her bright, suntouched hair and the mysterious depths of her eyes. "Did it not? I can see you are still not used to men who look at each woman who comes under their influence as possible bedmates. No doubt Ali Dey was not easy enough on this throne to let his mind wander strongly in such a direction at the time, but I would take care how I put myself in his power again."

"You sound as if you do not approve of Ali Dey as a ruler," Julia observed.

"Did I say so?" the other woman asked, her eyes wide. She glanced about as though she expected to see listeners who might report what was said to the dey. There were none. The roof opened wide around them, except for the house's solid walls that rose on two sides, lending the shade in which they sat. There was no one near, though Basim hovered somewhere inside the room from which they had reached the roof garden, waiting within call against the time when Julia would be ready to leave. Jawharah went on with emphasis, "I certainly did not mean to cast doubts upon the ability of Ali Dey. He is a strong man such as is needed in the post. I have no fault to find with him, none whatever."

"Nor I," Julia said, as much from conviction as because of Jawharah's frantic signal. She was as aware as the other woman that spies were everywhere. She had simply thought it not quite so imperative to be wary here in a private home as in the palace.

"Ali Dey is a vastly better ruler for us than Kemal, the once fat, would have been. Do you not agree?"

"Undoubtedly," Julia answered, puzzled by the curious epithet Jawharah had given Kemal.

"It would be a good thing if matters were so arranged that there could be no danger of Kemal succeeding to the honors of his grandfather, or of his cousin, Ali Dey."

"This is so," Julia answered, and waited. So much lip service to the excellence of the present dey must have some further point.

"If Ali Dey could be informed of the presence of Kemal, he would surely destroy his cousin's hopes of replacing him."

"He has been searching for him diligently these many weeks for just such a purpose," Julia agreed.

"Verily, and the quarry hidden away beneath his nose," Jawharah whispered as one awestruck.

Why could the woman not come straight out and say what she meant? Would it spoil the pleasure of having information to impart, decrease the importance of it? Or would it simply make it too easy for eavesdroppers to understand? How tired she was of these devious twists of the mind. "You mean you know where Kemal is?"

"Not so loud," Jawharah hissed, her eyes narrowing. "I have no wish to become involved again with the business of the mighty. My simple life with my husband and the prospect of a child to enliven my days satisfy me. I bestir myself to jeopardize such a peaceful existence only that I may, by so doing, pay the debt I owe you and to Ali Dey, and make my present way of life more secure. Kemal has a vicious temper and a long memory. No doubt he knows, or suspects, that you were instrumental in his downfall, and he has been in a position these last few months to notice that we, you and I, are still friends. Such a close connection with his enemy would not be ignored if he returned to the throne."

"You mean you fear reprisal because you associate with me, if Kemal should come to power?"

"I fear it not only for myself, but for my husband and my child."

"If that is so, I am sorry," Julia said. "But you must tell me what you mean by your hints. Have you seen the once-fat relative of him who is in paradise, that you can describe him? Is this one somewhere close in hiding that he has seen the visits I make to your house?"

"You have penetrated to the truth. On the occasions when I went with you and the Lady Fatima to sit behind the viewing screen over the audience chamber, I took careful note of the features of Kemal. There, too, I saw the Frankistani of the sharp eyes and the full lips who is the hireling of the French consul. It is possible I would not have recognized Kemal if I had not seen the other also."

"Where?" Julia insisted. "When?"

"I saw them once together, entering the coffee house in the alley which leads from this street below. It is a poor place where the thick fog of opium smoke rolls from the door. It may be that Kemal has a room above it, for I also saw him once coming from the alley alone, without the

Frankistani. If you were to see him, you would not credit that it was he. Even I, who have had much training in the recognition of men's faces, nearly passed over him as an Arab street beggar. He is thinner by far than when last we saw him. His face is sunburned, his clothing dirty, and the nails on his hands broken and black with grime."

"You are certain it was he?"

"I am certain. I watched him from this roof for the space of time it takes to come from the end of the street to this alley. There could be no mistake."

Julia drew a deep breath. "If it is so, and Reuben can carry this information to Ali Dey, it may be that in his gratitude the dey will allow Reuben and me to return to our homeland."

"If this comes to pass, Jullanar, my dove, my heart will beat with gladness for you, though tears may fill my eyes."

"And I shall miss you and long for your sage counsel wherever I may be," Julia replied. "Still, you will understand if I depart from you in haste now?"

"I will understand," Jawharah said, and embraced her. Stepping back, she clapped her hands, a signal to Basim that his mistress was ready to depart.

Once away from the house, Basim moved close to the curtains of Julia's litter. "My Lady Jullanar, do I have your permission to speak?" he asked, his voice low.

"Certainly, Basim."

"Touching upon this matter of importance of which you and the Lady Jawharah spoke. Might it not require more investigation before the subject is broached to Reuben Effendi?"

With resignation, Julia accepted the fact that Basim had listened to their conversation. His suggestion had merit. "What did you have in mind?"

"A child playing near this coffee house of which the wife of the rug dealer spoke might see much, and if in his innocence he were to find entry, he might hear more."

It would be a relief to have the identity of Kemal confirmed by someone who had seen him many more times than Jawharah. Julia did not doubt Basim's ability to appear to be a small boy; still, it was a dangerous undertaking. If Basim could recognize Kemal in his disguise, the reverse might also be true. "Is it worth the risk?" she asked.

"As a matter of vengeance, yes, a hundred times over. As a matter of service to you, fair mistress, then yes, a thousand times."

The dwarf had been silent in the main concerning his treatment at the hands of Kemal, and concerning the crime of which he had been accused. His feet had healed, recovering their quick movement, and, officially, all was forgotten. But sometimes his soft eyes would grow hard and he would finger his small scimitar as if in urgent need of some outlet for his anger.

Julia drew a deep breath. "You are a man, Basim. You must do as you will."

The decision, so quickly made, tormented Julia, though she would not have unsaid it if she could. Basim was no slave of hers, or of Rud's. For all his small size, he was a free Mussulman. His allegiance had been to Mehemet Dey; he served her only because of the duty imposed upon him by the old dey as he lay upon his deathbed. Nevertheless, when night fell without the reappearance of the dwarf, she grew pale with worry. He could be so easily disarmed by those larger and stronger than he. To kill him would be no more difficult than snuffing out the life of a child. If anything happened to him, she would hold herself responsible for the rest of her days.

The moon rose, pouring its golden light into the sleeping chamber. Julia, lying awake beside Rud's sleeping form, listened for some sound that would indicate Basim's return. There was none. She tortured herself with wondering if she should wake her husband and explain what had happened, leaving the weighty problems of whether to inform Ali Dey of Jawharah's suspicions on his shoulders. But what if Rud told Ali, and it all came to nothing? Would the dey not think less of Rud for listening to the tales of women? What if he retaliated in some manner for the false report, perhaps with reprimands and demotion? His behavior, if he was made to look foolish because of unnecessary precautions, was unpredictable. No, she could not bring herself to risk it. Not yet.

At breakfast, Rud asked, "Where is Basim? He did not serve us last night at dinner, and is not in evidence this morning."

"I don't know," Julia answered. "It may be he had business of his own to occupy him away from the palace."

"He has never had any before," Rud pointed out.

The need to inform Rud of what was happening and ask his advice warred with caution in her mind. The result was an irritation of the nerves which made her answer sharper than it might otherwise have been. "Basim is not a slave. He does not have to answer to us for his comings and goings, nor am I responsible for his whereabouts."

Rud looked at her with a frown between his brows. "What is the matter with you? Your tossing and turning kept me awake half the night, and you look like death this morning."

"There is nothing whatever the matter with me," Julia replied, angered, unreasonably, by both his acumen and his obtuseness. Any other husband would have failed to notice her haggard looks, or if he had, would have immediately attributed them to monthly causes or the confinement of her present position.

Rud stared at her a moment longer, his blue eyes cool, then got to his feet. Taking up his scimitar, he strapped it about his waist. With swift sure movements, he wrapped the turban of muslin he was now entitled to wear about his head and tucked the end into place.

With some idea of reaching him quickly if necessary, Julia asked, "Where will you be today?"

"With the dey, as usual," he answered. Moving toward her, he gave her a hard, unsmiling kiss. As he turned toward the door, a serving woman rushed to open the panel for him and close it quietly behind him. If it had not been for the woman's aid, Julia thought, he might have slammed from the apartments.

Waiting. It was all she seemed to do. Without doubt, it was the lot of women who must depend upon men to play the active part in the drama of their lives. Was it any

407

wonder that sometimes, when they could, women took their revenge by forcing men to wait upon them?

The garden was in shadow and the heat of the day was already leaving the stone walls under the dews of evening when Basim at last appeared. He was white about the mouth, and his bow was somewhat stiff as he presented himself to her, although he seemed unhurt.

"Basim," she cried, getting to her feet and giving him her hand to kiss. "I have been sick with worry. Are you well?"

"I am as you see me, well indeed, my lady Jullanar," he answered. "I would have been with you much sooner except for stupidity and ill fortune."

"You are here now," Julia said. "Be seated, and tell me what has occurred."

As she returned to her bench in the garden, Basim folded his legs and sank down at her feet. "My lady, it happened in this manner. I altered my appearance and went to the coffee house mentioned by the Lady Jawharah. There I found Kemal, just as she had said. He was changed, but recognizable. No sooner had I ascertained this than the Frankistani who is his ally also arrived. Together they mounted the stairs to a chamber above. In good time, I followed. They were, however, most careful. It was not easy to come upon them at a listening distance. Yet, with patience and agility, I did so by way of the balconies. With my own ears, I heard Kemal and the Frankistani plotting with a third person, who was, I think, the favorite boy of Kemal. They plan to enter the palace in one night's time and strangle the dey with the tasseled ropes of his bedcurtains while he sleeps."

Julia drew a sharp breath. "Could such a thing be done? Could they enter the palace, get past the guards?"

"Money is a key which opens many doors. Those guards who will not look the other way must be overcome. At the time when the deed will have been done, the followers loyal to Kemal are to attack the palace, surging into the breach left behind by the others. They hope for quick victory with surprise on their side. They expect the Janissaries, when they find Kemal in possession of the palace and supported by the French government, to give him their blessing."

"I see," Julia said thoughtfully.

"It is at this point in my adventure that my renowned magic deserted me. With the information for which I had come in my posesssion, I left the balcony and thought to return back through a sleeping chamber and down the stairs to the main room of the coffee house and into the street. When I was halfway across the sleeping chamber, I heard someone approaching, about to enter. Quickly, I lifted the lid of a clothing chest and slipped inside, burrowing beneath hot woolen burnooses scented with camphor, and a multitude of soiled pantaloons. Kemal and his favorite entered and laid themselves upon the couch. They did not rise until noon. I might have crept out in the night if I had not myself fallen asleep during the long wait for them to cease their play. My magic was still not returned, for by some ill chance Kemal chose that very sleeping chamber in which to hold a meeting of the commanders of his followers. The details of their attack made for interesting listening, but I was most uncomfortable, I do assure you, my lady. It was only an hour ago that I was able to leave my suffocating prison. I fear the clothing in the chest will never be worn by a fastidious man again, though I absolve Kemal of all claim to such a title. In any case, when I deliver my message this night he will no longer have need of his winter wardrobe."

This night? Of course. Basim had heard the plan of attack the night before. This very evening was the time of Ali Dey's great danger. "What are you waiting for?" Julia cried. "You must go at once to warn the dey!"

"Think you he would trust me after I have been accused of poisoning his uncle? I think it much more likely that he would put me to the test of pain first to be certain my tongue speaks the truth."

"Surely not?"

"It is not a chance I would like to take. Those in mortal pain can enjoy vengeance very little."

"What do you suggest, then?" Julia asked.

"If you will write a letter, using the extraordinary wisdom you possess, for a woman, of this art, I will take it to Reuben Effendi. Ali Dey once heeded a warning from you and profited by it. He may do so again, especially if it is delivered in the person of your master."

Julia did not care for that designation, but this was no time to argue. "Very well," she said, and clapped her hands, calling for pen and paper.

Basim did not return. The only indication Julia had that he had reached Rud with her message was the fact that Rud did not leave the side of the dey to return to the apartments either. It seemed to her overwrought mind that there was an uneasy quiet about the palace. After dinner, her serving women retired for the night, leaving her alone in the quiet emptiness of the *gulphor*. She took up a book of Persian love poems and put it down again, unable to concentrate. Her fingers stiff with nerves, she made a botch of her needlework and cast it aside also. Unable to stand the closed-in feeling of walls around her, she stepped out into the garden, breathing the soft night air.

It was there that she heard the first cries echoing across the vast complex of courtyards. "The dey has been attacked! Someone has tried to kill the dey!"

Like a beehive that has been invaded, the palace erupted with noise and confusion. The clatter of running footsteps came from all directions, as hard upon one catastrophe came another, an assault upon one of the main gates to the palace. The rattle and clash of musketry could be heard once more, as it had so short a time ago. The tread of marching men sounded outside the entrance to Julia's apartments, then an order was barked. When Julia looked out, she saw the eunuchs, who had stood for so many days outside like guardian statues, being marched away at a quick step.

The urge to follow was nearly overpowering. She wanted so badly to know what was happening; if Basim and Rud had managed to warn the dey in time, if the would-be assassins had been caught, and if anyone had been injured in the attempt. For all she knew, Rud and Basim and Ali Dey might be lying dead somewhere and the palace filled with Kemal's men. No, that could not be true, she tried to reassure herself, for then the cry that had gone up would not have been that someone had tried to kill the dey, but that the dey was dead. No doubt everyone who could was fighting to prevent the takeover by Kemal's followers. She must not get in their way.

She paced the floor, beating the palms of her hands together. The sound of fighting and of men hurrying here and there had died away, and still no one came. Once more, she walked out into the garden and stood straining to hear. She sniffed the night wind for the taint of smoke, but this time there was none. Above her the multistoried towers of the palace rose into the calm night sky. Here and there windows glowed from the light within. Sometimes the light dimmed as though a figure had passed between the lamp and the window, but no fiery tongues of flame leaped at the walls. All was serene.

Despite that appearance, Julia still felt the tingling of nerves beneath her skin. So acute was her apprehension that she shied at the feathery touch of a large moth that blundered past her as she turned back toward the lighted *gulphor*. Castigating herself for a silly fool, she stepped into the room.

A whisper of sound, a faint rustle of clothing, was her only warning. Before she could react, a muscular arm caught her from behind, clamping about her waist. The knife she wore at her side was plucked from its scabbard and sent spinning across the room to land with a clatter against the wall. In the same instant she was given a hard shove that sent her stumbling, to sprawl onto the divan.

Julia twisted to her side, flinging the hair back from her face so she could see. A man stood between her and the garden door with a vicious smile drawing his full lips back over his teeth. As she stared at him, he reached behind him to take up a kurbash, which leaned against the wall where he had placed it.

"Yes, Julia, *ma chère*," Marcel de Gruys drawled. "It is I. At last the time has come for which I have long waited. We are alone, and I have in my hands the means to settle old scores, and new ones." He slashed the

411

rhinoceros-hide whip through the air so that it sang with an evil whine. "Do you flinch, my lovely, untouchable Julia? Do you cringe with dread? Well you might, for I intend to take my toll of your lovely white skin. This time you have no weapon with which to thwart me, for I have seen to that. I will now exact from you in pain the price of a knife wound in the back and a ball in the chest, and also the pleasure which you denied me of being known as the man who saved the world from Napoleon Bonaparte, and for the failure to secure here in Algiers a puppet ruler for France. Oh yes, I know whom I have to thank for the destruction of my plans. I told that fool Kemal he was taking too great a chance, remaining hidden so close to a place where you came and went, so close to the abode of one who had been of the palace. He laughed at me, certain his disguise could not be penetrated. Hadn't you passed us in the streets a half dozen times without a hint of recognition? Each time I wanted to take you by force and eliminate you in my own way. Such pleasure was denied to me. You were not that important, he contended, but important enough that your disappearance would cause a thorough search of the section of the city where we were hiding. He promised to give you to me to do with you as I would when he was in power, to finish what was between us at my leisure. Imbecile! That I listened to him is my shame. No matter, I will not be cheated of my due though a Moorish princeling lies in chains and Islamic dogs bay at my heels! I will hear you beg for mercy and see you writhing at my feet if it is my last sight on earth! And when that is done and the sight has sufficiently whetted my desire, I will have you while you whimper and cry under me!"

His eyes blazing, he swung his arm back. As he began the downward slash, Julia gathered her muscles and rolled over the backless divan. The whip bit down into the covering where she had lain, slicing into it like the sharp edge of a knife. She bounded to her feet, and as Marcel started for her over the divan, she made a dash to where the blade of her knife gleamed in the far corner.

Marcel also saw her objective. He leaped in the same direction, and as she reached out for the knife, the kurbash came down across her outstretched fingers.

Her hand went numb, then a sickening wave of pain washed over her. Before she could recover, the kurbash swung again, slashing into the bare skin about her waist. The third blow ripped into the thin muslin of her pantaloons to curl about her hips. A red haze of agony rose before her eyes. Instinctively, she turned her back, trying to protect her soft underbelly, and the tender globes of her breasts. She received the full weight of a cracking blow across her shoulder blades, and her body was gripped in the sudden paroxysm of unbearable anguish. Blindly, she put out her hand, holding to the wall for support, sagging against the cool stone.

Abruptly the blows ceased. She heard the slow, assured footsteps as Marcel approached her. She could feel the warm trickle of blood where the kurbash had bitten into bare skin. By a supreme effort of will, she raised her head and pushed away from the wall, turning like an animal at bay to face Marcel.

He smiled, his black eyes holding hers as he thrust the whip under his arm and drew a knife from the sheath at his side. "As much as I am enjoying this, I believe my pleasure would be greater if you were somewhat less well clothed."

With ludicrous care, he inserted the tip of the knife beneath the fastening of her bodice between her breasts. With one quick upward flick, he sliced it through. The sharp blade caught in the chain she wore, however, cutting the soft pure gold with ease. The yellow diamond, and also her gold bee worn with it when she went unveiled, fell to the floor. Marcel scarcely noticed as he used the blade to flip the two sections of her bodice open, exposing the firm, warm treasure to his darkling gaze. Julia drew in her breath, flattening her stomach as his attention turned downward. There was nothing she could do with a knife pressed against her abdomen. Gold and silver beads scattered, bouncing over the floor, as her girdle parted, allowing her pantaloons to settle about her ankles.

Reaching out, Marcel caught her wrist, jerking her forward away from her clothing on the floor. As he stripped the bodice down her arms and tossed it aside, she stood before him as naked as the day she had been born. He ran his tongue over his lips, devouring her with his eyes. "Soon," he said. "Soon now you will beg me to stop, promise me anything to spare you the pain. I may be tempted to call a halt before I am done if you beg prettily enough and offer yourself with the proper abandon."

What reservoir of strength she drew upon she did not know, but in an instant, her eyes blazed with scorn. In defiance of the memory of Mariyah under the whip and the keening scream that had come finally from the Circassian's lips, she said, "Never! Never, though I die for it!" And in the same instant, she brought up her free hand in a swinging blow that snapped his head back.

"One more thing for which you must pay," Marcel grunted, and wrenching her arm behind her back, he bent over her, smearing his hot lips over her face as he tried to cover hers.

Julia strained away, though her elbow and shoulder were on fire with pain. She pushed at him, the air caught tight in her lungs against the nauseating slickness of his groping mouth and the smell of his breath. To kick out at him was her one thought. She jerked up her right knee, trying to find his ankle. Her knee struck between his legs, and the effect was instantaneous. Marcel gave a gasping yell and threw her bodily from him. She struck the wall and fell heavily on her side. Before she could recover, the whining whip bit into her shoulder and her flank.

At that moment there came a soft sound from behind them in the direction of the kitchen. A serving woman stood in the doorway of the gulphor. Her eyes grew wide with horror as they fastened upon Julia, and then as Marcel swung around with a curse, the woman backed away, scuttling out of sight.

Minor though the distraction was, it was enough. Never for an instant had Julia been unaware of where her knife
414

lay. Now she scrambled to her hands and knees and lunged for it. As she felt her fingers curl around the cool, jewel-encrusted metal, she felt a surge of strength. It would not last long, she knew, but perhaps it would last long enough.

Her sudden movement brought Marcel around. He checked at the sight of the weapon in her grasp, then relaxed. "So you have your knife," he jeered. "Much good may it do you. This time I am doubly armed against you; I have a weapon and I know your mind. To damage me with your toy, you must first get close, and I think you will find that my reach is far longer than yours."

To prove his point, he drew his arm back and sent the kurbash slicing down at her once more. It was a mistake, for it gave her an open target. Without hesitation, she turned the knife so that the blade was in her fingers. And then as Jawharah had shown her once in the spring sunlight, she sent it flashing straight at his chest.

Perhaps her strength was not as great as she thought. Perhaps the trembling in her arm betrayed her aim. Whatever the cause, the handle of the knife struck first with a thud. The useless blade clattered to the floor.

Marcel's grin of triumph, coming as it did after a moment of sheerest terror, was an evil thing to see. He had shuddered to a halt as he was struck, and now once more he sent his arm back to flay her.

The blow never landed. Like a trio of furies, the two serving women and the cook erupted from the kitchen area. They were armed with a broom and a carving knife, a pan and a fire poker, a skillet and a mallet. Alarm spread over Marcel's face. He tried to hold his ground, cutting the air with the kurbash. The broom served as a good defense against his blows, however, and he was backed slowly toward the door, with the women yelling, screaming, shrieking insults at the top of their lungs. Turning his back to find the handle of the door was a mistake. A sharp blow from the pan to the side of his head sent him to his knees, and he was beaten to the floor under a rain of blows.

Julia tried to speak, to tell the women to stop short of

killing him, but she could not command her voice. Instead, she began to laugh, and at the same time tears began to stream from her eyes. Raising shaking hands to her face, she bowed her head onto her knees. When next she looked up, one of the serving women was placing a blanket about her while a eunuch guard stood to one side. She had not been aware of losing consciousness, and yet she must have, for Marcel was nowhere in sight.

When she was covered, the guard picked her up and carried her from the apartments. Where they were going she did not know. She wanted to protest, to object to the chafing of the blanket against her raw skin and the movement that sent black arrows of pain through her brain, wanted to declare her unwillingness to leave Rud's apartments. The words would not quite form themselves upon her tongue. There was a strange gray fog gathering around her. Through it she was looming nearer and nearer the great carved cedar doors of the harem of the dey. They opened wide, swallowed her up, and were slammed shut behind her.

```
┌─────────────────────┐
│                     │
│      Chapter        │
│    Twenty-Two       │
│                     │
└─────────────────────┘
```

Footsteps, whispers, the overpowering, smoky smell of perfume censers, the sleepy chirp of the captive birds disturbed in their rest. These familiar things assaulted Julia's senses as she was carried through the vastness of the common room. The guard turned down a corridor that reeked of hot oil from the lamps burning at intervals. A few strides more, and they ducked through the heavy swags of beaded curtains. Julia saw around her once more the confining walls of a cubicle such as she had thought never to see again. She was placed on the yielding soft-ness of a couch. The guard bowed himself from her pres-ence, and she was alone.

Her solitude did not last. Before the curtains had stopped swinging behind the guard, Ismael, the Arab physician, stepped through. He removed the blindfold he had worn as he was guided through the harem and handed it to the serving woman waiting outside. Then he turned to Julia. With gentle hands, he cleansed her stripes and soothed their pain with a healing balm. He spoke little as he turned her this way and that, though his mouth was grim and sometimes he made a sound of mingled sym-pathy and anger that he was unable to suppress. He mixed a draft which Julia recognized as having the dis-tinctive odor of the fruit of the poppy and placed it in her hand.

"No musk this time?" Julia inquired, phantoms of

memory dancing in her amber eyes in the flickering light of the lamp.

"No musk," he replied as he watched her drink and took the cup away. With cool, passionless fingers, he drew a linen coverlet over her, then sat beside her until she slept.

Julia awakened to a quiet but steady tapping. She raised curiously heavy eyelids to see a woman standing over her. She was blond, plump, and in a high state of irritation. Her lips were thin, her eyes hard, and her slippered foot patted the floor with a monotonously regular sound. It was Isabel.

In the weeks since Julia had last seen her, she had lost her air of naiveté.

"So, you have returned to your old place," the girl said as she saw Julia's gaze sharpen with consciousness.

Julia moistened her lips. "It begins to look that way."

"Why? You were not happy here before. I know, because you told me so yourself. Why have you put yourself in the way of the dey again?"

Surely it was not jealousy that caused the sharp tone in Isabel's voice. "I did not put myself in the way of the dey. In fact, I have no idea why I am here, except perhaps to make it easier for Ismael the physician to come to me."

"You lie. The order to bring you here was given to your guard by the commander of the eunuchs. You, of all people, must know that this man acts only on the orders of his master, and mine."

"I swear I have had no communication with Ali Dey. I am here because of these," Julia said, and threw back the coverlet to reveal her whip marks.

Isabel sucked in her breath. "You—you must have displeased Reuben Effendi mightily."

"The effendi did not do this," Julia said sharply. "It was another, who came last night while the guards were called away, the Frankistani called de Gruys, who was involved in the attempt upon the life of the dey."

"Ah, this one has been placed under arrest." The other girl looked thoughtful. "It may be that the dey sought to protect you, then, while Reuben Effendi was busy with other things. There is much respect between the illustrious ruler of Algiers and the Frankistani who was once my master."

Julia nodded without reply. She had no strength to argue. Her lash marks gave her surprisingly little pain, however. She was sore, but the burning and inflammation had gone, taken away by the ointment Ismael had used.

"There is still no reason to bring you here," Isabel persisted. "You could have been guarded as easily in the quarters of Reuben Effendi as here. You would have been safe enough with your guards returned to duty."

"What are you suggesting?"

"I think Ali Dey may have seen a way of wresting you from Reuben Effendi. You have always excited his interest. He gave you the yellow diamond, did he not? I have watched from hiding and seen him gaze upon you when he thought no one was looking. He envied his friend the possession of you, for you are like the rare gem which all men wish to own."

"It is kind of you to say so," Julia replied in a dry tone, "but I am sure you are wrong. Ali Dey was too occupied with the assassination attempt and the revolt to trouble with any woman. It is as I said, a case of bringing the patient to the physician."

"No," Isabel said stubbornly. "Tell me, when you were in the harem did you ever know of a woman of the dey to be examined in her cubicle?"

Julia saw the trend of the question at once. Reluctantly, she answered, "No, they were always carried to a special chamber fitted with a curtain."

"And the examination was conducted through the curtain by touch alone," Isabel added.

"It is so."

"Why, then, was Ismael the physician blindfolded, led to your chamber, then permitted to view your nakedness?"

"It would not be the first time," Julia said wearily, and went on to explain.

Isabel gave a decided shake of her head. "That would make no difference. A slave dealer sees a woman who is bought by the dey before the sale, and yet, if he sets eyes on her afterward without knowledge and permission of her master, he may be blinded, even killed. And this, I think, is the answer. The dey gave his permission because he greatly feared to see your body scarred by the kurbash, and he knew it would be impossible to treat such injuries by touch."

"Isabel, please," Julia said, closing her eyes. "I do not know why I am here, nor why I have been treated differently. I only know I do not intend to compete with you for the favor of Ali Dey."

"I believe you mean what you say. I also know you may not be able to help yourself."

This was indisputable. Julia swallowed hard, trying to ease the tight feeling in her chest. She heard Isabel turn and stride to the grilled window. After a time, she opened her eyes. Making a great effort, she asked, "Have you news of Reuben Effendi, and perhaps of Basim the dwarf?"

"I have not heard of their deaths, if that is what you mean," Isabel said over her shoulder.

It was not precisely what she had meant, but the information was welcome. Had Rud returned to their quarters? What had he thought to find her gone? Did he know what had happened and where she had been taken? Did he care? They had parted in coolness after an exchange of words. What had it been about? Oh yes, the whereabouts of Basim. Rud had sensed something was wrong. It had been a mistake to keep it from him. She should have known he would do nothing to jeopardize his position. With more advance warning, the efforts to prevent the attack could have been much better planned. Marcel might never have escaped the net spread to catch him.

Abruptly, Isabel turned. "Kemal and his accomplices will be brought before Ali Dey in the audience chamber this morning. The wives of the dey have been given permission to attend, and also myself. There will be no objection, I think, if you wish to come also."

"Brought before the dey—to be judged?"

"Even so. There can be no question of their guilt, for

they were seen in the act of trying to strangle the slave who occupied the bed of Ali Dey. In the struggle to capture them, the Frankistani made his escape, but Kemal was taken with the—the young man who has been his favorite. Greatly wroth, the grandson of the old dey cursed Ali Dey and lamented that his attempt to kill him had been unsuccessful."

Julia raised herself so that she could look at the other girl. "This young man who was taken with Kemal, Isabel. Was he—could he have been your twin brother who was bought by Kemal and separated from you?"

"Your memory is long, Jullanar. It is indeed he who came with me from my mother's womb."

"Then he is no more than a child, a boy of fifteen! What will happen to him?"

Isabel's face was grim, and suddenly older. "I have the promise of Ali Dey that he will not be killed. Some punishment there must be, but it will not be fatal or crippling. When it is over, my brother will be allowed to go free. I fear that my importunings in this matter may have angered the dey, but I could not remain silent, I could not! It—it is for this reason that I fear the Illustrious One may look about him for another woman to take my place. It would not be fair, for I have held it for so short a time and come so near to attaining what I most desired, to be his wife."

"I am sorry also," Julia replied, "though I cannot think I would have done otherwise in your place."

"Now I must go to the audience and make certain that Ali Dey keeps his word to me concerning this of my brother. So, Jullanar, will you come?"

Rud must be there surely, and Basim. She would learn at first hand what had occurred and what would be done with those who had engaged in this disastrous plot. "Yes, I would like to very much. Thank you, Isabel."

"Good. It shall be arranged."

The audience chamber was much as it had been that day long ago when Julia had first been given the privilege of sitting behind the pierced screen. It was dim, the air heavy with lantern smoke and the emanations of the perfume censers. Jewels, gold and silver, silk and satins shimmered in the gloom as impatient men shifted. The dey sat in straight-backed splendor upon his royal divan, his presence stern and fearsome, and the scimitar at his side glittering with every movement.

Scanning the crowd below, Julia found Rud. The magnificence of his raiment, his turban held by a large sapphire, his midnight-blue brocade tunic slashed to reveal one of peach silk beneath, and his cream pantaloons pushed into soft leather boots sewn with gold thread gave him the look of a Turkish pasha of great wealth and power. His stance was commanding, and there was a grim look about his mouth. As Julia stared at him, he lifted his eyes to the pierced screen, and she had the curious feeling that he was aware of her hidden behind it. There was a tightness in her throat that grew until she thought she would have to cry out to relieve the pain of being so close, and yet so distant.

Beside Rud, coming barely to his thigh, was a childish figure dressed splendidly in cloth-of-gold. Seeing him, Julia smiled, blinking at the rise of foolish tears to her eyes. Basim had survived.

The women had hardly seated themselves before Kemal was led into the room. His anger, and the courage it had given him to curse Ali Dey, had passed. So great was his terror now that his eyes were unfocused, rolling in his head, and he had to be supported on either side by his guards. His clothing, still that of an Arab street beggar, was torn and dusty, and his beard and hair were unkempt. Behind him came a blond youth, the brother of Isabel, who drew in her breath at the sight of him. He was in little better case than his master. After these two came Marcel de Gruys, with his head thrown back and a look of rage in his bruised and battered countenance.

The three men were placed in a line before the dais. They salaamed, each according to his temper. Marcel's bow was curt, almost European. The blond boy's obeisance was profound, while Kemal sank to his haunches, touching his head to the floor, and had to be hauled bodily upward again.

Had Kemal been tortured? Julia could see little sign of it beneath his Arab robes, although he was far from strong. She swallowed, thinking of it, trying to tell herself that it was a small thing compared to what Kemal had done to the women of the harem, and had attempted to do to Ali Dey; that it was no more than he deserved for the evil of his life. Such justification helped little.

A long statement was read by the grand vizier, listing the crimes of which the men were accused and the manner in which they had been apprehended. Against Marcel had been leveled the charge, in addition to those against Kemal, of willful damage of the property of another, his attack upon Julia. Otherwise, the assault upon the dey appeared to have occurred much as Isabel had indicated.

When the grand vizier had stepped back into his place, Ali Dey looked down upon the three men. "Have you anything to say in your defense?" he queried.

Marcel stepped forward. "I am a free Christian attached to the French consulate in this country. You do not have the right to hold me, nor do you have jurisdiction over my actions. I demand the right of diplomatic immunity as guaranteed under international law."

"You have papers to support your claim?"

"They are at my lodging in the city," Marcel said, his expression impatient.

Ali Dey turned to the grand vizier. "These papers have been found?"

"No, O illustrious dey, they have not. A thorough search was made. No such documents were revealed," the court official declared.

"Then they were stolen or destroyed," Marcel accused. "But it does not matter. Proof of what I say can be obtained by the simple means of a message to the French consul."

"Let this be done then," the dey decreed.

The grand vizier said, "Knowing your great love of justice, O Ruler of the Time, your command was anticipated. We have already applied to the French consul. His answer to us is as follows: Although one Marcel de Gruys has made himself useful in and about the consular offices, he has no official connection with the consulate. They take no responsibility for his behavior, nor do they wish to become involved in his defense."

As the import of the grand vizier's words reached Marcel, the blood had receded from his face. His country, for which he had risked so much, had disavowed him. If he had been successful they would have lauded his exploits and weighted him with honors. As it was, they wanted no part of his failure. He was an embarrassment to them, a liability which they had jettisoned without a second's hesitation. Had employees of the French consulate gone into his rooms and removed his papers to weaken the embarrassing connection, or had the deed been done by the men of the guard at the orders of either the grand vizier or Ali Dey himself? The answer might never be known.

"Is there anything more you wish to say?" Ali Dey asked, his manner imperious and faintly sardonic.

Marcel de Gruys shook his head. Kemal, taking heart, staggered forward a step. "Have mercy," he bleated.

Ali Dey stared down upon his cousin. "You must apply to Allah, whose name be exalted, for mercy. I have none for you."

From somewhere in the depths of the room, a gong sounded. Quiet descended over the gathered men. When not so much as a fly stirred, the dey of Algiers spoke. "It is my decision that the slave boy of Kemal, because of his youth and his station, which did not allow him to refuse the criminal orders of his master, be given over to the bastinado, thereafter to be taken into my service. The other two before me I sentence to be strangled, the fate they had planned for me."

Kemal moaned, sagging between his guards. Marcel began to struggle. "You can't do this, not to me," he shouted. "I am a citizen of France. You have no right. I will not submit to your sentence."

Ali Dey made a weary gesture. Kemal's slave boy, with

tears streaming down his face, was taken away. The other two men remained in place. A buzz of comment ran through the audience chamber, then all was quiet once more. In the hush could be heard the sound of marching feet. Four large-muscled men with their bare arms folded across their chests entered the chamber. As the crowd parted before them, they advanced toward the throne.

Salaaming, the men positioned themselves, two on either side of the condemned prisoners. As they unfolded their arms, they revealed the slender cords of stout hemp they held in their fingers. A sighing gasp traveled over the room. Behind the screen, one of the wives of the dey suddenly tittered with nerves, a sound that ended on an indrawn breath.

Marcel, silent now, looked around him with a trapped, frantic gaze. His eyes were drawn in disbelief to the hempen cord dangling in front of him. Kemal, completely unable to control himself, began to sob.

Once more Ali Dey moved his imperial hand. The cords were fitted over the heads of the men. There came a gurgling grunt, a shriek suddenly cut off. Silence.

Julia clapped her hand to her mouth and leaned over, resting her forehead on her knees. She could not watch, could not feel the same vicious satisfaction that she sensed around her in the other women. If she had dreamed she would be called upon to witness such a savage spectacle, she would never have come. Despite what Marcel had done to her, she would not have wished this fate upon him. She did not look up again until she heard the scuffle of footsteps and the dragging scrape of burdens being carried from the chamber.

"My next duty is a much more pleasant one," Ali Dey said when the great doors had clanged shut upon the guards and executioners and the room was still once more. "I must reward my good friend Reuben for his extraordinary service to the throne. In token of my enormous gratitude, I hereby present to him these few baubles."

The dey clapped his hands, and from a rear entrance came a procession of slaves, each laden with a gift. There was a coffer filled with jewels, another filled with gold, and another with silver. There was a pair of pure white Arabian horses, a stallion and a mare, with gentle eyes and perfect lines. There were works of art and bundles of rugs and carpets, and last of all, a small model of a ship with the rakish lines of a Baltimore clipper. Rud's gaze rested longest upon this last gift, which was but a symbol of the ship which lay in the harbor, now his to possess. He did not look happy.

Rud bowed. "You do me too much honor, O Illustrious Ruler of the Age. The magnificence of your reward overwhelms me. I have no words adequate to express my gratitude."

"Do not be so hasty," Ali Dey replied. "I have not yet done with gifts. I have saved that which I am sure you will consider most valuable until last."

Rud's blue glance flicked in the direction of the pierced screen, then returned to the face of Ali Dey. "Your generosity shall be noted with awe a thousand years hence, O Mighty Ruler," he said at last.

"Perhaps," Ali Dey answered, pleased, "or it may be said I was a foolish ruler who cut off his own right hand. The gift of which I speak, O Reuben of the strong arm and stout heart, is one which I know you crave, the freedom to return to your own country."

Julia saw Rud's eyes narrow momentarily, as though he was certain of a trap in such affability. His response was smooth and polished, however, expressing in courtly terms his reluctance to leave the sun of Ali Dey's presence. In the same sonorous fashion, his royal friend assured him of a welcome, with much music and feasting, if he should ever return.

When the dey had finished, Rud lifted his head and squared his shoulders. "There is one boon more I must ask, if I may presume upon your generosity, Most Illustrious One. I would beg your permission to take with me, when I go, the Frankistani slave girl, Jullanar."

A black scowl crossed the face of the dey. Quiet fell once more over the room, positive testimony to the efficiency of the news system of the palace, and of the interest those present had in the decision regarding Julia's fate. Julia herself sat perfectly still, breathing not at all.

At last Ali Dey spoke. "You know the woman was brought under the mantle of my protection when she was left alone and unguarded. What else was I to think except that you did not value her as you should? She has suffered much for your neglect."

"It was not my wish or command which left her unprotected," Rud declared. "I regret that my duty to the throne left me ignorant of her plight, but I feel her pain as my own, and would soothe it with my love. She is as necessary to me as life itself, and I will sorrow all my days if these eyes never behold the loveliness of her face again."

"Well spoken, my friend, but does she feel the same? Would she choose to return to her own country with you, or would she choose in good time to become the wife of the dey of Algiers? This is a question which I think can be answered by the beauteous Jullanar alone. A message shall be sent to her in the harem. If she chooses to go with you, I will see personally that she is transported in safety and comfort to your ship in the harbor. If she does not come, then you will know that she decided to remain, and you must sail without her."

The disbelief in the faces below her echoed that in Julia's own mind. That the all-powerful dey of Algiers would allow a slave girl to decide her own destiny and control the gratification of his desires defied all tradition and knowledge of the personality of the man who sat upon the dais. Rud must also have realized this; still, there was nothing he could do except bow in acquiescence.

"You are all-wise," Rud answered. "Whatever the decision, I shall know it is the will of Allah, and I shall sail as the sun sets into the sea."

"So be it," Ali Dey said.

At the small sign of dismissal, Rud departed the audience chamber, his strides long and purposeful.

Rud loved her. He had declared it before the dey and the supercilious nobles of the court, risking everything on the chance that she might be free. If she was never allowed to see him again, she would have that much to remember.

As the hours passed, following the return of the women to the harem, it began to look as though that was all she would ever have. No message came to her. No choice was presented for her decision. She was left alone in her cubicle to contemplate the walls and to remember. Her disappointment was not great, as she had never dared allow herself to hope. At least, this was what she told herself. And yet, as the sun dropped like a copper weight down the sky, her heart grew constricted in her chest. The purple stillness of the twilight creeping in from the garden, bringing shadows into the room, found her lying on her couch with one clenched fist held to her lips and her eyes liquid with desolation.

At full dark, a serving woman came to light the lantern on its chain. Isabel followed her, standing to one side until the woman had gone out again. Her manner was so stiff and silent that Julia turned her head.

"What is it?" she asked in a voice thick with unshed tears.

"The ship of Reuben Effendi is no longer in the harbor."

Julia stared at her. In her mind's eye she could visualize the ship skimming westward with the light of the dying sun red upon her sails. Would Rud stand upon the quarterdeck and strain backward toward Algiers? Would he suspect that she had been detained against her will, or would he think that she had chosen the sybaritic life of the harem, with the artificial grandeur of being the wife of the dey?

"He is gone," she whispered experimentally, trying to bring some reality to her brain. What else had she expected? Did she want him to endanger his life by mounting an assault upon the palace to rescue her? No, that would be foolhardy. It was impossible for him to demand that the dey release her, with Ali Dey declaring that she had stayed of her own free choice. What else was there for him to do except to bow his head and sail away?

He could have stayed, her heart whispered. He could

have stayed and shared her exile, waiting for another opportunity to take her with him.

"Do not despair," Isabel said, dropping to her knees beside the couch, her voice so low it would not be audible for more than a few inches away. "If you will take your courage in both hands, there is still a chance you can escape the clutches of our master."

"What do you mean?" Julia's voice was soft, a zephyr of sound.

"A message has come to you through the serving women. The sender was Basim the dwarf, beloved bringer of good luck to all. He bids you make ready. He will come to you in the night in obedience to the orders of his old master, Mehemet Dey, who rests tonight in paradise in the arms of houris he would pretend are you."

When the girl did not go on, Julia said, "Is that all? He did not say how he would come, or when I might expect him?"

"He did not, though if he comes it must be through the garden. As to the time, it must either be before moonrise or after its set. You must hold yourself ready."

"Why has the message come through you?" It occurred to Julia how convenient it would be for Isabel if she were gone. For the girl's purpose, it would not matter if she escaped or was merely caught in the attempt. The effect would be the same, for if she was caught the dey would have little choice but to kill her; all-powerful he might be, but only within the customs and laws of Islam. Isabel would have the attention of the dey to herself, until the next attractive slave girl chanced upon his sight.

"I do not blame you for your suspicions," Isabel said. "In your place I would be the same. The message came to me because I am known to the serving woman who is a sister of one of the women given to Reuben Effendi by the dey, and because the woman could not come to your chamber without attracting attention that might be remembered later. It was also given, perhaps a little, because I am expected to be sympathetic to your cause, both for the debt I owe you for helping me to my place, and for my interest in removing you as a rival. There is no way I can prove that I will not betray you. I can only swear by the Most Exalted Name that it is so, and hope that you will believe me."

It was the wry self-knowledge of the last sentence which caused Julia to relax and extend her trust. Their whispered consultation lasted a few moments more, and then the girl slipped away.

Julia refused the evening meal. The thought of food was sickening to her, and she had no desire to face the other women in the common room. In addition, although she did not think Ali Dey would force himself upon her in her present condition, while stiff and sore from her whipping, it seemed best to prepare in this manner a tale that she was ill, too ill to obey a summons.

She had nothing to do, nothing to gather together. She had only the clothing she had on, and it did not in truth belong to her. Not that she was troubled by the lack. The only thing she would miss would be her gold bee, though doubtless the yellow diamond would have come in handy in the months ahead. She wondered what had become of them, who had picked them up from where they had landed on the floor. Had they been given to Rud, or were they reposing now in some servant's pocket?

What would she do when she had quitted the palace? Where would she go, and how? She must trust to Basim and hope he had some definite plan in mind, perhaps a plan suggested months ago by Mehemet Dey for use under other circumstances. Before, she had thought to travel overland until she was well away from Algiers, and then at some other seaport along the coast of Africa take a ship to either Malta or Gibraltar, where an English or American ship might lie at anchor. This might still be possible. There would be many problems, not the least of which would be that she would be a woman traveling virtually alone in a country where women hardly dared step outside their doors without an armed guard. Despite these things, the more she thought of it, the more her spirits unfurled and began to rise. She felt no fear or uncertainty, only a great readiness. Someday, months from now, she must at last set foot on English soil and make her way to the home of Thaddeus and Lucinda Baxter. What would her welcome be? Would Rud be there? Would he be angry that she had not come to him before? Would he believe that she could not? Would he, perhaps, welcome her with widespread arms? Such questions would have to wait upon that day for an answer.

A whisper of sound brought her up off the couch. The oil lamp overhead had spluttered and died long ago, but in the hallway outside the lanterns still burned. Isabel was outlined in their flickering glow. Julia stepped into her slippers and glided to the door, slipping through the curtains with scarcely the clatter of a single bead to mark her passing. The other girl put her forefinger to her lips, then reached out and took Julia's hand. Into the palm she pressed something small and hard. Julia did not need to look to recognize the shape of her gold bee. Had Basim sent it as a sign that it was he who waited? The precaution had not been necessary, but she was glad to have the tiny brooch returned to her. She and it had been through much together.

Isabel turned, moving ahead of Julia down the dim corridor toward the common room.

The solid blinds which closed off the common room at night were standing slightly ajar, just as they had been on that evening when Julia had surprised Mariyah returning from a midnight outing. Now Isabel stood aside and permitted Julia to go first into the garden. She quietly pulled the door to behind them.

The moon had not yet risen, but still the night was filled with gently moving shadows, each of which accelerated Julia's heartbeat. The air was like velvet, absorbing sound so that it seemed they floated instead of walked to the end of the large, wall-enclosed rectangle. Basim stepped from behind a stone bench as they approached. He salaamed in mute greeting and turned away at once to the wall behind him.

Against the stone, still warm from the sun, were the espaliered peach trees. Their gnarled, outspread branches, fastened to the wall, were covered with dark-green leaves that rustled as the dwarf set his foot to the limbs and climbed them like steps. At the top of the wall, he gestured to Julia to ascend by the same path.

Julia turned to Isabel. "Your debt is paid. As I helped set you toward the wish of your heart, you have set me toward mine. Here we must part. I hope you find great happiness, Isabel, and become the mother of many children, all with your frank and generous soul."

"Take care, Jullanar," the girl replied. "There are many surprises in this world, some agreeable, some not. I would like to wish that all your surprises are pleasant ones."

Julia felt a stab of apprehension at the strangeness of the girl's words. There was no time for thought, however. With a quick embrace, she said a last goodbye and turned to the peach-tree ladder. The branches gave alarmingly beneath her feet; she was not as light as Basim. The leaves were damp-edged with dew and slippery, hiding the footholds from her groping feet. For an instant, she balanced on the iron-spiked top of the high wall. Looking over her shoulder, she saw the shadow that was Isabel near the door that led back into the harem. The girl did not look back.

On the other side of the wall was another garden. There were no convenient peach trees here, only a rope with knots tied at intervals along its length, and a loop thrown over one of the iron spikes. Basim already stood on the ground below, patiently holding the rope taut. Julia did not pause to consider and grow nervous. She balanced, crouching with her feet between the spikes while she caught the rope, then she gripped tight and cast herself out and down. The rope burned the palm of her hands. She half-fell, caught herself, and slipped again, descending by swift and jerky degrees. After an age of time, she felt dew-damp grass beneath the soles of her thin slippers.

Basim took the rope from her tight grasp. Stepping back, he gave it a hard snap which lifted the loop from the spike and brought the rope curling down upon them. Rolling it about his arm, he set off toward the dark bulk of another wing of the palace.

"This way, fair mistress," he called softly.

Under their feet rose now the smell of crushed herbs. Breathing deep of their aroma, Julia decided that the garden they were in opened from the kitchens, deserted at this hour. They passed below the branches of pear and plum trees and brushed against the milky, odorous leaves of figs. Stepping carefully through a small patch of melons, they came at last to a section which had been allowed to grow wild. Here, weeds and thorn seedlings grew up to a sagging, little-used door.

The panel stood open a few inches, inviting entrance into a storeroom piled high with cracked oil jars, split baskets, and shrunken barrels with the staves falling in. They threaded their careful way through the refuse, halting at another door that gave onto a passageway. Basim peered around it, and finding the way clear, motioned her forward. They followed the passageway into a narrow corridor that branched and meandered for what seemed like miles through the nether regions of the great pile of stone. They passed hundreds of dark, windowless, cave-like chambers hardly large enough for a sleeping mat. These were the quarters of the kitchen slaves who provided the vast quantity of food and drink consumed daily in the palace. Without exception, these were dark, occupied by human beings sunk in the deep sleep of exhaustion.

At last they reached what could only be a rear entrance, a postern gate where every morning the suppliers of victuals brought their wares, the hundreds of chickens and squabs, the dozens of lambs, the tons of wheat and rice and dried and fresh fruits, and the myriad other rich comestibles. It was quiet and deserted now, except for a lone guard, an old man who barely glanced at them before accepting the purse Basim threw him, getting to his feet, and ambling off into the shadows.

They were still not safe. There were the stables for the dey's horses and the steeds of the officers of the Janissaries, along with the men who stood guard among the beasts against theft. They ghosted through this maze of pens and feeding troughs with the utmost care, knowing that here were vigilant sentries. Beyond these was an area of open palace drains filled with wastes. It was a noisome place and therefore deserted. Julia bore it without complaint.

Suddenly a dog began to bark behind them in the stable area. Basim reached to catch her hand. Abandoning all pretense of stealth, they began to run. They swung into a dark space that turned out to be a refuse-strewn alley. Their footsteps pounded along its curving length until ahead they could see a faint light at the opening into another street. In that opening sat a litter, with its bearers standing alert on either side and a linkboy with a burning lantern in front of it.

Basim gave an exclamation of satisfaction. Coming to a halt beside the litter, he held the curtain to one side for Julia. The instant she settled inside, the poles were taken up and the bearers began a jolting run. A part of Julia wanted to urge them to go ever faster, while another part cringed at the thought of attracting any kind of attention. They did not know for certain that they had not been seen leaving the vicinity of the palace. It was unlikely, now that they were drawing away, that a common livestock guard would connect the litter with the disturbance of the dog. Why arouse suspicion by acting in a way that could be thought peculiar? She looked out once to remonstrate with Basim, who was trotting along beside the litter. At the sight of him, she decided against it. He would not put himself to the effort of keeping up on his short legs unless he considered it necessary.

Well beyond the palace, the litter slowed. Behind them, the streets were quiet; there was no sign of pursuit. Taking the winding back alleys, they traversed the city, passing shuttered houses with beggars sleeping in the doorways, mongrel dogs sneaking out to lap from the public watering troughs, and now and then a skulking figure that melted away, no more anxious to be seen than they.

They came at last to the wider thoroughfares of the outlying section. The litter rounded the wall of an imposing dwelling place which could have been the abode of a rich merchant, and entered at an open gate. It continued to the rear of the complex of buildings. The place was quiet. No lanterns gleamed, not even in the gatehouse, where a guard should have been posted, or in the servants quarters. It was, to all appearances, deserted. Here the litter was set down. Even before Julia stepped out, she recognized the familiar smell of horses. They stood saddled and waiting, good beasts, Arabian mixed with Barb, and finely caparisoned. Across the saddle of one lay a cloak, which Basim caught by the hem and drew down, presenting it to Julia.

The covering was welcome. Her silken bodice and pantaloons, though suitable enough for the harem, were not designed for the night air, even such a fine summer night as this. Also, she was not unaware of the interest of the bearers of the litter in her scanty attire and un-veiled state. While she was donning the cloak, Basim paid off the bearers and linkboy. Their grunts gave evidence of the satisfactory size of their payment. The money disappeared into their rags. If their curiosity was not as satisfied, they gave no further sign, taking up the litter and moving off as quickly as they had come.

Seeing Julia staring after them, Basim said, "Fear not, my Lady Jullanar. To aid a Christian slave in escape is a crime for which the punishment is severe. They will not remember they saw you any longer than it takes them to leave your sight."

Julia nodded, accepting the word of the dwarf without question. She gestured toward the house. "This place, is it abandoned?"

"No, fair mistress."

"To whom does it belong, then, that they allowed you to keep the horses in wait here?"

"It was built many years ago as a retreat for Mehemet Dey, my Lady Jullanar. The key has been in my keeping for many months, awaiting your hour of need. In perfect truth, the house is now the property of Ali Dey, but he has not felt the need of solitude, and may never do so. Contemplation is not in his nature."

She must remember to say a prayer for the repose of the soul of Mehemet Dey, Julia told herself, and turned away.

With few exceptions, the women of the east did not ride horseback, traveling when they must behind the curtained seclusion and protection of a palanquin. For this reason the sidesaddle for ladies was unknown. The horses that waited carried the heavy high-pommeled saddles of Araby. Julia did not hesitate, however. It would not be the first time she had ridden astride. She mounted by the simple expedient of stepping upon Basim's bent back. When she was settled, the dwarf caught his stirrup, swarming upward like a sailor climbing into rigging. It was obvious from the way in which he sat his horse that, though palace-bred, he was at home in the saddle.

"Where do we ride, O small man of the large heart?" Julia inquired, gathering up the reins.

Basim observed her seat as candidly as she had judged his, and appeared to find no fault. His teeth flashed in the first light of the rising moon as he smiled. "First we leave Algiers, then we ride to freedom!"

It was not a full answer; still, it was enough. As he swung his horse around and set his heels into its sides, Julia did the same. She felt deep inside the rise of exhilaration, of returning life after a long winter of the soul. She would not despair and she would not be afraid. She was going to achieve what she wanted, no matter who tried to stop her. She would not be beaten.

Her thoughts kept time with the pounding of the horses' hooves. The refrain sang in her blood and drummed in her mind so loudly that it was some time before she grew aware that a part of the sound came from behind them. Looking back, she saw two horsemen. When had they begun to follow them? How long had they been there? She did not know. For now, they made no attempt to come up to them, but held back at a distance of a little less than a hundred yards. This did not ease Julia's mind, however. Something, perhaps the purposeful way in which they appeared to be maintaining the same pace as Basim and herself, sent a chill of distress down her spine.

"Basim, there are men, riders—"

"I see them, fair mistress."

"Let us spur forward and leave them."

"Do not be afraid. If they have been sent after us they will only give chase; if not, we would tire our horses for nothing. The night is short and the journey long."

"Must we wait for them to make the first move?" she asked, with heat caused by strained nerves and an aching back chafed already to rawness by the woolen robe.

"If I am correct, there may be no move to be made at all."

This cryptic statement did nothing to satisfy Julia. Nevertheless, she subsided, forcing herself to accept Basim's estimation.

They left the last mud hovels of Algiers behind them. The city was lost to view, and still the horsemen that followed came on. The dust of their progress rose behind them and was blown away on the night wind. Breathing deep, they forced fresh, clean air into their lungs, trying to forget the stench of Algiers and the palace. The wind seemed to be faintly tainted with salt from the sea away somewhere to their right. As the moonlight brightened and the miles passed beneath their horses' hooves, the ride with their ghostly pursuers took on the aspect of a waking nightmare. Gradually, almost imperceptibly, Julia increased the pace of her mount, and Basim's mare stayed even, unwilling to be left to the rear.

If Ali Dey wanted her, Julia told herself, he was going to have to exert himself to catch her. She would not be intimidated into spineless surrender, no matter what he might be accustomed to with other women. How she wished she had the knife Rud had given her! She would prepare a small surprise for the dey. Would he set out to chase her down himself? He was a man of action who enjoyed the hunt. Or would he send his minions? No, she decided, it must be the Illustrious One himself. She could not feature a mere soldier prolonging the chase in this diabolical fashion. The dey would want to exact the last ounce of vengeance for her insult in daring to prefer freedom to his couch. Would he kill her? His honor would decree it, as well as the law. The question was when, after what travail.

How had he discovered her absence? How had he come

so quickly upon her trail? Had Isabel betrayed her? Was this the surprise of which she had spoken? How could she think Julia would find it anything but unpleasant? Surely with her knowledge of the harem she must know that Ali Dey could not ignore what she had done and return her to her former place. No, she must not think so of Isabel. The alarm had been given near the stables. That had to be the answer.

Now the sound of hooves grew louder. A quick glance over her shoulder showed that the horsemen had kicked their mounts into a hard gallop. The sand of the road thrown up by their speed shone like gold dust in the glow of the moon. They were gaining.

Julia leaned low over the neck of her horse, speaking into her ear. Pain forgotten, she threw herself into the race. Beside her Basim rode, a frown on his face as he looked back. He straightened to stare ahead, then looked back again.

Following his forward gaze, Julia saw the sparkle of the night-dark sea where the road wound around to parallel the coast. The ground was higher here than the shoreline, the dirt track of the road running along a low cliff of rocky sand covered with sea grasses. Abruptly Basim pointed at a break in the escarpment. It was a trough formed by wind and rain into a long ramp to the beach. He turned his horse in that direction. Julia plunged after him, holding her horse in as he floundered in deep, rocky sand, letting him have his head as they reached the hard-packed beach at the water's edge.

And then, far down the line of the sea's edge, Julia saw their objective. It was a ship anchored out from shore, silvered by moonlight. A longboat from the vessel lay beached on the sand. From this distance the ship had the look of a phantom, a dream-conjured vision with the lines of a Baltimore clipper, the duplicate of a vessel long sunk beneath the waves of a far-flung ocean. She had the look of the *Sea Jade,* a ship lost forever. The rigging was the same, the shape of the bow and figurehead, even the paint. It could not be, and yet it was. Rud's ship, given to him by Ali Dey. He had sailed away in her, but not to stay. He had returned. For her.

Now she and Basim drummed their horses with their heels, flying like the sea wind toward the safe haven before them. The damp sand was thrown in clods as high as their heads, and they raced the lapping waves along the shore, now missing them, now kicking the water into spray. Behind them streamed their pursuers, demons of persistence, riding hard now that they saw their quarry about to slip through their fingers. Slowly the gap began to close.

Julia drew ahead of Basim. As she looked back at him she could have sworn he was drawing in. Was his horse failing? Had his oriental mind accepted that it was his fate to be run down by the dey of Algiers? Her mouth tightened. She would not give up so easily.

The leader of the two horsemen was outdistancing the other, his white Arabian stallion like molten silver in the glow of the full, sailing moon. With cloak flying, he sped past Basim, closing in upon Julia's flying mount. His horse was superior. There could be no doubt of the issue. She had been right. Until now he had been playing a game of nerves with her. He could have overtaken her at any time.

She turned her gaze forward, fastening her amber eyes upon the ship as on a talisman, willing Rud to sense her plight, wondering in a flash of amazement that there were no men to guard the longboat, men who might come to her defense.

The thunder of hooves was in her ears, a sound that blended with the beat of her heart. She felt the rush of wind as the silver-white Arabian drew in beside her gelding. As if drawn by a force she could not resist, she turned her head.

Rud. Rud racing beside her, his blue eyes glittering with reckless joy, his lips drawn back in a ferocious pleasure. Her heart leaped, and as he checked his mount to keep pace with hers, she sent him a dazzling smile. Together they bore down upon the longboat, their cloaks lifting like wings behind them.

They drew rein beside the craft, sending sand scattering in every direction. Rud leaped from his horse and ducked under its head. Julia slid into his waiting arms. He held her close as his chest swelled, his eyes searching the shining oval of her face, finding there a bright glory more wondrous than the light of the moon over his shoulder.

"Julia," he said, his voice low and vibrant. "You came!"

"Did you think I would not?"

"With you, I could not know. And now, speak quickly, for the time for riddles and evasion is past and the time for explaining is not yet. I love you beyond the thinking of sane men or the dreaming of women. My need of you burns within me like a flame. But that is not enough. I must know before we go farther—do you love me, Julia?"

It was the remembrance of his declaration of love before Ali Dey which allowed her to answer with the truth. "I love you, Rudyard Thorpe."

"Will you leave this godforsaken land and live with me in my country, braving time, the curious, and the woman who passes as my mother, remaining in my heart without parting for our lifetimes?"

"I ask nothing more."

"And I nothing less. For so long I have waited to take you away, passing opportunities without number of going alone. Now the time has come, and I find I cannot bear to take you from here only to lose you again. Better to return to Algiers and brave the wrath of Ali Dey for the chance to keep you as my slave than to be forced to let you go when we reach England."

"This sword cuts both ways," Julia answered. "I, too, could have gone alone, as was arranged for me by Mehemet Dey before his death. I would not, because it meant leaving you behind. Today I thought you were gone, and I meant to follow you, even to the edge of the world if need be. If I am to be the prisoner of your heart, then know you will also be mine!"

The tightness in his face did not ease. "How can I let myself believe, when tonight even Basim was more certain than I that you would come? With O'Toole, the only member of my crew I could trust—all the rest are Muslims—I agreed to wait here. I grew impatient and, I will admit, anxious. I decided to ride into the city and await your passing that I might serve as a rear guard. Seeing me behind you, you tried to run away. As always, you advance toward me, then retreat. Tell me why?"

"Because I love you. What other reason can there be? Feeling safe in your affection, I advance; doubting it, I retreat. As to just now," she went on, her golden eyes dark with the memory of fear, "I did not know you had sent Basim. I thought you were Ali Dey, riding to take me back."

"Julia, beloved," he breathed in apology and gladness, drawing her once more into the haven of his arms. The moon was blotted out by the promise in his eyes and the sweet and fearsome enchantment of his kiss.

O'Toole and Basim had come up now and dismounted. Averting their eyes from the man and woman standing in the sand, they dragged the longboat into the edge of the tideless sea. It was Basim, when all stood ready, who moved to tug at Rud's elbow.

"My Lord Reuben, would you be taken by the men of the dey in the throes of life's greatest joy? The boat awaits, and all else that is before you and the Lady Jullanar, Keeper of the Honey."

Rud turned, casting a rueful glance at Julia for their moment of forgetfulness. "And you, Basim? What is before you?" he inquired. "Will you come with us and share our future?"

"My heart goes with you and your lady, effendi, but my poor self must remain where all is known and familiar, and where my ears may be ready to hear, and my body to answer, the call of the faithful to prayer."

"If you are certain, O great one, then accept from me, if you will, the gift of the Arabian stallion to carry you like the winged horse of fame to where safety lies for you. I ask that you take the mare also, and care for them both, for there is no time to put them aboard my ship once again. The other mounts you may dispose of as you will."

"You are all that is generous, effendi," the dwarf said,

his eyes bright as he bowed low. "I will take them with the greatest joy in their possession. Touching on another matter, however, you must tell me what I am to do now with the wealth entrusted to me by Mehemet Dey for the care of his cherished slave, Jullanar."

From somewhere about his clothing, the dwarf drew forth a pouch and, opening it, poured a glittering stream of loose jewels, the transportable wealth of the east, into his cupped hand. They filled it to heaping with flashing points of fire.

Rud looked to Julia, by his silence passing the decision to her for whom the gift was meant.

Julia looked from her husband to the dwarf, and then out across the sparkling sea. At last she said, "Give me a few stones, no more than a fourth of the number, that I may have them placed in an ornament which will remind me of the boon of freedom, and serve to keep me from complete dependence upon any man again, even the one I love. For the rest, take them, that you also, Basim, may never call another man master."

Basim fell to his knees. Taking the hem of her cloak, he raised it to his lips. "Fair mistress," he said, "There are no words to express my gratitude. I can only promise to honor you all my days and direct the *baraka* of my body, if such I truly possess, to assure you a life abundant in happiness!"

The exchange of the jewels was made in accordance with Julia's instructions. Taking the handful the dwarf passed to her, Julia wrapped them in a twist of cloth and tucked them into her bodice, settling them between her breasts.

Mounting the back of the stallion, Basim gathered up the reins of the other horses. He lifted his hand in a last salute, then sent the Arabian plunging away along the shore in the opposite direction from Algiers.

Rud and Julia swung to O'Toole, who stood grinning, holding the longboat precariously to the shore with the grip of one hand. He ducked his head at the first opportunity offered him to greet Julia, and she gave him a brilliant smile in return.

"Shall we go?" Rud inquired, as though there was all of time before them.

"It might be wise," Julia agreed.

"Praise be," O'Toole said fervently.

Rud handed Julia into the boat, and she moved to a seat in the prow. O'Toole pushed off as Rud stepped in and then scrambled aboard. The two men settled themselves to the oars, sending the boat toward the moon-silvered shape of the ship.

Julia smiled, looking back at her husband. Casually, she stretched to tug the turban from his head and drop it over the side of the boat. The jewel holding its folds shone with a dark-blue gleam before the water-soaked muslin sank out of sight. The night wind off the sea ruffled the crisp black waves of Rud's hair, making him look more himself, more the man she married.

"You owe me a sapphire," he said, his mouth curving in a grin.

"You may collect it—later," she answered, her eyes bright with promise. Turning in her seat, she set her face homeward.

The possibility of a plot to free Napoleon from his island prison of St. Helena is not a fictional contrivance. From the time of his incarceration in October 1815 until the report of his death in May 1821, numerous such plans were hatched by his followers. Foremost among these was an elaborate scheme to set up in the Americas a Bonapartist camp where loyal soldiers and officers could gather, train, and arrange to buy and outfit ships in preparation for a military offensive to wrest the emperor from his jailers by force. Following his release, Napoleon would be offered the position of ruler of Mexico by the revolutionary party in that country. There were three ringleaders behind this endeavor: General Brayer, Colonel Latapie, and a renegade British officer, Lord Cochrane. Such a major operation, involving so many, was difficult to keep quiet. The arrest of Latapie disclosed the plot. Acting on information obtained from him, the Mexican government sent an armed force into Texas to obliterate the French camp called Champ d'Asile, and so the plan came to nothing.

Napoleon's brother Joseph, formerly king of Spain, who settled in New Jersey after the defeat at Waterloo, was implicated in several escape plans, as was Madame de Ranchope (née Pauline Fourès), one of the emperor's former mistresses. And then there is the well-documented conspiracy formulated by New Orleans businessmen-Bonapartists led by Major Nicholas Girod. This group financed the building of a schooner, the *Seraphine*, and erected a house suitable for the great man. Located in the Vieux Carré, or French Quarter, at the corner of Chartres and St. Louis, the imposing mansion still stands, a monument to their dedication. The news of Napoleon's death brought this expedition to an end.

The greatest bar to a belief in the emperor's escape from St. Helena is the lack of evidence that he ever reappeared on the continent of Europe or anywhere else in the world. Several legends seek to explain away this point. One holds that, tiring of war and the world's ingratitude, he retired in obscurity to the United States, perhaps joining his brother Joseph. Another states that he channeled his energies and accumulated wealth into a career as a diamond merchant in Belgium. And then there is the unsubstantiated report that he was killed while trying to gain a secret meeting with his son and heir, the duke of Reichstadt, who was being held virtual prisoner by his maternal grandfather, Francis I, emperor of Austria. The solution set forth in *The Storm and the Splendor* is based on nothing more than my own reading of the events and the possibilities inherent in the situation.

Anyone with the curiosity to delve deeper into the mystery will enjoy reading Thomas G. Wheeler's *Who Lies Here?* This fascinating and scholarly account of Napoleon's last years has been of invaluable help to me. Without it, my own book could not have been written.

Besides the emperor, several other historical personalities are portrayed or mentioned in the story. Foremost among these is Sir Hudson Lowe, Napoleon's keeper. Far from receiving the honors he felt he deserved for his service to the crown, he became a scapegoat for the dissatisfaction of the English people with the government's callous treatment of the prisoner on St. Helena, and he died an embittered man. Lady Lowe shared his impoverished disgrace; however, her stepdaughter, Charlotte, married the Russian commissioner, Count Alexander de Balmain, in 1820 and left the St. Helena episode behind forever. The British physicians Stokoe and Arnott, William Balcombe and his daughter Betsy, and Lord and Lady Holland each played their appointed parts, as did the Baron de Gourgaud, Las Cases, Count Bertrand, the Count de Montholon and his wife Albine, along with her daughter Napoleone, and the emperor's valet, Marchand. All others are fictional characters—with the exception of Eugène Robeaud, who hovers somewhere between the imaginary and the factual.

By tradition, Robeaud was an actual soldier with duties much as described, because of his resemblance to his commander-in-chief. But though his name, rank, regiment, and birthplace are known, Wheeler indicates that there is no record of his existence in the small town in France where he was believed to be born. The documentation for the supposed year of his birth has disappeared, almost as though someone preferred that the question of his existence should remain unresolved.

Was Napoleon of average height for a European male of nearly eight generations ago—approximately five feet, seven inches, as I indicated—or only five feet, two inches, "and four lines" as so vaguely given in the records of the autopsy performed on St. Helena following his death? Contemporary accounts support the first estimation, while popular belief holds firmly to the image of him as a short man. At this distance in time, who can say which is right? And yet the autopsy reports contain enough discrepancies, notably concerning the emperor's bodily scars and the lack of sexual development in a man known as one of the greatest womanizers of his century, to puzzle the most determined skeptic.

In the second half of *The Storm and the Splendor* the men to whom I gave the title of Dey of Algiers are fictional characters, though the office itself, with its various obligations and privileges, was not. The Turkish reign over Algeria came to an end shortly after the period of this story, when France, finding it politically expedient to resent a blow with a fly whisk in the face of the French consul by the ruling dey, seized the country. It remained under French authority for the next 124 years, well into the twentieth century.